# CRUSH

# ALAN JACOBSON

## A KAREN VAIL NOVEL

Vanguard Press
A Member of the Perseus Books Group

Sherlock Holmes quotes used with permission of the Sir Arthur Conan Doyle Literary Estate

Published by Vanguard Press
A Member of the Perseus Books Group

Text design by Jeff Williams
Set in 11 point Galliard by the Perseus Books Group

Cataloging-in-Publication data for this book is available from the Library of Congress.
ISBN 13: 978-1-59315-548-3

Vanguard Press books are available at special discounts for bulk purchases in the U.S. by corporations, institutions, and other organizations. For more information, please contact the Special Markets Department at the Perseus Books Group, 2300 Chestnut Street, Suite 200, Philadelphia, PA 19103, or call (800) 810-4145, ext. 5000, or e-mail special.markets@perseusbooks.com.

10 9 8 7 6 5 4 3 2 1

For Corey, Matthew, and Danielle:
*You are the branches on my tree that keep on giving.*
And I'm the old stump.
*I love you all, to the moon and back.*

*"It is a capital mistake to theorize before one has data."*
—SIR ARTHUR CONAN DOYLE,
WRITING AS SHERLOCK HOLMES

*"You see, but you do not observe."*
—SIR ARTHUR CONAN DOYLE,
WRITING AS SHERLOCK HOLMES

*"In wine there is truth."*
—ROMAN PROVERB

*"O thou invisible spirit of wine, if thou hast no name
to be known by, let us call thee devil."*
—WILLIAM SHAKESPEARE

# PROLOGUE

675 15th Street NW
*Washington, DC*

"So the dick says to the woman, 'I got nothing.'"

Karen Vail burst out laughing. Here she was, out on the town with Detective Mandisa Manette—just about the unlikeliest of acquaintances she'd socialize with—and she was guffawing at another of Manette's crass jokes. But she noticed Manette was not enjoying her own punch line. In fact, Manette's face was hard, her gaze fixed. And her hand was slowly reaching inside her jacket. For her weapon.

"Don't wanna ruin your evening," Manette said, "but there's a guy packing, and he looks real nervous. Over your left shoulder."

Vail turned slowly and casually snatched a glimpse of the man. Six foot, broad, and as Manette noted, under duress. Sweating, eyes darting around the street. In a minute, his gaze would land on Vail and Manette. *The guy looks familiar. Why?* She watched his mannerisms and then, as his head turned three quarters toward them, she got a better look at him and—

*Oh, crap. I know who he is.* In a few seconds, he'd probably make them as cops, and then the shit would hit the fan. The image conjured up a mess—and that's what would no doubt result.

Vail quickly turned away. "Don't look at him. Definitely bad news, and stressed as hell. With good reason. That's Danny Michael Yates."

Manette's eyes widened. "No way. The goddamn cop killer? You sure?"

Vail slid her hand down to her Velcro pouch. "Damn sure. What do you want to do?"

Manette moved her hand behind her back, no doubt resting it on her pistol. "Make a call, DC Metro, let 'em know what we got here. I'm gonna circle around behind him."

Vail pulled out her phone and made the call. With her back to Yates, she watched him in the reflection of the Old Ebbitt Grill storefront. Meantime, she assessed the situation. The sidewalk was knotted with people waiting for tables, enjoying a drink with friends, spouses, and business associates. She wished she could yell, "Everyone down!" so they wouldn't get hurt. Because she had an intense feeling that this was going to get very ugly, very fast.

Vail ended the call and slipped the BlackBerry into her pocket, her right hand firmly on the Glock 23 that was buried in the pouch below her abdomen.

She made eye contact with Manette's reflection in the window and nodded, then stole a glance at Yates. He looked at Vail at precisely that moment, and *Fuck—he made me—*

Yates turned and pushed through the clot of people standing behind him. Vail followed, doing her best to navigate the tumbled bodies with her still-sore postsurgical knee. Manette, she figured, was also in pursuit. Manette was tall and thin, and she looked athletic—whether she was or not, Vail could only guess—but she had to be faster than Vail and her recently repaired leg.

She caught a glimpse of Yates as he turned left on H Street—and, yup, there was Manette, pumping away, in close proximity. Christ, this was not what she had in mind when she suggested they have a girls' night out.

Vail turned the corner and picked up Manette as she kept up her pursuit of Yates. The shine of Manette's handgun caught the streetlight's amber glow and suddenly a bad feeling crept down Vail's spine. They were extremely close to the White House, where Secret Service agents and police outnumbered the citizens in the immediate vicinity. Snipers were permanently stationed on the roof, and—here was a black woman, chasing a white man, a big gleaming pistol in her right hand. No uniform. No visible badge.

This was not going to turn out well, and Vail had a sinking feeling it would have nothing to do with Danny Michael Yates.

Yates veered left, into Lafayette Park, and damn, if the guy wasn't a stupid one—he was headed straight for the wrought iron of the White House gate. Stupid isn't quite the word . . . insane might be more like it. Vail heard Manette yell, "Police, freeze!"

It had no effect on Yates except to have him veer left, parallel to the iron fence—which he had to do anyway.

But Vail had her answer: Manette was apparently a superb athlete, because she was now only fifteen yards behind Yates, who was moving pretty well himself.

Lights snapped on. An alarm went off.

Vail fumbled to pull her credentials from her purse, then splayed them open in her left hand, held high above her head, the Glock in her right hand, bouncing along with her strides. Showing the snipers she was a federal agent, not a threat to the president. And hopefully, by association, they'd realize Manette was a cop, too.

But as she processed that thought, a gunshot stung her ears like a stab to her heart. And Manette went down. Only it wasn't a sniper or diligent Secret Service agent. It was Danny Michael Yates, who had turned and buried a round in Manette's groin. She went down hard and fast.

And she was writhing on the ground. DC Metro police appeared behind Yates and drew down on him. Half a dozen Secret Service agents traversed the White House lawn with guns drawn and suit coats flapping. Snipers on the roof swung their rifles toward the plaza, their red laser dots dancing on clothing and pavement.

Vail brought up the rear, huffing and puffing, the cold night DC air burning her throat. She was heaving, sucking oxygen, when a weak "FBI!" scraped from her throat. She stopped fifteen feet from Yates, who was inching closer to Manette.

"She's a cop," Vail yelled. "She's a cop!" She wanted all the law enforcement personnel on scene to understand what was going on. Manette was on the ground, her handgun a foot from her hand. But she was in no condition to reach for it. She was curled into a fetal position.

Yates took a step closer to her, and his gun—it looked like a Beretta—was raised slightly, pointing vaguely toward Manette. "Stop right there," Vail yelled. "Take another step and it'll be your last!"

"Just kill me now," Yates said. "Because there ain't no way you're taking me in. I killed a cop, you think I'll make it through the night alive in lockup?"

"I'll personally guarantee your safety, Danny." Vail stood there with her Glock now in both hands, her credentials case on the ground at her feet, spread open, her Bureau badge visible for all who cared to look. "I'll make sure you get your day in court. I understand the way you think, I know you didn't mean to kill that cop."

"Bullshit. I did mean to kill him! I fucking hate cops, they raped my mother. You bet I wanted to kill him!"

*Damn, he's a dumb shit. No hope for this one. Served up a valid defense for his actions and he tells me I'm wrong.*

"There's only one way this can end good, Danny. You put the gun down and let me help my partner there. You got that?"

Yates took another step forward, his Beretta now aimed point-blank at Manette. Vail brought up her Glock, tritium sights lined up on the perp's head.

"Now," Vail yelled. "Drop the fucking gun!"

But Yates's elbow straightened. His hand muscles stiffened.

Given the angle, no one else could see what she could see. He didn't 'drop the fucking gun,' so Vail shot him. Blasted him right in the head. And then she drilled him in the center mass, to knock him back, make sure he didn't accidentally unload on Manette as his brain went flat line. Two quick shots. Overkill? Maybe. But at the moment, truth be told, she didn't really care.

Yates fell to the ground. Vail ran to Manette. Grabbed her, cradled her. "Manny—Manny, you okay?"

Manette's face was drenched with sweat, pain contorted in the intense creases of her face.

And then Vail lost it. She felt the sudden release, the stress of the past couple of months hitting her with the force of a tornado, knocking her back against the lower stonework of the White House fence.

Commotion around her, frantic footsteps, shouting, jostling. Someone in a blue shirt and silver badge knelt in front of her and pried the Glock from her hand.

———

DARK-SUITED SECRET SERVICE AGENTS stood in front of the White House fence, stiff and tense. White, red, and blue Metro Police cars sat idling fifty yards away. Half a dozen motorcycle cops in white shirt/black pant uniforms milled about.

Thomas Gifford, the Assistant Special Agent-in-Charge who oversees the Behavioral Analysis Units, badged the nearby Secret Service agent and walked to the ambulance backed up against the short, concrete pillars that sprung from the pavement. Vail sat on the Metro Medical Response vehicle's flat bumper, her gaze fixed somewhere on the cement.

Gifford stopped a couple of feet in front of her and raked a hand through his hair, as if stalling for time because he didn't know what to say. "I thought you had dinner reservations. You told me when you left the office you had to leave early."

"Yeah. I did. And then we saw Yates, and I called it in—"

"Okay," Gifford said, holding up a hand. "Forget about all that for now. How are you doing?"

Vail stood up, uncoiled her body, and stretched. "I'm fine. Any news on Mandisa?"

"Going into surgery. Shattered pelvis. But the round missed the major arteries, so she'll be okay. She'll need some rehab, but she's lucky. She's lucky you were there."

"With all the snipers and Secret Service and DC police around? I think she would've been fine without me."

"That's not what I'm hearing. They were assessing the situation, moving into position, trying to sort out what the hell was going on. The snipers weren't going to act unless there was a perceived threat to the president. And callous as it may seem, Danny Michael Yates was only a threat to you and Detective Manette. After Yates said he'd killed a cop, Metro started to put it together. But I honestly don't know if any of them would've shot him before you did. You saved her life, Karen."

Vail took a deep, uneven breath. "I had a good angle, I saw his arm, his hand—I knew he was going to pull that trigger."

Gifford looked away, glancing around at all the on-scene law enforcement personnel. "You still seeing the shrink?"

Vail nodded.

"Good. First thing in the morning, I want you back in his office. Then get out of town for a while. Clear your head. A couple months after Dead Eyes, this is the last thing you needed."

A smile teased the ends of her mouth.

"What?" Gifford asked.

"It's not often we agree on anything. I usually have some smartass comeback for you. But in this case, I've got nothing."

Vail realized that had been the punch line of the joke Manette had told earlier in the evening. It didn't seem so funny now.

Vail headed for her car, looking forward to—finally—getting out of town. Where? Didn't matter. Anywhere but here.

# ONE

## St. Helena, California
*The Napa Valley*

*T*he crush of a grape is not unlike life itself: You press and squeeze until the juice flows from its essence, and it dies a sudden, pathetic death. Devoid of its lifeblood, its body shrivels and is then discarded. Scattered about. Used as fertilizer, returned to the earth. Dust in the wind.

But despite the region in which John Mayfield worked—the Napa Valley—the crush of death wasn't reserved just for grapes.

John Mayfield liked his name. It reminded him of harvest and sunny vineyards.

He had, however, made one minor modification: His mother hadn't given him a middle name, so he chose one himself—Wayne. Given his avocation, "John Wayne" implied a tough guy image with star power. It also was a play on John Wayne Gacy, a notorious serial killer. And serial killers almost always were known in the public consciousness by three names. His persona—soon to be realized worldwide—needed to be polished and prepared.

Mayfield surveyed the room. He looked down at the woman, no longer breathing, in short order to resemble the shriveled husk of a crushed grape. He switched on his camera and made sure the lens captured the blood draining from her arm, the thirsty soil beneath her drinking it up as if it had been waiting for centuries to be nourished. Her fluid pooled a bit, then was slowly sucked beneath the surface.

A noise nearby broke his trance. He didn't have much time. He could have chosen his kill zone differently, to remove all risk. But it wasn't about avoiding detection. There was so much more to it.

The woman didn't appreciate his greatness, his power. She didn't see him for the unique person that he was. Her loss.

Mayfield wiped the knife of fingerprints and, using the clean handkerchief, slipped the sharp utensil beneath the dead woman's lower back. He stood up, kicked the loose dirt aside beneath his feet, scattering his footprints, then backed away.

# TWO

s Karen Vail walked the grounds of the Mountain Crest Bed & Breakfast, holding the hand of Roberto Enrique Umberto Hernandez, she stopped at the edge of a neighboring vineyard. She looked out over the vines, the sun setting a hot orange in the March chill.

"You've been quiet since we got off the plane. Still thinking about your application to the Academy?"

"Am I that transparent?" Robby asked.

"Only to a sharp FBI profiler."

Robby cradled a tangle of vines in his large hand. "Yeah, that's what I'm thinking about."

"You'll get into the Academy, Robby. Maybe not right away, with the budget cutbacks, but I promise. You'll make the cut."

"Bledsoe said he could get me something with Fairfax County."

"Really? You didn't tell me that."

"I didn't want to say anything about it. I don't really want it. If I talk about it, it might come true."

"You don't really believe that."

He shrugged a shoulder.

"Fairfax would be a step up over Vienna. It's a huge department. Lots more action."

"I know. It's just that there's an eleven-year wait to become a profiler once I get into the Academy. The longer it takes to get into the Bureau, the longer I have to wait."

"Why don't you call Gifford," Vail asked. "I thought he owes you. Because of your mother. Because of their relationship."

"That was Gifford's perception, not mine. He promised her he'd look after me." Robby glanced off a moment, then said, "He doesn't owe me anything. And I don't want any favors."

"How about I look into it, quietly, under the radar, when we get home?"

Robby chewed on that. "Maybe."

"I can call first thing in the morning, put out a feeler."

"No. We're here on vacation, to get away from all that stuff. It'll wait."

They turned and walked toward their room, The Hot Date, which was in a separate building off the main house. According to the information on the website, it was the largest in the facility, featuring spacious main sleeping quarters, a sitting area with a private porch and view of the vines, and a jetted tub in the bathroom. A wooden sign, red with painted flames, hung dead center on the door.

Vail felt around in her pocket for the key they'd been given when they checked in fifteen minutes ago. "You sure?"

"Absolutely sure. I'm wiping it from my mind right now. Nothing but fun from here on out. Okay?"

Vail fit the key into the lock and turned it. "Works for me." She swung the door open and looked around at the frilly décor of the room. She kicked off her shoes, ran forward, and jumped onto the bed, bouncing up and down like a five-year-old kid. "This could be fun," she said with a wink.

Robby stood a few feet away, hands on his hips, grinning widely. "I've never seen you like this."

"Nothing but fun from here on out, right? Not a worry in the world? No serial killers dancing around in our heads, no ASACs or lieutenants ordering us around. No job decisions. And no excess testosterone floating on the air."

"The name of this room is The Hot Date, right? That should be our theme for the week."

"Count me in."

"That's good," Robby said. "Because a hot date for one isn't much fun."

Vail hopped to the side of the bed, stood up precariously on the edge, and grabbed Robby's collar with both hands. She fell forward into him, but at six foot seven, he easily swept her off the bed and onto the floor, then kissed her hard.

He leaned back and she looked up at his face. "You know," Vail said, "I flew cross-country to Napa for the fine wine and truffles, but that was pretty freaking good, Hernandez."

"Oh, yeah? That's just a tasting. If you want the whole bottle, it'll cost you."

As he leaned in for another kiss, her gaze caught sight of the wall clock. "Oh—" The word rode on his lips and made him pull away. "Our tour."

"Our what?"

"I told you. Don't you ever listen to me?"

"Uh, yeah, I, uh—"

"The wine cave thing, that tour we booked through your friend—"

"The tasting, the dinner in the cave." He smiled and raised his brow. "See, I do listen to you."

"We've gotta leave now. It's about twenty minutes away."

"You sure?" He nodded behind her. "Bed, Cabernet, chocolate, *sex* . . ."

She pushed him away in mock anger. "That's not fair, Robby. You know that? We've got this appointment, it's expensive, like two hundred bucks each, and you just want to blow it off?"

"I can think of something else to blow off."

Vail twisted her lips into a mock frown. "I guess five minutes won't hurt."

"We'll speed to make up the time. We're cops, right? If we're pulled over, we'll badge the officer—"

Vail placed a finger over his lips. "You're wasting time."

———

THEY ARRIVED FIVE MINUTES LATE. The California Highway Patrol was not on duty—at least along the strip of Route 29 they traversed quite a few miles per hour over the limit—and they pulled into the parking lot smelling of chocolate and, well, the perfume of intimacy.

They sat in the Silver Ridge Estates private tasting room around a table with a dozen others, listening to a sommelier expound the virtues of the wines they were about to taste. They learned about the different climates where the grapes were grown, why the region's wind patterns and mix of daytime heat and chilly evenings provided optimum conditions for growing premium grapes. Vail played footsie with Robby beneath the table, but Robby kept a stoic face, refusing to give in to her childish playfulness.

That is, until she realized she was reaching too far and had been stroking the leg of the graying fifty-something man beside Robby, whose name tag read "Bill (Oklahoma)." When Bill from Oklahoma turned to face her with a surprised look on his face, Vail realized her error and shaded the same red as the Pinot Noir on the table in front of them.

"Okay," the sommelier said. "We're going to go across the way into our wine cave, where we'll talk about the best temperatures for storing our wine. Then we'll do a tasting in a special room of the cave and discuss pairings, what we're about to eat, with which wine—and why— before dinner is served."

As they rose from the table, Robby leaned forward to ask the sommelier a question about the delicate color of the Pinot. Oklahoma Bill slid beside Vail, but before he could speak, she said, "My mistake, buddy. Not gonna happen."

Bill seemed to be mulling his options, planning a counterattack. But Vail put an end to any further pursuit by cutting him off with a slow, firm, "Don't even think about it."

Bill obviously sensed the tightness in her voice and backed away as if she had threatened him physically. Judging by the visible tension in Vail's forearm muscles, that probably wasn't far from the truth.

They shuffled through the breezeway of the winery, their tour guide explaining the various sculptures that were set back in alcoves in the walls, and how they had been gathered over the course of five decades, one from each continent. When they passed through the mouth of the wine cave, the drop in temperature was immediately discernable.

"The cave is a near-constant fifty-five degrees, which is perfect for storing our reds," the guide said. The group crowded into the side room that extended off the main corridor. "One thing about the way we grow our grapes," the woman said. "We plant more vines per square foot than your typical winery because we believe in stressing our vines, making them compete for water and nutrients. It forces their roots deeper into the ground and results in smaller fruit, which gives more skin surface area compared to the juice. And since the skin is what gives a red varietal most of its flavor, you can see why our wines are more complex and flavorful."

She stopped beside a color-true model of two grapevines that appeared poised to illustrate her point, but before she could continue her explanation, a male guide came from a deeper portion of the cave, ushering another group along toward the exit. He leaned into the female guide's ear and said something. Her eyes widened, then she moved forward, arms splayed wide like an eagle. "Okay, everyone, we have to go back into the tasting area for a while." She swallowed hard and cleared her throat, as if there was something caught, then said, "I'm terribly sorry for this interruption, but we'll make it worth your while, I promise."

Vail caught a glimpse of a husky Hispanic worker who was bringing up the rear. She elbowed Robby and nodded toward the guy. "Something's wrong, look at his face." She moved against the stream of exiting guests and grabbed the man's arm.

"What's going on?" Vail asked.

"Nothing, signora, all's good. Just a . . . the power is out, it's very dark. Please, go back to the tasting room—"

"It's okay," Robby said. "We're cops."

"Policia?"

"Something like that." Vail held up her FBI credentials and badge. "What's wrong?"

"Who say there is something wrong?"

"It's my job to read people. Your face tells a story, señor. Now—" she motioned with her fingers. "What's the deal?"

He looked toward the mouth of cave, where most of the guests had already exited. "I did not tell you, right?"

"Of course not. Now . . . tell us, what?"

"A body. A *dead* body. Back there," he said, motioning behind him with a thumb.

"How do you know the person's dead?"

"Because she cut up bad, señora. Her . . . uh, *los pechos* . . . her . . . tits—are cut off."

Robby looked over the guy's shoulder, off into the darkness. "Are you sure?"

"I found the body, yes, I am sure."

"What's your name?"

"Miguel Ortiz."

"You have a flashlight, Miguel?" Vail asked.

The large man rooted out a set of keys from his pocket, pulled off a small LED light and handed it to her.

"Wait here. Don't let anyone else past you. You have security at the winery?"

"Yes, ma'am."

"Then call them on your cell," Vail said, as she and Robby backed away, deeper into the tunnel. "Tell them to shut this place down tight. No one in or out. No one."

———

AS A FEDERAL AGENT, Karen Vail was required to carry her sidearm wherever she traveled. But Robby, being a state officer, transported his weapon in a locked box, and it had to remain there; he was not permitted to carry it on his person. This fact was not lost on Vail as she removed her sidearm from her Velcro fanny pack. She reached down to her ankle holster and pulled a smaller Glock 27 and handed it to Robby.

They moved slowly through the dim cave. The walls were roughened gunite, dirt brown and cold to the touch. The sprayed cement blend gave the sense of being in a real cave, save for its surface uniformity.

"You okay in here?" Robby asked.

"Don't ask. I'm trying not to think about it." But she had no choice. Vail had developed claustrophobia after the recent incident in the Dead Eyes Killer's lair. Though she never had experienced such intense anxiety, it was suddenly a prominent part of her life. Going into certain parking garages, through commuter tunnels, and even into crammed elevators became a fretful experience. But it wasn't consistent. Sometimes it was worse than others.

Overall, it was inconvenient—and no fun admitting you had such an irrational weakness. But she was now afflicted with the malady and she did her best to control it. *Control?* Not exactly. *It* controlled *her*. *Manage* it was more accurate. Take her mind off it, talk herself through it until she could move into roomier quarters.

Sometimes, though, she thought she might actually claw through walls to get out. Getting squeezed into an elevator was the worst. For some reason, people didn't mind cramming against you if the alternative meant waiting another minute or two for the next car.

Vail slung her purse over her shoulder so it rested on her back, then moved the weak light around, taking care not to tread on anything that might constitute evidence.

"Maybe we should call it in," Robby said. "Let the locals handle it."

"The locals? This isn't exactly Los Angeles, Robby. I seriously doubt they have a whole lot of murders out here. If the vic's been cut like Miguel says, the local cops'll be out of their league. They're going to look at the crime scene but won't know what they're seeing."

"Beyond the obvious, you mean."

"The obvious to me and the obvious to a homicide detective are not the same things, Robby. You know that. When you encounter something unusual—no matter what profession you're talking about— would you rather hire someone who's seen that unusual thing a thousand times, or someone who's only seen it once or twice?"

"If we do find something, we won't have a choice. We've got no jurisdiction here."

"Yeah, well, we'll cross that bridge when we come to it."

They turned left down another tunnel, which opened into a large storage room of approximately a thousand square feet. Hundreds of French oak barrels sat on their sides, stacked one atop the other, three rows high and what must've been fifty rows long. A few candelabras with low-output lightbulbs hung from above, providing dim illumination. The walls and ceiling were constructed of roughened multicolored brick, with multiple arched ceilings that rose and plunged and joined one another to form columns every fifteen feet, giving the feel of a room filled with majestic gazebos.

A forklift sat dormant on the left, pointing at an opening along the right wall, where, amidst a break in the barrels, was another room. They moved toward it, Vail shining the flashlight in a systematic manner from left to right as they walked. They stepped carefully, foot by foot, to avoid errant hoses and other objects like . . . a mutilated woman's body.

They entered the anteroom and saw a lump in the darkness on the ground.

Robby said, "That bridge you just mentioned? I think we just came to it."

"Shit," Vail said.

"You didn't think Miguel was pulling our leg, did you? He looked pretty freaked out."

"No, I figured he saw something. I was just hoping it was a sack of potatoes, and in some kind of wine-induced stupor, he thought it was a dead woman."

"With her breasts cut off?"

"Hey, I'm an optimist, okay?"

Robby looked at her. "You're an optimist?"

As they stood there, Vail couldn't take her eyes off the body. She'd come to Napa to relax, to get away from work. Yet lying on the cold ground a little over twenty feet away was an all-too-obvious reminder of what she'd come here to escape.

Then she mentally slapped herself. She was pissed at having her vacation ruined. The woman in front of her had her life ruined.

Vail took a deep breath. "You have cell service? We need to call this in."

Robby flipped open his phone. "No bars."

"No bars in Napa? Some other time and place, that would be funny." She shook her head. "I can't believe I just said that."

"Humor is the best defense mechanism. Honestly, this sucks, Karen. You needed the time away. It was my idea to come here. I'm sorry."

"As our colleague Mandisa Manette is fond of saying, 'Sometimes life just sucks the big one.'" Vail's thoughts momentarily shifted to Manette, how she was doing in recovery. It didn't last long, as the snap of Robby's phone closing brought her back to the here and now.

"Okay," Vail said, "one of us goes, just to see if she's alive. We don't want to totally destroy the crime scene."

"Might as well be you," Robby said. "Get a close look, see if you see anything worthwhile."

Vail stood there, but didn't move. "I already see stuff that's worthwhile." She sighed in resignation, then stepped forward. "Like you said earlier, nothing but fun from here on out."

# THREE

*V*ail crouched a few feet from the body, outside the penumbra of bloody soil, and shone the flashlight across the woman's face, then worked her way over the chest, and on down to the leather shoes.

Robby stood twenty feet away, well beyond the visible field. "Feel her pulse."

"Yeah, no need to. She's done. Too much blood loss. No color left in the face."

"Check it, just—just to be sure."

Vail frowned, shifted her weight, and said, "I know death, Robby. I'm sure. Dead as the wood in those oak barrels back there."

Vail continued surveying the body with the light. Miguel was correct—the woman's breasts were severed, but then she never truly doubted that Miguel saw what he thought he saw. It's kind of a hard thing to get wrong, even when stunned with fear.

"Sharp knife, probably a few inches in length." She examined the slices, which were surprisingly clean. "No hesitation marks. Definitely not the first time this UNSUB has killed," she said, using the law enforcement abbreviation for "Unknown Subject."

"Any ritual behaviors?" Robby asked.

"Ritual" was a term used by profilers to describe unique activities a serial killer engages in with his victim's body. Like a behavioral fingerprint, they were vital to understanding or identifying a particular killer.

Vail pointed at the victim's chest. "For one, severing the breasts is a biggie."

"Yeah," Robby said. He cleared his throat in embarrassment. "I mean, aside from that."

"Her pants and underwear are pulled down to her knees. If there was penetration of any sort, pulling down the pants wouldn't be ritualistic, but if there wasn't any sexual assault involved, then it would be. Follow me?"

"Yeah. If he pulled down her pants and . . . violated her, then there's a reason for pulling the pants down. If he didn't violate her, there's no reason to pull down her pants. In which case it's probably related to his messed up childhood."

"Righto. But keep in mind that it's hard to draw conclusions on only one finding. There could be staging involved, so it's impossible to say for sure just yet."

"Staging. To throw off the cops?"

Vail pulled a pen from her pocket and gently nudged away the woman's collar. "If he's killed before, he may try to create a different looking crime scene, or the appearance of a new motive, just to misdirect us. That's why we have to consider the totality of the circumstances."

"And what would those be?"

"Every behavior is analyzed and reconciled with the logic of the forensic evidence. You have to examine each aspect of the crime scene to see if the offender carried out each key attribute to its logical conclusion. Are they sequentially logical?"

"Because unless the offender is a cop or a CSI, he wouldn't know all the details of crime scene reconstruction."

"Exactly." Vail shifted her weight to the right, leaned forward, and shone the light over the groin. "We'll have to wait for the ME to tell us about penetration. Hard to tell."

"The breasts?"

"Don't see them." She twisted and motioned to the forklift behind them. "See if there are keys in that thing, maybe you can shed some light on the situation."

Robby turned and made his way out of the room to the forklift. He leaned in, and a second later the vehicle's engine purred to life and the headlamp glowed brightly.

Vail rose from her crouch and stepped out of the beam's way. She looked down at the body. *Doesn't look any better in the light.*

A man wielding a powerful flashlight swallowed the mouth of the room. Robby spun, ducking from the beam's painful brilliance, Vail's Glock out in front of him.

"This is a crime scene," Robby shouted. "Get back."

The man, silhouetted by the handheld and the glare of the forklift's headlamp, said, "Yeah, I got that. But I'm supposed to be here. You're not. Now lower that fucking gun or we're gonna have a big goddamn problem."

"You are?" Vail asked, holding up a hand to shield her eyes.

"Detective Lieutenant Redmond Brix, Napa County Sheriff's Department."

Vail moved her head to the side, still fighting the glare. "Karen Vail, FBI. And that man with the Glock in your face is Detective Robby Hernandez, Vienna PD."

"Vienna?" Brix asked. "Where the hell is Vienna?"

"Virginia," Robby said, as he lowered his weapon.

Brix dropped his flashlight out of Vail's line of sight. "Glad to meet you . . . Not really. Now, you mind getting outta my crime scene?"

Vail raised her hands in resignation, then backed away to Robby's side.

Brix, his attention still on Robby, said, "Mind telling me, Detective, what you're doing with a handgun in California?"

Robby handed the Glock to Vail.

"It's my backup piece," she said as she bent over to reholster it on her ankle.

Brix frowned. There was nothing more he could say.

"Crime scene's yours, Lieutenant." Vail rested her hands on her hips and watched as Brix stepped forward, following Vail's path to the body. He lowered his Maglite and ran the beam over the victim. When the brightness hit the area of severed breasts, Brix rocked back involuntarily. He caught his balance and looked away a moment, then seemed to force his eyes back to the body.

"God damn," Brix said. "Shit." He turned away, then marched out, into the large storage room. Vail and Robby followed. "You okay?" Vail asked.

Brix seemed to collect himself, then lifted his head and faced her.

"I'm fine." He extended a hand. "Thanks for securing the scene. Where are you staying? I'll need to get a more complete statement."

"Mountain Crest B&B."

"I know the place." He dug out his cell phone, flipped it open, and shone his flashlight in Vail's face. He pressed a button, it made a camera shutter click, then he did the same to Robby. As he snapped his phone closed, he said, "I'll be in touch. We'll take it from here now. You know your way out?"

Vail felt her blood pressure rising. This was usually the point where she said or did something she later regretted. Robby either sensed the tension or he'd gotten to know her pretty well, because his large hand clamped down on her elbow. He pulled her close against his body, then gently turned her around.

"We're fine, thanks," Robby said.

It was all happening slowly, Robby's voice somewhere in the background, as he led Vail through the tunnels. The next thing she knew, she was standing at the wine cave's entrance, the cold fresh air of a Napa evening blowing in her face.

# FOUR

*A*fter returning the flashlight to Miguel Ortiz, they got into their rental and rode in silence, at a considerably slower speed, along Highway 29. Although they were supposed to have been treated to an exceptional meal paired with exceptional wine, the winery offered them a refund or a rain check voucher and sent its guests home because of a "water main break deep in the cave." Vail almost laughed aloud when they were told of the reason for the sudden cancellation, but stopped herself. It didn't matter. After the discovery of the body, the excitement of the evening seemed to leave them like air escaping a leaky balloon.

Finally, with the sunset now only a distant memory from what seemed like a long-ago afternoon, Vail sighed deeply and said, "Where are we headed?"

"A restaurant my friend recommended. I don't know if we can get in, but he said it's worth the wait."

———

ROBBY PULLED THEIR NISSAN MURANO into the parking lot of Bistro Don Giovanni. Vail was busy thumbing the keyboard of her BlackBerry, texting a message to her fourteen-year-old son, Jonathan. Vail's Aunt Faye was visiting from New York and staying at her house with Jonathan while Vail was on vacation.

Vail hit Send, then slid the phone into its pouch.

They left the car and headed toward the restaurant. Vail saw clots of people sitting on an outdoor veranda that rimmed the bistro under a covered awning. They hovered in close quarters over flickering candles. Couples holding hands, friends laughing. Vail and Robby walked in and gave their name to the host, who had a thick Italian accent. The restaurant swelled with chattering conversation and clinking plates. It smelled of garlic, tomatoes, and olives.

"I think that may've been Don Giovanni," Robby said, as they walked back outside onto the deck. He flagged a waiter heading toward him. "Hey, is that Don Giovanni?"

The server, who had an olive complexion and spoke with an Italian accent, grinned. "There is no Don Giovanni, sir. Donna Scala owns the restaurant with her husband, Giovanni. And yes, that man is Giovanni."

"Got it," Robby said. "Don, Giovanni."

"Tell Giovanni his restaurant smells heavenly," Vail said.

Robby thanked the man and turned away. "Just a guess, Karen, but I'm sure he knows."

Vail's phone buzzed. She pulled it out, read the text, and smiled.

"Jonathan?" Robby asked.

"He's gotten his sense of humor back, which is good to see."

They continued on down the wood steps into a gardenlike setting, an expanse of grass surrounding a fountain sprouting surreal brass sculptures that towered above the ground: a frog, hind legs in the air as it landed on a square pedestal; an Italian soldier balancing on a tall pole with one hand while supporting a large white boulder in the other; and a chef ascending an angled ladder with the flag of Italy in his outstretched hand, as if he were reaching to place it in a holder.

Vail and Robby crunched gravel as they walked to the fountain's edge, then stood there examining the artwork.

She cocked her head to the side. "Interesting."

"Not sure what to make of it," Robby said.

"That soldier is balancing the delicate choices of life and death. Precariously suspended above the ocean, he holds a large boulder, which in reality he shouldn't be able to support, as he keeps himself horizontal. A metaphor for staying afloat."

Robby studied the scene before him. "Not sure how you got that, but okay."

"I tend to get a little philosophical after seeing a serial killer's handiwork while on vacation." She turned and sat down at one of the small nearby tables that were arranged around the fountain's periphery. "Sorry, I shouldn't have brought it up. Bad enough seeing it, no need to talk about it in such a beautiful setting."

Robby reached out and took her hand. "Violence is all around us, Karen. It's a fact of life. We see it all the time. That's our job. Can't escape it."

"What do you make of Brix?" she asked.

"Strange name."

"Strange guy. But that's not what I mean. There's more to this murder than Brix is telling. I saw his face, his reaction when he looked at the body. Like he's seen this before."

"You got that from his reaction?"

"Body language. Then he sends us on our way."

Robby lifted a shoulder. "Maybe. But it's not our investigation, Karen. We're not even in the mix here."

A woman from the restaurant approached them in silhouette from the bright restaurant lights against the garden's relative darkness. "Robby, your table is ready."

"I'm leaving this talk out here," Vail said as she rose from the chair.

Robby reached out and took her hand. "No argument from me."

# FIVE

*V*ail and Robby sat at the bed-and-breakfast's rectangular table as the hostess announced what she would be serving: stuffed French toast with fresh fruit preserves and maple syrup, orange juice squeezed this morning, and Greek yogurt.

Joining them were a young couple who looked like they'd enjoyed the firmness of their mattress, and an older couple who appeared to be looking forward to retirement.

"I'm Chuck," the gray-haired man said, "and this lovely lady here is Candace. Married thirty-five years tomorrow. And we lived to tell about it." He elbowed his wife, who took it in stride and bumped him back with her shoulder. "And that's Brandy, and her husband, Todd," Chuck said. "Second anniversary is next week. Boston, right?"

"They can speak for themselves," Candace said. "Sorry, Chuck sometimes likes to dominate conversations. Trick is to kick him in the shin." Chuck gave her a look. "What?" Candace said. "It's worked for thirty-five years."

"We met Chuck and Candace a couple days ago," Brandy said.

"Karen and Robby," Vail said. "Virginia."

"So what do you and Robby do?" Todd asked.

"Us?" Vail said. "I'm with the FBI—an agent out of a special unit you may have—"

"FBI," Todd said. "Really? You know, I've always wanted to ask a cop what it's like, but, well, I've never been in the right setting. Know what I mean? You can't walk right up to a cop on the street and just ask."

"Ask what?" Robby said.

Todd began nervously bouncing his left leg. "Well, what it's like. What it's like to shoot someone. Have you? Shot someone?"

"I have," Vail said, flashes of Danny Michael Yates momentarily blinding her thoughts.

Todd leaned forward slightly. "Ever killed anyone? I mean, what does that feel like?"

"Todd," Brandy said under her breath. "That's rude."

"Yes," Vail said, looking into Todd's eyes. "I have. But it's not something that comes up often in my line of work. Actually," she said with a chuckle, "that's not true. I killed a bank robber and then almost killed my ex-husband a couple months ago. And then, last week, right in front of the White House—"

Robby leaned forward and cleared his throat. He forced a laugh, then said, "Karen's got a very dry sense of humor . . ."

Apparently, Robby had taken Candace's advice seriously, because Vail felt a kick beneath the table, a not so subtle signal for her to cut it out. The others at the table looked at each other, apparently trying to ascertain if Vail's comments were something they should laugh at or take seriously.

"Joking aside," Robby quickly said, "Karen's a profiler."

"Like on those shows?" Brandy asked. "What was that one, it was on years ago, we used to watch it right after we met," she said, poking Todd in the arm.

"*Profiler*," Todd said. "I loved that show."

Brandy leaned back in her seat with folded arms. "You just thought the actress was hot."

"No, I really liked it, the way she could touch the clothing and see the killer. That was cool—"

"That was a lot of bullsh—a lot of *nonsense*, is what it was," Vail said. "We don't have special powers. Real life isn't usually as cool as Hollywood."

"But it is pretty interesting work," Robby said.

"What about that show *Criminal Minds*?" Candace asked.

"More like it," Vail said. "Except we don't have our own private jet. It was actually proposed about thirty years ago but it didn't fly because it cost too much."

"Good one," Todd said. "The private jet didn't fly."

"And what do you do?" Chuck asked.

"I'm a detective," Robby said.

"Sounds like you both see a lot of violence in your lives," Chuck said.

*We keep on this line of questioning and you're likely to see a bit of violence, yourself, Chuck.* Instead of translating that thought into action, Vail forced her friendliest smile, waved a hand, and said, "Enough about us. Let's hear about you."

And she and Robby heard about Chuck's work as the owner of an auto detail chain and Candace's career in banking. By the time the plates were cleared, Vail had lost track of the conversation. Her mind was elsewhere.

As Todd and Brandy stood to leave and wished everyone a "great time in the wine country," Robby whispered in Vail's ear. "What's gotten into you?"

Vail turned away from the departing guests. "I don't know, this thing with Manette affected me more than I thought, coming so soon after Dead Eyes. I'm just on edge, I guess."

As the hostess started clearing the table, Robby thanked her, then walked with Vail outside to their car. A heavy dew still hung in the air from a steady, light rain during the night.

"Then it's good we're here. We can relax, put all this stuff behind us—"

"We have to go see Brix."

"Karen, if you're all dialed up about what happened last week, then you need to let go of this wine cave thing. Someone else will deal with it."

"Not my style. It's in my DNA, I can't help it. It grabs hold of my brain and doesn't let go—I tossed and turned all night. Something's up with him. I need to ask him some questions, get some answers. See if there's any way we can help out."

"Didn't seem like he wanted our help."

Vail pulled open the car door. "Then we have to show him why he should."

# SIX

While Vail drove, Robby dialed the Napa County Sheriff's Office and asked for Lieutenant Brix. Though Vail wanted to drop in, Robby felt that they'd pissed on his turf once and didn't want to come off as confrontational.

"The courtesy of a phone call would go a ways toward defusing any animosity he may have toward us," Robby had said.

"Hey, we were there trying to help out as peace officers. We weren't trying to 'piss on his turf.'"

"He gets to his crime scene and finds a big-time FBI profiler hovering over a vic's body in his jurisdiction. That's not intimidating?"

"Well, that and I'm a woman. I'm sure that didn't help."

"I'm sure not."

Vail pursed her lips. "Fine," she said, "we'll do it your way."

So Robby called ahead. "Got it," he said into the phone, as he jotted something onto a scrap of paper. He hung up and said to Vail, "Brix isn't at the station. He's at a place called"—he consulted his notes—"Peju Province, a winery off 29."

Vail pulled out her pocket GPS and began poking the address into its display. "Stella will tell us how to get there."

"You named your GPS?"

"Better than saying 'it,'" she said. She handed Stella to Robby and put the Murano in gear. "So how do you want to play this?"

"This is your show, Karen. I'm just along for the ride."

———

THEY ARRIVED AT PEJU PROVINCE, drove down the tree-lined driveway, and pulled around the circle into the parking lot. They walked through the metal archway and entered the winery grounds, which were meticulously landscaped with a variety of shrubbery, lush grass, multicolored flowering plants, man-made reflecting pools, and mixed-media sculptures. They crunched along the curving, decomposed granite trail past a triangular white marble female figurine, then entered a paved path that led past a stucco and stone-faced two-story building with a pointed, weathered copper roof.

"Beautiful grounds," Vail said.

"Cool sculptures." Robby pulled on the wrought iron handle affixed to the oversize wood doors and they entered a gift shop area.

"Are you here for a tasting?" a smiling woman asked.

Vail held up her badge. "We're here for some answers."

The woman's face drooped faster than a Vegas slot swallows a quarter.

"It's okay," Robby said, holding up a hand. "We're looking for Lieutenant Brix."

"He's in the tasting room," she said, still looking a bit rattled. "Follow me."

Robby leaned down by Vail's ear. "Jesus, Karen, cool your jets. You nearly gave that woman a heart attack."

"I get this way when my internal alarms go off."

"This isn't our case, remember?"

The woman stopped in a large, high-ceilinged room containing a wall-sized dome-shaped stained glass window depicting the three Greek graces. Several Brazilian cherry cabinets and tasting bars lined the room. Sommeliers were pouring from red-topped wine bottles. And a man was yodeling.

"Is that guy yodeling?" Vail asked, nodding at a blonde-haired sommelier with a guitar strapped across his shoulder and scratching out a rhythm with a coin against a ribbed credit card.

"Not sure," Robby said. He listened a moment, then said, "Actually, I think he's rapping now."

Just then, the tasters huddled around his counter began clapping. And Vail caught sight of Redmond Brix. And Brix caught sight of Vail.

He stopped clapping and pushed past the customers to meet Vail and Robby. Poking a thumb over his shoulder, Brix said, "Guy's a trip, isn't he?"

Robby glanced back at the happy guests, who had pulled out their credit cards to buy wine. "Customers seem to enjoy his show."

"They make some damn fine wine here, too. Now, what is it you want?"

*Direct*, Vail thought. *Good. I like direct. But I'm not going to play that hand.* She got her first look at him in the light. His face was leathery and lined from too many years spent in the sun. *From policework? Possibly, but not likely.* "Your name," she said. "Brix. We passed a restaurant a few miles back called Brix. You own it?"

"Brix is a wine term. A measure of sugar content in the grape."

Vail stifled a laugh. "So your ancestors named themselves after sweet grapes?"

Brix fixed his jaw. "Name used to be Broxton. My great grandparents, Abner and Bella, lived in the old Chianti area of Tuscany and grew grapes for a living. Bella thought they were working too hard for too little and heard about a wine region in California. She wanted to move, but Abner resisted. She finally convinced him to go, and they sold their land and came here and bought a vineyard. They planted Sangiovese and Chianti vines they'd brought from Italy, and hit it big. Bella disappeared five years later. Never found her. Abner changed the family name from Broxton to Brix to honor Bella, since she was the reason they moved to Napa. And she was a very *sweet* woman."

"So I guess you don't own that restaurant," Robby said.

"No, I don't own that restaurant."

Vail tilted her head. "That's a very . . . sweet story."

"Yeah, I think so. Now, you didn't come over here to ask me about my name. What is it you really want?"

"Answers," Vail said. "About the murder."

"Why did I know I hadn't seen the last of you two?" He turned and pushed through the large light-ash doors a dozen feet to his right. They exited the copper-topped building onto a wide footbridge that spanned the man-made pond, then stopped a few feet away, where the sun was breaking through the clouds.

Brix folded his thick, hairy arms across his chest. "Talk."

"Your reaction to what you saw in the cave—"

"You mean the dead body?"

"The dead body," Vail said.

"And just what reaction would you be talking about?"

*I hate playing games.* "You tell me. Seemed to affect you."

"Yeah, it affected me. It was brutal. It just got to me."

Vail said, "Bullshit. You're a homicide detective. You've seen bad shit before." Vail decided to venture forward with what she really wanted to know. "I had a hard time sleeping last night. I kept replaying what happened in the cave, and I kept coming back to your body language, the look on your face when you saw the woman, the severed breasts—"

"I'm sorry my *reaction* bothered you. I hope you'll sleep better tonight. Now, is that it?"

"I'm curious—did you find the breasts at the crime scene?"

"No."

"Do you know what the killer did with them—and why? Because I do."

Brix's facial muscles tightened. "We'll figure it out, thank you very much."

"I sure hope so, because knowing what that means is important. Here's another important question: Have there been any other murders like this one?"

Brix snorted. "If there were, you'd know about it. A murder in the Napa Valley—with the woman's breasts cut off? Jesus H., it'd make national news."

Vail's eyebrows rose. "National news, really?"

"You know anything about this region, Agent Vail?"

"About as much as the average FBI profiler from Virginia visiting the area for the first time."

"Yeah," Brix said with a chuckle. "I'll translate that into 'not much.' So here's the deal. Napa's economy is a huge revenue generator for the state. Heck, even for the country as a whole. Aside from Disneyland and Disneyworld, Napa is the third most visited place in the country. See where I'm going with this? If anything happened to jeopardize that kind of tourism, that kind of *money*—you tell me:

Would there be a lot of media coverage? Would all the stops be pulled out—at the state or federal level to investigate and figure out what the hell's going on?"

Vail chewed on that one.

Robby said, "I see your point."

"That's assuming," Vail said, "that the good people of Napa want the media crawling around here. The national headlines. Would put a huge dent in the local trade to have a serial killer plying his trade in town. I did a little reading on the plane. You've still got some mom and pops here, but you've also got a lot of multinational corporations that have been buying up wineries. Billions of dollars at stake. See where *I'm* going with this?"

Brix's eyes narrowed. He stared long and hard at Vail, then said, "Always good to visit with colleagues from outta town. Remember, drinking and driving is against the law 'round here. And the California Highway Patrol ain't as friendly as I am."

With that, he stepped around them and headed into the parking lot.

# SEVEN

*V*ail pulled out her BlackBerry and started playing with it. They were still standing at Peju, Redmond Brix having disappeared into the parking lot.

"What are you doing?" Robby asked.

"Finding out where the local morgue is."

Robby placed both hands on his hips and craned his head around. "Karen, we're here on vacation, remember? In fact," he said as he consulted his watch, "you have a mud bath and massage in Calistoga in a couple hours. Paid in advance. You don't want to miss that. If nothing else, after Dead Eyes and Yates, you need it."

Vail glanced up at Robby. "We should be fine. Plenty of time." She turned and headed off toward the parking lot. "Let's go."

They arrived at the Napa County morgue on Airport Boulevard about twenty minutes later. The morgue was located on the ground floor of the Napa County Sheriff's Department, a recently constructed state-of-the-art building built of stucco and stone. With a round, windowed rotunda projecting up like a sentry over the complex, it had the majestic feel of a high-end winery, not unlike the architecture of the structure that housed Peju Province's tasting room. But the triad of American, state, and sheriff's department flags flapping out front set the record straight on the building's true purpose.

Through the front door, a cylindrical lobby sported butterscotch walls with strategic lighting every few feet. On the floor, tan tile surrounded inner concentric circles of dark chocolates and gray greens, moving centrally toward a star emblazoned with the words "Napa County Sheriff's Dept." Directly above was an atrium that rose the equivalent of another story, with skylights along its periphery.

Vail glanced to her right, where there were two marble-topped oak counters with tri-panes of bullet-resistant glass.

Robby followed her gaze. "You don't expect them to look at your creds and take us back to the body, do you?"

"Couldn't hurt to try." Before Robby could protest—and no doubt point out that it could, in fact, hurt to try—Vail walked up to the counter and engaged the clerk behind the glass.

"I'm Special Agent Karen Vail with the FBI," she said, holding up her credentials. She could see the reflection of her brass badge in the glass. "This is Detective Roberto Hernandez. We need to take a look at the body that was found last night at the Silver Ridge wine cave."

The woman squinted, then said, "I didn't realize the FBI is involved."

"We're the ones who found the body." Not entirely true, but it sounded good.

"You—uh—I thought—"

"I've got this," a graying, buzz-cut military-looking man in the background said. He stepped to the glass, dressed in a green uniform and tie and a taupe shirt. A brass star was pinned over his left breast. And bars on his shoulder. A person of authority. *Uh oh,* Vail thought. *Now I've done it.*

"What did you say your name was?"

She told him. "I'm a profiler—"

"I know who you are," the man said.

Vail glanced at Robby, who didn't look pleased. He no doubt sensed trouble, and was watching his vacation slip away into a morass of politics and hard-headed cop testosterone.

"Yeah, that's good," Vail stammered. "So, like I was saying, we'd like to take a look at the body, if that's—"

"You taught that class at the Academy, didn't you?"

Vail felt herself take a step backward. "I teach at the Academy, that's right." Then she grabbed a peek at his name tag and put it all together. This guy was the sheriff and he must've gone through the FBI's National Academy, a program run by the Bureau to educate law enforcement leaders from all over the world on ways to raise their department's standards, knowledge, and interagency cooperation. The highly respected eleven-week course has graduated over thirty-six thousand law enforcement professionals in its seventy-five-year existence.

"You were in one of my classes, at the National Academy," Vail said. A statement, not a question . . . feigning recognition. Who doesn't like to be remembered?

"Yeah, couple years ago. Damn good program, I gotta say. Your class on behavioral analysis was one of the more intriguing."

Vail smiled and turned to Robby, who looked like a guy who found himself the butt of a joke. He was not enjoying this.

"Thank you, thank you very much. That means a great deal to me. I like to think that being a profiler is one of the best jobs at the Bureau." *That is, when serial killers aren't trying to kill me.* "It's very rewarding, particularly when we can help catch an UNSUB who—"

Robby cleared his throat.

"Right—well, in any case, Detective Hernandez and I would really appreciate if we could see the body of the woman who was brought in last night. Sheriff—"

"Owens. Stan Owens. Call me Stan."

"Right. Sheriff—Stan—if we could have a few minutes, we won't bother you about this again." A promise she might not be able to keep, but again, it sounded good—and judging by the look on Owens's face, he seemed to like the idea, too.

"I don't suppose it'd hurt anything," he said, then nodded to the legal clerk beside him to make it happen.

Owens swiped his electronic proximity card over the sensor, then led Vail and Robby downstairs and into the morgue conference room on the first floor. There was an ovoid conference table surrounded by high-backed, burgundy office chairs. There was a periodic table hanging in the corner of one of the long walls, a TV/VCR setup mounted on the wall, and a large whiteboard.

Owens walked over to the whiteboard and slid it to the left, revealing a window into the morgue. Behind the glass and to their right stood two lab-coated technicians in front of a gurney that was parked by a stainless steel dissection table, above which was suspended a large scale for weighing resected organs. The sheriff pressed a wall-mounted intercom, and the woman behind the glass looked at him.

"Dr. Abbott, we're here to see the murder victim brought in last night. This is Special Agent Vail and Detective Hernandez." Owens turned to Vail and said, "Dr. Brooke Abbott."

Brooke Abbott wore a clear face shield, a Tyvek biohazard suit, disposable booties, and latex gloves, and was up to her elbows in—well, she was in the middle of an autopsy. But it was the body on the adjacent table that Vail and Robby had come to see.

Abbott handed the scalpel to the technician. "Continue just like I showed you. I'm going back to Jane." Abbott shuffled to her left, to the adjacent table, and, with the movement of a gloved hand, indicated the corpse. "Meet Jane Doe."

Owens moved his hands to a small remote control box to his left. He shifted the levers and the image on the closed circuit monitor above his head zoomed and rotated. "No ID yet?" Owens asked.

Abbott turned to the window. "Should have something soon."

Vail stepped closer. They hadn't gotten too far into the procedure, because the Y incision had not yet been made. That was good—she'd wanted a look at the body under better conditions—on a table, in an optimally lit environment.

"What can you tell me about her?" Vail asked. She craned her head toward the monitor and tried to orient herself.

Abbott tilted her head. "From the cursory exam, I'd say late forties, but fit and with good muscle tone. Well maintained teeth, evidence of facial makeup."

"So she cared about her appearance and was not a vagrant or high-risk victim."

"Fair assessment." Abbott nodded at the body. "But there is something a bit bizarre, right up your alley, I'd imagine. Look at the feet." Abbott angled her headlamp and brought up a magnifying lens. "Second toe, right foot. Nail's been ripped off the bed." She pointed with a probe.

Vail moved closer to the screen as Owens maneuvered the lever. "Are those tissue tags on the nail bed?"

"Yes."

"Definitely ripped off postmortem."

"Exactly."

Vail moved away from the monitor, trying to get a better view. "Can we come in? It's really difficult doing it this way."

"For evidence control—"

"I understand, Doctor. But I need to see nuances that might not be picked up by the camera."

Owens nodded. "Fine with me."

Abbott shrugged. "Send her in. Just her."

Robby waited in the conference room while Owens took Vail into the corridor, out through a door into another hallway that opened to where the bodies were off-loaded into refrigeration units, and then into the Clean Room. Vail slipped into a Tyvek suit, then donned a face shield and gloves.

Owens pointed the way into the Dirty Room. "Go past the scrub sink and around the bend. That'll take you directly into the morgue." Owens left her to return to the conference room, and Vail followed his instructions.

Morgues all have a familiar look and smell. They're never cheery, sometimes downright depressing, always chilly, and often utilitarian. In keeping with the overall building, however, this morgue was the most spacious and technologically advanced facility Vail had seen.

She walked into the large room and crossed the shiny taupe floor toward the far wall, where the gurneys were docked. To her right, on the other side of the window, stood Robby.

Robby leaned close to the glass. In a filtered voice, through the intercom, he said, "So we've got severed breasts and a torn-off toenail."

"You're looking for the behaviors," Owens said, standing to his right. "What's it called?"

Vail leaned back from the body. "Ritual behavior. The things the killer does with the body that aren't necessary for the successful commission of his crime. They're unique to each particular offender. He does them repetitively, and he doesn't change them—so you'll see them in every one of his kills." She looked to Owens. "If this UNSUB has struck before, it's likely these ritual behaviors will help us link his victims."

Owens was nodding. "Hate that. If you don't use this stuff regularly, you forget it."

"There's a lot to it," Vail said. "And we're always learning more, expanding our knowledge base." She nodded at Abbott. "Anything you can tell us?"

"I haven't gotten too far into it—uh, I mean her—but both wrists were sliced. Very sharp utensil, which is . . ." She reached beneath the stainless autopsy table to a lower shelf and lifted a plastic-wrapped and evidence-labeled knife. "This."

Vail didn't take it, but she visually inspected it.

"Must've brought it with him," Vail said. "Not the kind of thing you find in a wine cave."

"Definitely not," Owens said through the intercom.

Vail turned back to the body. "Anything else?"

"Knife was found beneath the lower back. He wanted us to find it."

"Apparently. COD?"

"Asphyxiation, actually." She moved the light to the woman's neck. "See?" Abbott pointed with a gloved index finger. "Hallmark injuries to the lower jaw. Man strangs. The victim was moving her head back and forth, producing those abrasions. If I had to guess, he used a blunt object, possibly even a forearm, like a bar arm, to crush her trachea."

Vail looked over at Robby, who was craning his neck to look at the monitor. "*Crush* her trachea?" he asked.

Vail leaned in for a look. "That's a new one. I don't think I've seen that before. Usually the offender uses manual strangulation, or a ligature. But crushing the trachea . . . that'd take an awful lot of force. I mean, there's a lot of tissue there. You've got the thyroid and cricoid cartilage in front of it and the spinal column behind it. And the trachea itself is pretty tough cartilage."

Abbott was nodding. "It was a very violent act."

"Was a device of some sort used—a bar or pipe?"

Abbott looked down at the body, considering the question. "I'm not sure. There are no tool marks. I'll look to see if there are any traces of metal or paint embedded in the skin, but I didn't find anything unusual during the initial exam. Then again, I couldn't guarantee you'd find anything. Especially if it's wrapped in something."

Vail leaned forward and looked at the eyes. "Petechial hemorrhages?"

"Yes."

Vail nodded. *Makes sense.* "Any scrape marks on her back?"

Abbott stepped back, eyebrows raised. "Yeah, as a matter of fact, there are. Upper back and the parietal region of the skull. Pretty deep, actually."

"He pushed her against the cave wall as he cut off her air supply. And the lips—inside, indentation marks?"

"You mean from cupping her mouth?" Robby asked.

"Exactly."

"Let's check." Abbott gently parted the lips and rolled the upper portion into position. Shined her light. "Yup."

"Okay, so he confronts her face on," Vail said.

"So he might've known her," Robby said, "or sweet-talked her, to get close enough."

Vail nodded. "Reasonable conclusion."

"So what do you think is going on?" Owens asked.

"Hard to say," Vail said. "Not enough information to formulate an opinion."

"Best guess?"

Vail looked back at the body. She understood the desire of cops to know what she was thinking, but she also hated being pressured into drawing conclusions before there was enough information to make an accurate assessment.

But it did give her the opportunity to ask a question for which she still wanted an answer. "Have there been other murders like this one?"

"If there was a woman murdered with her breasts cut off, even you would probably have heard about it, all the way at Quantico. You gotta realize we don't have many murders here. About two a year. That's it. Been that way far back as I can remember."

Vail looked over at Robby through the window. "And you think Vienna is quiet." To Owens: "Sheriff, right now, all I can say is the guy is likely intelligent, organized, and confident. More than that will have to wait." Vail turned to Abbott. "Thanks for the look. Technically, I guess, I wasn't here."

She found her way back down the hall to the conference room and pushed through the door. She pulled a card from her pocket and handed it to Owens. "If you find anything else we should know about, would you give me a call?"

Owens took the card. "Sure thing. But . . . and I probably should've asked this up front . . . how are you involved with this case?"

Robby cleared his throat. "We're not."

"But we found the body in the cave," Vail said. "We secured the scene until Lieutenant Brix could get there."

"Redd Brix?"

Robby said, "Yeah, know him?"

"Not many people in this town don't know Redd."

"He doesn't seem to be too cooperative," Robby said.

"He doesn't like outsiders looking over his shoulder. Can't say I blame him."

"Don't take this the wrong way," Vail said, "but a killing like this could be a big problem. And with only two murders a year, you guys may not be . . . equipped to handle this type of thing. Nothing to be ashamed about, it's just a matter of getting some help from someone who's been down this path before."

"Tell you the truth, if it was up to me, I'd give your ASAC a ring and get you hooked up here. But I have to tread carefully. Don't wanna step on toes. You know what I'm saying."

"I do, but—"

Owens held up a hand. "Let me do my thing behind the scenes. Be patient. If it's meant to be, it'll happen."

# EIGHT

With nothing to do but wait, Vail and Robby headed to Calistoga Day Spa, where Vail would take in a mud bath, hot springs, and hour massage. It was a pampering to which she was unaccustomed—in fact, had never had, in her life.

Robby dropped her at the spa and had the next few hours to himself. When he returned to pick up Vail, she walked into the glass enclosed lobby by the front desk with her hair back in a headband and a smile on her face.

"Good time?"

"If I closed my eyes, I could sleep for hours."

He carried her duffle to the car and tossed it into the back seat. "So how was the mud bath?"

"Interesting. I mean, I'm lying there, totally relaxed, then I realized that I'm lying in a pile of warm cow shit. And I paid a lot of money for it."

"Did you enjoy it?"

"Once I got the thought out of my mind, it was very soothing. Not as relaxing as the massage. I had this hunk named Pedro, and he had these really strong hands—"

"Do I want to hear this?" Robby asked.

"Apparently not." She looked over at him and grinned. "Jealous?"

Before Robby could answer, Vail's phone started ringing. She reached into the rear seat and fished it out of the duffel. "Karen Vail."

"Yeah, this is Stan, Stan Owens."

"Stan . . . you got something for us?"

"Sort of. I had a chat with Redd Brix. I think you should go and talk to him, see if you can get him to request the BAU's involvement."

"You think he'll go for it?"

"I softened him up for you, told him about my experience with the National Academy. He did a lot of listening, didn't say much. Thanked me for the call."

"Well, thanks, Stan. We'll go chat with him right now. Any idea where he is?"

"Matter of fact, yes. It's his day off. He's at a buddy's house digging out an old wine cave."

"Digging out an old wine cave? Is that like spelunking?"

"Not sure what that is, but that cave is legendary stuff here in the valley. A hundred years ago there was an earthquake that caused a cave-in at one of the premiere wineries in the region. Black Knoll Vineyards, been around since 1861. Legend is that there were some special bottles in that cave, and when the earthquake hit, they were buried alive, so to speak. Some old geezer convinced his neighbor he knew where the cave was located, and it happens to be on land belonging to Brix's friend."

Vail took down the address, thanked him, and plugged it into their GPS.

"You don't really want to go there now," Robby said. "You're oiled, massaged, and relaxed. Let's go shower, get dressed, have a nice dinner—"

"Proceed to the highlighted route," Stella's GPS voice announced.

Vail shrugged. "You heard the lady."

# NINE

"You have arrived at your destination, on the left," Stella said.

Vail compared the address to her notes and said, "Indeed we have."

Robby nodded at the portable electronic device in Vail's hands. "You like that thing, don't you?"

"She's grown on me." Seeing Robby's twisted mouth, she said, "What, don't tell me you're intimidated by a female voice telling you where to go."

"You tell me where to go all the time."

"Exactly. Turn right." Vail thumbed a hand at the signpost. The numbers were lettered in block gold leaf on the label of a magnum wine bottle in the hands of a large statue of a waiter dressed in a tuxedo.

"Something tells me this is going to be interesting," Robby said as he swung the Murano onto the driveway.

They drove a hundred feet before they came to an electric gate, which sat splayed open. To the right was a well-maintained mushroom-colored guard shack, which stood empty.

"Guess we just let ourselves in," Vail said.

Just past the small security shed was a cutout in the fine gravel and compacted dirt that lined the paved roadway. A silver Ford sat parked parallel to the path in one of the available slots.

"Wanna walk?" Robby asked. "We don't know where Brix is on the property, might as well explore." He slid the Murano into the spot in front of the Ford and they hiked along the asphalt toward the house, which sat thirty yards ahead.

"Gorgeous property," Vail said. Exquisitely maintained vineyards, arranged in precise rows, lined the land to the north and south. "My feeling is that if we go to the front door, good chance they'll tell us to go home."

"But if we wander around, we're just a couple of bumbling idiots looking for Brix."

"Exactly."

The house was a gray, four-story, stone-faced structure with mature palms fanning out from either side of the entrance. A six-car garage sat to the left of the main building, attached by a covered walkway with vine-covered columns. Vail and Robby hung a left by the palms and moved down a graveled path for about fifty paces.

They stopped and surveyed the landscape. Ahead of them lay closely cropped grass-covered rolling hills, with a sharp drop-off slightly to their right. Robby pointed in the direction he felt they should proceed, and they made their way down the sharp grade, moving sideways to control their descent.

"You okay?" he asked.

"Knee's a little sore, but no problem."

The land flattened out, and further right, behind the house now and a hundred yards away, was a group of nine men holding shovels, perched beside a rectangular thirty-foot hole in the ground. A conical mound of overturned dirt sat along the far edge of the pit. A large, covered, blue-and-white wheeled cooler reclined at an angle on a secondary pile of dry soil.

As Robby and Vail neared, Vail made out Redmond Brix, beer in one hand and the handle of a shovel in the other, the tip stuck into the grass.

"Can I help you?" asked a man in a security uniform standing beside Brix, a two-way fastened to his belt. "This is private property."

"Front gate was open."

Brix turned. His face drooped as he caught sight of Vail. He frowned, then motioned to a man in jeans, leather gloves, and designer sunglasses. "This is one of my closest friends, Al Toland. He owns this property. Al, this is FBI Agent Vail and Detective Hernandez, from Virginia." Brix introduced the rest of the men, other friends and hired workers, who dipped their chins and tipped their hats in acknowledgment.

One of them had a high-end digital SLR camera around his neck, *Nikon D700* embroidered into the strap.

"Good to meet all of you," Robby said. "Sorry to intrude."

"Goddamn right," Brix said. "It's my day off. Can't a guy get a break?"

"Hey, this is our *vacation*," Vail said.

Brix cocked his head. "No one's asking you to keep sticking your nose in places you don't belong."

"Can't argue with that," Robby said.

Vail threw him a look.

"Javi," Toland said to the uniformed security guard, "go shut the front gate, please."

The security guard immediately headed off in the direction from which Vail and Robby had come. Brix stuck his shovel deeper into the dirt and trudged toward them, then motioned them to an area a few yards from the other men.

Vail faced Brix and said, "Look, we're just trying to help, that's it. If there's some information we can offer to help catch the guy who filleted that woman, then we've done our job."

"Your job? You have no job here. Do us all a favor, Agent Vail, go and visit some wineries, enjoy your time in the wine country with Detective Hernandez. Once you get home, it's back to the grind."

Vail couldn't help but think that this could've been Robby uttering those same words. And in another sense, Brix was right. What the hell was she doing here? She was on vacation. She should've been enjoying the beauty of the Napa Valley, tasting some of the world's best wine, decompressing, letting her knee heal. That was the plan. But some killer with a sharp knife had shredded those plans.

"You don't know what you're dealing with here, Lieutenant. If this guy has killed before, and I think that's very likely, this is something you don't want to fool around with. You need to get out in front of it now, before it's too late. Ask Sheriff Owens. He's been through the FBI's National Academy program. He's been exposed to this type of killer."

"Then I'll know who to ask if we find another body."

"The woman from Silver Ridge Estates had a missing toenail. Second digit, forcibly removed."

"Yeah, I heard all about it. Stan called me. You were at the morgue. Those are some balls you got there, Agent Vail. You sure know how to endear yourself with the locals."

"We've offered our help, but you haven't exactly been open to what we have to offer."

"We're not small-town cops. We can do our job just fine without the FBI's help. Thanks for your concern." He took a quick pull from his beer, then pointed the mouth of the bottle to a spot behind them. "Why don't you two run along now and have a nice day." He turned away, then walked back to his shovel and pulled it from the ground. "Let's get back to it, guys, we're losing light."

Vail sucked on her lip but didn't move.

"Come on, Karen," Robby said, gently taking her hand and leading her away.

———

"WE'VE DONE EVERYTHING WE CAN," Robby said, as they hiked past the six-car garage, headed toward the Murano.

"He doesn't know what he's dealing with. And that means more women are going to be killed because he can't put his ego aside."

"Sheriff Owens understands. Let him do his thing, maybe he can talk Brix into asking the BAU for help."

Vail sighed. "Fine. We've done everything we can, right?"

"Right."

She squeezed his hand. "So there's nothing left for us to do but enjoy our time together."

"Right again."

As they neared their car, the gate at the end of the road was closed. And Javi was by the guard shack reaching for his two-way.

"Gate is closed, yes sir."

"Don't let anyone in," the filtered voice of Redmond Brix said. "We've found a body buried down here. At least, part of a body. I'm gonna call in CSI. His name's Matthew Aaron. Let him through when he gets here."

"Roger," Javi said. "Uh, that FBI agent and detective are here. You want me to send them back?"

There was a long silence. Robby and Vail exchanged a glance.

Robby was holding Vail's hand tightly; she was sure he was keeping her from turning around and running back to where they'd come from.

"Send them back," Brix's filtered voice finally said.

Vail detected a note of dejection in his tone. But it didn't matter. She was already en route.

# TEN

When they arrived, the men were ringing the large pit, kneeling and staring at something at the far end. Brix was blocking their view, but judging from his body language, he was not pleased. He was on one knee and his head was bowed. The guy with the camera was snapping away, his flash bursting like lightning in a night sky.

As Vail moved closer to the hole's boundary, two of the men stood and moved out of her way. That's when she saw it: Two dirt-crusted feet were protruding from the edge of the opening, the flesh partially decomposed.

"Hey," Vail said to the man with the Nikon. "What are you doing? Why are you taking pictures?"

"I'm with the *Napa Valley Press*. I was covering the excavation of the cave. It's historic. I didn't think we'd find a—a dead body."

*Yeah, dipshit. I'm sure no one here expected that.* Vail thought of telling him to shove his lens where the light doesn't shine, but then figured the photos could be useful to their investigation. Besides, she had no right to tell him not to take photos. That was Brix's job.

Robby joined Vail and got down on his stomach to get as close a look at the feet as possible. Brix rose and moved back, then wiped at his sweat-pimpled forehead with the back of his leather work glove.

"Karen," Robby said. "Come closer. Take a look at this."

In the burst of light from the flash, she saw what drew Robby's attention. The second toenail of the right foot was missing.

———

THEY WERE ALL SILENT A MOMENT before Vail said, "Lieutenant, can you get these men out of here?"

Brix complied without comment, giving head signals to the workers. Toland followed. "I'm gonna have to ask you not to go public with those photos, Randy."

The *Press* photographer chortled as his gaze flicked between Brix and Vail. "We can discuss that later."

"Nothing to discuss," Brix said. "I invited you here as a guest because I thought you'd appreciate the exclusive on the cave. If you want to come back when we finish this thing, you'll honor my request."

Randy gave him a hard look, but nodded.

Brix extended a hand. "The memory card."

Vail could see Randy's facial muscles contracting as he flipped open the side compartment and withdrew the compact flash card.

Brix took it from him. "I'll make sure you get this back."

"Yeah, whatever," Randy said, then walked off.

When he was out of earshot, Vail said, "Well, guess that answers our question. This guy has killed before."

Brix's shoulders were rolled forward and his gloved hands hung at his sides. He spoke without meeting her eyes. "What's the procedure for bringing the profiling unit on board?"

"It's a pretty informal process. If an agency wants help from the BAU, they'd either call the unit and talk with an agent, or contact their local FBI office. Since I'm already here, all you had to do was ask. I'll call my supervisor for approval. Be a good idea to write me a formal request on letterhead for the file. But that's all just a red-tape formality. I'm here, and I want to help. Let's not waste any time."

"We've got a major crimes task force. Obviously, this is top priority. We'll start in the morning. I've got your number, I'll text you the info."

# ELEVEN

*J*ohn Wayne Mayfield sat in his idling white Jeep in the parking lot of Dean & Deluca, munching on a veggie sandwich. Country music was pouring from the dash speakers, the vocals pining about hating his job but not having a choice because he needed the money for alimony.

Mayfield didn't have the alimony problem, but it made him think of his job, and how he always strived to do it the best he could—but was it too much to ask that he wanted to enjoy himself, too? Sometimes he did, but oftentimes he did not—the reasons were obvious, but there was nothing he could do about it. He was given a task to complete and if he didn't complete it successfully, he didn't get paid. Simple as that.

It was a common dilemma with workers all over the world, he imagined: the desire to do something you enjoyed doing, but still earn a living doing it. In his case, it was not always possible to accomplish both.

But his hobbies, those were where he was able to feed his hunger, where he satisfied his desires.

As he bit into his sandwich, he saw a blonde exit the store, a white bag hanging from her hand. Diamond ring on her finger, but no male companion in sight. Was he waiting for her in their car? Mayfield watched her as she traversed the parking lot, passing right in front of his truck. His eyes were riveted to the sway of her hips, the slink of her thighs as they rhythmically moved through space. She stopped at a dark blue Mercedes and got into the passenger seat.

Mayfield swallowed, then took another bite of his sandwich. All in all, it wasn't a bad existence. And to be able to live in the area where he lived, in the house that he owned, that had to be factored into the equation. Some people killed for the sport, some killed over drugs, or money, or sex, or anger. Those were largely unfulfilling, without any of the satisfaction and sense of accomplishment he sought when he stalked his victims, and then ended their lives.

Unfulfilling, but necessary. Some things just had to be done, whether you liked it or not. For John Wayne Mayfield, this was both fulfilling and enjoyable. He crumpled the paper wrapping of his sandwich and shoved his truck into gear.

There was work to be done.

# TWELVE

They ate dinner at Angèle, which abutted the recently refurbished Napa River embankment. The food was exquisitely tasteful. But Robby was unusually quiet. Vail sensed he was frustrated that she had pushed so hard to be included in the investigation, and now the task force.

"I ruined our vacation," she said over a sip of Duckhorn Merlot.

Robby put down his fork and sat back. "No, the UNSUB ruined it. Wrong place, wrong time." He chewed a moment, then added, "But that doesn't mean you had to pursue it so aggressively."

"I had to."

"Karen, there are murders all across the country—hell, all across the world—and you can't be at every crime scene. You can't draw up a profile on every UNSUB. You can't help catch every psychosexual offender who's on the loose."

"I know that."

He splayed out his large hands. "So then what gives?"

Vail took another sip of wine. She put it down, studied the glass, then said, "I don't know. I saw that body, the—well, the behaviors—and my mind switched into work mode. I—this is what I do, and I've got very specialized knowledge that can help apprehend this guy before more women are killed. Am I wrong to want to help prevent that?"

Robby looked to his left, out the window at the Napa River. The sun had set and a blue-orange blush reflected off the water. The lights along the river's edge began glowing.

"No. I don't know. Maybe. I mean, you have to be allowed to have a life."

"Things would've been fine if we hadn't gone to Silver Ridge. We wouldn't have heard anything about it and we would've gone about our vacation."

Robby looked at her. "Are you saying this whole thing is my fault because I hooked you up with my friend to get us those wine-pairing tickets?"

"Of course not. I'm just saying that maybe this was meant to be. Maybe some higher power put us there at that time, same time as the killer, so we could do our thing and help catch this guy."

Robby furrowed his brow. "Wow, you're getting religious on me. I'm surprised."

"I don't know what to make of it, Robby. But we're here for a reason. Maybe that reason is to help put this guy away before he kills someone else."

The waitress appeared and leaned across the table to clear the used dishes.

Robby swirled his glass of Patz and Hall Pinot Noir, then lifted it and watched the liquid spin. As it came to rest, he said, "Basically, our vacation is over. You're now working this case. And that's fine, I guess. Maybe you can get Gifford to jigger your vacation time so you don't lose it. You can take another trip when you get back."

Vail finished off her wine. "So that means my vacation time won't correspond with yours because yours is now, and there's no reason for you to be working this case."

"Exactly. So I guess we'll have to enjoy whatever time we have when you're not working the case."

She reached across the table and took his hand. "I'm sorry. I didn't mean for this to happen. But we'll make the best of what we do have. Deal?"

Robby nodded slowly. "Deal."

"How about we start with tonight?" she said, leaning forward and planting a soft kiss on his lips.

# THIRTEEN

**V**ail and Robby ate breakfast with their B&B mates—plus another couple who'd arrived last night—and after putting down their forks and draining their coffee, were the first to leave. Vail had to be at the task force at 9 a.m., and she didn't want to be late.

While en route to the sheriff's department, Vail thought about asking Robby to call the Vienna police chief to ask permission for him to participate on the task force. But Robby, being a Virginia state law enforcement officer, had no jurisdiction in California. His chief would never go for it: He would say that the locals had plenty of homicide investigators to work the case—and he would be correct. Vail, however, was a different situation. She had a unique skill set the police here didn't have.

When they arrived at the sheriff's department, Robby pulled to the curb by the front of the building. "Call me when you're done."

Vail's door was open, the car audibly purring. "What are you going to do?"

"It's Napa." He held up a *Wine Country News* magazine. "No shortage of places to explore. Don't worry about me, I'll be fine."

---

VAIL WALKED INTO the conference room used by the Napa County Major Crimes Task Force. Located on the second floor of the sheriff's department, it was a well-appointed meeting space with a generous oak chair rail lining the walls and numerous gray ergonomic stenographer seats surrounding a sectional faux-marble taupe-and-gray table. A laptop sat in the middle of the table beside a few stacks of printed pages and a plastic container of muffins. County map posters hung beside an expansive pane of one-way glass. A large-format printer sat in the corner beside a wall-sized whiteboard.

Not surprisingly, Vail was the only woman in the room. All heads swiveled in her direction as she strode to a vacant seat. As she sat down, everyone resumed their conversations. Redmond Brix was standing at the whiteboard chatting with a young male in uniform.

"You must be Karen Vail."

Vail turned to see a man in his late twenties or early thirties, styled hair and thumbs hooked through the loops in his belt . . . wearing polished chestnut boots.

She extended a hand. "Yeah, that's me. Don't tell me I forgot to take off my name tag again." She smiled sheepishly and feigned a look at her shirt.

"Sheriff Owens mentioned you'd be here. I'm Scott Fuller. Detective Scott Fuller, Napa County SD."

"Sheriff's a good man. Small world, actually. He took my class on Behavioral Science at the FBI's National Academy—"

"I know all about it. I'm enrolled to start the program in a couple months."

"I'll see you back in Virginia, then."

"Do you know anyone else on the task force?"

"Just walked in a minute ago."

"Well, then let me do the intros." He turned, stuck his fingers in his lips and whistled. Everyone turned. "This is Special Agent Karen Vail, from the FBI's Behavioral Sciences Unit in Quantico," Fuller said. "She's here to help us with the wine cave murder."

"Glad to meet all of you," Vail said. "Actually, I'm with the Behavioral *Analysis* Unit, and we're a few minutes down the road from Quantico, in Aquia. We moved out of Quantico a little over ten years ago. But Scott's right, I'm here to help. If there's anything I can contribute, please don't hesitate to ask."

"That's Sergeant Ray Lugo, with St. Helena PD," Fuller said, indicating a Hispanic male as wide in the shoulders as he was in the gut—a refrigerator came to mind.

Vail nodded acknowledgment.

"And you already know Detective Lieutenant Brix," Fuller said. "He's the Incident Commander for this . . . uh . . ."

"Incident?"

Fuller frowned. "For this murder."

The door swung open hard and in walked a petite blonde in a tightly cut short-sleeve blouse and professional knee-length skirt. She strode to the front of the room and took a seat near the head of the oval conference table. Every male head followed her movement, and she behaved as if she knew it.

"And that's Roxxann Dixon," Fuller said.

Dixon tossed a thick binder on the table and looked up at Vail. "And you are?"

"Karen Vail, FBI."

Dixon looked around at the attentive male faces. "And why is the Bureau here?" she asked.

Vail waited for someone else to answer. Meanwhile, she was sizing up Dixon. Was she being antagonistic because she enjoyed being the only female on the task force, or was she merely the inquisitive, controlling type? Light blue eyes with unusually muscular arms and legs for a female, so she hit the weights regularly, and her short sleeves in the cooler weather meant she liked to let everyone know it. She was either into health and fitness and working out, compensating for something, or she felt she needed the bulk to compete with the men in her department. *I can relate to that,* Vail thought.

"Agent Vail is here on my request," Brix said. "This case has some unusual elements to it and I think she can help. She's out here on vacation and was . . . in the vicinity when the body was discovered."

Dixon nodded slowly. Vail could tell she was doing what Vail had done to her: sizing her up, measuring her potential adversary, determining whether she'd truly be an asset, competition for male attention on the task force, or an extreme annoyance with some political heft and an attitude. *I'm probably all of the above.*

"Which agency are you with?" Vail asked.

"I'm an investigator with the Napa County District Attorney's office."

"I'm actually a profiler with Behavioral Analysis Unit," Vail said.

"Oh," Dixon said.

*'Oh?' What does that mean?*

"Okay," Brix said, "let's get started." He took a step forward and handed Vail a thick card. "Electronic key. The proximity card will give you admittance to the building and restricted areas. Feel free to use it while you're here, but we'll need the prox card back when you leave."

Vail took it and shoved it into her purse.

"I've sent all of you the email with what we had as of last night," Brix said, passing a stapled sheaf of papers to Vail. The others had official county binders in front of them with requisite materials fastened and punched. "I've got a few updates, and some pictures of the victim." He nodded to Fuller, who took a seat at the conference table in front of the laptop.

Fuller reached around his binder and fingered the touchpad. The screen awoke and displayed photos of the Silver Ridge Estates wine cave interior. Fuller hit a button on a nearby remote. A screen unfurled from the ceiling and the blue light from a projector splashed across it. Fuller pressed a couple of keys and the enlarged image appeared for all to see.

Brix took the group through the crime scene, describing what they were seeing as a supplement to the email he had sent them. Vail studied the photos. They were no doubt taken a short time after she and Robby had left the Silver Ridge wine cave. "Coroner says both wrists were sliced deeply. She bled out fairly slowly because it was done postmortem. Looks like she was strangled." He nodded to Fuller, who pressed a button on his remote. The slide changed to a close-up of the woman's neck. Bruising was evident across the skin. "A knife was found beneath the woman's lower back. Scott."

Fuller advanced to the next slide. A glistening stainless steel blade filled the screen. "Coroner said it was incredibly sharp, like it had never been used. Problem is, it's a pretty common kitchen knife made by Henckels." Nodded to Fuller. Next slide. "And something of interest to Agent Vail . . . the victim's second toenail on the right foot was torn from the nail bed. Agent Vail?"

Vail leaned forward. "Yes. Well, the fact that the killer did this means that it had some significance to him. What that is, we don't know yet. But briefly, this is what we call—"

"Signature," Fuller said.

"Well, we used to call it signature," Vail corrected. "But we now refer to it as ritual, or ritual behavior. That means it's something the Unknown Subject, or UNSUB, does with the body that's superfluous to his primary goal, which is killing his victim. In other words, it doesn't result in the victim's death, and it doesn't help him avoid being caught. So it really has no relevance to anything—except that it's deeply significant, and symbolic, for the killer. It feeds a deep-seated psychosexual need."

She glanced over at Fuller, whose mouth was twisted and his gaze elsewhere—in his binder, to be exact. *Maybe he didn't like being corrected in front of the team. Great, more group dynamics to have to deal with.*

"What I can tell you," Vail said, "is that it's my strong opinion this UNSUB has killed before."

"How do you get that?" Dixon asked.

"Forget, for a moment, the other body we unearthed. If we just look at the wine cave kill, there were no hesitation marks with the blade. He strangled the vic, then sliced her wrists to allow the blood to drain. He then severed the breasts and removed the toenail. Very organized, efficient approach." Vail curled some red hair behind her ear. "Something I think we all need to consider is that the key to this case could be access."

"Access?" Brix asked.

"When you're dealing with a murdered prostitute or druggie, you're generally talking about publicly accessible places. But this is a cave, a wine cave that costs money—a lot of money—to get into. So we can narrow our offender pool of suspects by looking at who has access to the cave. This is an isolated location with a limited list of potential suspects.

"What's more, statistically speaking, we can eliminate women, because with extremely rare exceptions, they're not serial killers." She paused a moment to gather herself; painful memories bubbled to the surface, but she forced them down. "And our killer is probably in his twenties or early thirties. Again, that's going with percentages." Vail looked around. She had everyone's attention. "Another way we can narrow the offender's age range is to assume this offender is physically fit. He's able to efficiently subdue his victim, without her making much, if any, noise. And then crush her windpipe. So, again, we're looking at a younger person."

"Ray," Brix said to Sergeant Lugo, "get with the Silver Ridge admin people and get their guest list. The people who go on those tours, whether it's daytime or nighttime, pay a fair amount, so they'll have used credit cards. Roxxi, make sure Ray has the search warrant he'll need for that list. And their employee roster, past and present. Then narrow it down using Vail's parameters."

They both nodded. Brix made a note of their assignments on the whiteboard. "And, as Incident Commander, I'm naming you lead investigator. That good with you?"

Dixon looked up, appearing both surprised and pleased. "Yeah, I'm good with that."

Fuller leaned back in his seat, his mouth making contorting movements. Vail didn't think he was particularly thrilled with Dixon's assignment.

Brix wrote it on the board.

"Something else to keep in mind," Vail said. She waited a beat for Brix to turn around. "It's likely the offender knows the cave and has been there before."

"How can you make that assumption?" Fuller asked.

"It's a much higher risk for him to take a victim somewhere without knowing what—or who—he's going to find there. It's reasonable to assume, for now, that he had intel on the location, so that suggests some connection to the winery. If he knew anything about that place, he knew they conducted nighttime wine cave tours. He wanted that body found, he wanted maximum impact and shock when that tour came through. That suggests he was familiar with the winery. He'd either been there before or worked there in some capacity. So first order of business would be to look at the workers they have on staff."

Lugo spoke up. "That's a minefield if we go down that road."

"How so?"

"Migrant workers make up a significant percentage of the Napa Valley work force—they tend the vineyards, pick the grapes. A lot of them are illegal, and they move around. And they're undocumented."

"That makes our job a bit harder," Vail said. They mulled Lugo's comment a moment before she continued. "There is one caveat I should point out."

"'Caveat'? As in a 'save my ass' exception?" Fuller asked with a chuckle.

"This isn't about my ass and it's not about me," Vail said. "I'm just telling you there's a potential exception to consider. Nothing is foolproof, especially behavioral analysis." She stared down Fuller, then continued. "So as I was saying. There are some killers who engage in high-risk kills because it's all about the thrills. So they partake in high-risk behavior—which goes against what I just said about him having prior knowledge, or intel, about the cave."

"That doesn't make it any easier," Brix said.

Vail nodded in conciliation. "One thing that may help is that serial killers don't wake up one day and start killing. They learn, through trial and error, what works and what doesn't. What feeds their inner fantasies best. They experiment, learn how to stalk, how to kill. During this time, the killer is developing his interest in killing."

"How does this help us?" Dixon asked.

"His early killing career will likely comprise failures, victims that fought back and required either more force or greater resourcefulness on his part to be successful. So his early murders will be unsolved crimes; we can look for unsolved murders in the region. But they'll be tough to link to our UNSUB because his MO won't look like it does now, because he wasn't the same killer he eventually became. He may even move to another community, once he's learned what he needs to learn to kill efficiently. We'd need to know particulars of the case, especially behaviors he engaged in with the body. Those behaviors, the ritual behaviors I mentioned a few minutes ago, don't change whether it's his first kill or, God forbid, his fiftieth."

"So are you saying we expand our search?" Brix asked.

"We should contact all local police and sheriff departments within a reasonable radius to find out what unsolved female murders they've had in, say, the past twenty years, with ritual behaviors like the ones we've found here. The severed breasts, the toenail, and the slicing of the wrists."

"Only female?"

"As I said, almost every serial killer is male," Vail said. "Most victims are female. But not always. Some serial killers, if they're gay, will kill other males. And some will kill males because they're in the house and they're obstacles to getting to the chosen prize. So they blitz-kill the male, get him out of the way, then have their way with the woman."

"I think we're gonna need some help if we're expanding our potential suspect pool," Lugo said.

"We can use the resources of the Bureau to help in this search. It's not a panacea, but it'll give us a good head start. It's called VICAP, Violent Criminal Apprehension Program."

"Robert Ressler," Fuller said. "He started VICAP."

"Correct," Vail said. "Anyone here know what VICAP is?"

Only Fuller and Brix raised their hands.

"It's a central databank maintained by the FBI. Police departments send in reports on crimes in their jurisdictions, and we can sort and search the data based on unique qualifiers. So we can plug in certain parameters involving a crime and see if the same characteristics have been found in other murders in other states. Like the toenail. That's an unusual characteristic of this killer. If we also find it in the VICAP database regarding a case down in Los Angeles, we might be able to link that murder with the ones up here."

"Great," Brix said. "You'll take care of that?"

"Today. But understand its limitations. The database is only as good as the info it gets from PDs across the country. If they don't take the time to fill out the form and submit it to us, VICAP will never know about it."

"We'll take what we can get," Brix said. He turned to the board and wrote "VICAP: Vail." Over his shoulder, while writing, he said, "If we start to zero in on a suspect or suspects and we need help, we can tap the NSIB—that's Napa Special Investigations Bureau," he said to Vail. "They'll help us out with surveillance. They're part of the standing task force, and they'll do their part when needed."

"Something else, before I forget." Vail looked at the photo of the victim on the screen. "Can you advance it to the autopsy photos? A close-up of the neck."

Fuller pressed the remote and found the picture Vail wanted.

"There. See the marks on the neck? Your coroner, Abbott, she said the UNSUB used an object, like his forearm, across the neck to choke the victim. Sergeant," Vail said to Fuller, "can you stand for a minute?"

Fuller smiled sheepishly, slid back his chair, then rose. Vail led him over to the nearby wall and spoke to Fuller, though she was addressing all in the room. "Watch this," she said. "I'm the UNSUB, Fuller is the victim."

Lugo laughed. Fuller shaded red.

"This is not funny, guys. Now, watch." She took her left forearm and shoved it into Fuller's neck, while pushing him up and back with the side of her hip. Fuller's torso slammed into the wall and his head not-so-gently snapped back. They stood face-to-face, her eyes two inches from his.

Fuller did not look happy.

"I'm face-to-face with my victim," Vail said, maintaining eye contact with Fuller. "She's looking into my eyes. And I'm looking into hers." Vail kept her gaze on Fuller, then suddenly moved back and spun to face the others. Fuller swallowed hard and whipped his neck from side to side, but didn't dare rub it in front of his peers.

"Do you see where I'm headed with this?"

Dixon leaned back in her chair. "You're trying to embarrass Scott?"

Vail looked around. They all looked a tad miffed at her demonstration. "No. No, nothing like that. Think about the killer. Think about the victim. What's our UNSUB doing?" She waited, but there were no answers. "He's up close and personal. Confident. Controlling her. He's killing her, taking her life, while she stares into his eyes. While she watches. For killers like this, it's the ultimate in superiority. Complete arrogance. He's drinking it in, watching the life drain out of her eyes." Vail stopped, looked around. They were all looking intently at her, processing what she was saying. "Here's something else. He could've chosen a lower risk victim and confronted her somewhere else, where he'd have multiple escape routes. But he didn't. There are killers who get off on the thrill of the kill, because engaging in these kinds of high-risk stakes is part of the thrill. All that tells me we may—and I emphasize *may*—be dealing with a narcissistic killer."

They all took a moment to digest that.

"So he's in love with himself," Brix said. "How does that help us?"

Vail, then Fuller, returned to their seats.

"Everything we learn about this guy helps. When we catch him, if he is a narcissist, it'll require a special kind of interview technique to get him to confess. But if we do it right, he will confess. Because he wants to take credit for what he's done. That's what I think the toenail is about. If I had to guess—and that's all I'm doing now—the toenail could be his calling card, his way of telling us, 'This is my kill. Give me credit.'"

"You gotta be shittin' me," Dixon said.

"BTK Strangler, remember him? A few years ago the trail went cold, but he contacted police when someone was ready to publish a book. He was basically saying, Hey, I'm still here. All those kills were mine. I'm the guy you want. Again, all this goes to understanding who we're dealing with. The more we know, the more likely we'll be able to narrow our suspect pool and get closer to identifying who this asshole is."

"Any ideas on how to catch him?" Brix asked.

"She can't help us catch him," Fuller said. "She can only help us to eliminate suspects once we have some."

"That's true—sort of." Vail leaned forward in her chair. She was sure what she was about to suggest would go over as well as suggesting they pair a fine Cabernet with a fast food burger. "If I'm right, if this guy is a narcissist, then we can draw him out."

"You got my attention," Lugo said. "How?"

"Narcissists think they're superior to everyone else, and they want to be acknowledged for their work. They seek attention, and because of that, they're more risky in their behaviors and actions. By keeping a lid on this murder, you may even be facilitating his need to kill more. He may keep killing till you publicly acknowledge his work, stroke his ego."

They all laughed. One chuckled. Brix was shaking his head.

"I understand that going public with this has other implications for your community—"

Brix stepped forward. "Ain't gonna happen, Agent Vail. I told you what's at stake, both locally, at the state and federal levels—"

Vail held up a hand. "It's my job to give you information. What you do with the information is your decision."

"We could be destroying, or at least crippling, an entire industry," Dixon said. "We have to weigh our actions extremely carefully. There's gotta be another way to get to this guy."

"Then you have to look at victimology. Who your victims are, then try to figure out why these two women fell into this man's crosshairs."

"Any idea when we'll get an ID on the vics?" Lugo asked.

Brix walked over to the wall phone and punched in an extension. "It's Brix," he said into the handset. "Brooke, any chance you can get us an ID on the wine cave woman brought in last night in the—you do?" Brix listened a moment, then his eyes widened. "You sure about that?" He glanced at the faces in the room. "Keep that to yourself, Brooke. Very important. I don't want to see that name on any paperwork." He listened a second, then said, "As long as possible. Delay it. Lose it. We have to deal with this the right way." He said thank you, then hung up.

Brix turned, picked up a marker, touched it to the whiteboard, then stopped and recapped the marker. He said, "It's Victoria Cameron."

Vail watched the reaction of those in the room. Clearly, Victoria Cameron was someone they were acquainted with. "Obviously, this means something," Vail said.

"Yeah," Dixon said. "Bad news for us, is what it means. Victoria Cameron is—*was*—the daughter of one of the most influential winemakers in the valley. Frederick Montalvo."

"She's married," Vail said.

"She is," Fuller said, "to . . . what's that guy's name?"

"Kevin Cameron," Lugo said.

Brix sighed heavily. "Okay." He sucked on his upper lip, then leaned on the conference table with both hands. "We gotta do our jobs real well, because there's gonna be some heat no matter what happens. If we fuck up . . . well, I don't even want to think about it. But we need to control this information as best we can, so effective immediately, I'm putting a gag order on this building. We also need to inform next of kin. I've never met the lady or her family. Anyone want to handle that?"

"I got it," Lugo said. "I went to school with one of the Montalvo brothers. I knew Victoria. I know Kevin. I know the whole family."

Brix wrote the assignment on the board beside Lugo's name. "Roxxi, you're already getting the Silver Ridge warrant drawn. Why don't you pick up their guest list, too?"

"Will do."

Brix moved the task to Dixon's column. "One other thing. We've canvassed the area around the cave, and no one saw anything unusual. Of course, that would've been too easy." He tossed the marker onto the table. "Let's meet back here at four o'clock." He grabbed a piece of paper from his binder and passed it to Fuller. "Write down all your contact info. I'll run copies for all of you before you leave. Anything comes up, call me and I'll make sure everyone knows."

Vail signed the sheet, passed it on, then stepped over to Brix. "I'm gonna need to ride with someone. Or I can do my thing with Detective Hernandez, if you don't mind."

Brix chuckled. "As long as you don't tell him who the vic is, I don't care what you do."

"You still don't want me here, do you?"

"What I want doesn't really matter, does it? I think you've got some valuable insight we could use. Is it gonna catch us a killer? I have no fucking idea."

"Profiling isn't gonna catch us a killer, Brix. It's just another weapon at our disposal."

He closed his binder and slung it under his wrist. "Let's hope that weapon is locked and loaded. We may very well need to use it."

# FOURTEEN

Vail walked outside into the cool air and took a deep breath. The scent of American oak barrels filled with fermenting Cabernet grapes floated on the air like the background perfume of an expensive day spa in Calistoga, miles down the road.

Then again, maybe she was just imagining it. She gave Robby a call to see where he was, but he didn't answer his cell. She left a message, then called her ASAC, Thomas Gifford.

A moment later, she was put through to his desk. "So how's your vacation? How's the weather out there? Been raining nonstop here since you left. I think you should come home, give us a break." He chortled a bit, in surprisingly good spirits.

She hesitated. "Weather's been good. Vacation was good, too. But . . ."

"I don't think I like the sound of this, Karen. But what?"

She and Gifford didn't agree on much, and they'd had their share of arguments, but this was not likely to sit well with him, given what had happened with Yates, and, of course, Dead Eyes. Given the work the profilers did, the mental health of those in his units was a top priority. "Well, we kind of stumbled onto something here."

"What kind of 'something'?"

"Something like a dead body. Both breasts severed and removed from the scene—"

"Ah, Jesus Christ, Karen. What are you, a serial killer magnet?"

"Yeah, that's a good one, boss. Remind me to put that on my new personalized license plate."

"Serious, Karen. I sent you away to *get* away, get your mind off this shit."

"Believe me, I wasn't looking for it. It was a 'wrong place, wrong time' kind of thing." *Maybe I am some sort of psychosexual offender magnet.*

"So let me guess. You told the detective assigned to the case that you should help out, because you're the great Karen Vail, super agent who thinks she can absorb all sorts of psychological trauma and keep on ticking."

"Not in so many words."

"So now he wants BAU support."

"Right again, sir. Did you eat your Wheaties this morning? You're on a roll."

Silence. *Ooops. I must've gone a tad too far. Why do I always do that?*

Finally, Gifford said, "So you think this is a serial offender?"

"I do. Not his first kill. Pretty brazen, possibly narcissistic."

"Fine, you're there, you take the case. But I don't want you staying longer than your vacation. And when you get back, I want you to take a real vacation. Maybe we'll put you in a cement overcoat, suspend you by crane over the Potomac, where you can't get into trouble."

"If you think it'll help."

"Honestly, I don't. Somehow trouble will find you."

"I'll have the Incident Commander send you a formal note on letterhead. And hey, the sheriff here went to the National Academy."

"Well, *hey,* that really makes my day, Karen. That makes me so happy. Glad to hear it. Just . . . just keep me up to date on what's going on."

Before she could reply, she realized the line was dead. But she still needed the VICAP run, so she called back. Asked for a colleague of hers, Frank Del Monaco. He answered on the third ring.

"Frank, it's Karen." She heard an audible sigh. "Something wrong?"

"I was having such a nice day before you called, is all."

"And now?"

"Not so much. Wait—aren't you in California on vacation?"

"Well, you got the first part right. Listen, I need you to run something through VICAP."

"What do I look like, your servant?"

"Frank, I'm three thousand miles away. If I could do it myself, and not have to ask you for anything, I'd do it. Now, I need you to run the following parameters. The UNSUB we're looking for—"

"You're on vacation and you're working a case?"

"Yes, Frank. And I don't need any shit from you. Just run this or I'll call Rooney or Hutchings."

"Rooney's in California, too. But, fine, whatever."

Vail gave him the details of the behaviors she had observed. Del Monaco said he would run the report when he was done with his meetings and get back to her when he had the results.

She hung up and tried Robby again. Voice mail. She went back into the sheriff's department and tracked down Brix. "I need a car or I need to ride with someone."

"What about Hernandez?"

"He's off doing his own thing. He's not answering his phone."

"Smart guy, probably tasting wine and enjoying himself."

She ignored his swipe. "So—car or not?"

"Not. You can ride with Dixon." He told Vail to wait there, then disappeared back into the task force conference room, down the hall. He emerged a moment later with a reluctant Dixon. Vail couldn't hear what was being said, but from Dixon's hand movements, it appeared she was asking, "Why me?"

After her apparently futile argument, Dixon moved back into the room while Brix held open the door. Dixon appeared seconds later with her binder clutched in her left hand. She made her way down the corridor to Vail. Her body was stiff, her face tight.

"Guess I'm chauffeuring you around today," Dixon said.

"Just for a bit, till my friend gets my voice mail, then you can be rid of me."

They walked outside to Dixon's county-issued vehicle, a Ford Crown Victoria. She got in and unlocked the doors.

As Vail sorted herself out, Dixon snapped her seat belt and said, "Now what?"

"This is your investigation," Vail said. "I'm here to help, that's it. If there's some insight I can offer that'll help narrow our pool of suspects, that's my specialty."

Dixon put the car in drive and headed out of the lot. "Problem is, we have no pool of suspects."

"At this point, we don't even have a pond."

Dixon stifled a laugh. "Yeah, no pond."

"I put in a call to Quantico and we should have a report on the VI-CAP results later. Meanwhile, let's make use of our time."

"How about we start where all crimes start? Motive."

Vail knew that motive for a serial killer was a much different animal from that which a traditional criminal exhibits. But she decided to go with Dixon, see where it would lead. "Keep in mind that most murders are between individuals who know each other. Serial offenders are traditionally stranger on stranger crimes, which makes it harder. Motive isn't always visible to us."

"Noted," Dixon said. "But we have one thing going for us. Victimology—in this case Victoria Cameron and the Jane Doe. Start with basic investigative policework: Who would want her dead? Had she had any arguments with anyone? What was her relationship with her husband like? Do any of these things have to do with the Jane Doe lying in the morgue?"

"All good stuff," Vail said. "We may want to extend that to looking into where Victoria shopped, places she frequented on a regular basis, people she did business with, and so on. Once we get an ID on the corpse Brix unearthed, we'll do the same for her. That'll generate a suspect pool and then I can be a little more helpful."

"I thought your info was pretty helpful."

Vail tried not to let the surprise show on her face. "Thanks, Roxxann. I appreciate that."

———

WHILE DRIVING, Dixon activated her visor-mounted Bluetooth and called her office. She spoke with the deputy district attorney and explained why they needed a search warrant drawn for Silver Ridge Estates, and told her that Brix would be drafting the probable cause statement. She was promised an executed warrant within the hour.

"So what's the scoop on the guys on the task force?"

Dixon chuckled. "What am I, the school gossip queen?"

"It's best to know who I'm dealing with so I don't put my foot in my mouth." Vail threw up a hand. "Scratch that. I'm gonna put my foot in my mouth anyway. But I'd still like to know who these people are."

"Haven't you profiled everyone in that room already?"

Vail couldn't help but let a smile tilt her lips. "I try not to do that. Makes it hard to get along with people." She shook her head. "Scratch that, too. Guess it doesn't help. But to answer your question, yeah, I can't help but do it. Like Scott Fuller. He seems like a know-it-all."

"Oh, yeah. Boy Wonder, everything handed to him on a gold platter. He's read all the books, can probably even recite what chapters that shit comes from. But he's light on experience."

"Book smarts, not street smarts. He's certainly got the profiling stuff down—but it's textbook stuff, dated info, like he read all the Underwood, Douglas, and Ressler books and committed them to memory."

Dixon nodded. "But here's the wrinkle. He's the stepson of Stan Owens."

Vail tilted her head. "Really. See, now that's good to know."

"Which is how he's ascended the ranks so quickly."

"And one to be careful around," Vail said.

"But Ray Lugo's a good guy. Been here all his life, started out as an underage migrant field worker picking grapes. Parents were illegal, but he was born here, so he's a U.S. citizen. He worked hard, did well in school, and went to the Academy, became a cop."

"And here he is, a sergeant. Very impressive."

"Whereas Fuller had it handed to him, Ray's earned it."

"And you?" Vail asked.

"Me? I don't like to talk about myself."

"Neither do I. But—"

"But if you had to draw conclusions about me—"

"I'd say you're intuitive. You're diligent, detail oriented. You've been doing this job awhile but you're not bored with it. And . . ."

Dixon slowed for a stopped truck in front of her. "And what?"

"And you're intimidated by being a woman in a male-dominated profession."

"Is that some sort of . . . what do they call it, projection?"

Vail laughed. "Maybe."

"But you're right. Sort of. Still, I have no trouble putting one of these guys in their place if they get out of line. But it really hasn't been a problem."

"But it was, once."

"Once."

That's all she said, and Vail let it drop. She watched more vineyards roll by, then asked, "So how long have you been with the DA's office?"

"A few months."

Vail lifted an eyebrow. "I take it you were in law enforcement before that."

Dixon glanced at Vail.

Vail knew the look: Dixon was measuring her answer. There was a story behind this, and she was deciding how fine a filter to use . . . how much she would share and how much she would hold back.

"In a nutshell," Dixon finally said, "I was born and raised here, in the valley. I was with the sheriff's department for five years, then took a job with Vallejo PD. I was promoted to detective and a few years later I transferred to the DA's office. So there you go. My law enforcement pedigree."

Vail figured she had Dixon's reaction pegged correctly: A detective did not usually transfer out of her department to become an investigator for the district attorney unless she was retiring from that agency, or injured, or in search of a quieter, safer existence. There was definitely more to her transfer than she was relating.

But Vail didn't want to press it, since it was their first time having a conversation—and because Dixon was turning right at Montalvo Villa Estate Wines, a large winery set back from Highway 29, majestic in its pristine setting and architecture. Its landmark sign established its founding in 1931.

Vail and Dixon drove down the long, paved roadway lined by impeccably maintained vineyards. Placards mounted on a wood fence that ran the length of the road labeled the vineyards with what Vail assumed were family names: Genevieve's Family Vineyard, and, fifty yards further, Mona's Estate Vineyard.

"Anything I need to know about the family?"

"They've got three residences on-site. The parents, Frederick and Mona, have the main house. The two smaller houses, if you can even use the word 'small' in this setting, belong to their daughter Genevieve and her husband, and their son Phillip and his wife. The other son lives off-site, as did Victoria and her husband, Kevin."

"Any reason why two siblings get to live on the family estate and two don't?"

"No idea. They're private people, for the most part. But Victoria and her husband purchased their own winery, so maybe that ruffled some family feathers. Frederick has been around in the region a lot longer than someone like Robert Mondavi, but he never got the attention or the respect Mondavi got. I'm not singing the blues for Frederick, though. He's done just fine lurking in the shadows, so to speak."

"If he values his privacy and shrouds himself in mystery, he can't take on the persona of a colorful, influential personality. Sounds like that isn't what he wants."

Dixon pulled the car into a spot and shoved the gearshift forward. "Oh, he wants it. But he wants it to come to him. The attention, that is. But he won't go in search of it. I guess it's a different way of going about getting attention: His behavior, the mystery and privacy, has promoted some of the attention he claims to want to avoid. People wonder. The lack of access produces greater interest."

They got out of the car, walked to the winery's administrative offices, identified themselves, and asked to see Frederick Montalvo. The office manager raised an eyebrow as she perused Vail's credentials, then was on the phone to her boss. A moment later, she said, "I'll take you back."

They were led through strategically lit, walnut-paneled, high-ceilinged corridors. The woman stopped at a room at the far end of the hall, rapped the wooden door three times, then opened it. Vail stepped in after Dixon, and the scene before her stopped her short. The entire far wall consisted of what appeared to be one expansive glass pane—possibly twenty feet wide and fifteen feet high. Beyond the window stood the vines of an endless vineyard, stretching back and ending at a steep climbing hill, itself covered with neat rows of grapevines. Vail thought she was looking at a three-dimensional painting of unrivaled beauty.

Dixon reached out and shook the hand of a thin, silver-haired man seated at a desk that was half the size of the window, impressive in its own right: hand-carved legs with a front that was, in relief, a depiction of a group of men tending to vines on rolling hills. She quickly realized she was looking at a carpenter's representation of the view beyond the glass.

At first glance, the man looked to be about seventy, but something about the way he moved made Vail think he might've been older, or stricken with a muscle-wasting disease. He leveraged himself with both hands on his desk to rise slowly from his leather chair. "Any news on my daughter?"

Dixon stepped forward. She was the local cop here; she would be the one to deliver the news.

But before she could speak, the phone buzzed. Montalvo looked down at the desk, thought about whether to answer it, then lifted the receiver. "Yes."

He listened a moment—Vail could hear a loud, distressed male voice at the other end of the line—and she realized what must be happening. Lugo had just informed Kevin Cameron of his wife's death. Frederick Montalvo, family patriarch and the woman's father, got the first call.

Montalvo's face drained of color, his left hand slipped from the desktop, and the phone dropped from his grip as his legs gave out. He hit the carpeted floor with a thud—with Dixon and Vail quickly at his side.

Vail tossed down her purse, then checked Montalvo's pulse while Dixon lifted his legs. His skin was clammy, but judging by his slow and regular pulse, Vail felt he had fainted rather than had a heart attack. He opened his eyes, blinked, and stared at Vail, who was hovering over his face.

"Mr. Montalvo, are you okay?" she asked.

"I—my daughter. Is she—is she? . . ."

"Yes. We're deeply sorry." She cradled the back of his neck. "Come on, let's sit up. Slowly."

Montalvo, with Vail's help, moved into a seated position, still on the floor. He put his head between his knees while Vail supported his back. And then he began to weep.

Vail and Dixon shared a look. Vail could tell that Dixon hated this as much as she did. There was just no good way to deliver this kind of news. The reaction often ranged from outright disbelief to massive heart attacks, and everything in between.

Dixon lifted the fallen receiver from the desk. She had apparently surmised what had happened as well, because she said, "Mr. Cameron, are you there?" She waited, then said, "No, he's fine. He'll be fine. I'm sorry for your loss." She listened a moment, then said, "Of course we will," then hung up.

"How did it happen?"

Montalvo's voice was weak, frail.

"I think all we should say at this point is that she crossed paths with a killer and we're doing our best to track him down. We have a task force already set up—"

"You're not answering my question," he said, more forcefully. He turned away from Vail's supportive hold, rolled to his right side, and struggled to get to his feet. He swayed a second, then found his chair and sat down heavily.

"She was murdered," Vail said. "That's all you need to know. The details are unimportant. And you have to trust me on that. I help track these killers for a living. And I can tell you that we're doing everything we can to find this guy. That's a promise."

"Where? Where did you find her?"

"In the wine cave at Silver Ridge Estates."

Montalvo sighed, then shook his head. "That doesn't make sense."

Vail bent down, retrieved her purse, then slung it over her shoulder. "Why's that?"

"They're a competitor, of sorts. Worse than that, perhaps. We've had some difficulty with the family."

Dixon moved closer. "What kind of difficulty? Which members of the family?"

"The disagreement goes back a very, very long time. I doubt it's related. It wasn't violent. Just business."

"How long is a very, very long time?"

"Decades. About forty years."

Dixon looked at Vail, then at Montalvo. "Tell us more about—"

"It's got nothing to do with anything, Ms. Dixon. And no, I don't care to discuss it. It's family business, that's all."

"With all due respect, sir," Vail said, "that's for us to determine. You can't possibly know what's related and what's not. That's our job."

Montalvo sat there, the fire gone from his eyes, his shoulders slumped forward, his gaze downcast. "I've said all I'm going to say. Now . . . please, leave me alone. I have to go tell my wife that her daughter . . . that her daughter . . ." His bloodshot eyes started to tear up. "I'll call you if I come across anything you need to know."

Vail doubted they would hear again from Frederick Montalvo, but there was nothing more they were going to get from him at present. At least they had something to dig into.

They again offered their condolences, then left the way they came in.

# FIFTEEN

*J*ohn Wayne Mayfield stood beside his vehicle, peering intently at the entrance to the administration building of Montalvo Villa Estates Winery. No one would question his presence, yet because of who he was, he was as conspicuous as a pus pimple on the tip of a nose.

Didn't matter, though. He could easily deflect anyone who came his way and asked why he was there. His job gave him that power and authority.

Less than twenty minutes after arriving, the two women left the building; a looker redhead and a well-put-together blond. Mayfield didn't know who they were, but he would make it a point to find out. They looked official, but he hadn't seen them around—he most certainly would've remembered them.

He should have expected this. But this was where it got interesting— which was good; this was something he'd never had to deal with, and he welcomed a challenge.

Mayfield reached into his shirt pocket, pulled out a notepad, and began writing. A moment later, he watched as the women settled themselves into their Ford. They remained there a few minutes, talking and making a phone call. He walked to his vehicle and then followed them down the road, off the property, and onto 29, keeping a discreet distance.

The duties of his real occupation would have to wait. For the rest of the day, he had a new job.

———

VAIL CLOSED HER DOOR and turned to Dixon, who was staring

through the windshield. She made no effort to insert the key into the ignition.

"So what do you make of that?" Vail asked.

"Hard to say. There are a lot of families who've been here decades. Bragging rights, competitive posturing—even among family members. There are rifts, feuds, politics . . . so this disagreement Montalvo talked about, it's nothing to write home about." She raked her hair back off her face. "But it could be motive."

Vail wasn't sure about that, but said, "We should at least check it out."

Dixon pulled out her phone, and dialed Lugo. It rang through her car's hands-free speaker. He answered on the second ring. "Ray, we're on our way over to Kevin Cameron's place. You still there?"

"Yeah, why?"

"We've got some questions for him." Dixon turned over the engine and drew back the gearshift. "Give me the address. We'll be there in ten."

Dixon turned onto 29 and took the nearest cross street that went through to Silverado Trail, a gently winding picturesque road that was largely untouched by tourist spoils, restaurants, and city buildings: only vineyards, smaller production wineries, scenic foothills, and the occasional well-financed home set back on a hillside perch.

They turned left and headed down a private road that snaked uphill into the drive of a generously sized Tudor home. It wasn't as pretentious as Montalvo Villa Estates, but it was, nevertheless, a multimillion-dollar structure.

Vail followed Dixon to the front door, where Dixon pressed the chime. It sounded large and cavernous inside, and when the wooden entry door swung open, it didn't disappoint. A spacious great room stood before them, with a wall-sized stained glass window, similar in style to the one at Peju—only larger—directly ahead.

Ray Lugo stood grasping the highly polished brass knob. His face was long and he looked like he had been crying.

"You okay?" Dixon asked.

"Kevin took it hard."

*You don't look so good yourself.* Vail stepped in and Lugo closed the door behind them. In a low voice, Vail said, "Frederick Montalvo mentioned some kind of disagreement they've had with the family that owns Silver Ridge Estates. Supposedly goes back four decades."

Lugo straightened, moving from family friend back to detective. "You're thinking motive?"

"Doesn't really fit what we saw at the crime scene," Vail said. "Still, worth checking out."

Dixon matched Vail's low volume. "We need to ask Kevin if he knows anything about this feud."

Lugo looked over his shoulder nervously, then turned back to Dixon. "He's kind of in a bad way. Later may be better."

"If this is a straight murder, then any delay could compromise our ability to close the case," Vail said. "If it's a serial, like I think it is, and this feud is unrelated, then it's better we get out in front of it ASAP." Sensing Lugo's persisting hesitation, she said, "Don't worry, we'll go easy on him."

Lugo turned and led them left, down a hall that fed into an expansive, tiled family room. "Kevin," Lugo said to the man sitting stone-faced on a desk chair. Kevin didn't appear to be aware of their presence. He was staring ahead, shoulders slumped and jaw hanging slack.

Depression, shock, disbelief.

Vail had seen the look many times before. She moved in front of Kevin Cameron and sat down. "Mr. Cameron, I'm Special Agent Karen Vail with the FBI and this is Investigator Dixon. You spoke to her on the phone a little while ago." She leaned forward slightly. "I'm sorry about Victoria's death. But we need your help if we're going to catch the guy who . . . took her life. Will you help us?"

Kevin's eyes, glazed and red, canted upward to Vail. He examined her face, then his gaze moved to Dixon, and he did the same with her. "Yes," he finally said in a near whisper.

"We know about the feud your wife's family's had with the family that owns Silver Ridge Estates. Can you tell us who your disagreement is with, and what it was all about?"

He stared ahead for a long moment, then refocused his eyes. "It goes back to the parents, Harold and Anna. That's when the whole thing started. It all had to do with typical wine industry stuff. Frederick was just taking over the business from his father, Gerard, and he was aggressive coming out of the gate. He wanted to really inject some energy into the brand, which he felt was stale, not growing, and maybe losing market share." Kevin stopped, shuddered as he took an uneven breath.

"Silver Ridge had won a lot of wine competitions, and they were kind of full of themselves. Frederick wanted to make a splash, so he set his sights on Silver Ridge's up and coming star winemaker. He spent a year trying to lure him away but the guy was loyal to Harold and Anna. Fifteen years later, Silver Ridge hit a tough spot. Harold had a stroke and Anna had some health problems, too. The sons, who didn't get along too well to begin with, took over day-to-day operation of the winery. So with all that uncertainty, and with Montalvo doing better but still not reaching its potential, Frederick swooped in and snagged the winemaker."

Vail added all this up to motive. But there were still disconnects. "The family feud is obvious. But how malignant did it get—how bad were the feelings between the families?"

Kevin shrugged. "I'm relaying all this as it was told to me. I wasn't around, so I can't really judge. But from what Victoria said, and from what Frederick told me once, it was pretty poisonous stuff. They had some arguments over the years that the AVA board had to step in to resolve."

"AVA?" Vail asked.

"American Viticultural Area. It's a designation determined by the Bureau of Alcohol, Tobacco and Firearms to specify where a wine is grown and made. Think of it like a branding. When it says *Napa Valley* on the label, you know that at least 75 percent of the grapes used in that wine are from the Napa Valley."

"Why wouldn't all the grapes come from the valley?"

Dixon chuckled. "Sticky question. Grape prices are lower, as you'd imagine, in other regions of California that don't have the cachet of Napa. Some would say the *quality* of Napa. So it's okay to mix some grapes from, say, the Central Valley, provided 75 percent of the grapes used are from Napa. It protects their brand."

"How many AVAs are there?"

Dixon deferred to Kevin, who shrugged. "Well over a hundred," he said. "Probably closer to a hundred twenty-five, hundred thirty. The better known ones are Stags Leap District, Russian River Valley, Anderson Valley, and so on."

Vail looked at Dixon, who indicated she had all she needed. Vail placed a hand on Kevin's shoulder. "Thanks for all your help. I know this wasn't easy. If you think of anything that might help us find . . . the person we're looking for, would you give Investigator Dixon or Sergeant Lugo a call?"

Dixon handed him her card. Lugo made no such move. He and Kevin were friends, and Kevin undoubtedly had Lugo's number. In fact, without question, Kevin's call—should he make one—would go to his buddy.

Lugo led them to the front door. Out of earshot of Kevin, he said, "I don't think this feud is related to the murder."

"Too soon to say for sure," Vail said. "But the odds are strongly against it."

Dixon held out a hand. "I wouldn't discount it just yet. The body was found at their winery. But we don't have enough info yet. We need to dig more before we make any decisions."

———

BACK AT THEIR CAR, Dixon stood at the driver's door and looked across the vehicle at Vail. "The things that were done to the body could be taken as being a personal attack. Severing the breasts, for one."

Vail shook her head. "Severing the breasts is probably not personal."

"Overkill, right? Excessive violence shows a relationship between the offender and the victim."

"Up until very recently, that was our operating theory. We automatically considered overkill to be rooted in anger, and then we extrapolated that into a personal relationship. If the offender's angry, he had to have something against that person. Bingo. He knew the vic, hated her or was pissed at her for something. But the new thinking is that psychopaths, who don't feel any anger at all, are not necessarily angry at the victim. They're angry at someone else and projecting onto the victim.

"Even more significant is that we've found that some psychopaths enjoy inflicting damage and injury—for them, there's no anger or projection involved. So we have to be careful with calling severe violence 'overkill.' It could be a sign of anger, but not always. The other thing to consider," Vail continued, "is that serial killers target strangers. There's no relationship with the victim. It's not personal because they don't know the victim personally."

"So you're not buying this feud as a motive."

"First of all, anger is not a motive. Revenge is, but anger is an affect, not a motive." Vail looked over at the house. "The feud was a disagreement between the patriarchs, right? It's what, forty years old? There's just no energy left in the feud. So if we're looking at revenge as the motive, and not anger, why wait all these decades to act? Montalvo's an old guy. Unless we're missing something, it doesn't look like it filtered down to the kids. It might have to some degree—but at the same intensity? They're aware of it, of the history, but it's not really their battle—certainly not enough to kill over."

"We need to dig deeper," Dixon said. "Make sure you're right."

"Here's something else to consider. There were no defensive injuries on the vic; at the same time, there was a lot of control involved in her capture, and the killing, as well as the postmortem mutilation of the body. The UNSUB was very much in control of Victoria and of himself. He was methodical and careful. He didn't hack at the breasts with a machete, but he excised them neatly. That reinforces my feeling that there's no anger in the crime scene. And the killer's definitely satisfied with what he did there."

"So if Victoria was killed because of a personal feud, you're saying we'd see more damage, more anger, possibly even rage. But what if the killer got interrupted and had to leave?"

Vail smiled. "I had a case like that very recently. Dead Eyes. You hear of it?"

"I read some stuff about it. Several women killed. Virginia, right? A couple months ago?"

"Yeah." *Doesn't come close to summing it up, but that's good enough for now.*

"That was you?" Dixon snapped her fingers. "With the state senator—"

"Yes again." Vail waved her hand. She wasn't sure if she was waving it to get off the topic or to . . . get off the topic. "So yeah, it's possible the UNSUB heard something and freaked, like you said. But there's the issue of the other body we dug out of that collapsed wine cave that was missing the toenail. So I don't think that's what we're looking at here."

"The choking, crushing injury is pretty violent. That could be a sign of anger."

Vail considered that. "True. Let's wait and see what your coroner tells us about the other body. Then we can make some additional judgments, build on our profile. Right now, with just two vics, it's hard to be accurate in our conclusions. I can only tell you what it looks like, but the odds of me being wrong are higher with so few bodies. We need more bodies, more behavior, to evaluate." Vail shook her head. "That didn't come out right. I'm not wishing we had more bodies—"

"I know what you meant," Dixon said.

"I can draw one conclusion with reasonable certainty. We're dealing with an organized offender. Intelligent and potentially socially adept. Since there were no defensive wounds, it appears he was able to co-opt his victim in such a way that she doesn't see him as a threat. In other words, he was capable of emotionally disarming her so she'd go along with him until he could strike. If she had any objections, he successfully neutralized them."

Dixon's phone began vibrating on her belt. She flipped it open and listened a moment. "Okay, meet me over there."

She closed the phone and turned to Vail. "Warrant's ready. Clerk is delivering it to Silver Ridge."

———

VAIL AND DIXON arrived at the winery a moment ahead of the law clerk, who handed over the warrant in the parking lot.

"You sure we're going to need that?" Vail asked. "We're not talking about protected information."

"Not personally. But it's proprietary information important to Silver Ridge's business. A place like this is going to want to protect its guest list. Eventually, they'd turn it over. But this makes it a whole lot faster and easier."

As they got out of the car, Vail sighed and shook her head. "This is where my vacation started. And ended."

"How so?"

"We were first on the scene, so to speak. We were on the tour and pairings dinner."

"How'd you score a Silver Ridge tour? Pretty exclusive. And expensive."

"It's both. Robby's got a friend here who's got connections."

"Nice friend to have."

They took the warrant into the main building, walked through the large, windowed tasting room with low-hanging fiber-optic lights, and asked for the administration office. After Dixon badged the secretary, they were handed off to the wine sales manager.

A tall woman with chic black-rimmed glasses, she leaned back in her chair and appraised Vail and Dixon.

"I take it you're not here to join our wine club."

Vail glanced at the placard on the woman's desk. "Thanks, Catherine. Perhaps another time. We would, however, like a copy of your guest list, specifically those people who've purchased tickets for wine cave tours or the wine-pairing dinners during the past five years."

Catherine removed her glasses and studied Vail's face. "You were here the other night, when Miguel found—"

"The dead body, yes," Vail said. "I don't know why, but wherever I go, violence seems to follow me. Let's hope history doesn't repeat itself."

Catherine gave her a look Vail took to be somewhat hostile.

"So," Dixon said. "Your guest list. We'll also need a list of all your employees going back ten years."

Catherine thinned her lips into a tense smile. "That's not going to happen. I'm sure our customers don't want their names ending up in some police file associated with a murder investigation—"

"I thought you might say that," Dixon said. "So I had this pre-pared. Just for you." Dixon grinned politely, then handed over the warrant as if it was a gift certificate.

But, of course, it wasn't. The woman perused the document, then gave Dixon the same look she'd previously reserved for Vail. It didn't look any better the second time around.

Catherine leaned forward, pressed two buttons on her phone, then lifted the receiver. "I need you to do something for me." She pro-ceeded to give the person instructions on what to print and where to find it. She tossed the warrant back at Dixon, who fumbled it before getting it in her grasp. To Dixon's credit, she merely refolded the doc-ument and placed it on the desk. "No, no," she said. "This is yours, for you to keep. Our gift to you."

"Thanks so much for your cooperation," Vail said. "It's people like you that make our job just a tad bit tougher."

———

TWENTY MINUTES LATER, lists in hand, they started back toward their car. Vail shoved the paperwork in her purse, then stopped as they passed through the tasting room. She went over to a sommelier who was handing a customer his just-purchased case of wine.

"Would you like a tasting?" the man asked.

*I sure would. That's one reason I came to Napa. That and a vacation with Robby—who, come to think of it, still hasn't returned my call.*

"I'd love one," Vail said.

Dixon joined her at the counter and gave her a questioning look.

The sommelier—whose name tag read Claude, turned to the wall of wine bottles behind him. Vail leaned closer to Dixon. "Go with me on this," she said.

"Oh," Claude said, now facing them. "I'm sorry, will that be two tastings?"

"Just the one," Vail said. "My partner doesn't drink."

Dixon cleared her throat.

Claude lifted a bottle and cradled it in two hands so they could view the label. "I'm starting you off with our Pinot Noir, from our vineyard in the Carneros region."

Claude poured it. Vail lifted the glass to her lips.

"No, no," Dixon said. "I may not drink," she said, eyeing Vail with a sharp look, "but I sure know how to taste wine." She took the glass from Vail, placed it on the countertop, then swirled it rapidly. The red liquid shot centrifugally around the edges before coming to rest. "Aerates it," Dixon said. "Releases the nose." She handed the glass back to Vail.

"The nose?" Vail asked.

"The scent," Claude said.

Come to think of it, Claude's nose was a bit outstanding as well. Large and bulbous.

Vail took a sip. It slid across her tongue and down her throat effortlessly. "Very nice. Strawberries and . . . peach?"

"Yes, yes," the man said. "Very good."

Vail flared her nostrils. "A big, broad nose, too."

Dixon rolled her eyes.

"Go ahead and take another sip. This time let it flow over the palate, see how the taste buds on different areas of your tongue pick up different flavors."

Vail brought the glass to her mouth. Stopped, sniffed the wine. "So tell me a little about the winery," Vail said. "Who owns it?"

"Oh," Claude said, his face brightening. "It's owned by two brothers and their sister, but Gray is the main one. He's here every day—in fact, he was in here not five minutes before you came in."

"Does Gray have a last name?"

"He's always gone by Gray, or Grayson. He's very friendly with all the staff. Good man, I've known him about eleven years now."

Vail lifted the glass again to her lips. "Good to know. And Grayson's last name?" She tilted the glass and took a mouthful, as Claude instructed. Concentrated on tasting it—couldn't really see a difference—then swallowed.

"Oh, sorry," Claude said. "Brix. Grayson Brix."

Vail started coughing. Violent hacking, struggling to take a breath. She put her hand out and grabbed the counter, then bent forward to steady herself as she fought to keep her throat from closing from the burn of alcohol.

Dixon took the wineglass from her, then said to the sommelier, "Did you say Grayson *Brix*?"

"Is there a problem?" Claude asked.

Vail cleared her throat. In a raspy voice, she asked, "Any relation to Redmond Brix?"

"Anilise is their sister. Redd is the other brother, the silent partner. He's also a lieutenant at the Napa County Sheriff's Department—"

"Yeah, we got that part," Vail said. She turned to Dixon and, still trying to get the burning edge off her throat, said, "I think we'd better get back."

They turned and started to leave. Claude called after them. "The tasting fee is ten dollars—"

"Yeah, about that," Vail said as she neared the doorway. "Tell *Lieutenant* Brix it's on him."

———

THEY WALKED IN SILENCE to the car. Vail's hands were clenched and she was walking briskly through the parking lot.

As they approached the vehicle, Dixon said, "Well that's kind of disturbing."

"How could he keep that from us? He's a cop, doesn't he realize he has an obligation to be straight with us?"

They got into the Ford and Dixon started the engine. "I assume we're headed back to the sheriff's department?"

"Oh, yeah," Vail said. The twenty minute ride would do her good. Right now she felt a pulsing in her temples. That meant her blood pressure was high. And that meant she needed some cooling off time before she confronted Brix. It was likely going to be somewhat contentious.

# SIXTEEN

As they drove down Highway 29, the wineries of Niebaum-Coppola on her right and Opus One flying by to her left, Vail turned to Dixon. "How solid is Brix?"

"You mean, can he be mixed up in this somehow? A serial killer?"

"No," Vail said, "that makes no sense."

"He doesn't seem like the serial killer type."

Vail hiked her brow. "No, he doesn't."

"Still, he may have a motive."

"How well do you know him?"

Dixon shrugged. "Had a case with him a couple years ago. Since then, I've seen him around town from time to time. I like the guy. We shoot the breeze, bullshit. Cop talk. Nothing deep."

They drove on another mile. "Are those railroad tracks?" Vail said, craning her neck to the right.

"Napa Valley Wine Train. It's an old restored train that goes up and down the tracks, maybe an hour and a half each way, while people eat lunch or dinner. I did it once."

"Looks like fun." Vail reached for her phone to check for missed calls. None. "It's not likely Brix is involved," she said, "but it's our job to consider him a potential suspect. Keep an eye on him."

Vail removed the employee and guest lists, then shoved her purse beneath the seat. "You mind?"

Dixon shook her head. "I keep the car locked. Mine's in the glovebox. Just push it all the way under."

She drove on another minute, then Vail said, "You know, Brix really should recuse himself from the investigation."

Dixon chuckled. "Good luck with that. Still, it might be better keeping him close, where we can keep half an eye on him."

———

VAIL WAS THE FIRST through the front doors. She walked up to the desk, as she had the day earlier, only this time the clerk knew who she was. Nevertheless, the woman took a few seconds to acknowledge her.

When she finally came over to the desk, Vail asked, "Where's Lieutenant Brix?"

"Would you like me to page him for you?"

Dixon came up behind Vail. "Come on, I know where he is." She held up her cell phone. "Just spoke to him." Dixon swiped her prox card and proceeded down the hall.

"You didn't say anything about—"

"I told him we were in the building and we had something to discuss with him."

They walked into the Major Crimes Task Force room. Redmond Brix was seated at the head of the conference table, a file splayed open in front of him. Beside him was a uniformed officer.

"Give us a moment," Vail said to the cop.

The man looked at Vail, then Dixon, before coming to rest on Brix, who made the same rounds with his gaze. Brix nodded and the officer left.

Brix leaned back in his seat. "What's up?"

"Oh, I don't know," Vail said. "How about you own the winery where the vic was murdered, a winery that's been locked in a decades-long family feud with Frederick Montalvo? And how about you . . . uh . . . *forgot* to mention any of this?"

"First of all, I'm more of an investor—"

"Bullshit," Vail said. She placed both palms on the desk in front of her and peered at Brix. "You and your brother own it. True or false?"

"It's not black and white—"

"Answer my question. Please," she added.

"True."

"Did you have anything to do with the murder of Victoria

Cameron? Anything at all, ordering or facilitating a contract hit, killing her yourself, assisting your brother or anyone else—"

Brix rose from his seat. "Who the fuck do you think you are?"

"I'm part of a task force investigating the murder of a young woman. And you, a Lieutenant and the senior cop heading the investigation, decided to willfully hide facts from the rest of us."

"I didn't hide anything," Brix said. "It's just not relevant."

"Redd," Dixon said softly, "that's for all of us to decide."

"Scott knows. Stan knows. It's not a secret."

"Look," Dixon said, "as soon as we discovered the vic was Victoria Cameron, you should've disclosed your ownership of the rival winery to *everyone* on the task force."

"And you should recuse yourself from the investigation," Vail said.

"Bull-shit," he sang, drawing out the word.

Vail rested her hands on her hips. "How could you stay on, given what—"

"It's not our call," Dixon said. "If he wants to stay on the investigation, it's not our decision."

Vail had to concede that point. She had no authority here, other than to help and advise. But Dixon, as lead investigator, could have pressed the issue. Dixon had apparently decided not to pursue it—so Vail let it drop. "Fine," she said. "Whatever. Any other secrets half the task force knows and the other half doesn't?"

Brix ground his molars, perhaps waiting for his anger to fade. He turned to Vail with a heavy stare. "I've never had my integrity questioned. Never. And I'm not about to allow a Fibbie to dictate to me, or anyone else—"

"That's enough."

They all turned to the door, where Sheriff Stan Owens was standing.

"I don't want to hear any more of that derogatory bullshit. I know the FBI doesn't always get along with cops, and vice versa. But I respect both state and federal law enforcement. We're all in it together. Learn to play on the same field." He surveyed their faces. "Now, is there something you want to share with me?"

Vail looked at Brix. She wanted to disclose Brix's conflict of interest.

But she didn't want to be seen in the wrong light, particularly after Owens's admonishment. Besides, this was Dixon's fight, if she chose to take it on.

Dixon said nothing. Brix said nothing.

Owens nodded slowly. "Fine." He disappeared out the door.

"Anything else worth reporting?" Brix asked.

Vail dropped the guest and employee list printouts on the table. "We'll fill you in at four," she said. "That way *everyone* knows what's going on. For a change." She walked out of the room, leaving Dixon behind.

# SEVENTEEN

John Wayne Mayfield pulled into the Napa County Sheriff's Department parking lot and backed into a spot opposite the morgue's access gate. A moment later, the two foxes got out of their Ford and walked toward the building's entrance.

The redhead was moving faster. Urgent. Angry.

Interesting. She'd looked angry when they left Silver Ridge. What had gotten under her skin so deeply that it was still bothering her? He'd have to find out, take a look around tonight, when no one was on duty.

He pulled the pad from his breast pocket and opened it to the next page. Clicked his pen and began making notes. He needed to find out who they were, but he was almost sure they were working on the Victoria Cameron murder. Which meant they were looking for him.

"Right here," he said under his breath. "Better come get me before I come get you-ou," he sang.

———

VAIL LEFT THE SHERIFF'S DEPARTMENT and stood outside, waiting for Dixon. A few minutes later, Dixon walked through the front doors carrying a small brown bag. She tossed it to Vail, then got in the car.

"Late lunch," Dixon said. "There's turkey and veggie."

Vail opened the bag, peered in. "Either's fine."

"I'll take turkey. I need the protein for my workouts." She took the sandwich from Vail and put the Ford in gear. Peeled back the wrapping, took a bite.

Their phones rang simultaneously. Vail pulled her BlackBerry—a text message from Ray Lugo:

Another vic. Meet me.

It was followed by the address.

"You know where that is?" Vail asked.

Dixon nodded, then depressed the gas pedal, sandwich in one hand and steering wheel in the other.

---

VALLEJO, CALIFORNIA, was a straight shot south down Highway 29, a fifteen-minute ride under normal circumstances. But with her lightcube flashing, Dixon downed her sandwich in four minutes and arrived at the Vallejo Police Department seven minutes after that.

Vallejo is part of the San Francisco Bay Area, one of the more expensive regions in the country in which to live. But Vallejo, at the lower end of the income spectrum, provided affordable housing for those not able to purchase the more ritzy addresses of a Silicon Valley or North Bay neighborhood. Still, its location, on San Pablo Bay and within a short drive of the Napa Valley as well as the greater Bay Area, provided picturesque views and prime weather patterns.

Home to the Six Flags Discovery Kingdom, the decommissioned Mare Island Naval Shipyard, and the third largest Filipino American population in the United States, the city has the little-known distinction of briefly serving as California's state capital from 1852 to 1853.

"You're very quiet," Dixon said.

"Just thinking."

"You clammed up soon as I told you we were headed to Vallejo. I'm betting you're dialed into the Zodiac. Concerned our case is related."

Vallejo was the site, four decades ago, of two victims of the Zodiac killer. The Zodiac was never apprehended, and the investigation, which was mothballed in 2004, was reopened in 2007. In 2009, a woman came forward claiming her deceased father had been the killer and that she had been present during some of the murders.

"Regardless of his true identity," Vail said, "he's either dead or incarcerated. He's been inactive for forty years. Besides, MO's different. Ritual's all wrong." She unbuckled as Dixon parked. "But yeah, that's what I've been thinking about."

They walked into the police department and headed to the Detective Division. "Still, there are similarities," Vail said. "Zodiac was a narcissist, just like our UNSUB. He contacted the police after his kills, claiming credit. Mailed cryptograms to the newspapers."

"I've heard the stories," Dixon said. "Before my time."

As they walked into the Detective Division, Ray Lugo caught their attention from across the room. Vail and Dixon headed toward him.

"Oh, Jesus," Dixon said under her breath.

Vail looked at her, but before she could inquire about the remark, another man, seated behind Lugo, rose from his chair. Dark complected, possibly Asian, maybe Filipino.

"Well, well, well," the man said. "If it isn't Buff Barbie."

"Eddie," Dixon said, a surprisingly measured and civil response. "Should've known you'd be here."

Vail sensed a failed relationship. She watched them staring at one another, that awkward look pregnant with transparent communication.

"Well," she finally said, "I'm Special Agent Karen Vail. FBI. I take it you're Eddie."

He kept his eyes on Dixon but extended his hand in Vail's direction. "Detective Eddie Agbayani." He finally pulled his gaze over to Vail as they shook. "Good to meet you."

"So where's this new vic?" Vail asked.

Lugo held up a case file. "*Probable* new victim." He handed Vail the manila folder. "Before I went over to Kevin Cameron's, I sent out a text blast to all my LEO buddies," he said, using the acronym for Law Enforcement Officer. "I've lived here all my life, I've got a fair number of law enforcement contacts. I figured you never know, something may turn up."

"And it did," Agbayani said. "Almost three years ago we found a DB in South Vallejo, in a tony neighborhood. It was a body dump. The area's got the most expensive real estate in the city, so it scared the crap out of them. We never solved it."

"And what ties it to our UNSUB?" Vail asked.

"Severed breasts and missing toenail," Lugo said. "That's what I put in the text message. I thought, of all things that's unique about this killer, that sums it up."

Vail opened the case file. "Good thinking, Ray. Exactly right." She backed off to a nearby chair while the other three talked. Vail heard snippets like "So how've you been?" that came from Agbayani, followed by Dixon's response, then his comment: "I've missed you." Vail tuned it out and focused on the reports in front of her.

Coroner's report: ". . . *thirty-five-year-old woman, brunette, 157.5 cm. Apparent homicide victim. COD looks to be crushing wound to the trachea; fractured hyoid bone. Bilateral breast tissue excision, with well-defined margins suggesting a sharp knife or scalpel . . .*" Vail skipped a bit but came across the item that brought her here: *"the toenail of victim's right second digit is missing, apparently forcibly removed due to . . ."*

Vail thumbed through the rest of the file. No known suspects identified. No witnesses to the murder. No forensics other than tire tracks lifted nearby that might or might not have been from the assailant's vehicle. The pattern matched that of a mass produced tire from a major brand manufacturer. Over a million of these tires were sold in the Bay Area proper during the previous three years. Victim ID was Maryanne Bernal. Served for three years on a nonprofit board. Executive director of Falling Leaf Winery in the Georges Valley District. Employees all cleared. Not married, no known enemies, no disgruntled boyfriends.

Vail closed the folder.

"Not much help," Lugo said.

"Actually, that's not entirely true." Vail joined the three of them by Agbayani's desk. "This is further proof this offender has killed before. It allows us to begin creating a geographic kill zone, a geoprofile."

"That helps us how?" Dixon asked.

"Well, right now, it doesn't help us at all because our sampling size is too small."

"The more victims the better," Lugo said.

"In a warped sense," Vail said, "yes. So . . . Maryanne Bernal. What do we know about her?"

"Last seen leaving a house she was renting in Northgate—"

"Northgate? Where's that?"

"In Vallejo."

"She worked at a winery in Napa and lived in Vallejo?"

"Not unusual," Agbayani said. "Relatively quick off-hours commute. Prices are better. She may've had the house before getting the Napa job."

"Okay," Vail said, accepting that explanation. "What else?"

Agbayani continued: "We don't know where she went after. Far as we could tell, she didn't visit or talk to any of her friends after leaving home. She more or less disappeared from the living. At some point, her path crossed with the killer's, and that was it. We were never able to establish any kind of suspect list based on where she worked or people she knew. She didn't date much and didn't have any arguments with anyone."

"We now know this is a serial offender case," Vail said. "They're almost always stranger-on-stranger crimes, so Maryanne probably didn't know the killer, not well. She may've met him somewhere, someplace meaningless to her . . . standing in line in the bank, at work in passing. Meant nothing to her, but she was suddenly on his radar. He either took her soon after or followed and tracked her for awhile. Given that this guy appears to be an organized offender, he probably planned his attack on her."

Agbayani sat down heavily. His chair creaked. "Well, I'm glad we've got some activity to work with on this. Maybe we'll catch this fucker."

Vail's phone rang. She pulled it from her belt and checked the display: Robby. "Excuse me, I've gotta take this."

---

VAIL ANSWERED THE CALL as she headed back out to the parking lot the way she'd come. "Hey, stranger."

"How's your day been?"

Vail sighed. "I'm working. Learned some stuff about the wine industry you're not likely to get from one of the tastings we had planned."

"Yeah?"

"And you?"

"Oh, been tooling around, visited a few wineries. Took a tour of this castle winery, pretty cool actually."

"Tell me about it over dinner. Wanna meet around six?"

"I can do that. Want me to pick you up?"

"I can get someone to drop me off. Where do you want to meet?"

"Back at the B&B. We'll go from there."

There was a noise over her shoulder. Dixon and Lugo walking toward her.

"Gotta go. See you later. Miss you." She ended the call and reholstered her phone. "So, good work, Ray. This is an important discovery."

"I'd much rather find already dead bodies from this killer than fresh ones."

Vail shielded her eyes from the glare of the sun, which was breaking through the clouds. "I have a feeling there are more. Looks like this guy's been operating in the area for a while. That means he's comfortable here. Knows his way around, works here, lives here."

"So the question is," Dixon said, "where's his base of operation?"

"That's a loaded question. We'd need at least an hour to answer it in theory, and a few more victims to answer it in practice."

Dixon pulled out her car keys. "So for now, we just keep adding to the profile."

Vail nodded. "Exactly."

Their phones buzzed simultaneously. Vail pulled her BlackBerry: a text from Brix. They were to report back now to the task force op center.

Lugo turned toward his vehicle. "See you two in fifteen."

# EIGHTEEN

Vail followed Dixon and Lugo into the conference room the Major Crimes task force was currently occupying. A number of suited guests were standing in front of the whiteboard. Redmond Brix was conducting class, gesturing to the group of bureaucrat-looking officials.

"Who are these people?" Vail whispered to Dixon.

Dixon turned her back to Brix and said, "Let's put it this way. They're not friendlies."

Brix looked past the shoulder of one of his guests and locked on Vail and Dixon. Lugo had already taken his seat.

Vail felt the coolness of Brix's look, even across the room. She and Dixon made their way to the front of the room. Each of the guests turned to face Vail. The men glanced at Dixon—men could never help but look at a beautiful woman—but their gazes returned to Vail. She felt as if she had done something wrong and was facing her accusers.

"This is Roxxann Dixon, investigator with the DA's office, and Special Agent Karen Vail, FBI," Brix said. He gestured to the suits and said, "And this is Mayor Prisco, Board of Supervisors president Zimbrowski, and Timothy Nance, District Director for Congressman Emmanuel Church."

Vail absorbed this information, hoping she hadn't contorted her face too badly; she wasn't one to effectively mask her emotions, particularly when it came to bureaucrats and politicians. Trying to behave, she shook each of their hands with a firm greeting.

"This is a pretty impressive showing," Vail said.

"This is a pretty important case," Timothy Nance said.

*Politically,* Vail mused. *This is a pretty important case politically.*

Brix consulted his watch, then spread both hands. "Why don't we take our seats, get started." He held up a sheaf of papers. "I had our names and contact numbers typed up and hole punched. I also had copies made of the autopsy report on Victoria Cameron. Take one of each and pass it on."

The politicos sat in chairs placed in the front of the room, off to the side. Sheriff Stan Owens walked in, clapped hands with the mayor, said something to Zimbrowski and Nance, then took a seat beside them. Vail sat where she had earlier, at the midpoint of the oblong table, to Brix's right, who stood at the head. Dixon was beside Vail, followed by Lugo at the far end, facing Brix. Scott Fuller perched himself on the other side, opposite Vail and slightly to her left.

"Everyone's been introduced to our guests," Brix said, "so let's move on. We have a number of follow-ups to cover, but first, let's hear about this new vic."

"That's mine," Lugo said. He took the papers making the rounds and peeled off a copy of each document as he spoke. "Lived and worked in Vallejo, killed three years ago. Body dumped in an upper class South Vallejo neighborhood. Nothing to go on, case unsolved."

"Severed breasts and second right toenail removed postmortem," Vail said. "That provides us with linkage to Victoria Cameron and the unidentified vic from the excavation site. So that gives him three victims that we know of, and there are going to be more."

"You know that how?" This from the board of supervisors president, Zimbrowski.

"From my years of experience studying serial killers," Vail said firmly.

"Whoa," Nance said, leaning forward in his seat. He looked at the room's door, as if to make sure it was closed. In a lowered voice, he said, "Let's not throw around terms like 'serial killer.' That's volatile stuff. We don't know that's what we're dealing with here."

"I'm with the Behavioral Analysis Unit," Vail said. "A profiler."

"Profiling. I've always wondered about that," Nance said. "Is there any validity to that stuff?"

Vail chuckled. "You know, you bring up a valid point, Mr. Nance.

I've had the same doubts. I've always thought my career was a waste of time and taxpayer money."

The room was silent. Nance dropped his head and leaned back in embarrassment, clearly realizing how stupid his question was. At least, that was Vail's initial interpretation of his reaction. Now that she thought about it, however, he could've been thinking, *Who's this bitch and how can I get rid of her?*

"Agent Vail has a way with words," Brix said, breaking the odd quiet that had draped the room like dense smoke.

"I've found her analysis useful so far," Dixon said.

Lugo nodded. "Because of her input, I was able to find that Vallejo vic."

"That's dandy," Nance said, a bit louder. "Has it caught us a killer?"

"Look," Vail said, "I'm not here to debate the merits of profiling. But I'm here. And to answer your question, yes, there's validity to it."

"Why *are* you here?"

"I wasn't—"

"I asked for her help," Brix said.

Vail looked at him, and again, tried to disguise her facial expression, which probably bordered on wide-mouthed shock.

"This is something beyond our knowledge base," Brix said. "We probably could've done a decent job, muddled through it, missed some important nuances about this killer, and eventually caught the guy. But in my estimation, we've got a volatile situation here. And since we're dealing with the lives of young women, I felt it was best to bring in the FBI. Before we had more victims, new victims, to deal with."

Nance started to object. Brix held up a hand. "I don't like Agent Vail's methods, but she knows her shit. So unless Sheriff Owens has a problem, Vail stays and we move on. Sheriff?" Brix turned to Owens.

"I've been to the National Academy at Quantico," he said, speaking ahead, not looking at the dignitaries. "Agent Vail was one of my instructors. She's got my vote."

Brix's eyes scanned his guests' faces. Hearing no objection, he said, "Okay, then. Let's follow up on our assignments."

"One observation," Vail said, "before we go any further. This new victim helps us build on that 'access concept' I mentioned after we found Victoria Cameron. We now have three likely vics of the same offender. They were each found in different locations. That means we have three different access lists to evaluate. Access population A, the Silver Ridge wine cave; population B, the excavated Black Knoll cave; and population C, Vallejo. Unfortunately, because Vallejo was a body dump, we don't know where she was killed. If we can reopen that investigation and determine where she was murdered, we can look for overlap on who'd have access to these three crime scenes. That'd help narrow the suspect pool."

"Interesting," Nance said.

Dixon nodded. "We can start with population A. Karen and I obtained the guest lists from Silver Ridge."

Vail locked eyes with Brix, waiting for him to disclose to the group his ownership interest. He met her stare and held it until she looked away. Then he said, "The guest lists are being cross-referenced by officers I've got working the case behind the scenes. So far, nothing unusual has shown up. Only a handful of locals, half of them women. The others are being looked at. They'll be interviewed to see if they've got alibis for the time in question. I'll let you know if we get anything interesting."

Fuller said, "Population B, the excavated cave, is a problem. There's a gate on the property, but anyone could realistically bypass it. But if we're assuming it's not leaky, you're looking at a lot of potential people, from housecleaners to caterers, to gardeners, to maintenance people. All will be granted access without much resistance. I don't think your access theory is going to get us anywhere."

Vail entertained thoughts of responding, but before she could speak, Lugo said, "I met with Kevin Cameron. Karen and Roxxann joined me and we asked him all the standard questions. He didn't know anyone who'd want to harm Victoria. There was something about a family disagreement going back forty years or so between the owners of Silver Ridge and the Montalvo family."

"And we spoke with Frederick Montalvo," Dixon said. "We delivered the news, and he was pretty broken up, as you'd imagine. Karen and I didn't feel there's much to this disagreement—"

"Hold on a second," Mayor Prisco said. "The Montalvos and the owners of Silver Ridge have had a long-running feud and you don't think it's relevant?"

"We're looking into everything," Vail said. "But since we're dealing with a serial killer, and since these types of things—bad blood between families—don't fit with the psychopathy seen in the behaviors at the crime scene, it's unlikely there's a relationship. But as I said, we're looking into it." She again glanced at Brix.

Brix cleared his throat. "Just . . . have confidence that we know how to run an investigation. We're good at this type of thing, Mayor."

Prisco's eyebrows rose. "I didn't mean to imply otherwise. I'm sorry. I'll—I'm just concerned, is all."

"We're all concerned," Owens said. "That's why we're taking this very seriously."

"And it's why I think we need to take the next step," Vail said. "If we want to accelerate this investigation, we want to push this killer into the open. We want to play to his weaknesses."

Zimbrowski pushed his glasses up on his nose. "What weaknesses?"

"He's a narcissist," Vail said.

Fuller sat forward. "We don't know that for sure."

"I think we do. At least from what we've seen, there's a good chance that's what we're dealing with."

"And how does this impact your investigation?" Prisco asked.

"Narcissists feel they're superior to everyone else. They recognize that what they're doing is wrong, but they just don't care. And they want credit for what they've done. One such case you may be familiar with is the Zodiac Killer from nineteen—"

"Don't even say it," Zimbrowski said.

"That case is still unsolved," Prisco said. "If you start talking like that around here, people will absolutely freak out—"

"I don't want to hear those words again," Nance said. "In this room or outside it."

Vail looked around the room, waiting for someone to object. All the cops were looking down at the table or stimming with pens or the edge of their binders.

Finally, Vail said, "No disrespect, but I'm giving you advice on how to catch this killer. I can't be swayed by your sensibilities about— whatever it is you're worried about. Because this killer, if we can get him to communicate with us, will reveal information about himself we can use to catch him. And that's vital, because right now, we've got shit. And *that's* something to be worried about."

There was quiet before the mayor asked, "How do we get him to communicate with us if we don't know who he is?"

"We go public with this, we go on TV, the newspapers—"

"Are you out of your mind?" Fuller asked. "We'll have widespread panic."

Vail crossed her arms. "Sounds to me like you've read all of the Douglas and Ressler and Underwood books on profiling, Scott. You know what I'm saying is right."

"I don't know that. Those books don't talk much about narcissism. Besides, you don't know for sure this guy is a narcissist, so going public now is the wrong thing to do. Let's get more evidence first, see more behaviors before we can determine if he's really got Narcissistic Personality Disorder."

Fuller, in throwing around medical terms, sounded authoritative and, judging by the way the suits were looking at him, had captured their attention. He also appeared to be saying what they wanted to hear.

"More behavior," Vail said, "means more bodies. How long do you think you can keep this under wraps? And how upset are people going to be when they find out you knew you had a serial killer loose and you failed to warn them?"

"I challenge your theory of a serial killer," Nance said.

Vail shook her head. "I'm not a politician, okay? I'm a cop. But I see what's going on here. Understand this: I'm not worried about tourism levels or income to the state, or the federal government. I'm concerned with catching this guy before he kills again."

"Thank you, Agent Vail," Brix said. "And we appreciate your input. But this is our community, and we have to live with all the various interests and forces that govern our local economy. Putting out a public notice may save the life of one person, but it'll have a profound effect on thousands of people's lives. If not tens of thousands. A lot of family businesses depend on the wine-growing and wine-selling economy. Sales tax on purchases, bed-and-breakfast room taxes, income taxes from the booming trade of people just being in town: restaurants, gift shops, stores. We tip that scale the wrong way, we may never recover."

Nance added, "There's a lot of competition from wine regions all over the world now. Washington state, Argentina, Chile, France, Italy. Not to mention other areas in California. We don't want to jump the gun and cripple the Napa Valley in a way it might not be able to recover from financially."

"We need more to go on before we go public," Prisco said.

"And we need to be sure that going public is the right thing," Fuller said. "I mean, contacting this guy may be the wrong way to go. He could look at it as a challenge, and really go off the deep end. And go on a killing spree. You see what I'm thinking?"

*A killing spree? What the hell is Fuller talking about?*

"What I'm *thinking* is that a little knowledge is very dangerous," Vail said. "You've asked me here to help. I hate to say it, but sooner or later you're going to have to go public with this. It's our best chance at catching this killer."

"I want you to promise," Nance said, "that you won't act without seeking the proper permission from the sheriff, whose office is spearheading this investigation and who personally bears ultimate responsibility for the disposition of the case and its impact on the community." He looked over at Owens, who did not react one way or another. "Do I need to make myself clearer, or do you understand what I'm saying?"

Vail stifled a chuckle. "I'm not an imbecile, Mr. Nance. I understand what's driving you and I know exactly where you're coming from. As to promising you what I will or will not do, I'm not going to do any such thing. I'm part of this task force. I don't work for you and I don't work for Congressman Church. I work for the federal government. And for the victims, for the People. I'm sorry if that bothers you." She rose from her chair and pushed it tight against the table. "No, check that. I'm not sorry at all."

———

VAIL WALKED OUTSIDE and descended the first flight of stairs directly ahead of her. She turned and leaned against the metal railing and looked up at the three flags blowing hard in the wind. The sky was now deep blue, a few barely visible clouds dotting the expanse. She closed her eyes and let the gentle breeze slink through her red hair. *This was supposed to be a vacation. What the hell was I thinking? All I can do is advise, I can't make these people do the right thing.*

She put her head back. The coolness of the evening's arrival relaxed her, cleared her mind.

"You have a knack."

Vail opened her eyes and spun around. Dixon was standing there. "A knack?"

"For pissing people off. I thought I was the only one."

"Oh, no, I've perfected it." Vail grinned, then let the smile fade. "I don't do it on purpose. But I challenge people. I don't hold back what I'm thinking. Good or bad, it's who I am." She took a deep breath and looked around. "I'm not trying to piss anyone off. This is something I know about and feel strongly about. I do have a knack, a kind of sixth sense, I guess. I don't know how to describe it. I just understand these killers. It's not like reading a textbook, like Fuller. I've seen it, I've been down in the trenches."

"I hear you."

"There's a saying in my unit, one of our profilers started using it maybe a dozen years ago and it stuck: Knee deep in the blood and guts. That kind of describes what we do. After a while, you get dragged down in the muck, and you start to slog your way through it, and pretty soon you're emotionally and physically stuck in it. And it affects you." She stopped, thought a moment, then continued. "But more than that, you begin to see things you didn't see before, have a better understanding of what you're looking at when you see these behaviors. I've talked to these killers, I've sat a foot from their faces, I've asked them questions, I've made them cry. And in all those interviews, all these years, they add up to a deep understanding of who these assholes are. I don't know if that makes any sense, but being inside their heads affected me."

Vail pushed away from the railing, then checked her watch. She didn't realize how late it was; Robby would be arriving in a few minutes. "Can you drop me at my B&B?"

"Where are you staying?"

"Mountain Crest, in St. Helena."

Dixon looked back over her shoulder at the sheriff's department building, as Fuller, Lugo, and Brix were walking through the door. The meeting had ended.

Dixon turned back. "Sure, let's go. I live out that way anyway."

---

JOHN WAYNE MAYFIELD waited until the two women got into their car. He was now sure they were cops—detectives, actually, because they weren't in uniform. But they had the look, he decided. Other men in suits left the building, too. He wasn't sure if they were with the women, but the fact that they were leaving, and not entering, made the task ahead easier.

He got out of his vehicle and walked up the two flights of stairs to the entrance. He had nothing to fear; he'd been in this building many times before and would not be out of place. But he'd never been here to do what he was about to do. And that made him nervous.

But he was good at handling himself and defusing potentially hazardous situations. He knew what to say if someone stopped him. *But they've got no reason to stop me.*

Mayfield pushed through the door and moved down the hall, nodded at the legal clerk behind the glass, then swiped his prox card and walked through the door. He surveyed the nearby rooms on either side of him. He needed to look confident, like he was supposed to be here and not snooping or doing anything nefarious or suspicious. So he opened the first door he came to on the left and stepped in. Looked around. Nothing of interest.

Moved back out into the hall and tried the next door. He knew one of these rooms had to be where the cops met, where they kept their case files and notes. Over the years, he had read about the Major Crimes task force that convened to track fleeing felons, bank robbers, kidnappers, and the like. He figured this task force had already met to discuss him. Maybe that's what those women were doing. And those men.

But this building was a maze of the worst kind: The hallways and doors all looked alike, save for the teal and white placards mounted outside each door. As he continued to wander the hallway, he read the little signs looking for some kind of task force notation . . . or a large meeting room of some sort.

As he made his way around yet another bend, he was beginning to doubt he would find what he was looking for. And the longer he was here, the more likely he'd run into trouble. But he was sure he had blown them away with the wine cave murder. He left it for everyone to see. They *had* to be working his case. They had to be. He was surprised there was nothing in the newspaper. Not even a death notice.

He paused beside another door, whose teal placard read, Conference Room # 3. Mayfield pushed through and walked in. The motion sensors fired and turned on the lights. This was it, the base of operations. A whiteboard with a grid. Names, what looked like tasks and assignments. *Oh, yes. Very good.* He fished around his deep pocket for the digital camera. He aimed and depressed the shutter. Once, twice, three times.

This was too much—it was all about him! *Of course it was.*

Then something caught his eye. The word "Vallejo." So they knew about Vallejo and Detective Edward Agbayani. Well, that was impressive.

He looked over the names on the whiteboard. Brix and Lugo: no introduction necessary. Dixon, Vail, Fuller—he needed to look those up.

Mayfield walked around the room, realizing he'd already gotten most of the info he needed. Best to get out of there. While he could explain away his presence, why take the risk?

As he turned to leave, he saw a laptop beside scattered papers lying on the conference table. He grabbed a sheet off the top and glanced at it. Names and phone numbers. Neatly typed into a grid, hole-punched for binders.

Very good.

He folded the paper into his pocket and walked out. Moved down

the hall to find a computer he could use. The laptop in the conference room would have sufficed, but if any of the task force members
walked in on him, that would be a lot more difficult to explain than if
he was discovered in front of a PC somewhere else, in an unoccupied
office.

But it was late in the day, and most of the clerical staff had clocked
out. He wasn't looking to hack into anyone's terminal . . . just a computer with Internet access he could safely use that wouldn't leave behind search results traceable to him. He turned the corner into a large,
cubicle-filled room. The dividers were tall, nearly ceiling height, and he
couldn't see over them. He walked around, turned the corner, and entered the main aisle that cut through and past all the desks. He kept his
head forward, not wanting to look suspicious. But the area was largely
deserted, except for a black-haired head thirty feet away.

He slid into the cubicle and faced the monitor. Turned it on, hit the
spacebar, and the screen lit up. It looked like a plain vanilla Windows
desktop. No password screen, so it was likely a standalone computer,
not connected to the county network. Exactly what he needed.

He opened Internet Explorer, and in the Live Search field, typed
"Roxxann Dixon Napa California." Got several hits, including one that
contained a photo of her and a brief bio of her position with the district attorney's office. It said she served on the Major Crimes Task
Force. *Bingo. This is the blonde I saw.*

Next he typed in "Karen Vail Napa California." No relevant hits.
Narrowed the search to "Karen Vail." And got references to the Federal Bureau of Investigation. Clicked on one: *"FBI Profiler Karen Vail,
fresh off the case of the Dead Eyes killer, the notorious serial killer who ter-
rorized women in the Virginia area . . ."*

Mayfield slid back his chair. "Whoa." He said it aloud then quickly
snapped his flapping lips shut. *FBI. A profiler. They are taking this seriously. I must've scared the shit out of them. That's why they haven't told the
media. They're afraid they don't know what they're dealing with.*

His eyes were drawn again to the words "FBI Profiler." *A federal
case. As it should be. John Wayne Mayfield deserves nationwide coverage.
But there's no fun in spoon feeding them the story. They have to realize*

themselves *what they have here. Once enough pressure's applied, it'll reach a point where they can't contain it anymore. Then the newspapers and TV would find out. Everyone would know. It would blow up into a huge story.*

A broad smile spread Mayfield's lips.

He looked back at the screen, fingered the mouse. Time to turn up the heat. And he had just the thing to get their attention. Something that would drive them nuts.

# NINETEEN

Vail and Dixon pulled into Mountain Crest's small gravel lot beside Robby's Murano. His brake lights were still glowing.

Vail had the door open before Dixon brought the Ford to a stop. "Hey, come out for a sec. I want you to meet someone."

Vail jumped out of the car and into Robby's arms. He gave her a big embrace, then seemed to notice Dixon standing there and released his grip.

"Oh—this is Roxxann Dixon," Vail said. "We're working together on the task force."

Robby straightened up, then reached out to shake. "Robby Hernandez."

"Good to meet you."

"So . . ." Robby said. "How was your day?"

Vail and Dixon shared a look before Dixon said, "Let's just say it was . . . productive and leave it at that."

"Uh huh." Robby squinted and shifted his gaze from Dixon to Vail, then decided to heed Dixon's advice.

Dixon backed away. "You two have a great evening. Pick you up tomorrow? Eight-thirty?"

"Sure," Vail said. "See you in the morning."

Dixon got in her car and drove off.

Vail tilted her head at Robby the way a mother looks at a son expecting an explanation.

"What?"

"You found her attractive," she said. "I can tell."

"Well, yeah. She is. Is that up for debate?"

Vail slapped him in the arm. "Wrong answer."

"I'm just saying. It is what it is. I didn't say I was attracted *to* her. I said she was attractive."

"Is there a difference?" Vail asked.

"Yeah. But to set the record straight, yes, I was attracted to her. I'm a man, she's a beautiful woman. But you're more beautiful. Besides, you've got my heart."

She reached out and grabbed his groin. "That's not all I've got."

Robby raised his eyebrows, then guiltily glanced around the parking lot, which was now bathed in fading light. He said, "I think I should take this inside."

———

AND THAT'S EXACTLY what he did. Afterwards, Vail rolled off him and stared at the ceiling. "That makes up for what turned out to be a tough day."

"You have to learn to play well with others," Robby said.

"How did you know what happened?"

He gave her a look that said, Come on. "Give me some credit. I think I know you pretty well, Karen."

She yawned. "You know what, I don't even care anymore. About today. I'm hungry . . . starved. But I'm so . . . I feel so rested. I don't want to move."

Robby got off the bed and drew the curtains. It was now ink black outside, the sun having set and the woods filtering whatever stray light might be emanating from the moon. "Let's order room service," Vail said, her speech groggy.

"Good one," Robby said as he slipped on his pants. "How about I go out, get something, and bring it back?"

"Sounds good to me," she mumbled. "Wake me when you get back . . ."

———

VAIL WAS ASLEEP, dreaming of yodeling sommeliers, the oak barrel scent of raspberry-nosed Pinot Noir, the weight of Robby lying atop her, the heat of the Day Spa sauna . . . hot . . .

Sweating . . .

So hot . . .

And the stench of gasoline. *Gasoline?*

Nose stings, hard to breath, smoke—

Vail woke from her stupor, lifted her head, and saw nothing. Blackness like a velvet coffin enveloped her. Cocoonlike in its confinement, thick. She felt around—she was on the bed. Asleep. Robby—he went for food.

Felt her fanny pack on the night table, with the Glock's prominent bulge.

*Can't see.* Cough! *What's the layout of the room?* She couldn't remember—but just then, something blasted through the small window, a fireball, flames—feeding on the once-delicate frilly curtains, conflagrating upwards toward the ceiling. Covering the walls.

Vail snatched the fanny pack and tossed the strap over her head. Wrapped a robe around herself and stumbled off the bed. Ran for the door—grabbed the knob and—*fuck!* Hotter than hot. Found a piece of clothing, wrapped it around her hand and tried to turn it. Locked? *Jammed?* She slammed against it with her shoulder. It rattled but didn't budge. *The door opens from the inside—it'd have to be pushed open from the outside.*

She turned toward the window—only way out—but a wall of flames stared back. Angry, ferocious fire lunged at her.

*The smoke, so thick. Get down, crawl*—she fell to her knees, more because of her inability to breathe than a memory of what to do in the case of fires, which was suddenly plucked from some deep reach of consciousness.

She started toward the bathroom, but the air . . . so thick with particulates she tasted it on her tongue. *Go, go, toward the bathroom. Window?* Can't remember . . .

*Get out of here!*

Made it to the bathroom, reached up—doorknob hot, burning hot—can't open it. *Hot doorknob means fire inside the room.*

Turned back toward the front door, need a chair, smash through it . . .

But as she crawled along the floor, her chest felt heavy, tight—
*no air.*

*Robby!* she screamed in her mind. *Jonathan . . .*

*No, keep going. Cover mouth, keep going . . .*

As she fought the intense heat, flames all around her, crackling, black smoke—the room door burst open. She couldn't lift her head but two arms grabbed her and yanked her hard, and she felt herself being lifted into the air and thrown against a body. *Robby . . . thank God . . .*

She was bouncing up and down, helpless, a rag doll bobbing about on Robby's back as he ran away from the burning building, the adjacent hedges now lit up like a bonfire.

coughing—

hair in her face—

and an explosion behind her—a fireball rose up into the sky, wood shards slamming into her back and above her, to the side, all around, and—

*Robby, move faster!*

He kept going, the smoke still thick, and she kept bouncing around as he ran into the graveled parking lot. Eyes burning. Tearing. Can't see—

Off in the distance, a siren.

Vail lifted her head.

Forced her eyes open, then closed, then open . . .

. . . saw two blurred headlights jumping in the darkness. They stopped, someone running toward her, and she was suddenly laid down on the gravel, looking up and seeing—

"Karen! Oh my god—what happened?"

She looked up, blinked repeatedly, eyes thick, and Robby was only a few feet away, running toward her. And then he was leaning over her, lifted her up and embraced her, held her close.

"Are you okay?" He pushed her away, held her at arm's length, looking at her. "Karen—Karen, are you okay?"

Vail coughed, hard, nodded, her senses coming back to her with the cleaner air starting to infiltrate her lungs. With her pulled hard against his body, his long arm and large hand wrapped around her body, grabbing her hip, Robby led her farther away, toward his car. But he stopped, turned, and said, "Are you okay?"

"Fine."

Coughing.

"I'll be fine."

And then he was moving her toward the car again.

———

JOHN WAYNE MAYFIELD sat in the thicket, a pair of Carson Super-Zoom binoculars pressed against his face. Normally, seeing in the distance at night would require a specialized night vision apparatus. But he didn't have such equipment—and with the intense illumination given off by the fire, the area was lit just fine for his needs.

He had never experimented with fire, but watching the flames jump and consume and *devour*—he had to admit, it carried a certain excitement. A certain power.

But how would you leave your mark? How would others know it was *you* who set the fire?

Most of all, it was so distant, so removed from the action. The thrill just wasn't there, at least not the same level of thrill he sought. That he *craved*. He was a tactile person. He needed to feel the death with his hands. And watch, up close.

As he sat there, he considered the virtues of various methods of killing. Guns, arson, poison . . . they all caused death but they just didn't possess the qualities he sought. Still, he had to admit, fire setting had its merits. To arsonists, the scene before him was, in fact, the kindling that stoked their desires. Their internal fires.

Mayfield lifted the binoculars back to his face and watched.

———

THE SIREN WAS LOUDER NOW, filling her ears, floodlights and headlights and movement all around her. Firefighters jumping off the truck, pulling hose, paramedics rushing to her side, grabbing her left arm, Robby steadying her on the right, moving her quickly, lifting her off the ground and carrying her away from the fire truck, away from the commotion, from the smoke.

They sat her down on the ambulance's bumper, strapped an oxygen mask to her face, and one of the men started examining her, bright light flicking across her eye as he checked her pupils.

Vail looked over at Robby. "Thank you, thank you . . ." she said through the mask. "You saved my life. You saved me . . ." As tears started rolling down her ash-covered and soot-stained face, the paramedic was saying something, turning her head back toward him.

She heard something. Robby was talking to her.

"Don't thank me."

*What?*

*Don't thank me.* That's what he said.

And then it registered. Vail turned her head away from the medic, focused on Robby's face. And noticed he was looking off to the left.

"Thank her," he said.

Standing in the flickering light of the fire engine's swirling light bar, with singed clothing and blackened face, was Roxxann Dixon.

# TWENTY

Vail sat there looking at Dixon, who was now bent at the waist, coughing hard. The other paramedic left Vail's side and helped Dixon to the ambulance's bumper, beside Vail. He reached inside and grabbed another oxygen mask, then strapped it over Dixon's face.

Vail pulled down her mask with a weak hand that felt like it weighed fifty pounds. "You? That was you?"

Dixon's eyes moved right, the whites in stark contrast to her soot-covered face—and they narrowed as she smiled. Then nodded.

Vail grinned too. A silent thanks.

———

AN HOUR LATER, with the blaze now doused and the fire chief, Brix, Lugo, and Fuller on scene, Vail and Dixon were breathing easier and refusing transport. Their eyes had been flushed, they'd been infused with oxygen, and a few second-degree burns on Vail's legs were dressed with Silvadene ointment.

Once Vail had her wits about her, she asked Dixon why she had inexplicably shown up at the bed-and-breakfast—not that she was complaining.

"You forgot your purse," Dixon had told her. "It was shoved under the seat. When I got home, I pulled mine out of the glovebox and remembered you'd stowed yours, too. I checked and it was still there. I figured your phone and wallet were probably inside, and it wasn't that far, so I thought I'd bring it by." She turned back toward the destroyed building. "I certainly wasn't expecting this."

Vail said, "This is the first time I'm glad I left my purse somewhere."

Now, half an hour later, Dixon was approaching the ambulance, her face smeared with black ash and streaked saline, giving it a running mascara appearance. "Okay," she said. "We're covered. Once the fire is out, the exigency under which we entered the scene is greatly diminished. Further search or scrutiny of the scene requires a search warrant or consent from the owner or agent in control of the premises. I had Ray contact the owner. She went to San Francisco for dinner. She's on her way back."

"What makes you think this is a crime scene?" Robby asked.

"Just being thorough. I think it's strange that right after you left, an aggressive fire breaks out and nearly kills Karen."

"I agree," Vail said. "So what's procedure out here?"

"Well, the firefighters are doing their bit, poking around, conducting an investigation to determine the ignition source and method to make sure the fire's really out, and that the cause of the fire no longer exists. That's their responsibility, and it's covered by the exigency under which they entered the premises. But because *we're* here, a defense attorney could make the case that the search is going beyond what is required by exigency and turning to the collection of criminal evidence."

"But since I paid for the room rental, don't I have the right to give consent for the search?"

"Hmm. I'll make a call. You may be right." Dixon pulled her cell phone. "By the way, one of the fire guys said he saw a gas can behind the building. Don't know if it's related, or if it's from a lawn mower, or whatever. To be safe, they backed off and waited for Brix to get here."

"Brix is here? Didn't even see him."

"Behind the structure," Dixon said, tilting her head back over her shoulder. "There's another guy with him from the Napa sheriff's office. I don't know who he is, but they've been pointing at things, talking a lot." She turned and punched a speed dial number into her phone.

Vail sighed. "All our stuff was in that room. We've got nothing to wear."

"Just stuff," Robby said. "Replaceable."

The noise of crunching boots on gravel made them turn. Walking toward them was Brix, alongside a short, squat man in a suit. His legs were so thick he rocked a bit from side to side as he approached.

Brix nodded at Dixon, then gestured to the man. "Burt Gordon, Napa County arson investigator."

Gordon acknowledged Vail, Dixon, and Robby. "This look familiar?" He held up a plastic bag. Inside was a dinged, dull-metal butane lighter.

Vail and Robby shook their heads.

"Should it?" Robby asked.

"I'm here with an investigator from CalFire. We rely on them to determine cause and origin, and he's pretty sure this here lighter is what was used to start it. That and gasoline. Found a can back behind the building. We'll know more by morning, once we've had a chance to run it all through the lab."

"Arson," Vail said. *Jesus Christ. What have I gotten myself into?*

"Looks that way. When so much fire spreads that quickly, the cause is automatically suspicious." Gordon handed the evidence bags to a nearby assistant. "Building was a freestanding structure, so no one else was at risk. All the other renters got out without a problem. So the question begging to be asked is, Any idea who'd want to kill you?"

"We just got to town a couple days ago," Robby said. "Not enough time for anyone to get to know us, let alone want to kill us."

Vail rose from the bumper. "I wouldn't exactly say that."

Robby gave her a pleading look. "I don't think I want to know."

Dixon shoved her cell back into her pocket. To Vail, she said, "We're good for the search. You were right." She looked up at Robby. "As to any . . . disputes Karen may have had, they would've been with law enforcement officers. None of them would've done this."

Vail nodded slowly. "I've pushed some buttons, but Roxxann's right."

"We talking about people *here*, on-site?"

Vail nodded. "The task force. Brix, mostly. I said some things the mayor, board of supervisors president, and Congressman Church's District Director took offense to."

"Again," Dixon said, "not the kind of people who'd be involved with something like this."

Gordon sucked on his teeth, then nodded slowly. "Okay, here's what I'm gonna do. I'm going to meet with each one of these people, on-site, right now. Get alibis, statements from each of them—"

"Mayor Prisco, Supervisor Zimbroski, and Tim Nance aren't here," Dixon said.

"Then I'll send someone to go find them. This is serious goddamn shit, Investigator Dixon. And I take my job seriously. Which means I gotta ask you, where were you tonight?"

Dixon set her jaw, then said, "I went home after dropping Karen off here."

"Anyone who can corroborate that?"

"My dog. He's a standard poodle. He's very smart."

Gordon's eyes narrowed.

"But," Dixon said, "I suggest a recorded statement. His handwriting's paw. I mean, *poor*."

Gordon stared at her. "I'll get you a pad and pen and you can give me your statement. I suggest you leave out that bullshit about your dog." He hobbled off toward the now doused but still simmering structure.

Dixon watched him until he walked sufficiently out of range, then said, "What kind of bullshit is that? Thinking I had something to do with this. He pissed me off."

Robby rubbed his eyes. "Not your fault. Karen's got a way of rubbing off on people."

"Don't talk about me like I'm not here," Vail said. She then shivered, grabbed a blanket the paramedic had given her earlier and wrapped it around her shoulders. "My backup piece was in there."

"Yeah, well, it's probably toast." Robby winced. "Sorry."

"Better it than me." Vail wiggled her fingers at him. "Can I have your phone? Mine's now an expensive paperweight, assuming they ever find it."

Robby handed her his cell. She dialed Thomas Gifford's direct line and left him a message, briefly telling him what happened, knowing he wouldn't get it until he arrived in the morning. That was fine—there was nothing for him to do, but if she didn't keep him informed of a potential attempt on her life, he would not be pleased. She handed

Robby back the cell, rewrapped the blanket, and said, "So . . . no clean clothes and no place to sleep."

"You guys can stay with me," Dixon said. She gave Vail a quick once-over. "You're a little taller, but I've got something you can wear until you can go shopping."

"Guess I know what I'm doing tomorrow," Robby said.

"Hey, let me borrow your phone again." Robby handed it back to Vail, and she began dialing. "Who are you calling?"

"Jonathan." She glanced over and saw Robby look at his watch, no doubt doing the time calculation. "I just need to hear his voice," she said. "He's a teen, he'll fall right back to sleep." But he didn't answer. His cell went straight to voicemail. She listened to his recorded greeting, grinned, then left a message, told him she loved him, and that she'd call him when she had a moment.

As Vail handed her phone back to Robby, Dixon yawned wide and loud, then said, "Let me go write up my statement, then we can get the hell out of here."

After Dixon walked off, Vail cuddled into Robby's chest, watching the firefighters mill about, rolling hoses, packing air tanks, and stowing tools.

Gordon's question echoed in her thoughts: *Any idea who'd want to kill you?* It was a question for which she had no rational answer.

Yet.

# TWENTY-ONE

$S$omeone was shoving her. Pushing her shoulder. *What. Who—*

It was Robby, lying beside her in the double bed of Roxxann Dixon's guest bedroom. Because of Robby's breadth and the mattress's small size, they were jammed up against one another most of the night. That is, once Vail stopped hacking and fell asleep sometime around 1 a.m.

Robby was handing her his cell phone. "Your boss."

"I didn't even hear it ring."

Vail pushed herself up on an elbow—and launched into a coughing fit. She rolled out of bed, hurried into the bathroom, and spit up a glob of soot-infused mucus. She swallowed some water, leaned on the sink a moment, then turned. Robby was standing there.

"You okay?" Robby asked.

"Peachy." She took the phone, cleared her throat, and said, "Yes, sir."

"You sound about as good as my eighty-year-old father," Thomas Gifford said. "Smoked two packs a day for fifty years."

"Thank you, sir. That's good to know."

"I got your message. Thanks for keeping me abreast of the situation. Wish you'd called me at home—"

"There was nothing you could've done. With the time difference, I would've woken you. No point."

"True. Okay, here's what I've set in motion. Art's been in L.A. testifying in that Blue Lake Killer case. He was due to fly back to Quantico this afternoon, but I had him switch flights. He's gonna stop off in Napa on his way. Just a quick visit."

Art Rooney was a sharp profiler, someone Vail respected, and the person to whom Gifford assigned most of their serial arson cases. His input could only help.

"But this is not a serial," Vail said.

"You sure?"

Actually, she had no idea. "I'll check on that. I never asked."

"Do you need any medical attention? Are you okay?"

"A paramedic worked on me, I should probably follow up with someone here."

"Good. Do it. I've also made arrangements for you to get a new phone. An agent from the Santa Rosa Resident Agency is picking up Art at the Napa Valley Airport, so he'll give the phone to Art, who'll give it to you. A new badge will be overnighted to you. Which brings me to the next item." He waited a few seconds before saying, "Do you think this fire was targeting you?"

"Hard to say at this point, sir. No obvious suspects."

"Fine, keep me posted. And . . . I feel like I'm always saying this to you, but . . . be careful, will you?"

*What, no "arson magnet" comment?*

"Yes, sir. I'll do my best."

———

HAVING ATTEMPTED to make herself presentable in Roxxann Dixon's clothing, and despite Dixon's claim she had something that would fit, Vail appraised herself in the mirror and frowned. It was hard enough for a woman to put on work attire each day and feel good about herself. Wearing someone else's clothing—particularly with the figure of a Roxxann Dixon—made it more maddening.

But the reminder crept into her thoughts again—she survived the fire and that was all that mattered.

Robby came up behind her, pecked her on the neck, and, dressed in the clothing he'd worn yesterday, told her she looked great.

*Why do women always want to hear such drivel? Because it makes us feel better.* She knew she didn't look great, but those simple words, uttered by her boyfriend, lifted her spirits. How strange the human psyche.

They met Dixon in the kitchen, grabbed some cereal for breakfast, and went their separate ways. Robby headed to the Napa outlet stores to put together a wardrobe for both of them, armed with Vail's instructions on where to shop and what sizes and styles to buy. He seemed a little out of sorts, but she told him to find a clerk about her age and ask her opinion. It was the best she could do given the circumstances. Besides, it was only a few outfits. Chances are, he'd find some blouses and pants that fit decently. Generally she wasn't that difficult a fit. That is, when she wasn't trying to look good in clothing worn by a woman Detective Agbayani had referred to as "Buff Barbie."

Vail and Dixon headed for the sheriff's department, but Vail wanted to stop first at the bed-and-breakfast to poke around in the light. Since the meeting was scheduled for ten, they had a little time to peruse the grounds.

As they approached the driveway, Vail said, "So it seemed like you knew Eddie Agbayani."

Dixon chuckled. "Yeah, you could say that. We dated for a year, but we ran into some problems." She hung a left into the bed-and-breakfast's parking lot. "It was good for a while, but there was always an edge to our relationship. Still, we love each other. It's hard. We hit a wall when we ran into some . . . dominance issues."

*Dominance issues.* Vail wondered who was the aggressor, but from Vail's observations, and the greeting Agbayani had for Dixon when they saw each other, she figured it was probably Agbayani's insecurity with their relationship that caused the problems. Male testosterone and ego getting in the way. As Vail pushed open her car door, she realized that wasn't necessarily a fair assessment. What did she really have to go on, anyway? It was hard for her, as a profiler, to refrain from making psychological assessments off the clock. The constant analysis, the evaluation of body language and vocal tones and facial tension sometimes made it tough to sit back and casually converse with someone.

"When did you two call it off?" Vail asked.

"*I* called it off, not *we*. I'm not a typical woman, whatever that is. I'm headstrong, I know that. And sometimes we clashed because Eddie likes to call the shots, too. We had a balance for a while, but it shifted when I started spending more time at the gym than with him. I just, I had a couple stressful cases and working out helped settle my mind, put things in perspective.

"So I guess some of that was my fault. But toward the end we were always at each other's throats, and I felt it was best we took a rest." They got out of the Ford and headed down the gravel path. "It's been hard. I've missed him a lot. But time passes, distance opens up between you, and before you know it . . ." She shook her head. "It's been almost four months."

*That coincides roughly with her shift from Vallejo PD to the district attorney's office.* The smell of burnt wood and gasoline sat heavy on the air like cheap perfume, and made Vail's nostrils flare. "Wonder how long till this stench dissipates."

Dixon scrunched her nose. "Probably not till they bring in a demo crew and get this shit out of here."

Approximately a quarter of the structure was still intact, no doubt due to the fire department's rapid response. What was left was charred charcoal black, a ghostlike shell with fragments of flowery wallpaper stuck to odd-shaped wall fragments untouched by flame but doused by water.

Vail walked the periphery, stepping carefully through the ash that carpeted the ground. Dixon's shoes were half a size small, which made them uncomfortable, but not unmanageable. Still, Vail was aware of each step she took.

She stopped beside Dixon, who had her hands on her hips, surveying the lay of the land: Off to the left, there was another building, once a garage that had been converted to the more lucrative Cabernet Truffle Room, as noted by a hand-painted sign above the door. A larger, two-story structure extended perpendicular to it, deeper into the wooded area, containing another four rooms.

At her feet lay the charred Hot Date sign that had hung on their door only a couple of days ago. Ironically, the painted flames were nearly burned away, reduced to ashes, much like the promise of her vacation.

Vail mused at the luck of their having taken the one solitary room, tucked away in its own building. If the aim of the arsonist had been to harm her, and she and Robby had been booked into the Cabernet Truffle Room, some of the other guests might not have survived.

Vail shook off the thought, then started coughing again. Too much residual smoke still riding on the air. She headed back to the Crown Vic, hacking away, with Dixon behind her.

They drove a mile down the road, before Dixon pulled over beside a large rolling vineyard. Vail got out and coughed long and hard, bent over at the waist and holding onto the wire fence that separated the vines from the roadway. A moment later, the spell subsided. She stood up, cautiously took a deep breath of the fresh air, then blew it through her lips.

She got back into the car, her forehead pimpled with perspiration. "Well. That was great fun."

Dixon eyed her. "You okay?"

"Couldn't be better." Vail nodded at the road ahead. "Let's go."

THEY WALKED INTO the conference room and took their seats. Absent were their guests from yesterday, save for Timothy Nance. Sitting off to the side, his face was tight, etched with concern. His tie was pulled to the side, and he looked like he hadn't slept much. Vail knew how he felt.

Brix walked in and strode to the front of the room, dropped his thickening binder on the desk and put his hands on his hips. He, too, looked frazzled. His hair was hastily combed, his uniform was not as crisp as it had been and he had dark, loose skin beneath his eyes.

He put his teeth together and whistled loudly. Everyone came to order. "Okay, I'm really pissed off at the night's events. Someone's targeted us, people, and I intend to find out who. It's no secret I've had a problem with Special Agent Vail and her . . . attitude and methods . . . but she's one of our team, and we don't gotta like everyone, we just have to work effectively with them. If someone takes a swipe at her, they take a swipe at all of us. So I want to catch this fucker. And I want to catch this goddamn serial killer. And I want to do both sooner, rather than later. That's not too much to ask, is it?"

He looked around, making eye contact with Lugo, Dixon, Fuller,

Vail—holding her gaze a few seconds longer for acknowledgment—which she gave him with a slight smile—before coming to rest on Tim Nance.

Brix looked down at his hand, which held an envelope and a FedEx overnight pack. "Karen, these are for you. Front desk clerk gave them to me." He passed them to Nance, who handed them off down the line toward Vail. "I've been in contact with Karen's boss and we've got an Alcohol, Tobacco, and Firearms agent on his way to pay us a visit. Karen, you want to fill us in?"

Vail laid the envelope on the table in front of her and glanced at the airbill on the FedEx package. "The BAU has two ATF agents in an Arson and Bombing Investigative Services subunit that we started twenty years ago. They were trained as profilers and primarily work ATF cases but they consult on all serial murder cases because, well, because they're really good profilers." She grabbed the tab, ripped open the package, and slid out her new badge. "Special Agent Supervisor Art Rooney is the guy who'll be here sometime today. His input will help us, I'm sure."

"He's actually here," Brix said. "He and Detective Gordon are at the site right now, taking a quick look around."

Brix lifted the wall phone and punched in an extension. "Yeah, it's Brix. Send in Matt." He replaced the handset, then said, "Before Gordon and Rooney arrive, I've got a few updates for you. First, we've got an ID on the body we excavated from the collapsed wine cave."

The door opened and in walked a lanky, balding man in a lab coat. Matthew Aaron stepped in and Brix introduced him to the attendees.

"Well," Aaron said, clapping his hands together. "This was a very challenging case because of the state of decomp of the body. Dental x-rays didn't give us any hits and missing persons reports were a dead end because we lacked identifying characteristics to establish a match. And since the body wasn't prepared for burial, most of the flesh was a goner long ago."

"But," Aaron said, raising an index finger, "the skin on one of her hands was partially preserved, for some reason. Still, I couldn't figure out how to lift a fingerprint we could put in the system. Then I remembered this case I read about involving a 1948 military plane crash.

For decades, one of the victims went unidentified. They tried everything, including DNA. But a George Washington University forensic science professor soaked the man's hand in a chemical they used to ID Katrina victims. Eventually, he was able to rehydrate the skin and secure a print from the index pad."

"And . . ." Brix said.

Aaron smiled and leaned back. "And that's what I did. And presto. We have an ID."

Brix raised his eyebrows, asking the question silently.

"Oh—the victim's name is Ursula Robbins." Aaron reached into his deep pocket and pulled out a notepad. Flipped a page and said, "Robbins went missing and was presumed dead a little over two years ago. No children, early fifties. I'm working on getting a photo for all of you. All I know is she was the chief executive of a winery in the Georges Valley District."

"Okay," Brix said, "Ray, that's yours."

"A few more things, then I'll be out of your way," Aaron said. "About that toenail thing—very interesting, actually. I've never seen that before. But it takes a few years for a buried body, one that's not prepared or preserved in any way, to skeletalize completely. By that I mean for it to turn completely to bone, no soft tissue left. Nails are protein, keratin to be precise, like hair, so they stick around for a while. In this case, your victim had nail polish on her toes, preserving them and keeping them intact. Otherwise, once putrefaction gets underway, the skin on the hands and feet can slip off intact, a process called degloving."

"Degloving, cool," Fuller said.

Aaron looked over at Fuller and squinted confusion. "Yeah, okay. Well, the fact that the victim used nail polish means the other nails remained intact."

Vail said, "Hang on a minute. We don't know if the victim put on the nail polish or if the killer did it. If the killer has some knowledge of forensic anthropology, he might've known the skin and nails would slough off, so he put the nail polish on to keep all the nails intact—except for the one he pulled off."

Brix lifted his eyebrows. "I'm not sure what to do with that. Let's keep that in mind. Our UNSUB might have a knowledge of forensic anthropology. So he could be a pathologist."

Vail shrugged. "Possible. Or a forensic scientist."

A few heads turned toward Aaron.

Brix pointed at Lugo. "Ray, you've got that too. Get some help if you need it. Run all the people in the area who've had training in those fields. Including the ones in our office." He glanced at Aaron. "See if any have a record—mental illness, drug habits, propensity toward violence—"

"Got it," Lugo said.

Fuller said, "We already know that these two vics, and the one in Vallejo, were done by the same guy. If we can find some commonalities in these three women's victimologies, I say we got this UNSUB."

Vail scrunched her face. "Well . . . let's just say that these vics are *probably* done by the same guy and that evaluating the victimologies might *help us* identify him."

Fuller rolled his eyes, as if to say Vail's comment was merely a difference in semantics.

"But I come back to access," Vail said. "Access might be the commonality we're looking for."

There was a knock at the door. It swung open and in walked Burt Gordon, followed by Art Rooney. Vail couldn't help but smile. Seeing Rooney in this setting gave her a sense of warmth and comfort.

Brix nodded at Gordon and said, "Take a seat, gentlemen." As they were complying, he turned to the whiteboard and wrote "Vic 2 Ursula Robbins–Ray Lugo." He spun back to the conference table and said, "I want to thank Special Agent Rooney for taking the time to help us out."

"Karen Vail is a very valuable member of our unit," Rooney said in his southern drawl. "If someone tries to fry her ass, it really pisses me off. Since I've spent nineteen years studying arson and bombings, I think it's fair to say there might be something I can offer that'll help identify the type of person who did this."

"Don't take this the wrong way," Fuller said. "But why are you here? I mean, don't you deal with *serial* arsonists? Looks likely he might've only set this one fire."

"Only one fire," Rooney said. He nodded slowly, as if he was considering Fuller's point. "I see where you're coming from. After all, it's just one fire, why make such a big deal over it. Right?" Rooney grinned broadly, leaned back in his chair. His military style crew cut, chiseled features and trim body gave him a formidable appearance. He didn't need to act intimidating to *be* intimidating. "What's your name, son?"

"Scott Fuller. Detective."

"Good to meet you, Detective. I can certainly understand your confusion over the need for me to be here. And I don't think any less of you for asking such a misinformed question. So let me answer you, so you won't make the same mistake again." Rooney slowly rose from his chair. "I am with the ATF. That stands for Alcohol. Tobacco. And Firearms. See, we deal with alcohol—this here's wine country, so you might think there's a connection there. But no. No, that's not why I'm here. And then there's tobacco, and, clearly, tobacco's not why I'm here, either. So we get to the last letter in the acronym. Firearms. That covers bombs, incendiary devices, terrorism related offenses, and criminally set fires." Rooney grabbed the back of the chair with two large hands. "Now let me ask you something, son. Where did you hear the word 'serial' in that description?" He narrowed his eyes, kept his gaze fixed on Fuller, who was staring back, his jaw set, lips tight and thin.

Vail shared a glance with Rooney. She was thinking: *Man, I wish I could do that as well as you can.* Her look said: Boy, I'm glad you're on my side.

"So," Rooney said. "Let me get back to where I was headed. I'm an ATF agent, but I'm also trained as a profiler. That's important because the FBI has no jurisdiction over arson, but obviously it falls right into the sweet spot of the ATF's authority. For Detective Fuller's edification, that would be the 'firearms' part." He walked to the whiteboard and motioned to the marker. "May I?"

Brix handed it to him. Rooney uncapped it, and moved to a blank area on the board. "Let me give you some background on the type of person who is most likely to have committed this crime. Problem is, there haven't been a whole lot of studies done on arson. But we've been able to pool all our knowledge based on the studies and offender interviews that *have* been done, and we've arrived at a *typology* of arsonists. It's based primarily on motivation, the motives behind the crime. Now we're categorizing this fire as arson because it meets the three established criteria."

Rooney held up a hand and ticked off each item on a finger: "First, property has been burned; second, the burning is incendiary and a device of some sort has been found at the scene; and third, the act was committed with malice, with the intent to destroy. I've been to the crime scene with Detective Gordon, and based on what we saw there and what he saw last night, this officially qualifies as arson." He swiveled toward Gordon and said, "Is that right, Detective?"

"Yes, it is."

"So here's what we know," Rooney said. "Shortly after Detective Hernandez left Agent Vail alone, the place went up in flames. We found a gas can in the back, in a well-concealed area that's not visible from another room, the parking lot, or adjacent property. We found a cigarette lighter, likely used to ignite the trigger—the gasoline. But we also found something that we can't explain." Rooney nodded at Gordon.

Gordon scratched the back of his head. "Yeah, it's damn strange. There was a well-defined area around the structure, which served as a barrier to the blaze." He stopped for effect, then said, "And what looks like some sort of fire retardant chemical on the ground was laid out along the periphery."

Dixon tilted her head and asked, "So you mean he meant to stop the fire at the one building?"

Gordon nodded. "That's what it looks like. And no, nothing special about the chemical used. We're still looking at it in the lab, but I think it's widely available Class A foam, from fire extinguishers. It's used to contain small brush and grass fires by creating a fire break."

"So," Rooney said, "armed with that knowledge, let's talk about what we know about the people who start these fires. We classify them according to their motives: vandalism, excitement, revenge, crime concealment, profit, and extremist. All are self-explanatory."

"Excitement?" Dixon asked.

"They get off on setting fire. They're seeking thrills, attention, recognition, even sexual gratification—but the sexual component is pretty rare."

Dixon said, "So are you saying we need to investigate each of these potential motives so we can eliminate them as possibilities, then narrow our suspect pool to those who are likely to have the remaining motive?"

"That's one approach," Vail said. "But rather than running in six different directions while still trying to zero in on this wine cave killer, I think we can logically eliminate crime concealment and extremist. There was no other crime he could've been trying to hide. Unless someone is aware of something, I don't see a social, religious, or political conflict. Is there anything you know of I'm not seeing?"

"Nothing I'm aware of," Brix said. He looked around. No one offered up anything.

Ray Lugo said, "If there was a profit motive, why just burn down the one structure?"

"Doesn't make sense, I agree," Rooney said. "Still, be worth looking into the owners, see if they're in financial distress. Do they have a business partner with a beef? Have there been offers to buy the property that've been rebuffed by the owner? Anyone who'd stand to benefit by burning down the structure? An architect or contractor who was talking with the owner about a remodel the owner didn't want to do? All this needs to be ruled out. Remember, the offender doesn't think he's going to get caught. He doesn't think he's leaving any clues for us."

"Yeah, but . . ." Vail stopped, then shook her head. "Why would he go to such efforts to ensure the other structures wouldn't also get destroyed?"

"An important question, for sure, but one we can't answer right now," Rooney said. "We'll eventually know the answer, but for now it's another thing to stick up on the whiteboard." He turned and wrote "Arson," then, below it, listed the question Vail had asked. "Another thing to keep in mind is that I've given you a very basic primer on arson—a number of those categories we discussed have *sub*categories. And then you have mixed motive offenders, too. But let's keep it simple for now and expand as you gather more information and eliminate other factors."

Fuller leaned forward, both forearms on the table. "Since you're a profiler and your job is to profile, how about telling us who we should be looking for?"

"That's really putting him on the spot, Scott," Vail said.

Rooney held up a hand. "No, no. That's a fair question, Detective." He folded his arms across his chest and thought about it a moment. "If we go with the percentages, we're looking for a younger white male, between eighteen and thirty, with a generally poor marital history. That suggests this UNSUB has a history of unstable interpersonal relationships. And a guy like this will have average or higher intelligence, and between a tenth- and twelfth-grade education level. There's a fifty-fifty chance he'll have one or more tattoos."

"Will this guy have a sheet?" Brix asked.

"Highly probable. You're looking at about a 90 percent chance he's had a felony arrest and better than 60 percent chance he's had multiple felony arrests. So, yeah, that'd be a good place to start: known offenders with potential motives for wanting that structure—or Agent Vail—in ashes."

"Speaking of which," Vail said, "were you able to tell anything about the front door?"

"In what way," Gordon asked.

"I'm not sure, but it may've been jammed shut. I couldn't open it."

"There wasn't much left of the structure, let alone the front door. But we can go back over there, take another look. You sure about it being jammed?"

"I was pretty freaked. The knob was very hot. Burned my hand." She stole a glance at her palm. It was red and it hurt, but nothing serious. "I'm not sure, but I couldn't open it."

"Check it out," Brix said to Gordon. "Anything else on the profile?" he asked Rooney.

Vail said, "There'll probably be a history of some form of institutionalization. Not just prison—orphanages, juvenile homes, or detention, even mental health institutions."

"But," Rooney said, "unlike serial killers, a majority of arsonists come from intact and comfortable family units."

"That makes me feel real good," Dixon said. "Something went wrong somewhere."

"Here's something else you won't like," Rooney said. "Nation-wide, law enforcement has a clearance rate on arsons of only about 20 percent, give or take. So we've got our jobs cut out for us." He handed the marker back to Brix, then walked toward his seat. "If we find out this guy's set other fires, there's more to this equation, because then he'd be serial, and that brings in some other trends that'd help us catch this guy."

"Like what?" Fuller asked.

"Like most serial arsonists walk to the scene of the fires they set, and they usually live within two miles, so they're familiar with the neighborhood. About a third stay at the scene and a quarter of them go somewhere nearby where they can watch the fire department do their thing. Forty percent leave the scene."

"But," Gordon said, "almost all return to the scene from twenty-four hours to a week afterwards. So we've got an undercover watching the area to see if anyone comes by."

"In case anyone's wondering, the other guests have been placed at other B&Bs," Brix said.

"We're assuming," Rooney said, "that we're dealing with an honest to goodness arsonist. But if the intent was pure and simple, kill Karen Vail, then a lot of this goes out the window."

There was quiet while everyone considered that.

"Any questions?" Rooney finally asked.

Fuller leaned back and stretched his arms upward. "Yeah, I've got one. How long are you gonna be in town?"

"I'm not. I'm headed to SFO for a flight back to Quantico. But I'm reachable on my cell." He waited a minute, looked around the room, and saw there were no questions. "Karen, will you walk me out?"

While Vail rose, Rooney reached out to shake Gordon's hand. "Pleasure, Detective. Please, keep me in the loop. You need some-thing, anything, ATF will get it for you."

"Appreciate that."

"Oh—one more thing. An agent is on his way over from the San Francisco ATF Field Division office. I'd really appreciate it if you'd include him on your task force. Name's Austin Mann." He consulted his watch. "Should be here any—"

He stopped at the rapping of knuckles against the door.

Brix yelled out, "It's open."

The door swung in and revealed a suited man of average height, but heavy around the shoulders and thighs. He stepped in and nodded at Rooney. "Sorry to interrupt."

"This is Agent Mann," Rooney said. He then proceeded to introduce everyone in the room to him.

Vail couldn't help but notice Mann had scarring on the left side of his face and a prosthesis—an artificial left hand. This was odd, to say the least. Vail would have thought such a condition would result in a forced retirement due to medical disability. Then again, she knew of agents with severe injuries who were permitted to remain on the job— but that was rare and usually due to their exceptional service records.

However, there was one thing she could be reasonably sure of: An ATF agent missing an extremity meant it had been blown off while defusing an IED on the job.

Mann turned to face her. "You're Agent Vail?"

"Karen, yes. Good to meet you."

"Karen was just about to walk me out to the car. You okay here?"

"They can get me up to speed." Mann extended his right hand and Rooney took it. "I'll keep you posted once you get back."

Vail slipped the new FBI badge onto her belt, grabbed the envelope from the table and left the room with Rooney. As they cleared the front door to the building, Rooney reached into his inside suit coat pocket and handed her a new BlackBerry. "It's activated and ready to go. Same number."

She turned it on and waited as it booted up. "Thanks."

"Watch that kid in there. Fuller," Rooney said. "I've seen his type, knows it all, young buck who's gotten where he's at because of favors or nepotism or both. Book smart, street dumb."

Vail marveled at Rooney's ability to read people. She knew he was good, but that was impressive.

"He bugs me," Rooney said. "Could be trouble."

"Noted. What do you know about Austin Mann?"

"Hell of an agent. Loyal to the job like guys aren't loyal anymore." He nodded at the Bureau car down the street, headed toward them. His ride to SFO, Vail surmised.

Rooney said, "You noticed the prosthesis, I'm sure. Got it OTJ, defusing a bomb. Lucky that's all he lost. I worked with him years ago in North Carolina. I was there when . . . when it happened. I hope you never have to see something like that. It was awful. A guy like that, tough as they come, squealing like a pig." He shook his head. "Anyway, he took this assignment in Frisco and he's been good. He's been happy."

The dark blue Crown Victoria pulled up to the curb.

"Is it a prosthetic hand, or his whole arm?"

"What?"

"Agent Mann's prosthesis. How extensive is it?"

Rooney's eyes narrowed. "Hand and forearm. Why?"

Vail stood there thinking a second too long.

"Karen, what is it?"

She laughed and waved a hand. "Nothing. Just tired."

Rooney placed a hand on Vail's arm and gave it a squeeze. "I want you to get back to Quantico in one piece, you hear? No more fires or other shit you seem to get yourself into."

"Are you implying something, Art?"

"Implying? Hell, no. I think your record speaks for itself." He stepped off the curb and opened the door. "See you back home soon."

# TWENTY-TWO

*V*ail watched the BuCar swing a wide arc in the street and head off down the road. She liked Rooney, and because she was about a dozen years younger than he, she sometimes thought of him like an older brother. She never felt that way about anyone in the unit—or anywhere else, for that matter.

But Austin Mann's prosthesis began to bother her. When crushing a trachea, the "bar arm" move would be vastly more efficient if the offender had a hard prosthetic forearm. She would have to look into that. Carefully. One of her mentors had just vouched for the ATF agent. One thing she did not want to do was investigate a fellow LEO—a man with a distinguished service record—and have it get back to Rooney.

She turned to head back into the building, realized she was still holding the envelope Brix had given her, and turned it over. *Agent Karen Vail* was printed in black laser ink. She tore it open, and, while starting up the two flights of stairs, began to read:

Hey there, Agent Vail. You don't know me, but I'm betting you wish you did. I know you're a profiler who's been brought in to catch the guy who killed that woman in the wine cave. And I know you've found the one in Vallejo and the one in that old Black Knoll Vineyards cave. That was a nice touch, actually, don't you think? They've talked for years about getting at that vintage wine that was supposedly buried there, so I figured they'd eventually find my handiwork. It just happened sooner than I figured. I wanted it to be a total surprise, like, out of the blue, a holy shit moment, where everyone freaks out and says, "Oh, my god, another woman's been killed by the same guy!" Ah, so the first question might be, am I a guy, or am I a woman? I'm not going to tell you. I'll let you figure it out. I'm sure by now you've already got your theories. I'm sure you're all thinking about me, talking about me. You, and Lieutenant Brix and Detective Fuller, Investigator Dixon, and Sergeant Lugo, and whoever else you're going to bring on board. The more the better. You're going to need it. But I'm wasting your time, and it's not right to waste taxpayer money. So here's the deal. I'm willing to work with you, but under some conditions. Are you sitting down?

No, Vail was definitely not sitting down. She was, at the moment, flying up the second flight of stairs, then bursting through the front doors, swiping her prox card, sprinting toward the task force conference room, and then—inside and out of breath, coughing like a two-pack-per-day smoker—holding the letter out in front of her.

All heads turned toward her—how could they not, she was hacking away and no one could hear anything else.

"You okay?" Mann asked, rising from his chair and helping her to her seat. Brix handed her a cup of water from the cooler in the corner.

Vail, holding the letter out away from her to protect it from trace contamination, took the drink from him with her other hand and did her best to swallow between coughs. As the spasm passed, she held up the letter and envelope and said, "I need a pair of gloves. Letter from the offender."

Lugo reached into his pocket and rooted out a crumpled latex glove and handed it to Vail, who pulled it on.

"I'll need to give Matt Aaron my prints as an exemplar. I was holding the letter before I realized what it was."

Vail would be the only one to handle the letter for the moment, and only with her gloved hand. "We should obviously dust it in case the UNSUB handled it. There might be contact DNA on the paper or in the saliva on the adhesive of the envelope. Can your lab run DNA?"

"We've got it covered," Dixon said. She wiggled her index finger at the letter. "What does it say?"

Vail read it to them, up to the point where she had left off. She then continued: "I want you to release news of my work to the media. You will refer to me as the Napa Crush Killer. Get it—the crush of grapes, the crush of the windpipe—I figure it's a fitting name. Here's what else I want from you.

"To show me you've agreed to my demands, you will have the newspaper publish a front page article about me. Use my name in the headline. Do that and we'll talk about the rest of my demands. Oh—I know, I have to give you something in return. I'll stop killing. Okay? Is that fair? I thought you might think so. Tomorrow's *Napa Valley Press*—and post it on the *Press's* website, on their home page, lead story, by noon today."

"Where did that letter come from?" Dixon asked.

Brix lifted the room phone. "Good question." Into the handset, he said, "Someone took possession of an envelope addressed to Special Agent Karen Vail last night or this morning. I need you to ask around to find out who dropped it off." He listened a moment, then said, "That's right. Check the surveillance tapes, get back to me ASAP. It was left by the killer we're tracking . . . yeah, that's right. He was in our goddamn building." He slammed the phone onto the wall receptacle. "Christ."

"He was here," Lugo said, "right under our fucking noses and we didn't even know about it."

"Pretty ballsy," Dixon said.

"That fits," Fuller said. "A narcissistic killer feels invulnerable to getting caught. He's better than everyone else. Superior. There's nothing we can do to catch him. Isn't that right, Vail?"

Vail nodded slowly. "Yeah, that about sums it up."

"So the question is," Dixon said, "What do we do about his demands?"

Mann said, "One of many questions. Is this UNSUB the same guy who set the fire? All to get attention?"

Vail looked at Mann, examined his demeanor and body language. If he was the UNSUB, he wasn't giving anything away.

Dixon sat forward. "If he's the same guy, why would he send Vail a letter if he jammed the door to kill her? She'd be dead if he was successful."

"We don't know for sure the door was jammed shut," Brix said.

"And maybe he was hanging around the periphery, knew she survived, and left the letter after the fact."

Dixon nodded slowly.

"So," Mann said. "Back to my question. Same guy?"

Vail hiked her eyebrows. "Entirely possible. Though there isn't generally a crossover between arson and serial killers. Then again, the longer I'm in this business, the more I've come to realize we can't blind ourselves to new and previously unseen, or unidentified, behaviors. Just because we haven't observed something doesn't mean it doesn't exist. It's something we've discussed many times at the unit. We want to pigeonhole offenders into our neat categories, but there are some who lie outside our observed patterns. This Crush Killer could be one of those."

"Back to the *other* question, then," Dixon said. "Do we go along with what he's demanding?"

"Yes and no," Vail said. "I suggest we do just enough to keep the line of communication open. We negotiate. But the bottom line is we keep him talking to us. The more we learn about him from his communications, the better it'll be for us. At some point he'll give us something he's not aware he's giving us. And that could lead us to him."

Brix looked around the room. "Comments?"

Fuller shrugged. "Vail was pushing for us to give this to the media, which would've been a disaster for the community. And instead of doing that, the guy contacts us."

Dixon said, "What are you saying, Scott?"

"That maybe it's not always best to listen to what she's telling us to do. Before she got here, we did just fine handling murders."

"You have, what, two murders a *year?*" Vail paused, realizing she may have inadvertently insulted them. She bowed her head and said, "Look, I'm only here to help. You can take my advice, or not."

"Help," Fuller said. "Now we have an arson to investigate, too. That kind of help we don't need."

"That's not fair," Lugo said. "She didn't ask to almost be burned alive. Let's not lose sight of the fact that we're all here for the same reason. To catch this goddamn killer. Because I don't know about you, but I think this is a big fucking problem. And if we're not careful, this

guy is going to go on a spree and then we won't have control of anything. But we'll have a lot of uncomfortable questions to answer."

Vail didn't agree with the "spree" terminology, but the sentiment
behind Lugo's comment was accurate. She decided to sit back and not
force the issue; let them come back to her.

Timothy Nance, who had been stealthily observing the discussion,
stood up and approached the table. "Congressman Church is very
concerned about what's going on. I don't want to report back to him
that his own Major Crimes task force is at odds about what to do. I
need to tell him we've got things handled, and that you people are all
on the same page and that you have a valid plan of attack. Now, I don't
know about you, but it seems to me the FBI's had a lot of experience
dealing with serial killers. And this guy is a serial killer, am I right,
Agent Vail?"

"Yes, sir."

"Then I would like to see us seriously consider what she has to say.
Let's talk about it. Debate it. But in the end, I want what we decide to
make sense, and leave the politics and egos out of the equation."

Vail silently applauded Nance's speech. Perhaps she had the guy
pegged wrong. Perhaps he was merely providing the political voice his
boss needed and expected.

"Okay," Brix said. He approached the whiteboard. "This is what I
want to do. We've got two investigations going, the murder and the
arson. I want to make sure we handle both properly, but I don't want
one interfering with the other. So we're going to split the task force:
Gordon, you and Mann will run the arson investigation. If you need
bodies, let me know and I'll assign some people. Whatever you need,
I'll make sure you get it."

"I think between us and CalFire, we'll be fine."

"Good. Check in with me regularly in case the two crimes were both
committed by the same asshole. The rest of you, you're staying on the
Crush Killer with me." He turned to his right, where an overhead projector arm was mounted to the desk. "Karen, bring that letter over here.
Let's look at these demands and figure out how we're going to reply."

DIXON SWUNG THE CAR along the curving road that led from the sheriff's department building to Highway 29, headed toward downtown and a quick lunch.

Before leaving, Vail had suggested they meet only a portion of the killer's demands. They would know in a short time whether it satisfied his needs. There was debate—Lugo thought it best to give him what he wanted—if he truly stopped the killing, that would accomplish their goal in the short term while they continued to search for him.

But Vail insisted he would not comply—he would kill again, because he had to. Even if he honestly intended to honor his agreement, he couldn't. Killing, to him, was a deeply seated psychosexual need, one that he wasn't fully aware of. So his offer was not valid. Instead, Vail stressed that the goal was to keep him talking with them. And what she devised was designed to do just that. It also risked angering him in a way that could trigger another murder. But there was nothing she could do about that. Because if they didn't catch him, there would be *many* more murders, not just the one she may or may not have instigated. They had to keep him engaged and talking with them.

Lugo continued his objections, however. He said that if they don't give the killer what he wants, what's stopping the guy from calling up the TV station, identifying himself as the Napa Crush Killer, and telling them about Victoria Cameron's murder? The story would be assigned to a reporter, who'd follow up with the speed of an Olympic sprinter. They'd make a few calls and it would be a national story in the space of an hour. So they may as well try to get a deal out of it, he reasoned, because maybe, just maybe, he would honor his word.

Vail couldn't help but shoot him down. If the killer was going to contact the media, she explained, he would've already called them. But there was no fun doing it that way. He wanted to force their hand, have the story come from them, from a police department acceding to the demands of a killer because they were helpless against his genius. With narcissistic killers, they needed to feel that others recognized their superiority.

Lugo steamed silently. And Brix decided they would go forward, for now, with Vail's plan.

They filtered into the parking lot, with Brix, Fuller, Lugo, Mann, and Gordon going their separate ways.

"We've got forty-five minutes," Vail said, as Dixon accelerated onto 29. "By the time we finish lunch, I have a feeling we'll know if this was the right way to go."

———

JOHN WAYNE MAYFIELD sat in his vehicle, eyes on his cell phone clock, which he knew was accurate. When the digital display read 12:00, he headed into the Java PC cybercafé in downtown Napa. There were no surveillance cameras—he had already checked.

He bought a fifteen-minute pass in cash, logged in, and went to the *Napa Valley Press* website. Scrolled down, then up, and down again. Refreshed the page. Nothing there about him. He glanced at his phone: 12:05. Navigated to a different website, then back again to the *Press*. And there it was.

The headline read: Napa Crush Lays Down Roots in Community.

*What?*

He read the teaser paragraph. It said something about a startup company that was launching a new soft drink that had roots in the valley, a rebirth of the wine cooler—

He fisted his right hand and was shaking it, holding back, wanting to pulverize the monitor but knowing that would draw attention—and possibly the police.

Instead, he shoved his curled fingers into his mouth and bit down. Waited for the anger to subside. Finally, he calmed enough to turn his attention back to the screen. There had to be something here. Why else would they post this article if there wasn't information contained within to address his demands?

He read the article, looking for an embedded message of some sort. Then he found it: a quote attributed to Karen Vail, the company's director of marketing and promotion. "We thought long and hard about how to launch this product, and we had demands that we couldn't comply with. But we're willing to work with the local leadership to show them how much we respect them and their abilities.

We're looking for ways of working with them so all parties can be satisfied. Anyone interested in contacting me can do so at NapaCrush@live.com."

Mayfield logged off, rose from his chair and walked stiffly toward his vehicle. He had to get out of there before he did something people would notice. He drove down the road, reached beneath his seat, and pulled out a case. With one hand, he flipped open the lock and lifted the lid. Gleaming knives were nestled in soft velvet holders, blades down, ready to be used.

He had a victim he'd marked for killing, and there was a date by which he had planned to act. It was still a week off—but doing it now would be dramatic. And it would send a powerful message to Karen Vail, FBI profiler and "director of marketing and promotion."

The concept of sending a message appealed to him. Figuratively—and literally. He pulled over to the side of the road as cars sped by. Tourists and wine aficionados out for a memorable time on the town. *I'll do my bit for making it memorable, no need to worry.*

He reached into his pocket and extracted a disposable cell phone. He turned it on and waited for it to find its cell service. Then he went about his business.

He shoved the phone back in his pocket, yanked the gearshift back into Drive, and returned to the highway. *I'm in promotion, too, Agent Vail. Of my own services and handiwork. So be prepared, because sooner or later you'll want to make me happy. You'll come around. You'll have to.*

He reached over, then removed one knife from the case and lifted it toward his face. The bright sun glinted off the highly polished chrome.

*Promote this, Agent Vail.*

———

FOLLOWING LUNCH, Vail and Dixon were killing time, awaiting word the UNSUB had gotten the message. An email, a phone call to the sheriff's department. Something.

"I'll give you a tour of Silverado Trail," Dixon had said. "Beautiful road."

As they passed notable wineries, Dixon played tour guide: Hagafen

Vineyards—"an award winning kosher winery"; Regusci—"they fooled the Feds by operating secretly during Prohibition to produce bootleg wine"; and, "There, coming up on your left, is Baldacci Family Vineyards. Their vines go back ninety years and give some of the best Cabernet—"

"It's 12:24, Roxxann."

Dixon glanced over at her. "I'm just trying to take your mind off it."

Vail's elbow rested on the window frame while she rubbed at her forehead. "He's seen it by now."

"Probably," Dixon said. As she drove past Baldacci, she said, "What do you think will be his next move?"

"He probably knows the sheriff's department is on alert, monitoring the entrance and lobby area. Watching for him. Let's hope he reads the article and sends me an email."

Just then, Vail's BlackBerry buzzed on her belt. She leaned left and pulled the device from its holster. "He just texted me."

"Texted?" Dixon asked. "How is that possible? You didn't put your cell number in the article."

Vail stared at the screen. Her body had broken out into a nervous sweat. "I don't know," she heard herself saying in response to Dixon's question. Because she didn't know—but it would be something she'd have to think hard about. Her larger concern at the moment, however, was the message she received.

She closed her eyes. "He said we didn't comply, so we should expect a new victim in the next few hours. And to expect a surprise."

"I don't like surprises," Dixon said.

Vail didn't reply. Her mind was flooded with emotions ranging from fury to guilt to anxiety-ridden frustration.

"We knew the risks," Dixon said. "You can't feel responsible for what this asshole does."

"I know that intellectually, and I still feel it was the right way to go. But when I stare at the next woman's mutilated body, I can't help but ask myself if it needed to happen. Was I responsible?"

"The guilt. Comes with the territory, I guess. A perk of the job."

Vail sat back. She thought about the killer stalking his victim. If he was organized, as she was sure he was, he would've already had his next target chosen. He might have been stalking her, waiting for an excuse to strike. And she just gave it to him.

Yes, this emotional torture did come with the territory. Vail knew the risks. But to remain effective on the job, she had to tell herself that this was the right thing to do, that the goal of catching the offender before he killed on a grander scale was more important than this one life.

It didn't help. And there was nothing she could do now but wait for the call.

---

IT CAME EXACTLY three hours later. Brix sent a text message blast to the task force members that was as chilling as it was short:

new vic. meet me.

And he gave them the address.

Dixon made it there in ten minutes, driving the speed limit—keeping it a low profile approach, at Vail's urging—despite her desire to floor it, lights blazing.

When they drove up, Vail noted that the parking lot to Crooked Oak Vineyards in the Georges Valley District was full of unmarked county vehicles. Even Lugo was in a plain vanilla white Chevy Impala. Vail and Dixon got out and walked past the parked cars, looking for their comrades. Approximately a hundred feet away, amidst an adjacent, well-kept vineyard, they were all huddled around something, their heads down, hung low. *Looking at a body,* Vail surmised.

But as she and Dixon got closer, Vail was not prepared for what she saw.

---

VAIL STOOD OVER THE BODY trying to process what she was seeing. But no matter how hard she tried to focus, she couldn't hone in on what she was feeling, what she was thinking. *Come on, Karen. They're all looking at you—to you—for answers.*

*But I've got nothing.*

"Karen," Brix said again. She barely heard his voice, off in the distance. Then a hand on her shoulder. "Karen, what's the deal?"

Vail kept her gaze on the victim. On the male body that lay before her. The right shoe and sock were removed. And the second toenail had been forcibly extracted.

---

VAIL KNELT BESIDE THE BODY. Buying time. Trying to figure out what the hell was going on here. "Forensics?" she asked.

Lugo said, "On the way."

"This vic, he's a *guy*," Brix said.

"Yeah, I got that. Thanks for pointing it out." Vail tried to push the confusion from her thoughts. She needed to focus. *Look at the body. See it. See the behaviors.* Her mental checklist said: right second toenail missing. Breasts—or where they would be had the victim been female—had been sliced away. Bruising over the neck, so they would likely find a crushed trachea. There was linkage to the other murders—the toenail was a detail only those on the task force knew about. And the coroner.

"We've got linkage," she said, hoping that talking aloud would help put it together and bring her to a logical conclusion. "The toenail, the . . . breasts, and the COD—I think we're going to find out his trachea was crushed. Just like the others."

"But the others were women," Brix said.

Vail fought the urge to respond with a sharp retort. Brix was merely looking for answers, and it was anger at her own inability to mentally process this victim that was threatening to bubble to the surface.

"I don't know," Vail finally said. She looked up at everyone. They were huddled over the body, looking down at her. "I don't understand it."

They seemed to slump en masse. Or maybe she was projecting her sense of inadequacy onto them. Imagining their disappointment. Perhaps she was giving herself too much credit and they were thinking nothing of the sort. They were professionals. Cops, investigators. This was their business.

But they hadn't dealt with serial crime. Not like this.

And, Vail suddenly realized, neither had she.

# TWENTY-THREE

V ail looked over the immediate vicinity: well-pruned rows of leafy grapevines stretched a few football fields into the distance, leading up to tree-dense mountains that rippled the muscular countryside.

The new victim was nestled in the gently concave dirt floor of the area between the vines, with a dark blood puddle pooled beneath the body, the liquid having largely been absorbed into the porous earth. Vail closed her eyes and cleared her mind. "It's not unheard of for a male to be a victim of a serial killer," Vail said. "But like I told you yesterday, there are specific circumstances. Usually it's a killer who targets homosexuals. Or the offender takes out the male in the house to get at his real target, the woman. But when he kills the male, he does it in the quickest way possible and he doesn't engage in postmortem activity with the body. The behaviors—the things he leaves for us at the crime scene that we see with the female—just aren't there."

Everyone stood there, silently absorbing Vail's analysis.

"Okay," Brix said. "So let's figure out what we have here. Same killer, right?"

Vail opened her eyes. "Looks like it, yes."

"He killed again, right after we spurned his demand to go public," Brix said.

"Not to mention the text message," Dixon said.

Fuller asked, "What text message?"

"Karen got a text message," Dixon said, "about three hours ago, after the article was posted to the *Press*'s website."

Brix shot her a look. Vail interpreted it as, *Why weren't we told about this?*

"There was no point in notifying everyone," Dixon said. "There was nothing we could do but wait for something to happen."

"Well, something happened," Fuller said.

Vail stood up. "You're the one who reads all the profiling books, Wonder Boy. What do you have to say about this?"

Fuller's face flushed the burgundy side of Cabernet. His eyes surveyed the faces of everyone, who were now looking at him, as if they were expecting an answer. "I—the texts don't address this."

"I can tell you this," Vail said. "His actions fit those of a narcissistic killer, and I think it's important we start treating him like one. It's entirely possible this kill was meant to get our attention, a response to our decision to reject his demands."

"*Your* decision," Fuller said.

"*My* decision," Brix said. "We discussed it, and based on what we had, I felt this was the way to go. No one has all the answers. But goddamn it, we're doing the best we can."

"I need some time to digest this," Vail said. "For now, let's get back to basics. First off, I don't think the victim was killed here."

"Why not?" Lugo asked. "The body's here, and obviously the blood drained underneath it."

"Yes, the blood," she said, motioning to the soaked soil. "So it's safe to say this is where the cutting was done. But assuming the guy's MO hasn't changed, we'll find that the trachea was crushed. Like I demonstrated back at the sheriff's department, he'd need to force the victim up against a wall using his forearm, remember? That's his MO, and it's worked well so far, so no need to change it. But there's no place for him to do that here. So I think he was killed somewhere else, somewhere close, then brought here and sliced and diced."

Dixon said, "But we've got something new here. It's a guy, which means, theoretically, at least, he chose a victim that wasn't as easily subdued."

Vail nodded. "That's part of what bothers me. Why he suddenly changed. Could mean our UNSUB is extremely confident that he could overpower his victims. He's either skilled in some form of martial art that enables him to efficiently control or debilitate an individual, or—"

"He knows them," Brix said.

"Exactly. He knows them, so they don't see him as a threat. Could also be he's a person of authority or standing, so he can get close without someone seeing him as a threat."

"If that were the case," Brix said, "how does that fit with the wine cave at Silver Ridge?"

"Hard to say at this point. Someone of authority in a place like that would stand out, the employees would tend to remember him. Unless, of course, it's someone they're accustomed to seeing there."

Brix stared at her.

Vail figured he thought that comment was intended for him—which it was—but only as a jab, not because she thought he was the offender.

"This guy could be changing his appearance, too," Lugo said. "He may've worn a uniform for this kill, but regular clothing for the wine cave murder so he wouldn't stand out."

"Uniform," Fuller said. "You saying it's a cop?"

Lugo squinted at his colleague. "Lots of people wear uniforms, Scott. Gas, electric, water department workers, security guards. But yeah, it could be a law enforcement officer. Why not?"

"We've got nothing that says it's a LEO. That's why not."

"A bigger question," Vail said, "is how he got my cell number. The only place that's listed—other than at the Bureau—is at the sheriff's department. If it's not a cop, it could be support personnel."

Lugo nodded. "I'll get a list, see if it leads anywhere." He started to turn, then stopped. "What about data backups? Where are they kept?"

Brix raised his brow. "Don't know. But that's a good point. Check it out."

"Who found the body?" Dixon asked.

Brix knelt and pointed at the ground, where paw prints were evident. "Dog must've smelled the blood and tracked through it. When he went over to that house out there," Brix said, indicating the structure where they had all parked, "he had blood all over his paws. The owner freaked out, thought her dog was hurt. She cleaned him up and saw it wasn't coming from him. She called 911 and dispatch called me.

I've already spoken to her about the importance of not telling anyone about this."

"Did she seem cooperative?" Vail asked.

"I was pretty firm about it, gave her a little incentive." He used his fingers as imaginary quotation marks. "I don't think she'll be a problem."

A loud whistle came down the long dirt row between the vines. Trudging toward them with his thumb and middle finger between his lips was the tall and thin CSI, Matthew Aaron. He stopped a few feet from the body and looked down. "Looks like we've got a freaking party here. Sure you don't want to extend the invitation? I think we need more bodies trampling through my crime scene."

"Just do your thing and let us know what you find," Brix said.

He surveyed the immediate area, then chose a spot to set down his toolbox. "I'm gonna need each of you to retrace your steps outta here. And stop by the lab at some point today so I can get castings of each of your shoes."

As they moved out of the vineyard and back to the parking lot, Vail's phone rang. It was Frank Del Monaco.

"VICAP?" Vail asked.

"VICAP," Del Monaco said. "So here's the deal. The toenail thing is unique as far as the database is concerned. So either no one thought much of reporting a missing toenail, or none of the murders that involved a missing toenail were submitted to VICAP. Or these are the only kills this UNSUB's committed."

"Makes sense, because I'd never seen or heard of it before."

"And I'm looking into that other thing."

Vail joined the knot of task force members, who had congregated around Brix's vehicle. "What other thing?"

"Rooney asked me to look into something. He was at the airport, dialed me up and said I got to look into some guy you're working with. A Detective Scott Fuller."

Vail was standing five feet away from Fuller. She glanced over at him to see if he'd heard his name. She couldn't tell. "Hang a sec." Vail moved off a few paces and said, "What exactly did Art want you to look into? And why? The guy's a bit of a showoff, trying to impress everyone with his knowledge. But he's harmless, nothing I can't handle."

"Rooney was a little more concerned than that. You know how he is. Someone crosses him, he goes for the jugular."

She made a mental reminder never to get on Rooney's bad side. "Okay, but what's there to look into?"

"He sent me on a fishing expedition. Anything and everything I can find on the guy."

Vail glanced over at Fuller. "I think he's overreacting."

Del Monaco laughed. "You want me to tell him that when he gets here?"

"No," Vail said a little too quickly. "Leave it be. I don't know what he saw, but I assume something caught his attention."

"Yeah, and he might've been right. A sealed record. Have no idea what it is, but I'm on it."

"Could be nothing." *Or, it could be something.* "Keep me posted." She ended the call, put away the phone, and stood there observing. The late afternoon wind blew her hair back off her face. What was it Rooney saw that she hadn't seen? Was it something obvious, something she should've recognized, or merely a feeling he'd gotten in their brief interchange in the conference room?

Whatever it was—or wasn't—she would keep her eyes open, but carry on until she heard otherwise. There were too many things she had to deal with, and this, at the moment, seemed like a distraction.

She walked over to the others and got the sense they were still talking about the new victim when her phone rang again. It was Robby.

"Hey there. What've you been up to?"

"Went to the outlets and did some fabulous shopping, bought you the most marvelous clothing and a dear—"

"Robby, the gay thing doesn't work for you."

"No? Fine. I got you some clothes. Hope you like 'em, but I gotta say it was a bit of a crapshoot."

"Much better," Vail said. "I'm sure whatever you got will work for another few days. And what about a place to stay?"

"I booked us into this darling inn with a wonderfully frilly duvet and cherry—"

"Robby?"

"Cut it out, right?"

Vail rubbed her eyes with thumb and index finger. "Yeah."

"Okay. I got us a room at the Heartland B&B in Yountville, a few blocks from downtown." He gave her the address. "Meet me there in an hour? Or do you want to go straight to dinner? There are a few nice looking restaurants downtown, within walking distance."

"Works for me. I need to get out of these shoes. I'll meet you at the B&B, do a quick change, and then we can pick a place to eat."

She shoved the phone into its holder, then walked over to Dixon. "So what's the deal?"

"Aaron is still with the body." She glanced at the setting sun. "But he's gonna need some fixed lights brought in if he's gonna be here much longer."

Lugo closed his phone and said, "He said he'll be done in about twenty. He needs someone to hold the lantern for him."

"Unless you think he could be our UNSUB, I'll do it," Vail said. "I've got some time to kill before I can get into my B&B."

Brix slammed his trunk closed and said, "I've known Matt a dozen years. If he's our guy, he's fucking got me fooled. But if you're concerned about it—"

"I can handle it." She flashed momentarily on her recent romp with the Dead Eyes killer, but pushed it from her mind. She couldn't do her job effectively if she let things like that change the way she operates.

"Good," Brix said. "I've got a car arranged for you at St. Helena PD. A green Ford Taurus that was used by its investigator before the position was canned. It's yours. I'll have Aaron drop you off there when he's done. Keys will be in a magnetic case in the driver's wheel well."

Vail nodded her thanks, wished everyone a good evening, then headed out to the vineyard to assist Aaron. As it turned out, it was to be the start of an unexpectedly dangerous evening.

# TWENTY-FOUR

*J*ohn Wayne Mayfield stood on the hillside, Carson binoculars pressed against his face, watching the police try to make sense of his latest job. He couldn't make out fine details of their facial expressions at this distance—and in the fading light—but he could get a sense of what they were thinking and saying by their body language.

And they didn't look happy.

But he had warned them. He told them what would happen. Did they not believe him? Next time they had better listen or he'd make them pay again.

As he crouched and watched them debate what they had found, he realized that maybe he hadn't been convincing enough. Maybe he needed to speak louder for them to hear him.

———

As THE LAST of the task force members drove off, Vail watched a car pull up behind Matt Aaron's vehicle. At the wheel was Austin Mann.

"I'll be right back," Vail said.

"Wait—where are you going? I need you to hold—"

"I'll just be a couple minutes," Vail called back, and continued down the path toward Mann.

Mann slammed his door and maneuvered around the car. "I just got the text. Who's the vic?"

Vail stopped, blocking his path, and shoved her hands in her rear pockets. There he was, only a dozen feet away now. Prosthetic arm at his side. Vail pulled her gaze from the device and looked Mann in the eyes.

"Glad you're here." She had to handle this carefully, tactfully—a laughable thought. If there's one skill Karen Vail never could master, it was the art of diplomacy.

"Who's the vic?" Mann asked again, craning his head around her, toward where Matt Aaron was bent over the body.

"You sure you don't know?"

Mann swung his gaze to Vail. "Huh? Should I? Who is it?"

"It's a male. No ID yet."

Even in the fading light, Vail could see his eyes narrow. "So why should I—" He stopped. His body stiffened, and he seemed to lean back, away from her. Staring at her.

Vail did not speak. She remained still herself, measuring Mann's response. A brisk wind whipped through her shirt. *Damn, it's cold.*

"Vail," Aaron called out. "Get your ass back over here!"

Vail ignored him. She looked at Mann.

"Well," he finally said, "go ahead. Ask."

Vail folded her arms across her chest. She did it for warmth, but it served the dual purpose of exhibiting body language of someone in charge. "Where were you when each of our victims was killed?"

"That's not the question you want to ask me, Agent Vail. I'll give you another shot. Ask your question or get the fuck away from me. Now."

"Did you kill Victoria Cameron?"

"No."

"Did you kill Ursula Robbins?"

"No."

"Did you kill Maryanne Bernal?"

"No."

"How about the vic lying out in the vineyard behind me?"

"No. Satisfied?"

Vail snorted. "Not really."

"You've really got a set of balls, you know that? To question a person who's given his life and career, hell, his goddamn left arm for the job—you really think I could be your killer?"

Vail ground her teeth. "I have a job to do, Agent Mann. And part of that job is to look at this case logically, without bias. Our victims were killed by a crushing blow to the trachea. The coroner can't rule out the use of a tool or appliance. Something that'd make crushing the trachea—normally a tough thing to do—much easier. Then you walk in with a prosthesis. And yeah, I'm thinking, shit, that's pretty obvious. Too obvious. But I have to look into it, you hear me?"

Mann stared at her but did not reply.

"It's nothing personal. In fact, someone I respect a great deal vouched for you."

"You discussed this with Rooney—"

"No," Vail said. "I didn't. I've thought about it. I couldn't rule it out in my mind, beyond saying 'He's a great agent and great agents don't do this type of thing.' Well, that doesn't cut it when time comes to present my case. You know that. Don't you?"

"Yeah."

"So again. Nothing personal. Got that?"

"Yeah."

"So as to where you were—"

"I was out of town when you found Victoria Cameron's body. On ATF business. You can ask my partner, if you want."

"When did you get back?"

"We flew back from New Mexico yesterday morning. Two days after Mrs. Cameron was killed, if I'm not mistaken. Check it out with my partner. We were together just about every minute of the five-day trip."

"Vail!" Aaron said. "Now or never—"

"You insist it's not personal."

"It's not," Vail said. *Where's he going with this?*

"Have you brought this up to the task force? Have you or anyone else looked into *other* men in the vicinity who have prostheses? Because if you really think this makes it a slam dunk"—he held up his left arm—"then you would've checked into that. Did you?"

"No."

"Didn't think so. So don't fucking insult my intelligence."

Vail sighed. "I'm sorry. Honestly, I meant no disrespect." She extended a hand. Mann looked at it a long moment, then turned around and got back into his car.

MATT AARON DROVE UP to the police department, in the heart of downtown St. Helena, a one-story shared-use structure that also housed City Hall. Aaron pulled to the curb and dropped off Vail in front of the building.

Vail opened her door. "Thanks for the ride."

Aaron didn't bother turning to face her. "And thanks so much for your help."

She could tell he didn't mean it. Sarcasm. A dose of her own medicine.

Vail swung the door closed, but Aaron drove off before it had completely shut.

She pushed through the police department's front door and walked into a small anteroom separated from the rest of the office by a pane of bulletproof glass. She spoke to the community service officer and explained she was going to be taking the Taurus. The CSO told Vail where it was parked, then gave her directions to downtown Yountville.

As Vail pushed through the doors, her BlackBerry rang. It was Rooney. *Oh, god. Please tell me Austin Mann didn't call Art. That'd suck big time.*

"Karen, listen, we got some shit on Fuller. I had Frank look into it while I was in the air, then when I went wheels down, he called me."

*Fuller.* She shifted her brain out of panic mode and back to business. "Fuller, yeah, I know. Frank told me there was a sealed record."

"Not just a sealed record. Not by a fucking long shot."

Vail found the magnetic storage container, then unlocked the door and settled herself into the seat. The sun was now long gone and the air had taken on a typical March chill. A gray cast hovered in the sky, billowy clouds barely visible in the charcoal sky above.

"What was it?"

"Juvie record, Fuller was convicted of—wait for it—attempted arson. He was pissed at his teacher, so he set a school storage shed on fire. Janitor was on-site and saw Fuller, did a sketch, and picked him out of a lineup."

"Arson."

"I knew there was something about the kid."

"He's the sheriff's stepson, you know that."

"I don't give a shit. I'm sure the sheriff knows about this. And here we've got an arson in his town and he doesn't tell us about Fuller's history?"

"That's a fine line, Art. Asking a father to rat out his son."

"Hey, the fucker tried to kill you, Karen. This goes way beyond family. This kid's a killer."

"Okay, I'm with you on this. What now?"

"I want you to steer clear of it. I'll call Mann and have him coordinate with an agent in the San Francisco office. We'll handle this internally. I don't want Owens finding out, tipping off Fuller, and giving him a chance to cover up evidence, or bolt or whatever the hell he'll do. Wish I hadn't flown back."

"We can handle it from here."

"Not we, Karen."

"Yeah, okay." She depressed the brake pedal, then shoved the key in the ignition. A pair of headlights came on a few dozen feet behind her. She flipped the rearview mirror into night mode and pulled out of the parking lot, headed right, down Highway 29 toward Yountville. "Keep me posted, okay?" Rooney did not reply. She looked down at her BlackBerry. It had dropped the call. Didn't matter—she was sure he, or Mann, would let her know what was going down, and when.

Vail sighed. She had thought Fuller was annoying—but harmless. It now appeared she was wrong. Not that she was never wrong—but it didn't happen often, which was a good thing—because in her profession, being wrong often met with disastrous consequences.

She was looking forward to seeing Robby, to sharing a glass of wine with him and unwinding, telling him about Fuller. She was grateful that Rooney was such a hound dog with an acute intuitive sense.

So much had happened in the few days since they had arrived. And this was supposed to be a time for her to get away from the stress of the past couple months.

As she drove along 29, she thought about where she'd like to take her real vacation. But when would she go? She couldn't leave Jonathan again, certainly not right away; that wouldn't be fair to him. And they will have burned through Robby's vacation time. She'd gotten so caught up in the hunt—in the need to help—that she had selfishly, and foolishly, pursued this case at Robby's expense. This was supposed to be their time together, and she had ruined it. And at the moment, she wasn't even sure she had done the community any good. Like Gifford had said, she seemed to be a magnet that frequently sent the Shit-Happens Meter off the scale.

Perhaps she and Robby could steal a weekend here and there for an overnight or two. Maybe the Red Fox Inn in Middleburg—she'd forgotten about that place. Close to home, but far enough away that it would provide a needed change of scenery for both of them.

Vail was surprised at how few cars were on the road. She knew most wineries closed around 5 p.m., so the tourists were probably back at their bed-and-breakfasts, dressing for dinner and a relaxing night out—something she would be doing very shortly, as well.

Her headlights hit the sign ahead that announced Calistoga would be coming up in fifteen miles. Calistoga? Her Napa geography was fairly poor, but she remembered Calistoga being toward the top of the map—farther down the road, *after* St. Helena—meaning she should've turned left onto 29, not right.

She slowed to see where she could make a U-turn, but headlights in her mirror caught her attention. Same ones she saw a few moments ago when leaving the police department? Impossible to say—and normally she wouldn't give it much thought. But last night someone—Fuller?—had tried to turn her into a french fry and today a serial killer texted her phone. Her sense of awareness, always pretty good, was heightened. *Paranoid?* Realistic. Someone might be following her. She wasn't about to let whoever it was have the upper hand again.

A few yards ahead was Pratt Avenue. Without signaling, she hung a sharp right onto the narrow, two-lane road and accelerated, coming up quickly on Park Street. Swerved right again, then made an immediate left onto Crinella Drive. Residential.

Glanced up, saw nothing—no headlights. *All that for nothing.* She felt her heart rate moving at a good pace. Nothing like a little scare to get the blood pumping. She followed the road as it curved right, keeping an eye on her mirror, just in case. If nothing else, it'd be a long way around to getting back onto 29 in the correct direction.

Parked cars populated driveways and lengths of available curb space. To her right, a portable basketball standard stood poised for action, sandwiched between neatly placed garbage and recycling containers.

She followed Crinella as it proceeded straight, then hooked right again. *Perfect, a circle.* She would stay on it and loop back onto Park, then get back onto 29. Of all things—a detour when she desperately wanted to meet up with Robby and relax. If she told him about this, he'd laugh at her. Then again, given all they've been through lately, he probably would not find it amusing.

After turning right onto Park, she took a couple of deep breaths to slow her pulse rate. *This can't be healthy*, she thought. *Doesn't stress kill? A totally different kind of serial killer. One I'd never be able to catch.* She chuckled at the absurdity of her thought, how the mind turned to humor at strange times.

As she passed the opening of the Crinella loop, she caught a glimpse of a car sitting at the curb ahead of her, its headlights burning. *So what? It's just a mother who's running to the store for milk. Waiting for me to pass so she can turn onto Park.*

Vail continued along Park, headed toward Pratt. Looked in her side mirror. The car had turned onto Park but was several dozen feet behind her. *But what if it's not an innocent resident?*

She reasoned most people would turn left here, to get to the main drag, Highway 29. So she turned right, down toward a darker area. If the other vehicle stayed with her, the chances were greater its occupant was trailing her. She would then call Robby, have him drive toward her. *Enough of this shit.*

As she crossed a set of railroad tracks, Vail wished she had Stella with her. She didn't know her way around—especially in the dark—and the Taurus wasn't equipped with an in-dash GPS. She then realized she should've headed back to 29, a road she had been on and which was a main thoroughfare. Then she could have gone back to the police department.

As she mentally kicked herself, the two pinpricks of bright light appeared in her mirror. The car had turned right and was now behind her again. She accelerated hard, took it up to seventy for the next half mile as the road doglegged left. This had to open up somewhere, spill onto another road. If not, she'd need to find a street to turn around, then head back toward whoever was following her. She pressed her left forearm against her waist and felt her Glock.

While she mulled her options, Pratt dead-ended at what looked like a main road a hundred feet ahead. She remembered looking at the map when they were planning the trip and seeing another artery that paralleled Highway 29. Silver-something. It was the road she was on earlier today with Dixon.

Yellow traffic sign: Narrow Bridge. She slowed hard, then crossed the two-lane cement-walled overpass. Street sign—Silverado Trail. *Yes, that was it.*

She turned left while sneaking a peak in her mirror. No one there. No lights. Was he still behind her, running silent? She accelerated hard through the turn and brought the Taurus up to sixty, alternating her gaze between the road ahead and the rearview mirror. She flipped the signal bar forward and threw her headlights into the brights setting so they illuminated a wide arc on the asphalt ahead. They also stretched upward, reaching the lower branches of the tree-lined road.

She pulled out her BlackBerry and struggled to navigate to Robby's phone number. But because this was a new phone, none of her contacts were loaded. She'd have to go into her call history, to when he had called her. That's all she needed—to get into an accident by dividing her attention among three different tasks. But no one else appeared to be on the road, which was good. If those headlights appeared again, she would have to take action.

And as luck would have it, a few seconds later when she glanced up, she saw those fucking headlights appear in her mirror, turning onto Silverado from Park. She thought of texting the killer back on his number—but she had to keep her head about her. What would that accomplish? If it wasn't the Crush Killer following her—if it was Fuller, for example—she could set in motion a series of events that would be potentially disastrous. If she had her original phone, she could call Fuller and find out if it was him behind her.

Up ahead—a turnout. She cut her headlights and downshifted into low. The car lurched hard as it abruptly dropped into third gear. Vail yanked hard on the wheel, screeching round the bend onto a narrow, unmarked road—without applying the brakes. She wanted to give her pursuer the illusion her car had disappeared from existence. Beamed away into thin air—neat trick if it were possible, but this should work fine, too.

Vail swerved onto the narrow side street, regained control of the vehicle, then hung an abrupt U-turn, using the skills she had learned in the tactical driving course at the Academy. She brought the car around facing Silverado Trail and pulled hard right against the soft shoulder. Cut her lights and disabled the interior dome light—in case she had to exit the vehicle.

She sat there and counted. Based on the distance the car was behind her, she figured she had no more than four seconds before it would pass her. But she was ready.

The Taurus was in neutral, her foot off the brake and her head ducked down low to prevent the driver from seeing her—in case he was looking in her direction when he passed.

There! The car zoomed by, its headlights off now. Speeding, no doubt looking for where she had gone. Keeping her own lights off, she pulled the Ford into drive, accelerated hard and went into pursuit mode.

He was traveling fast—but with a dark dashboard, she could only guess at the speed. What mattered was she was losing ground. She glanced up—saw another car behind her—and ignored it. Focus on the task ahead.

She depressed the accelerator. The engine downshifted, hesitated, roared, surged. But the vehicle ahead was still expanding the distance. The roadway curved left, then right.

He blew through the flashing red, and with a quick glance at the intersecting street, Vail followed suit.

She wasn't sure he was aware of her presence; in the near-total darkness, she didn't think he'd be able to see her. He wasn't driving evasively; he was driving as if he was pursuing, searching. Wondering where the hell she had gone. Whoever he was, he was clearly motivated to find her.

*I'll bet you are, asshole.*

An oncoming truck was approaching in the opposing lane. In the glow of his headlights Vail could now see the silhouette of the driver of the car in front of her: a male, rotating his head from side to side. Looking for her, no doubt. His vehicle had the shape and smooth, curved lines of a Chrysler.

The light from the truck was a mixed blessing: It illuminated her pursuer, but it would also lay her bare as well, should he look in his rearview. And he must have done just that—because he suddenly switched on his headlights and slammed on the brakes.

*Christ!* The oncoming truck was passing her the instant Vail had to swerve left into his lane to avoid smashing into the Chrysler. She narrowly cleared the truck's rear and was now driving in the opposing lane.

Heart pounding hard in her ears. *Bam, bam, bam. Calm yourself, Karen. Focus!*

She reached for the switch to turn on her headlights—but the Chrysler swerved into her, pushing her Ford further left. Onto the shoulder.

Vail tightened her grip on the wheel and leaned right, as if that would help pull the car away from the oncoming tree line.

The two vehicles were of similar size and mass, so Vail had only one option available to her: She slammed on the brakes. Screeching tires . . . ripping scraping metal as her front fender tore along the left side of his sedan.

The Chrysler braked before she was able to clear the rear of his car. She yanked her wheel hard right and accelerated. Her engine groaned in protest.

But Vail had leverage on her side and the Chrysler whipped into a violent counterclockwise spin. He swung around and smashed into her left front fender, and they careened to Vail's right, off Silverado Trail, and slammed through the wire-and-wood fence. She struck a divot in the shoulder and went in nose-first, but the Chrysler hit the gully at an odd angle with greater force and flipped trunk-over-hood. It tumbled backward before coming to rest upside down. Vail's Ford wedged itself in the furrow, at the edge of a vineyard.

*Holy shit.*

She took a deep breath and seized into a coughing fit. Grabbed the dashboard to calm the spasm, then steadied herself. Eyes blurry with tears. Head aching.

She forced herself to assess the situation: Airbag did not deploy. Front end lodged in some kind of ditch. And it was dark.

She turned on her headlights; the lone working lamp illuminated a portion of the vineyard ahead of her. She caught a glimpse of her face in the rearview mirror, which was cocked at an odd angle. She had a gash on her forehead above the left eye. *Fuck it. Get out of the car and find the asshole who did this to you.*

Vail pushed the driver's door open and tumbled out of the Ford. A few yards off to the right, nestled among the vines, was the Chrysler, spouting a fog of smoky steam from the front grill. She pulled her Glock—which she should've done before exiting the Ford—and scrambled toward the overturned car, the pistol out in front of her.

Vail shooed away the smoke and peered through the windshield, which was diffusely lit by the brightness from her headlight. But it appeared to be empty. She swung around and fired a round into the lamp, throwing her—and her pursuer—into charcoal darkness. She then headed off in the opposite direction. If her pursuer was nearby, she didn't want him to have the advantage of seeing her. The risk of him hearing her gunshot, and thereby locating her, was fairly low. Unless he saw the muzzle blast, it was more difficult to pinpoint location based on a single shot you were not expecting.

Vail moved around the upended vehicle, encircling it, looking for signs of where its occupant could've gone. Just about impossible in the near-darkness. But out of the corner of her peripheral vision, she caught something—the blur of motion, perhaps, along with the rustle of leaves. She ran toward the object, her Glock firmly clasped in both hands out in front of her.

As she neared the approximate location, she sensed something slip past her, a row to her left. She dipped to the ground, rolled beneath the lowest hanging vines and cross-wires, then rolled through to the adjacent aisle. There—ahead, maybe thirty feet in the darkness, her brain combined the vague blur of motion with the shift of dirt being displaced by shoes.

Vail pushed forward, a bit more cautiously, sensing that her quarry had stopped moving. She felt the brush of nascent grape leaves against her cheek and she nearly unloaded her weapon into the unsuspecting vine. But she regrouped and kept moving down the aisle.

Absent a nearby city and a visible moon, there was scant external light. There had been times in her career when she wished she had another fully loaded magazine; at other times, she longed for the easy reach of her weapon—any weapon. Now all she wished for was her Maglite.

Something to the left—movement. She turned in its direction, brought her Glock up, and felt the rush of air by her cheek before a powerful punch exploded into her temple. She fell backward and went down, falling against a mess of vines and supporting cross-wires—which, although rough, served as a cradle. She lay there a second, dazed, until—somewhere off in the distance—she heard rustling leaves, then felt something swipe at her left arm, knocking the Glock from her grip. Two hands grabbed her by the blouse and yanked her up out of the tangle of branches.

Vail focused her eyes and saw the face of her pursuer. But she did not let the revelation of who it was delay her response. She brought her knee up hard, into Scott Fuller's groin, then, as he doubled over, she cupped her right fist and slammed her hands down onto the back of his neck. Now it was his turn to go down.

"You prick," she said, standing over him. "You fucking tried to kill me!" She thought of kicking him in the face, which would likely loosen a few teeth as well as render him unconscious—but she needed answers first. "I know about your juvie record, the arson," she said.

"You don't know shit," Fuller said between clenched teeth. He fought off the pain but rose into a stooped posture.

"I know it's enough to get you booted off the force. A cop convicted of arson as a teen investigating an arson committed against a federal agent that cop didn't like? Sounds pretty fucking bad, Scott."

She stepped to her left, hoping to come across her pistol before Fuller rushed her—or worse—pulled his sidearm. On her second step she felt a hard crunch. As Fuller moved toward her, she brought the weapon up and swung it in line with his chest. "Where were you the night of Victoria Cameron's murder?"

He did not raise his hands. Did not flinch. "Fuck you. I don't owe you any explanations."

"Did you set the fire to my room?"

A broad smile spread his lips.

"I guess that's my answer."

"Go pound sand, Vail."

"Fine, you don't want to talk to me, you can face your stepfather. I doubt the sheriff will be happy to hear my theories. Because pretty soon, we'll have all the evidence we need—"

That was all she got out—because in the next moment she felt a sharp prick, followed almost immediately by a dizzying sway. The ground moved beneath her. She lost her footing. And all went black.

# TWENTY-FIVE

An acrid scent stung her nose. A sour taste coated her tongue. A chill blew across her face. And her back felt wet.

Vail opened her eyes, but saw nothing. No, not nothing—she tracked left and right, and saw stars. She was lying supine, looking at the sky. She started to sit up—but a wave of nausea hit her like a bad flu. Vail lay back down and wondered where she was, why she was on the ground. She turned her head left—saw vines—and realized she was in a vineyard.

*How? Why?*

To her right she saw more of the same. Darkness. Flora. And a pair of boots. But not just any boots; they looked like the ones Scott Fuller wore. Fighting the dizziness, Vail forced herself onto her right side to get a better look, pushing up her torso with her left hand, slowly, into a sitting position. That's when she saw it.

Fuller was also on his back, and though it was dark, she could tell he was not moving. Incapacitated, like her. Her senses were slowly returning. Her head hurt and she brought a hand up to her temple. It felt bruised, swollen.

Something was irritating her nose. It was a scent she knew all too well. Blood.

Reached for her Glock. Not there. *Oh, this is not good. Weapon gone, unconscious in a field, blood somewhere nearby, and no fucking idea how I got here.*

"Scott, wake up," Vail said. She shut her eyes, trying to will away the dizziness. She leaned forward and got onto all fours, then began feeling around in the dirt, searching for her missing Glock.

*Wait. I was following another car. Headlights. . . .*

Felt around. Nothing. She swung around in another direction, to the right, trying to keep some sort of directional sense as to where she was going so she didn't double back on herself.

*Car tried to force me off the road. Went into a ditch, it flipped—*

Still failing to locate her pistol, she hung another right turn and crawled back toward her starting point.

*Fuller. Fuller in the other car. He tried to run me off the road. Rooney—sealed arson record on Fuller. Bastard.*

Vail crawled toward Fuller to get his handgun. Then she would wake him and find out what the hell he did to her—and why. Then, and only then, maybe she'd kill him. At least, that's what she felt like doing.

Vail came upon Fuller's boots, yanked on them. The movement made her nauseous. "Fuller, wake up!" But he didn't respond. She scrabbled forward, grabbed his shirt to give him a good shake, but it was wet. Not just wet, but slimy and thick. Blood.

*That's the blood I smelled. Fuller's?*

She drew back, wiped her hands on her blouse, then peered closer to try to get a better look at where he was bleeding. She felt for his wrist, for a pulse. But there was nothing. *Jesus Christ. What the hell happened here?*

*Argument with Fuller.* Sharp—she brought her right hand to her neck. Something stuck her neck. She remembered that. But Fuller? Dead? Why wasn't she killed, too?

And if Fuller had tried to burn her alive, then who'd want to kill him—and leave her among the living?

Cell phone—she needed to call someone. Robby. Dixon. Where did she keep it? *Come on, Karen, think.*

She felt around and located her BlackBerry. Couldn't find Robby's or Dixon's number. *New phone. Shit!* She paged to the call log. A DC number—Rooney. She hit Call and waited while it rang. He answered on the first ring.

"Karen. Everything okay?"

His voice was amplified, like he was on a headset. "No, Art, things are all fucked up. I—I don't know what happened. I think I was drugged—"

"Drugged—where are you?"

She slowly turned. It was dark . . . no lights of any kind. "I'm in the middle of nowhere. A vineyard, I'm in a vineyard. More than that, I don't know. I remember driving on—on Silver . . . Silverado. Silverado Trail. I remember that. I thought someone was following me. Turned out to be Scott Fuller. He tried to run me off the road, we crashed, I got out of my car, and—I'm not sure. We argued. About the arson. I was talking to him,"—*asking him whether he killed Victoria Cameron*— "I was asking him if he killed Victoria Cameron. Then I felt something sharp and I went down. When I woke up, I was on the ground, I was dizzy—and Fuller's dead."

"Dead? How?"

"I don't know—blood. There's blood on his chest, I checked for a pulse. But my phone, it's a new one after the fire, the one you gave me. And there's no contact list so I don't have anyone's number—"

"Karen. Listen to me. I'm going to call Detective Hernandez. Then I'll call Brix."

"Call Dixon, Roxxann Dixon."

"Okay. I'll call her. How are you, are you able to wait for them?"

"I'm . . . okay, I think. Just have Robby call me. I'll try to direct him to where I am."

"Need be, we'll track your cell signal. Meantime, be careful, Karen. Someone tried to kill you. And he's still out there."

"Actually, Art, the guy who tried to kill me is a few feet away from me. Dead. And whoever drugged me and killed him could just as easily have killed me, too. So I think he's got other plans."

"Maybe. If this guy's a narcissist, this could all be part of his game. Showing you how superior he is, that *he* controls things, not *you*. He could've easily killed you, but didn't. Maybe next time he will. We don't know what's going on yet. But we can't assume it's safe just because this one time keeping you alive served his purpose better."

Vail knew he was right. "Fine. I'll keep you posted. Just make sure they keep this stuff off the police band."

She hung up and waited for Robby to call her. Meantime, she didn't want to move—she'd already compromised the crime scene by crawling through it. At present, less was more. She kept her feet planted.

Robby's call came through two minutes later. She told him her location, as best she could estimate, then waited. A short time later, two cars pulled up simultaneously, approaching from opposite directions. As Dixon and Robby exited their vehicles, Vail called out to them. As they started toward her, Brix drove up. The three of them left their headlights burning and stood at the edge of the vineyard, twenty yards from Vail's Taurus. To their right sat Fuller's upended vehicle.

"Sorry," Vail called to them.

"For what?" Robby asked.

"The car. It only had thirty thousand miles on it."

"Are you okay?"

"I'm still groggy and dizzy, but I've been worse." Robby knew firsthand she was telling the truth.

Dixon turned on the black tactical flashlight she was holding and panned it around. She paused on Fuller's Chrysler. "What happened?"

"Fuller tried to kill me again."

"Again?" Brix asked.

Vail went through the sequence of events in as much detail as she remembered, including Rooney's discovery of the sealed record.

Brix and Dixon shared a look of disbelief.

"So that's what I mean by 'again.'"

"Until we know for sure," Brix said, "it's just a theory."

Vail let that slide. "Whatever," she said. "But you may want to notify Stan Owens. I'm sure he'll want to come down here, ID the body."

Brix pulled his phone. "Damn straight."

"Meantime, I've gotta find my sidearm without disturbing the area more than I already have."

"Get Matt Aaron down here," Brix said to Dixon. "And an ambulance for her."

"I don't need an ambulance," Vail said. "I'll be okay, I just need some time."

"You're getting the ambulance," Dixon said. "This is no time for tough guy theatrics. Sounds like you were injected with something. Until we get a better handle on what happened to you, we need to do this right."

Robby took the flashlight from Dixon, then stepped closer to Vail. "I don't know where the crime scene boundary is, but you think you can catch this?"

"I'm still kind of groggy and unsteady. Just stay there and shine the light on the ground. Maybe I'll get lucky."

After several minutes of doing a tight-beamed grid search, Vail saw something metallic at the base of a thick vine. "Over there." She pointed to the spot and Robby moved a step to his right, crouching lower to change the light's angle. "Got it." She stepped a few paces to her left, toward the handgun. "I'm gonna put my business card under a rock to mark where we found it."

Using the bottom, clean portion of her blouse, Vail picked up the Glock and blew on it to dislodge any loose dirt. She pulled the slide back and gave it another good infusion of air. Then she carefully slipped it into her fanny pack. "I'm gonna have to turn it in to the local resident agency. They'll send it on to the lab for processing."

"Did Fuller ever touch it?"

She thought a moment before answering. "I think he just knocked it out of my hand. I picked it up after, so I'm pretty sure there aren't any of his prints on there." She carefully made her way out of the vineyard, doing her best to avoid destroying any trace evidence or footprints.

When she reached Robby, they embraced.

"Ready to go home yet?" he asked by her ear.

Vail looked up at him, her expression hard, her jaw set. That was the only answer he needed.

"I'll call the resident agency, if you want. Which one is it?"

Vail stepped away and brushed back her hair. "Santa Rosa."

Robby strained to get a look at his watch. "Hopefully I'll catch someone working late." He pulled out his phone and started dialing.

The flash of a first responder's light bar flickered in the night sky, accompanied by a siren that pierced the countryside like an air raid warning. As Vail sat down on the bumper, a clean-cut paramedic in his late twenties jumped out and attended to her. "How are you doing, ma'am?"

The man's name was embroidered above his left pocket and read, Marcus. "Much better now," she said, giving him a quick once over. "Nothing like a man in uniform."

Marcus shifted his feet, grinned sheepishly, and probably blushed.

Robby snapped his phone shut. "Excuse me?"

Vail turned to Robby and said, "Second time in a week I find myself flirting with a medic. Fun as it might seem, I think I should get my kicks another way. Take up bowling, maybe. Or mahjong. What do you think?"

Robby looked over at the confused first responder and shrugged. "I don't know what it is about her, but she grows on you."

That seemed to fluster poor young Marcus even more, and he turned away and fumbled with his penlight to examine Vail's pupils.

Dixon walked over with Matt Aaron, who was toting his toolkit.

"What is it about you, Vail?" Aaron asked. "Things are generally pretty quiet around here. You come to town and I can't seem to have a night with my wife."

"If you ask my boss, I'm a serial killer magnet."

Aaron threw his head back. "A *what*?"

"Yeah, that's what I said." She twisted away from the medic, who was examining the welt on her temple. "DB's out there in the vineyard, to the left of that upended Chrysler. It's Scott Fuller."

"*Detective* Scott Fuller?"

"Is there another Scott Fuller in town?"

"I don't think this is very funny, Agent Vail. Scott was a colleague of ours."

"He's also a fucking arsonist. He tried to kill me. Twice. So forgive me if I don't share your warm fuzzies."

Aaron's eyes narrowed. He studied her a moment, seemed to compose himself, then said, "So what happened here? What should I be looking for out there?"

"He attacked me. Clocked me good," she said, then turned so her swollen temple was visible. "I recovered my handgun, which he'd knocked from my hand. I was questioning him when I felt a prick in my neck and that's the last I remember. When I woke up, Fuller was dead. I'm sorry if I fucked up your crime scene. I wasn't thinking clearly when I came to, and I was dizzy so I couldn't stand up. I crawled around trying to find my Glock. But obviously there was someone else out there, so I'd look for a third set of footprints."

"Obviously?"

"Whoever drugged me, he came up from behind."

Aaron gave her a look of disgust, then turned and trudged off toward his vehicle. "Don't go anywhere," he called into the night air. "I'll be back to do a GSR."

"Don't let him bother you," Dixon said. "I know you and Scott didn't hit it off, but he was part of the community. A lot of people saw him as a child prodigy. Some of that had to do with Stan Owens."

Tires crunched dirt behind them, followed by another swirling light bar and bright headlights.

"Speaking of which," Dixon said, "here he is." She turned to Vail, who winced as Marcus applied an icepack to her head. "Be prepared."

"For what?" Vail asked.

"Owens seems like a nice guy, but he can be a real bastard when he's pissed. And hearing his stepson's been murdered ain't gonna make him happy."

Owens spent a moment conferring with Brix, who had been helping unload klieg lights and tripods from Aaron's vehicle. With the icepack pressed to her head, Vail watched Owens's body language. His shoulders slumped, he brought his hands to his head, grabbed his hair, then walked forward toward the Chrysler. Brix put his arm out to stop him, said something, then Owens swung away, out of his friend's grasp. Red and tear-swollen eyes reflected in the swirling emergency lights. Then Owens turned toward Vail and they locked gazes. Vail had a feeling this was not going to go well.

As if sensing her thoughts, Robby said, "Oh, shit, here it comes."

Vail turned to Dixon. "I assume you're familiar with the saying, 'It's about to hit the fan'?"

Owens was approaching with a slow, deliberate gait, his eyes focused on Vail, who looked down at the ground. She felt bad for Owens and didn't want to be seen as confrontational.

"What the fuck did you do to my son?" Owens said, as he advanced on them.

Vail held up her free hand, and cocked her head to the side, as if to say, "It wasn't my fault." But Owens suddenly lunged at her and would've landed a hard right had Robby not stepped in front and knocked him backwards to the ground.

"I'm sorry for your loss, Sheriff," Robby said, looking down at him. "But you need to get your shit together. Agent Vail had nothing to do with your son's death. He attacked *her*. And if you can't deal with this rationally and objectively, haul your ass out of here and let your people do their jobs."

Vail placed a hand on Robby's shoulder. Owens got to his feet. He was average height, about five-ten, and that made him nine inches shorter than Robby. He wouldn't move against Vail again. Instead, he ground his molars. The incessant flickering of the red and blue lights lent an uneasy tension to the already edgy scene.

Brix was now at Owens's side. He put an arm around the sheriff's back and turned him, then led him away. Brix glanced over his shoulder at Vail. She couldn't read his expression. Apologetic? Disgust? It was too dark to make it out. Could've been either.

The paramedic knelt on a knee and started to pack up his case. Dixon held out a hand. "Hold it a second. I need you to draw a blood sample."

"A blood sam—I don't usually do that."

"I know. But I need it done. Now."

Marcus looked at the firm expressions worn by the people surrounding him, then knelt back down and opened his kit. He pulled out a plastic-encased syringe and tore it open. "What is it you want?"

Dixon looked out toward Aaron, who appeared to be moving with purpose off in the distance, then said, "I'll let you know in a second." She pulled her cell phone and called him. Vail watched as Aaron, now bathed in the bright lights trained on Fuller's body and the immediate vicinity, moved to answer his phone. He said something to Dixon, then shoved his phone back in his pocket.

Dixon hung up, turned to Marcus, and gave him specific instructions. To Vail, she said, "I'm hoping whatever you were drugged with will still be in your system. If we wait too long, it'll clear—"

"Yeah, got it," Vail said. "Thanks."

"Hey, just trying to keep my head about me, do the right things. Aaron said he'd be over in a bit to get the GSR."

Marcus reached out, took Vail's left forearm, and wedged it in his armpit, then, with gloved hands, tied a rubber strip around Vail's bicep as he prepared to do the blood draw. "When we're done here, I'll give you a sterile container. Go into the back of the rig, pee into it, then seal it. It's not ideal, but we're improvising here."

Robby stretched his neck back, rolled his shoulders. "So this UNSUB is getting bolder. He must've been shadowing you and followed you and Fuller here. Then he drugged you and killed Fuller."

"Until and unless we learn more, that seems like a reasonable conclusion," Dixon said. "But why would he leave Karen alive? And why kill Scott?"

*Good questions.* Vail unrolled her shirt sleeve and rose from the bumper. "Could simply be that he wanted to show us he can operate with impunity. Ultimate power. Kill a cop, he's got total control. As to why he chose to kill Fuller and not me, it might simply have been who had their back to him when he struck."

"The luck of the draw," Dixon said. "So to speak."

"Unless . . ." Vail shoved her hands into the back pockets of her pants and began to pace. "Unless that's not it at all."

"How do you mean?" Robby asked.

"We're missing something very important here." She pointed at Dixon. "Give me your phone." Dixon handed it over and Vail hit Send. Aaron answered. "It's Vail. How was Fuller killed?"

There was a moment's silence. Vail looked at the phone's display to see if the line was still active, then glanced off in Aaron's direction to see what he was doing. She didn't see him. *Was he still pissed at her? Or was he examining Fuller's body?*

"Aaron, you there?"

"Right here."

Vail turned, threw a hand up to her chest. "Jesus Christ, man, don't sneak up on me like that. My nerves are a little raw."

"I'll have to remember that." Aaron motioned to her and she handed the phone back to Dixon, then extended her arm. Aaron placed a number of adhesive gun-shot residue disks across the back of her hands, sleeves, chest, and torso. He drew a grid in his notebook and made notations as to where each of the round tabs had been placed.

"So how was Scott killed?" Dixon asked.

While Aaron continued his task, he said, "His trachea wasn't crushed, if that's what you're thinking. Looks like he took three forty-caliber rounds to the chest. One is up around the dicrotic notch; looks like stippling on the neck, indicating that shot was very close range, maybe around two feet. Another one looks to be from a little further away than the others. Most likely that was the shooter's first shot. But I'll know more once I get him to the lab and I can do a full workup."

"What about—"

"No. Toenails are intact."

"Okay," Vail said. "Figured as much. Thanks."

"Yeah, whatever." He pointed at her fanny pack. "You carry a forty-caliber pistol, correct?"

"A Glock 23."

Aaron pulled an evidence bag from his pocket and extended a hand. "Your weapon."

Vail shook her head. "Actually, it's going to the FBI lab."

"No," Aaron said, drawing it out as if it was a musical note, "it's going into *this* evidence bag and back to *my* lab."

Vail thought about that a moment, then said, "I'm a federal agent and I have to abide by federal rules and regulations. If you've got a problem with that, my ASAC is Thomas Gifford. I'm sure he can quote the appropriate section from the Manual of Administrative Operations Procedures. So my sidearm is going to the FBI lab. I'd imagine you can have it once they're done with it."

Aaron groaned—it sounded more like a growl—and walked off, back toward the lighted crime scene.

Vail stared off at the ground for a moment, lost in thought. "This isn't his typical kill," she finally said. "No ritual behaviors. He didn't choke Fuller and he didn't yank off a toenail. He used a handgun to kill him."

"So what are you saying?" Robby asked. "That this isn't our offender?"

Vail shook her head. "I'm not saying that."

"He could've been trying to make it look like you killed Fuller," Dixon said.

"Why would he do that?"

"I'm not saying he did." Dixon turned to Vail. "But how else would you explain what he did?"

Vail picked up the sterile urine specimen container Marcus had set aside. "If the UNSUB's motive was merely to fuck with our heads, show us he's in charge, then it doesn't matter how he kills Fuller. He was taking a big risk by following us, by entering this vineyard. Even though it was pitch black out, either of us could've heard him. But the way a narcissist thinks, he figures he can do this stuff and there's nothing we can do to stop him. Killing one of us is a big deal. The more shit he does like this, the more it starts to add up and it becomes more difficult for us to contain the fallout. I mean, he killed a cop—the sheriff's stepson. If he knew the relationships, then his choice was purposeful."

"He couldn't lose," Robby said. "The sheriff's stepson, a sergeant, or an FBI agent. Either way, that's big shit."

Vail was about to respond when Stan Owens appeared behind them. Brix was trailing a few paces back. "Stan," Brix called out. "Stan, think about this."

Owens stopped a few feet from Vail—a bit further than normal conversation typically occurs. But Robby was at Vail's left elbow, and Owens no doubt remembered his recent encounter with the large Vienna detective.

"I'm sorry for your loss, Sheriff."

"That right?" Owens said. "I don't know what happened here, but I will find out. I don't care what it takes, but I'll make sure you go down for this—"

"Stan," Brix said. "Stan, you're not seeing things objectively."

Owens spun on him. "I'm not? Well, you tell me what happened here. Vail's here, my son is here, she's already shown contempt for him, with plenty of witnesses—"

"I show contempt for a lot of people," Vail said. "When they de-serve it. Doesn't mean I meet them in a deserted vineyard at night and shoot them."

Owens turned fully back to Vail and set his jaw. "If you did this, I will personally come after you and do to you what you did to Scott. Count on it."

"Threatening a federal agent isn't smart," Vail said. "And it sure as hell isn't productive. Whoever did this—and it's likely our offender—is still out there."

"Convenient, isn't it? Some guy knocked me out and killed the other guy, then disappeared. They made a movie about that once."

"*The Fugitive*," Vail said. "Based on a real case. Dr. Sam Shepard was arrested and convicted for the murder of his wife."

"They caught him and we'll catch you, too."

"Here's the thing, Sheriff. Shepard was innocent. Someone really did knock him out and kill his wife."

Owens frowned and was about to reply when Brix clapped him on the shoulder. "C'mon. We've got work to do."

As he led Owens away, Vail turned to Robby and Dixon. "If this is our offender, we've gotta catch him. He's getting bolder. And if we don't do something to stop him, we may not have a choice."

"Go public," Dixon said.

Vail nodded. "Give him what he wants."

# TWENTY-SIX

*N*inety minutes later, the task force was convened at the request of Redmond Brix. Vail had already given her statement to Brix about the shooting and met with an agent from the Bureau's Santa Rosa Resident Agency to swap out her Glock. Her spent weapon—the one that might have been used to shoot Fuller—was placed in a chain-of-custody evidence bag. The agent provided Vail with an identical replacement.

Afterwards, in the ladies' restroom, Vail and Dixon splashed their faces with cold water. Dixon pulled a paper towel from the dispenser and wiped her face.

"You feel well enough to go in there?" Dixon asked.

"I'm not going to let you or anyone else try to defend me. I'll stand up to anything anyone wants to throw at me."

"That's what I thought you'd say."

Vail leaned over the vanity, close to the mirror, and looked at her swollen temple. She gently blotted it with the wet towel. It was extremely tender to touch. "We need to look into Fuller's background, who he knew, who his friends were. We need a search warrant for his place and any known places he might've stored things. If we can establish a link between him and the arson, we can close that case without bias."

"Better if I ask for those things. I don't know if your opinion—or requests—would carry much weight with the task force right now."

"I agree."

Dixon balled up her fist and crumpled the paper towel, then tossed it in the waste bin. "Let's do it."

Mann, Gordon, Dixon, Brix, Lugo, Nance, and Vail were seated around the conference table. Brix had scared up a sheriff's department shirt and a pair of uniform pants for Vail to wear so her blood-smeared clothing—rather, Dixon's blouse and pants—could be forensically tested. Given the late hour and circumstances, Robby was permitted to sit in on the meeting—which Brix promised would be brief and productive.

"You okay?" Lugo asked Vail, as he took his seat.

"I'm fine. Thanks for asking, Ray. I have a feeling my friends in this town are dwindling in numbers."

"I didn't realize you had friends," he said.

Vail wasn't sure how to take that. Lugo was probably joking, but she was tired and hungry and still wasn't completely back to herself—no doubt the drug she'd been given wasn't entirely out of her system.

"All right," Brix said. "I, for one, am going to miss Scott. Out of respect for him, the sheriff, and his family, we're going to put everything we've got behind this. If Karen and Roxxann are right, this is the work of our UNSUB. I'm not so sure of that, but I don't have a better explanation just yet."

"I think," Dixon said, "we should make every attempt to clear Scott's name. Let's look into his background, the people he knew, who his friends were. I'll get a search warrant for his place and cell phone and financial records and any associated locations where he might've stored his stuff."

"I'm not a cop," Nance said, "but seems to me we're investigating Scott instead of investigating who killed him."

Vail had to fight to keep her eyes from closing. Now that she was sitting, her lids felt heavy. If she could just close them for a few minutes—

"We've got two issues here," Brix said. "First is who torched the B&B and tried to roast Karen alive. Second is the Crush Killer, who may or may not have killed Scott."

Dixon clicked her pen and scribbled a note on her pad. "If we can rule out an obvious link between him and the arson, we'd go a long way toward clearing his name."

Nance spread his hands, palm up. "Sounds to me like you're trying to find a link, not rule one out."

"Depends on how you look at it," Vail said. She felt like her speech was slow, possibly even slurred—but no one seemed to be reacting, so maybe it was in her mind. She pressed on. "We're just trying to get at the truth. Wherever it leads"—she shrugged—"is where it leads. It's our job at this point to collect evidence, not interpret it. Interpretation will come soon enough."

"Hopefully," Dixon said, "our digging will lead to someone else, in which case we clear Scott's—Detective Fuller's—name."

Nance shook his head. "Witch hunt, that's what it is. Twist it any way you want, that's all it is."

Dixon tossed down her pen. "Look, Mr. Nance. You're here as a courtesy. As lead investigator, whether or not you're allowed to remain is my call. But let's get something straight. My generosity only goes so far. You need to understand that this is our investigation and we're going to run it professionally and efficiently. We're keeping you in the loop, but you don't have a say in what we do and how we do it. I'm not even sure why you care so much about how we handle Detective Fuller's death investigation."

"I care because Stan Owens is a friend of the congressman. I care because it's the right thing to do."

Dixon spread her hands. "Then let us do our jobs. We'll figure out what's going on. No one in this room is out to pin things on Detective Fuller or tarnish his reputation in any way."

His eyes flicked over to Vail. "I'm not so sure about that."

Vail heard Nance's comment, but it wasn't registering. She needed to go lie down. But first, she had to bring a matter to their attention. "There's something else we should look into," she said, keeping her eyes on the table in front of her. "Because of the way our victims are killed, we need to question those men in the area who have amputated upper limbs, who wear prostheses."

All heads rotated toward Austin Mann, who did not react. His gaze remained firmly on Vail.

"I know what you're thinking, and I've already had this discussion with Agent Mann. He's alibied." She glanced up and saw a mix of surprise and anger on the faces of her team members. *Fuck it. I had to come clean. It had to be said.* She brought a hand to the back of her neck and squeezed. "It's a bit of a long shot, but if we're being thorough, it shouldn't be overlooked. We need someone to follow up on this. Compile a list. Limit it to those men living within a seventy-five mile radius. That's a bit broad, but it'll eliminate error. If the list is too long, shorten it to fifty miles. Eliminate anyone younger than twenty-five and older than forty."

Brix cleared his throat. "I'll see if I can get someone from the Special Investigations Bureau on this."

Vail rose unsteadily from her chair. "I'm not feeling so great. I'm going to lie down for a few minutes, try to shake off this fog."

"Shift Change Room's right down the hall," Brix said. "Flip the sign to 'occupied' and no one'll bother you."

"I'll be back," Vail said. "Hopefully soon."

―――――――

JOHN WAYNE MAYFIELD fingered the pay-as-you-go phone—one of three he owned, none to be used more than once—and thought about what he would type.

It had gone exceedingly well with Vail and Fuller. He had been behind the car that was following Vail, before he realized the driver of the other vehicle was Scott Fuller. That was when an alternative plan began to take shape. He had the drug and syringe in his toolkit. Though he had never used it, he lived by the Boy Scout principle: Be prepared.

And so he was. He backed off his pursuit but remained close. Having Vail and Fuller tangle and force one another's collision facilitated his plan. In fact, it worked out better than he had sketched it out in his mind.

Fuller's death was the type of devastating loss that would put them back on their heels, keep them on the defensive. He would've loved to hang around and see their reactions when Vail awoke and tried to explain what had happened, how Fuller ended up murdered while she . . . slept, taken out by an unseen assailant. He wondered if they believed her.

But he had better things to do with his time than stick around just to see how they handled Karen Vail. More stunning things, things that would have vastly greater impact. Because he was just getting started.

He looked down at the phone and typed out a text message.

# TWENTY-SEVEN

*V*ail's trip to the Shift Change Room turned into a four-hour nap—still the result of the residual effects of the drugging. When she awoke, Dixon was standing over her with Dr. Brooke Abbott at her side.

A slice of light fell across her face. She squinted against the glare, then held up a hand to shield her eyes.

Vail blinked several times. "Roxxann." She sat up on the bottom bunk, but a rush of dizziness struck her like a sharp wave on a small dingy. She stuck out an arm to grab onto something. Dixon grabbed Vail's arm and caught her, held her steady. "Sorry. I guess whatever drug he used is still in my system."

Abbott chuckled. "That drug is BetaSomnol. Based on the tox screen we did from that blood sample the medic drew from you, and doing a little guesswork—because we don't know how long you were out before you called for help—it's likely you were injected with fifteen milligrams. Enough to put down someone your size and weight for about twenty minutes. That's a pretty hefty dosage. No wonder you've had lingering dizziness."

"I've never heard of this. Beta—"

"BetaSomnol. It's a super quick next-generation sedative, a mixture of a benzodiazepine—a drug like valium—and an antipsychotic."

"Who would have access to it?"

"Not many people. It was developed for use in ERs and mental institutions, where they need fast-acting preparations to quickly put down a thrashing, violent patient. BetaSomnol is gradually replacing the traditional mixture of Haldol and Ativan, which are just too slow.

And when someone's doing his best to take out your eye, you want him down PDQ."

"Is the tox screen you ran definitive?" Dixon asked.

"I've sent it out to a reference lab for a quantitative analysis. They'll do a high-sensitivity screen for several hundred licit and illicit drugs, as well as alcohol. Once we get that back, we'll have a definitive result. But that'll take days, maybe weeks."

Vail rubbed at her neck. "Any lasting effects of this BetaSomnol?"

"The drug metabolizes fairly quickly, so I wouldn't worry about it. You'll be fine."

Dixon stifled a yawn, then consulted her watch. "So the obvious question would be, where did the drug come from?"

"BetaSomnol is a pretty new product, so there's limited distribution."

"Perfect," Dixon said. "We should be able to find out fairly easily if any hospitals within a hundred miles reported a theft."

"Of fifteen milligrams?" Abbott asked. "If you've got access to these drugs, you could easily siphon off a few milligrams here and there and no one'd be the wiser."

Vail slowly swung her feet off the bed. "True—but you're missing the point. Theoretically, someone who'd have access to the drug would have to work there, as an employee or contractor. More than that, these drugs are locked away. They'd likely have to hold a position that gives them access. Again, theoretically, that narrows our suspect pool."

Abbott nodded. "I'll get right on it. I'll let you know what I find out." She turned and pushed through the door.

Vail leveraged herself off the bed, squared her shoulders, and faced a small mirror that hung on the adjacent wall. She ran her hands through her hair, turned her face to the side, then shook her head. "I look like shit."

"You had a car accident, went toe-to-toe with Scott Fuller, then got injected with an antipsychotic cocktail. Not to mention it's four-thirty in the morning. How did you expect to look?"

"C'mon, you know none of that matters. We can rationalize all we want, but is it ever okay for us not to look good?"

"I was just trying to make you feel better."

"Only thing that'll make me feel better is a hot shower, a comfortable bed. And Robby's body beside me." They walked out of the Shift Change Room and headed down the hall. "Speaking of Robby, where is he?"

"He's been working with Brix and Lugo."

Vail felt a buzz on her belt. She dug out her BlackBerry and blew off the dirt that had no doubt come from rolling around in the vineyard. Looked at the text. And stopped in midstride. She felt dizzy again—only this time it was not from a next-gen drug. It was raw fear. "Oh my God," she muttered.

Dixon stopped beside Vail and looked over her shoulder. "What is it?"

*Think, Karen. Calm down. What do I do? How do I—stop. Breathe. Concentrate.* She wiped at her eyes with two fingers. "Get Robby," was all she said.

Dixon ran off. Vail dialed Jonathan. It went right to voicemail. "Fuck!" She hung up and scrolled to speed dial looking for Paul Bledsoe's number. But there were no speed dial entries. *Damn it! Think. What's the number? 703 . . . come on . . .* She pressed her eyes shut and it came to her. Punched it in, hit Call.

Bledsoe, a friend and homicide detective with Fairfax County Police Department, answered on the third ring.

"Bledsoe, it's Karen. I know it's early—"

"Fuck, Karen, I was up half the night. I finally fell asleep sometime around three. What time is it?"

"Seven-thirty, your time."

"Seven—what do you mean, 'your time'? Where are—"

"California, working a case. I need your help."

He moaned. "Today's my day off. Call me back in a few hours—"

"No! Get your ass out of bed. He's targeting Jonathan—"

"Jonathan? Who's targeting—"

"Shut up and listen to me. Throw on your clothes and get ready to leave. I'll call you back in thirty seconds and tell you where you're going." She disconnected the call.

Vail stood there staring at the text message, her pulse pounding in her head. *Whoever you are, you goddamn fucking bastard—*

"Karen!"

Robby came running down the hall.

She pointed at him as he approached. "Have someone look up the next flight out to DC."

"DC? What's wrong?"

"Jonathan." She held up a hand. "Please, just do it."

Robby pulled his phone and started dialing. Vail pushed Talk on her BlackBerry and waited while it rang. Bledsoe picked up.

"Bledsoe, I'm putting you on speaker. I've got Robby here, too, and Roxxann Dixon, an investigator I'm working with." She pressed a button on her phone then held it out. "Can you hear me?"

"Yeah," Bledsoe said, his voice filtered and tinny. "Now what the hell's going on?"

"Start driving toward Jonathan's school. Lincoln Intermediate, you know where it is?"

"Yeah, but—"

"Just get in the car and I'll explain."

The crank of an engine turning over came through the speaker. "Already in the car, on my way."

Robby ended his call and stepped closer to Vail and Dixon.

"I just got a text from a serial killer we've been tracking here in Napa." She played with the device's joystick and brought up the message. "He said, and I'm quoting, 'I'm watching a very interesting young man. Reminds me of a young Karen Vail. He's on his way to school right now. Lincoln Intermediate is a lot nicer than the school I went to, which was a real shit hole. I'll be sure to say hi to Jonathan for you. Hope you enjoyed your little nap. A nap in Napa. LOL.'"

Dixon and Robby exchanged an uneasy glance. "Did you call Jonathan?" Robby asked.

"Went right to voicemail. He turns his phone off because the school confiscates it if it so much as vibrates."

"Well that worked out great," Bledsoe said. "Smart rule."

"I'll call the school," Robby said, flipping open his phone. "Have them go into lockdown."

"They can't go into lockdown before school starts," she said. Into her phone: "Bledsoe, you've gotta find him—"

"I'll find him, Karen. I'll be there in ten. I've got it handled, okay?"

*No, not okay. That's not quick enough.* "Yeah, sure. Thanks." She hung up, then leaned back against the wall and sank down to the floor.

# TWENTY-EIGHT

Robby's cell phone was clasped in his left hand as he knelt in front of Vail. He lifted her chin with a finger. "Karen, look at me." He waited until her eyes met his. "It's going to be okay. Bledsoe knows what he's doing."

She took a deep, uneven breath. Rage was building beneath the surface. Anger at having been so close to this killer, at having him over her shoulder—he touched her—and now, several hours later, he was within striking distance of her son.

*He could've killed me, but he didn't. Now he's flown across the country. Why? Control. Power. That's an awful lot of effort to go through to show her he's running the show. Unless he intends to kill Jonathan.*

She pulled herself to her feet, shook off Robby's attempt to help her.

"Karen," Dixon said. "There's nothing you can do but sit and wait. Let's go down the hall, get a cup of coffee."

Vail ground her molars. She knew Dixon was trying to help, to help her pass the time until Bledsoe called with news. *Of what? That Jonathan was safe? Or—*

She pulled her gun and swung her arm, backhanding the window in the door to her right. The glass shattered with a crisp, jolting crash.

"Jesus, Karen." Dixon grabbed her hand and forced the Glock toward the floor. "Calm the fuck down, will you?"

Vail yanked her hand free. "Goddamn bastard. No one threatens my son!"

Robby held up a hand. "Karen, look at me. Karen—" He waited while she focused on his face. "Put your weapon away."

Vail ripped open her fanny pack and shoved the Glock inside. "I swear, I'm gonna kill this guy. If he touches Jonathan, I will castrate the fucker."

"I hear you," Robby said.

"Then I'm going to put a bullet in his deranged brain."

Robby drew her close and enveloped her in his large torso.

"After he begs for his life," she mumbled into his chest.

Robby stroked her hair. "That's only if I don't get to him first. I won't be so nice about it."

Lugo and Brix were walking down the hall toward them. Brix said, "We heard a window—" His eyes followed the door down to the floor, where shards of glass had landed. "What the hell happened?"

"Bats," Dixon said.

Brix looked at her, then at Robby. "Bats?"

"Bats. Their sonar got fucked up."

Brix took a step to his left, saw Vail huddled in Robby's arms. "What's going on?"

"UNSUB says he's in Virginia," Dixon said. "He texted Karen. He's at her son's school."

"You're shitting me."

"I need to go," Vail said. She craned her neck up toward Robby. "When's the next flight?"

"There's a six-twenty-five out of SFO," Lugo said.

Robby shook his head. "Even if you left now, you probably wouldn't make the flight. Besides, it won't even get there till almost six, and that's if there are no delays. Then you have to get out of Dulles in rush hour."

"I don't care. I need to do something—"

"You called Bledsoe. He'll handle it—if there's even something to handle."

Vail's BlackBerry rang. She shoved Robby aside and fumbled the phone from her belt. Bledsoe's number. "Yeah."

"I'm on-site. Everything looks okay. I've got six officers en route, should be here any minute. We'll comb the place, make sure everything's cool. Then I'm gonna put someone on Jonathan, shadow him till you catch this guy. Good?"

She closed her eyes, took a deep breath. "Good. Thanks, Bledsoe. You're the best."

# TWENTY-NINE

*D*ixon and Vail sat in the break room around the small round table, on formed, yellow plastic chairs. Vail clutched a cup of hot tea.

Robby walked in and took a seat. He placed a hand atop Vail's. "I also asked Lugo to do a search for flights out of SFO that'd arrive in the DC metro area by morning. Just to see if it's even possible. Virgin has one, a 9:35 p.m. departure, arrives Dulles 5:30 a.m. I mapped out the timeline and it works out."

Vail bowed her head. "So he could be there."

"Yeah," Robby said. "If not him, an accomplice. Impossible to say."

"Call Virgin. Find out if they had anyone on that flight who looked suspicious."

Robby tilted his head. "You're kidding, right?"

"Just get a passenger manifest and we'll check 'em all out ourselves. And see if they've got any videotape of the terminal that we can examine."

"Already done. Lugo's calling the airline. And he's requesting video from SFO's security cameras, in case one of them caught the offender." Robby fought off a yawn. "Before it records over."

Dixon flipped her notepad to a clean page and clicked her pen. "Okay. Let's take a step back and look at this. You two have a personal stake here. But we can't let our feelings cloud our thoughts, affect our opinions."

Vail warmed her hands on the sides of the mug. "He let me live, then he went after my son. All the way across the country?"

"A lot of effort just to scare you," Dixon said. "Killing you would've accomplished the same thing if he was after control, to show his superiority."

Vail's phone buzzed, followed a second later by Dixon's. Vail figured it was regarding the same issue. They both answered simultaneously.

At the other end of Vail's call was Bledsoe. "I just wanted you to know I saw Jonathan and he's fine. He's in the classroom. School just started and I've got them in lockdown. There's an officer posted outside and he'll be Jonathan's shadow until we put this scumbag away. Okay? You can stop stressing."

"Why do you think I was stressing?"

"You don't really want an answer to that, do you?"

"No. And—Bledsoe . . . thanks. Unfortunately I don't have much info on this killer." She told him what she knew, then said, "I assume you'll want the unit's help on this. If the offender's now in your neck of the woods, you should pick up the investigation. Bring in Rooney and Del Monaco."

"How about we just leave it at Rooney?"

Vail chuckled. "Do me a favor and touch base with Gifford, let him know what's going on, okay?" Vail thanked him again, then hung up.

"I assume he found Jonathan," Robby said.

"He's fine. They're locked down. Bledsoe posted a cop."

Robby reached across the table and took her hand. "You okay?"

"Better. But I won't be 'okay' till we catch this bastard." She nodded at Dixon. "What was your call about?"

"Gordon and Mann are on their way in with a person of interest. They ran Fuller's LUDs and cell records. One number in particular kept coming up, and the two of them had some long conversations the morning of the fire. Number belongs to Walton Silva, a buddy of Fuller's. They went to his place with the K9 unit and got a hit outside an old cottage in the back.

"So they requested a warrant, and in the meantime they woke him up, gave him the bad news about Scott, and asked him to come down to the station to help us out. Once he was on county premises, they took his phone—gave him some bullshit story about new county guidelines because some workers in the building have pacemakers—and then executed the warrant on his wife. Searched the cottage and found chemical residue that looked and smelled like what was used around the building."

"Until the lab can make a definitive match," Vail said, "we don't have much."

"We can sweat him," Robby said.

Dixon flipped her notepad closed. "That's the plan. But there's a little twist." She looked at them. "Good, you're sitting. There were also calls to another number on Fuller's cell logs. And on Silva's. Right after Fuller talked to Silva, Silva called this other number. Every time. Care to guess who the number belongs to?"

Vail shrugged.

Dixon rose from her chair. "I'll let it be a surprise. C'mon, let's go. You're gonna want to see this."

# THIRTY

Vail and Robby made their way through the maze of corridors and into the task force conference room where Brix sat, waiting. On the wall-mounted television screen was the image of a man, shown from an angle above eye level.

Brix motioned to the monitor. "Meet Walton Silva. A thirty-one-year-old investment banker with Rutledge Warren Stone. He's a newbie in the firm."

"Does he know why he's here?" Dixon asked.

"I told him we needed help finding the guy who killed Scott Fuller, that we're all pretty shaken up about it, and that Sheriff Owens was on our backs to solve it quickly."

Dixon folded her arms. "Good."

"Mind if I do this with Roxxann?" Vail asked. "One of the things we do in the profiling unit is teach interview techniques."

Brix's jaw moved from side to side. He was considering the request. "Roxx, you're lead investigator. Your call."

Dixon pulled her attention from the television monitor. "We work well together."

"What's your plan?" Brix asked.

Vail tilted her head. "We'll need a printout of Fuller's mobile calls."

Brix reached over to the table and grabbed a manila folder. "It's all in here."

Vail snuck a look inside, then nodded. "Good. You got Silva's cell?"

Brix dug it out of his pocket. Vail slipped it into hers.

"I think we should keep it cordial for as long as possible," Vail said.

"Brix, when you see me pull out my BlackBerry, give me a minute, then come in and whisper in my ear. Nothing funny or cute."

A smile thinned Brix's lips, then he nodded knowingly. "I like that."

"I thought you might." Vail glanced over at Silva, then turned to Dixon. "Let's do this."

Moments later, after a brief strategy session in the hall, Vail and Dixon entered Interview Room 2, a small, six-by-eight room containing a square table topped with the same taupe and gray faux marble found in the conference room. Two black chairs. And that was it.

The size of the room injected Vail with an instant dose of claustrophobia. Her eyes did a quick once-over of the space, her mind measuring it and adding it up and knowing it was small, but willing her brain to think it was plenty big, with enough air. She stood beside the door, ready to make a quick exit if the need arose. *I can do this. No big deal.*

As Vail struggled with her unfounded anxieties, she looked over at Walton Silva, who was occupying one of the two seats in the room. Silva wore well-tailored sweats that probably never saw the inside of a gym.

Dixon introduced herself, then nodded at Vail and said simply, "This is my partner. Can we get you anything to drink?"

"Any reason this had to be done now?" Silva made no attempt to stop his yawn. "It's not even light out yet."

Dixon sat down opposite Silva. "The sheriff is really upset about his stepson. He's busting our butts. He's called everyone in. We don't want to let him down. And we're hoping you can help us."

Silva yawned again. "I'll help you anyway I can. But what can *I* do?"

"We need to know about Scott. We knew him around the station, but friends always know us better than our coworkers."

Silva shrugged.

"You're with Rutledge Warren Stone, right?"

"I started there about a year ago."

"How'd you do when the market tanked?"

"Like everyone else who had money in the market, I guess. I may be an investment banker, but I didn't have a crystal ball. I took a bath." His gaze drifted to Vail, who was standing still and quiet, across the room and to Dixon's right, Vail's shoulder beside the door. Back to Dixon: "But what's that got to do with Scott?"

"How close were the two of you?"

Silva lifted a shoulder. "We went to school together, hung out, that sort of thing. We kind of lost touch when I left for college. But as soon as I moved back to town, we started talking again."

"Scott was a good guy, wasn't he?"

Silva sucked his left cheek, paused a moment, then said, "Yeah."

"Did you two see a lot of one another?"

"About once or twice a month. We'd grab a beer when he got off shift. But we weren't as close as we were before I left."

"So you weren't that close."

"Nah, not like we were."

"Let me show you something, Walton. It's something Lieutenant Brix gave me a few minutes ago, and it doesn't make a whole lot of sense to me. Maybe you can help me understand it."

"Sure."

Dixon splayed open the manila folder Brix had given them, then turned it so Silva could see it. "These are phone logs for Scott's cell phone. Can you tell me if you recognize any numbers on it?"

Silva pulled the sheets closer and looked them over. His eyes seemed to hover a bit, then he moved on down the long list. "No, nothing that looks familiar."

Vail was moving now, catching Dixon's attention. Dixon glanced over her right shoulder at Vail as Vail punched in a number on her BlackBerry. Dixon turned back to Silva.

"You sure about that?"

Silva shrugged again. "Yeah." He looked at Vail and said, "I thought you're not supposed to use cell phones in this building."

Before Vail could answer, a musical ring tone sounded: the unmistakable strains of "Stairway to Heaven." Silva's eyes widened. Vail produced a thin-form Sanyo from her front pocket and held it up. A small red LED flashed on the top of the device.

Silva rose from his seat. "Hey, that's my phone—"

"Is it?" Vail pressed a button on her BlackBerry and seconds later the Sanyo went quiet. "See, I just dialed 555-4981—"

"Okay," Silva said. "I get what you're doing."

Dixon hiked her brow. "Really. What were we doing?"

Silva sat down slowly. "She—well, she called my number."

"That's funny," Dixon said. She slid the papers in front of her and placed an index finger in a specific spot. "That number, 555-4981, appears on Scott's phone logs. Every day, in fact."

"Yeah, so what?"

Dixon leaned forward on her forearms. "Well, you looked at this phone log not a minute ago and said you didn't recognize any of the numbers. And a minute before that, you said you weren't that close with Scott anymore, yet according to these logs, you talked to him pretty regularly."

"Obviously, I misspoke. It's really early. It's not even—"

"Not even light out, yeah, you told us."

*Come on, Brix,* Vail thought. *What'd you do, fall asleep out there?* Then the door opened. *Finally.* Vail leaned over and listened while Brix spoke softly into her ear. She nodded, made a point of raising her eyebrows, then thanked Brix. She glanced at Silva, just enough to get his blood pressure moving north, then stepped toward Dixon and whispered something to her. Dixon, too, nodded.

Silva looked from Dixon to Vail before settling back on Dixon. "Am I in some kind of trouble? Do I need a lawyer?"

"Nah," Dixon said with a wave of her hand. "We're just looking for answers and we could use all the help we can get. We like it when things fit together, and some things just aren't fitting together." Dixon let her fingers rest on Silva's forearm. His gaze moved down to her hand. "Walton, there's something else you can help us with. There was some scorched dirt mixed with a chemical residue near the cottage behind your house. We brought it to the lab for analysis and found that it contains a very specific substance called Class A foam."

"Thanks for the chemistry lesson," Silva said. "Can I go now? I'm really tired and I've got a full day ahead of me."

*Cool under pressure. Interesting. But he realizes we're heading in a direction he doesn't want to go.* "Yeah," Vail said, "I think you can go." *Not just yet, however . . .*

Dixon tightened her hand on Silva's forearm in case he was going to make a move to get up. "I've just got a couple more questions, if you don't mind."

Silva tilted his head in annoyance. "What?"

"Well, here's that thing I mentioned earlier, the thing I said you could help us with. That same Class A foam found around your cottage is only used in fire extinguishers. And, see, manufactures put specific markers in their branded chemicals so they can be forensically distinguished among one another. And that exact foam was the one found at the arson scene where a woman was nearly burned alive."

"I don't like what you're implying."

"I'm sorry," Dixon said, sitting back. "I didn't mean to imply anything. What did you think I was implying?"

Silva looked from Dixon to Vail. "I think it's time for me to call my lawyer."

"Did you do something wrong, Walton? Do you need an attorney?"

"You tell me."

Dixon turned to Vail. "Do you think he needs an attorney?"

Vail unfolded her arms, pleadingly holding out her hands. "We're just looking for help, trying to figure out who killed Scott. Did you kill Scott, Walton?"

He sat back in his chair. "Are you out of your minds? Scott was my friend."

Dixon nodded sympathetically. "Judging by how often you talked on the phone, I can see that. What did you talk about when he called you?"

Silva leaned his chair back on its two rear legs. "Stuff. You know, the market, where I saw things going."

"The stock market?"

"That's what I do. Securities, equities."

Dixon nodded. "Right. But, see, nothing's been going on in the market lately. Volatility mostly. Goes up, then down, then up. But you had this long conversation with him on the ninth. What was that about?"

"How am I supposed to remember what we talked about?"

"It wasn't that long ago."

Silva looked up at the ceiling. "I have lots of conversations every day. I can't remember what they're all about."

"This one I think you'd remember. Because it was right before the fire. And then you spoke again, right after the fire."

Silva let the chair fall forward onto all four legs. "Why do you keep asking me about this fire?"

Dixon leaned in close again, glanced back at Vail, as if she wanted to have a private conversation with Silva, out of the earshot of her partner. "Can I be totally honest with you, Walton?"

The man squinted. "Please."

"We did a preliminary rapid DNA screen on that foam. It's the latest in DNA technology, and it's not a hundred percent accurate—but it's close. The lab will be doing a more comprehensive test, but that'll take a few days. But the rapid screen, it showed your DNA mixed in with the Class A foam. You so much as breathe in the same room and it'll pick up your DNA. And, see, that foam was identified as an identical match for the one used in the fire. The arson."

Silva slapped the table. "Now wait a minute—"

"Calm down, Walton. Before you get upset, I have good news for you. I know it sounds like the evidence implicates you as the person who set the fire. But that's not what we're getting at."

"What are you getting at, then?" Silva asked.

"Well, Scott's death."

Silva rubbed his face with both hands. "I've had enough. I think I need an attorney."

"For what?" Vail asked. "We're trying to help you here. You bring in an attorney and the DA will, for sure, file charges against you. We don't care about the fire, you hear? We just want to find Scott's killer."

"And I told you. I can't help you there."

Vail stepped up to the table. "Sure you can," she said in a lilting voice. "We know Scott set the fire. He told us that shortly before he was killed."

"He did? Why—"

"Why he told us is unimportant. The point is, he did. But—can we—can we keep talking here, Walton? Because we know you didn't set the fire."

"Fine. So what is it you want?"

"Well," Vail said, "we just want to know why Scott set it. If we can figure that out, it may lead us to his killer. And that's all we're interested in."

"So I tell you what I know about that, and I can go. Right?"

Vail turned to Dixon. "Yeah."

Dixon shrugged agreement.

Silva chewed on this a moment, not saying anything, but his eyes were roaming the room, thinking, working it through.

*Come on, scumbag. Say something stupid.*

Finally, Silva leaned forward. "It was nothing, really. At least, my part wasn't that big a deal. Scott wanted to set this fire, like he told you, but he didn't want anyone getting hurt. So he asked me how he could control the fire so it wouldn't spread."

*Atta boy. That qualifies.* "Why would you know anything about that?"

"My dad was a chemical engineer at Dow for forty years. I asked him some questions one day. He's retired and gets bored easily. So I asked him how to do a controlled burn if all you had were household supplies lying around. He was all too happy to help me out. So, yeah, it was Class A foam. It prevented the fire from spreading, just what Scott wanted. That's the extent of my involvement."

"The scorched dirt near the cottage," Dixon said. "Did Scott do a test run? Just to make sure the foam would work?"

Silva's eyes flicked between Vail and Dixon. "Yeah. Scott was testing it."

"I'm sure Scott told you why he wanted to do this, to set this fire."

"All he told me was that an FBI agent was causing problems. She wanted to go public with this killer you people are after, and he couldn't let that happen."

"Couldn't let it happen, like silence her? Kill her?"

"I don't know. I didn't ask. I figured he just wanted to scare her."

*Bullshit. You fucking scumbag. I'd like to wring your goddamn neck—*

"Because it would destroy the tourism industry?" Dixon asked.

"The tourism industry?" Silva chuckled. "Heck no. He was worried about Congressman Church."

Dixon leaned forward. "Worried how? Why?"

"The congressman is going to run for governor."

Dixon sat back in her chair.

Vail's anger vanished like an extinguished candle. Her focus was immediately laser thin on Silva's words. And it wasn't good. She'd totally missed that one.

"So what if the guy wants to run for governor?" Dixon asked. "He's a politician."

But Vail suddenly got it. *If Church is in office, he takes his cadre with him. And he wouldn't be the first California governor to win the United States presidency.*

Silva spread his hands, as if even an imbecile should understand. "If he's elected governor," Silva said, "he takes his people along for the ride."

Vail was exhausted and felt weak, spacey. She needed caffeine, calories, and glucose for her brain to burn. But she couldn't walk out now. "Okay, Walton. I think I'm seeing this come into focus. Why don't you spell it out for me. Church—Congressman Church—is going to run for governor, and what happens then?"

"Scott would get a high-level law enforcement position, like Deputy Director of Homeland Security, I'd get Commissioner of Financial Institutions, and Tim would be his Chief of Staff."

"Tim," Vail repeated. *The "surprise" Dixon referenced earlier.* "Timothy Nance?"

"Yeah."

Dixon said, "And if Special Agent Vail, that FBI agent who was threatening to go public with this killer, went to the media, it'd hurt Congressman Church's chances?"

"Well, yeah," Silva said, as if it were obvious. "Any negative publicity would be a bad thing. Things get blown out of proportion in political campaigns. This serial killer happened under his watch. They'll say he didn't do enough to protect the People, didn't come down hard enough on the police to find the guy. Of all his territory, Napa is his top cut, the prime rib of his district."

"Okay, Walton." Vail nodded casually, as if it was all just a misunderstanding. No big deal. "I think we've got the picture. Get that agent out of the way, and the problem is eliminated."

"That's about it."

"But," Dixon said, "you didn't think 'elimination' meant death."

Silva looked from Vail to Dixon.

*Gotcha, asshole.*

He thrust his chin back, as if Dixon's comment was a most absurd conclusion. "Of course not."

"All right, Walton. Thanks so much. That does help." Dixon pulled a pad and pen from a drawer beneath the table and slid it across to Silva. "Go ahead and write all that down, starting with Scott planning the fire and what he wanted to accomplish. Don't leave anything out. When you're done, you can go." She rose from her chair. "Thanks again, Walton. You've really put this whole thing into focus for us."

Silva was already busy writing. Dixon walked out, following Vail into the conference room.

"That was a pleasure to watch," Brix said.

"I like that Class A foam shit," Robby said. "That chemical marker stuff was brilliant."

Brix laughed. "That rapid screen DNA was even better. Where did you get that?"

"That was good, wasn't it?" Vail said. "We thought of it right before we went in."

"Good work, Roxxi," Brix said. He sighed, rubbed his forehead. "So now we go pick up Nance, hopefully get his confession and wrap this thing up."

Vail turned to the monitor and watched Silva put down the pen. "I'll be right back." She headed into the interview room, glanced at the pad, and asked Silva to sign the bottom. After he scrawled his name and handed Vail the pad, he said, "Can I go now?"

"Absolutely. We've got a car and driver waiting outside for you." She extended a hand and Silva took it. "Thanks for your cooperation. I don't think we've been formally introduced. I'm Karen Vail. Special Agent Karen Vail. FBI."

Silva's hand went limp. "You—"

"Yeah, that's me. And yes, I'm fucking pissed." She forced a smile. "But it's been great meeting you, Walton. Have a pleasant stay in lockup."

Vail walked out and joined Robby in the conference room.

"You enjoyed that, didn't you?"

She looked over at the monitor, where Walton sat, grasping his hair with both hands.

Before Vail could respond, her BlackBerry buzzed. As she pulled it from her belt, Brix's and Dixon's phones chimed. She glanced at the display. A text message.

And another body.

# THIRTY-ONE

Walton Silva kept bemoaning that the sun had not yet risen when he was roused from bed. The task force members couldn't have made that complaint because, as they gathered around the fresh crime scene, the sky was brightening in the east, silhouetting the vineyard-tipped hills against pale yellow hues.

As Vail and Robby huffed up the steep rise, something that had been bothering Vail on the ride over continued clawing at her thoughts—but her brain function was fuzzy with sleep deprivation, and it took a while to fight through the fog.

"If this is the work of our Crush Killer, he can't be in Virginia," Vail said to Robby.

"That's a big 'if.' Let's first see what we've got, then we can draw some conclusions."

Vail looked over at Robby in the rising brightness. "That's something I would say, with some food in my stomach and sleep under my belt. You're absolutely right." She grabbed a peek at her watch, then said, "There's no reason for you to be here. You can go grab some shut-eye."

"As soon as we get a look at the body, figure out whether or not this is the same asshole, I'll take off, let Bledsoe know what's going down, and hit the sack."

"Wish I could hit that sack with you."

They joined the huddle of task force members—Dixon, Gordon, Mann, and Brix. Lugo stood at the periphery, rubbing his face with both hands, in obvious distress.

"What do we have?" Vail asked.

Lugo looked at her with a long face. "Same fucking thing. Breasts, windpipe, toenail. Go see for yourself."

Relief flooded over Vail—Jonathan was safe because it was now highly probable the killer was still in California—and she instantly felt deep remorse and embarrassment that she could be relieved over the discovery of a new victim. She cut herself some slack—lack of sleep did strange things to the way one processed information and stress—and moved past Lugo.

Matt Aaron was crouched over the body, his klieg lights creating the sense of an important event. And there, in the center of his stage, lit up like a diamond on display, was a woman who looked to be in her late thirties.

"TOD?" Vail asked.

Aaron did not shift his attention. "Maybe an hour ago."

"Jesus Christ," Brix said. "An hour?" He twisted his body, eyes scanning the countryside. "Where the hell is this guy?"

"Obviously not in Virginia," Robby said. He touched Vail's shoulder—she wished he'd lean over and give her a hug and kiss—she needed it. "I've still got those clothes I bought for you in my car. I'll leave the bags on Roxxann's trunk."

"Thanks."

He then walked off, toward his car.

Vail closed her eyes. She was so tired she thought she could fall asleep right here, right now, vertically suspended. But there would not be any sleep, not for a while.

"The bastard pulled one over on us, made us jump through hoops, made me think he was across the country stalking my son."

"Yeah, how about that?" Austin Mann asked.

Vail opened her eyes. "Smart guy. And out to show us just how smart he is, how superior he is, by tricking us—tricking me into thinking he was after my son. He knew that'd get a visceral, no-holds-barred response."

"But there'd be no way for him to know you'd actually fallen for it."

"What mother wouldn't? Who could take the chance? Of course I fell for it. He knew. He's a goddamn smart one. Organized." The beginnings of a profile were taking shape. "This guy will have a higher education. He owns a more expensive car, like a high-end Toyota or some other foreign make. He works in a job that doesn't recognize his true worth, and this frustrates him. He has to show us how intelligent he is to compensate for his failings in the real world."

Burt Gordon cleared his throat. "Doesn't help us much. We know the kind of person we may be looking for, but who is he? There can be hundreds of people who fit those parameters."

"Once we start getting a suspect pool, we can narrow it down using these guidelines."

Gordon gave a slight laugh, then looked to Aaron. "Any ID on the vic?"

"Nothing. No wallet, credit cards, license. I'll get you something as soon as I can run her prints, dental impressions—you know the deal."

"Knife under her lower back?"

Aaron inched closer, directed his flashlight at the body, and examined the area. "Can't tell. And I'm not sticking my hand underneath to find out. We'll know when it's time to move the body."

Vail's phone vibrated. She plucked it from its holster, glanced at the display, and lifted it to her face. "Vail."

"It's Bledsoe."

She reminded herself to enter in her contacts—not having caller ID configured for her phone numbers was a pain in the ass.

"Good news. We just found a fresh vic." *Did I just say that? Shit, I really need some sleep.*

"How is that good news?"

Vail rolled her head back, then side to side. "It's not, it's not. I just meant, if we found another vic in Napa—"

"How can that be, if the fucker's here, two thousand miles away?"

"Exactly. That seems to be the question of the day. Until we know for sure, we're assuming he's here in Napa, that his text last night was a ruse just to screw with our heads."

"Between you and me, it worked."

"I know it worked, Bledsoe. Thanks for pointing out the goddamn obvious." She noticed Dixon giving her a look. Vail turned away and walked off a few paces. "Sorry. I haven't had a whole lot of sleep."

"Takes a lot to piss me off, you know that."

"Now there's a quality I could use some of myself. Listen, can you put Jonathan on the phone?"

"I would if I was still there. I left the school a while ago. Everything was clean. My guy's on him. Trevor Greenwich. Give him a buzz."

"It's just—I just need to hear Jonathan's voice."

"No need to explain. Take care of yourself. Get some sleep. And call me if you need anything else, especially if your killer really is in my backyard."

"Count on it."

Bledsoe gave Vail the cop's cell and she immediately dialed through. As it was ringing, she realized she knew this officer. She'd had a run-in with the guy a couple of months ago. Not that it was his fault; he was just doing his job—but she was not in the mood to take any shit from the guy. When he answered, she identified herself—waiting for some sign of recognition—but got nothing. She plowed forward, not allowing too much room for him to comment, and asked him to pull Jonathan out of class for a moment. Greenwich didn't argue, nor did he question her as to why. Jonathan was on the line seconds later.

"Mom?"

"Hey, how are you?"

"Fine. What's the deal with the cop?"

"He's there to protect you. And please be polite. He's there as a favor, okay?"

"A favor for what? Everything's fine."

"It's not something I want to get into. I'll tell you when I get home. But for now, it's important you let the officer hang around close by. Okay?"

"Is this a big deal?"

"I hope not. I'll let you know if anything changes. And call me if you have any concerns, if anything doesn't feel right. Okay?"

"Yeah, okay. Whatever."

"I love you."

"You too."

Vail put away her phone and joined Dixon at the crime scene boundary.

"Everything okay?"

"I just needed to hear my son's voice." She turned to Dixon. "You have kids?"

"Me?" She laughed. "No. I'd like to, I think. But first I have to meet someone. I'm not into the single parent thing. Certainly not being a cop. You divorced?"

Vail took a moment before answering. "That's a long story I'd rather not get into right now. Better on a day when I'm awake and not dealing with a major case. Let's just say I *am* doing 'the single parent thing,' though that wasn't the plan. It just sort of . . . happened. And given how things turned out, it was probably for the best. Jonathan's father ended up being a bit more than I bargained for."

"It's nice, I think, having children. Watching them grow up, become people, have families of their own. And when you get old, you've got family around."

Vail couldn't help but look down at the corpse laid out in front of them. It seemed wrong to be having such a conversation in its presence. She turned and headed away. Dixon followed. "That sums it up," Vail said. "But that's only part of the deal. Lots of challenges along the way. Makes life interesting, to say the least."

"Is Jonathan your only child?"

Vail nodded. "Fourteen and full of angst. Overall, he's a good kid. But I'll be glad when he gets past the teen attitude."

Brix came up behind them. "Just got a call. Tim Nance is at the sheriff's department."

Vail sighed, long and slow. "This is going to be fun."

Brix rubbed at his forehead. "Yeah. Not so much."

# THIRTY-TWO

Vail had slipped on the shoes Robby had bought for her—they fit well, felt like tennis shoes, and were a welcome relief. She joined Dixon and they entered the sheriff's department facility. They were immediately met by Stan Owens, who was already having a less-than-friendly chat with Redmond Brix. As they approached, Vail's phone rang.

It was Gifford. He must have thought Vail had already programmed her new phone, or that she would recognize his voice, because he didn't bother identifying himself. "I guess this shouldn't surprise me, but you've dug yourself a new hole."

"Which hole are you referring to, sir?"

Gifford hesitated just a moment. "There's more than one?"

Vail smiled. She didn't mean to push his buttons. But it was, she had to admit, a bit of a kick.

"You know what?" he said. "Don't answer that. I don't want to know. I just got a call from the assistant director, who got a call from the director, who got a call from Congressman Church. Do you know who Congressman Church is?"

*Shit.* The conversation she just witnessed between Sheriff Owens and Brix was now coming into focus.

"I know *of* him. He represents Napa, as well as—"

"The correct answer is that Congressman Church is the man who's making my life miserable. And that means that he also happens to be the man who's now making your life miserable. Do you see where I'm going with this?"

"I'm beginning to get the picture."

"So what can you tell me about Church's district director, Timothy Nance?"

*My chance to douse this fire before it rages.* "I believe Nance was involved in the plot to kill me, sir. We got a confession from one of his friends who stated that he and Scott Fuller and—"

"Fuller's the dead LEO who was found a few feet from your body while you were . . . sleeping?"

*Obviously, he's already been briefed.* "I wasn't sleeping, sir. I was drugged. Someone—I believe it was the Crush Killer—came up from behind and injected me, then shot Fuller. Probably with my handgun."

There was a moment of silence. "And when did you think it was appropriate to inform me of this?"

"Don't take this the wrong way, sir, but I've been a little busy."

"We'll address that when you return. Meantime, I need to deal with this Nance issue."

Vail turned and saw Brix, Owens, and Dixon staring at her from down the hall. Whatever was about to happen was not going to be good. She swung back around. "With all due respect, there's no issue for you to deal with. Nance is a suspect in an attempted murder investigation. He was implicated by his purported accomplice. If he does the smart thing, he'll lawyer up and everything will be put into the court system here in California, where it'll be harder for congressmen and assistant directors and directors to influence the outcome of a properly conducted trial in front of a jury of the asshole's peers."

"Jesus Christ, Karen. You're shortening my life, you know that? Shaving away precious years."

"Not to sound unfeeling, but I'm the one who was nearly burned like a french fry. Talk about cutting one's life short. So let's keep things in perspective."

"How close are you to catching this Crush Killer?"

Vail sighed deeply. She needed some caffeine. And a vacation. *Oh yeah, this* was *my vacation.* "Not as close as I wish we were."

"I think your time in Napa is coming to a close. I want you to wrap things up and catch a flight out tomorrow night. I'll have Lenka email you the confirmation number for your flight."

"I can't just leave. We—"

"Karen, you're not doing anyone any good. For some reason, the killer seems to be playing off you. We remove you from the equation, maybe things will quiet down. I'll ask the San Ramon RA to send over an agent to monitor the situation and act as liaison."

*He can't do this. They'll never catch this asshole. But is Gifford right? Am I just serving to stir him up? Who am I to think I'm the only one who can catch this killer?*

"Karen, you hear me?"

"I—yes, I hear you."

"Good. Now you leave Timothy Nance alone and keep your ears clean till your flight leaves." And he hung up.

Vail stood there, her cell still pressed against her ear, eyes closed, drained of emotion and energy and, well, numb. She lowered her arm, put her phone away, and turned to walk down the hall.

"Everything okay?"

Dixon's voice. Vail looked up, saw Dixon, Brix, and Owens staring at her.

"Yeah, I just—I could use some coffee. Since sleep isn't coming any time soon, I need caffeine." She nodded down the corridor. "Are we going to meet with Nance?"

Brix shook his head. "He's going to lawyer up as soon as we start questioning him."

Vail nodded. "The congressman has already used some juice, trying to get us to back off."

"That's pretty strong juice," Owens said.

Vail folded her arms across her chest. "Damage control, is all it is. If his district director is dirty, Church is dirty by association. This is a man who has designs on running for governor. Any kind of association with an attempted murder could cause serious problems for those ambitions."

Owens was shaking his head. "We should let this lie low. We've got Walton Silva. Maybe that's enough for now."

"If Nance was a conspirator in trying to kill you, would nailing only one of them be enough? Because that's what happened here, Sheriff. Nance and Silva and, yes, your stepson, tried to fry me alive."

Owens shaded red, then stepped forward. "I've had just about enough of you!"

Dixon and Brix moved together, cutting off Owens's path toward Vail, who had staggered back.

Owens extended an arm through the blockade and pointed at Vail. "Their only crime was that they didn't succeed."

Vail recovered and stepped forward herself, daring Owens to come at her again. "You want to clear Scott's name, Sheriff? Question Nance, see what he says. Maybe Silva's lying. Maybe Scott had nothing to do with it." She desperately wanted to face Nance, see what he gave up. And better the order come from Owens, which would insulate her.

Owens shrugged off Dixon and Brix. "Scott wouldn't have anything to do with this. He's innocent—and now he's dead. For all I know, you're the one who shot him."

"C'mon now," Dixon said. "I've spent an awful lot of time with Karen these past few days and I can tell you, that's just not what she's about."

Owens turned away, strode a few paces down the hall. Wiped at his face, then placed both hands on his hips. Without turning around, he said, "Go. See if he'll talk to you."

<hr />

BRIX WALKED INTO the task force conference room, followed by Vail and Dixon. They took their seats around the table. Nance, in his requisite dark suit, white shirt, and maroon tie, was already there, pacing in front of the whiteboard.

"Mind telling me what this is about?"

Vail looked at him, trying to get a read on his demeanor and body language. Was he, in fact, a conspirator in trying to kill her?

"Do you know a Walton Silva?" Vail asked.

Nance advanced on her, walked just a bit too close for normal speaking distance. He put both hands on his hips and looked down at her. "You know I know him, Agent Vail, otherwise I wouldn't be here."

Brix held up a hand. "Okay, Tim. You know him. We did know that. Question is, how well do you know him?"

"Look, don't insult me. Just come out and ask what you want to ask."

Vail glanced at Brix, who nodded. She said, "Did you conspire with Scott Fuller and Walton Silva to set the fire that almost killed me?"

"No. Next question."

"So if we search your house, your garage, your cell phone records, text message transcripts, none of it will implicate you?"

"We were friends, that's it. I knew him from high school."

"And you had nothing to do with the fire," Brix said.

He looked at Brix with an unwavering gaze. "Nothing."

"Then maybe you can help us out. What can you tell us about Walton and Scott?"

"I knew Scott better. He was a good guy. Walt is, too, but I don't spend much time with him."

"What's he like?" Vail asked. "Someone who's likely to get into trouble? Honorable?"

"Pretty honorable, yeah. Never did anything a typical teen wouldn't do. Other than that, I've never seen him get into serious trouble."

Here's where it would get a little dicey—but she wanted to see his reaction. "That's interesting, Mr. Nance, because Walton said you and he and Scott worked together to set the fire that nearly killed me."

Nance leaned forward, invading Vail's space, and placed a hand on the table beside hers. He was now six inches from her face.

Vail was tempted to head butt him. A quick crack across the bridge of his nose. It would hurt like hell—but it'd also feel quite good. She did not take well to men intimidating her. An image of her ex-husband, Deacon, flashed through her thoughts. There's no way Nance would pull this on a man; she knew that.

"Bullshit," he said. "Why the hell would he say that?"

Vail rose from her chair, driving him backwards. She stepped forward, now invading his space and causing him to tilt ever so slightly onto his heels. "Oh, he did more than just say it, Mr. Nance. He wrote it. Three pages worth. Describing how, and why, you guys set the fire. Something to do with Congressman Church running for governor—

and taking the three of you along with him and naming you to important posts in his administration."

Nance tugged at his tie, loosened the knot. "First, it's all bullshit. And second, Walt wouldn't do that."

"Do what, write it all down or set the fire?"

Nance narrowed his eyes. "I don't believe you."

"Then I guess we're even," Vail said. "Because we don't believe you, either."

"And I'm done talking."

Brix rose from his chair. "Then that's two things we agree on. Because we're done talking, too."

———

LEAVING THE TIMOTHY NANCE MATTER to Sheriff Owens to sort out, Vail and Dixon headed out of the county building.

Dixon pushed open the front door. "What's your take?"

Vail held it open for a large man who was entering. "Nance is cool, no doubt about it. But Silva had no reason to lie. Nance is guilty, but whether or not you can prove it is another matter. And making a case against him might be difficult. Unless we find more forensics around his place, the case is Silva's word against Nance's. Who's the jury going to believe?"

Before Dixon answered, Ray Lugo came walking up the steps.

"You're late for the party," Dixon said.

"Oh, yeah? Judging by the look on your faces, it doesn't look like I missed anything. But here's something we don't want to miss." He held up his cell phone. "Just got a call. Kevin Cameron wants to talk."

# THIRTY-THREE

**K**evin Cameron had physically aged in the past two days. As he stood by his open front door, he had the darkness of depression in his eyes, which were puffed, glassy, and bloodshot. His hair was uncombed and his cuffed dress shirt had days-old wear-creases.

Ray Lugo gave Cameron a shoulder hug, then reintroduced him to Vail and Dixon. The four of them stood there, silent, until Lugo said, "Why don't we go for a walk?"

Cameron nodded, then motioned them to a path around the back of the house, which led to a compacted, decomposed granite path that cut through a rose garden. Twenty paces ahead was a well-tended vineyard. A couple of workers were down one of the aisles, huddled around a vine.

They walked in pairs, Lugo and Cameron ahead of Vail and Dixon. Their shoes crunched the walkway as they waited for Cameron to start talking. When he failed to initiate the conversation, Vail glanced at Dixon, who nodded. Vail said, "Kevin, Ray tells us there's something you want to talk about."

"Yeah."

But though he kept walking, he stopped talking. Finally, he reached a freshly painted wood structure. It was a small gazebo, built into the side of the path, and looked out upon the vineyard and vine-lined mountains in the near distance. From here, they looked like tight corn-rows on a smooth scalp.

Cameron stepped into the gazebo and took a seat. On the round table sat an opened bottle of 2003 F&M Georges Valley Family Estates Syrah beside a 2004 Opus One. Vail, Dixon, and Lugo took seats around the table. Cameron pulled the corks, then lifted both bottles and gestured to the glasses in front of them. Normally, law enforcement officers did not drink on duty, let alone in the morning. But Vail remembered reading about Opus One's world class wines and its price—somewhere near $200 a bottle. It was like the snake in a famous garden she'd heard about as a child. In fact, the setting, as beautiful as it was, probably was fitting. As idyllic as Eden?

She looked up at Cameron and pointed at his left hand, which held the uncorked bounty.

"Opus One," Vail said. "A competitor?"

"The CEO is a friend," Cameron said. He did not elaborate.

He tipped the bottle and the rich, garnet-tinted wine filled her glass. The others apparently felt she'd opened the door, because they all indicated their various preferences. Lugo no doubt feeling allegiance to his friend and not wanting to hurt his feelings, chose the Georges Valley Syrah. Dixon sided with Vail.

Vail brought the glass to her nose, as Dixon had instructed her, and sniffed. *Oh. This is heavenly.* She moved it to her lips and sipped. *No, this is heavenly.* Creamy, with cherry and spice—anise—caressing her tongue. Closed her eyes. Wished Robby was here enjoying this with her, that Dixon and Lugo and Cameron were not.

"So," Dixon said, swirling the wine and watching the law of centrifugal force play out in her glass. "You have information for us?"

Cameron took a long sip from his glass—he, too, chose the Syrah—and swallowed before answering. "I was thinking about the stuff I told you, about the feud."

"It goes back a long time," Vail said. "It's not likely the catalyst here."

Cameron nodded. "I know. You're probably right. But there's something more recent that happened, I remember Victoria talking about it. I mean, it wasn't a big deal. Or she didn't think so at first. But there was this phone call that really upset her."

"Who called?"

"All I know is that it was someone who knew about the disagreement on the AVA board. So someone with insider knowledge."

Vail set down her glass and leaned forward. "Back up a second. What disagreement?"

"The AVA board—"

She held up a hand. "This is the group that oversees various things that occur in a particular growing region. That's the AVA board, right? I'm just trying to remember what you told us last time."

"Yeah, that's it. It's a nonprofit group, a consortium set up to look after political issues that crop up, like enforcing the boundaries of the AVA's brand. And promotional stuff—tastings, press releases, website content, that sort of thing."

"These are elected positions?"

"Yes." Cameron took a drink. "But the AVA is a low-key group, working in the background to enhance the appellation's value. Battles erupt, but not very often."

"What kind of battles?" Dixon asked.

Cameron held up his glass to the sun and studied the remaining wine. Then he drained his glass and poured another.

"Political. There's something that's been going on for a long time now. There are a few vintners on the board that want to modify the federal government's regulations for our AVA. The current regulation, if enforced, would destroy our brands—and our businesses. So we've been fighting it."

"How would it destroy your brands?" Lugo asked.

"The law now requires a wine that puts itself out as being in the Georges Valley District to contain 85 percent grapes grown in Georges Valley. But a few of us want the government to change it so we can use the name Georges Valley without having to have 85 percent Georges Valley grapes in the wine."

Vail crossed her legs and leaned back in her chair. "Why would some vintners be opposed to that?"

Cameron tipped the glass and drank. He licked his lips, then said, "Because Georges Valley is a premium brand, with a well-established quality and cachet associated with it. The fear is new wineries could come into the region and turn out low-priced, high-volume produc- tion wines. They couldn't possibly get the yield they want from Georges Valley, so they would have to buy cheaper grapes from Contra Costa County, the Central Valley, and Livermore. They could then call their wine Georges Valley Reserve. But there wouldn't be any Georges Valley grapes in it."

"I haven't heard anything about this," Dixon said.

Lugo shook his head. "Me either."

Cameron forced a smile. "Bad publicity. We keep it under wraps, but it's gotten pretty contentious at times."

"We'll need the names of the players," Dixon said. "All the board members."

Cameron sat back. "I don't think it gets *that* heated, that anyone would want to kill over it."

"It's business," Vail said. "Business is money. Big money, is my guess. And people kill over money all the time." *But serial killers don't kill over money, and they kill strangers, not people they work with on local boards. So this still doesn't fit.*

"I'll have a list faxed over to your office," Cameron said.

Dixon took the last sip, then set down her empty glass. "Who sits on the AVA board? What type of people?"

Cameron poured more wine for himself, then offered it around the table. But the cops had had enough. "Just about all are winery executives. The president's position rotates every three years."

"Do all AVA boards operate this way?" Dixon asked.

"They all vary in how they work. Georges Valley is different than most, I think."

Vail was suddenly lost in thought, sifting through something her brain was trying to tell her. What was it? AVAs . . . winery executives . . . she had seen something somewhere . . . *Vallejo. Maryanne Bernal was a winery executive sitting on a nonprofit board.* She would have to check to see which one.

"Did you know Maryanne Bernal?" Vail asked.

Cameron looked at Vail. "Yeah, she was a friend of Victoria's. She was killed about three—" Cameron stopped himself. "You don't think the two are related—"

Vail pursed her lips. "Can't say, Kevin. Maybe, maybe not. But we'll check it out. Maryanne was on a nonprofit board. Do you know which one it was?"

"Yeah, the AVA board."

"Was she still on the board at the time of her death?"

"No, her time on the board went back a couple years before that, I think."

Vail looked away. She had hoped Bernal was an active board member—that might have helped provide a needed link. Still, it was worth looking into. Victoria was on the board and she was killed. Maryanne Bernal was on the board a couple years earlier and she was killed.

"Connection?" Dixon asked.

Lugo started bouncing his knee. "What about the Black Knoll vic? Ursula Robbins. Was she on the board?"

Cameron looked off into the vineyard, as if it'd hold the answer. "Not sure. Name doesn't ring a bell."

"We'll check it out," Dixon said. "Ray, you backgrounded her."

Lugo nodded. "I don't remember anything about her being on the board. But the winery she headed up is in Georges Valley. I'll look into it."

Cameron took a long drink. His cheeks were now flushed and his pupils were slightly dilated. Vail and Dixon shared a look.

"While you're checking that out," Cameron said, "there was something Victoria was working on. Something about corking. There was a lot of discussion about it."

"Corking?" Vail asked. "Like in corking wine bottles?"

"One thing this AVA does, which is unusual, is that they pool their resources. Normally the member wineries are friendly competitors. But they realized a few years ago that if they work together to negotiate deals with third parties, they could get significantly better prices. Power in numbers. Get two dozen wineries together, you've suddenly got pricing power when bottling, buying corks, labels, barrels, you name it."

"Corks," Vail said. "We'll look into it. Anything specific?"

Cameron took another drink. "Nope. I just remember her mentioning something about it. Maybe it's significant, maybe it's not." He looked down at his glass. "If you don't mind letting yourselves out, I think I'm just going to sit here and finish off these bottles."

Lugo rose, placed a hand on his friend's left shoulder, then led the others off the property.

# THIRTY-FOUR

On the way back to the car, Dixon called Detective Eddie Agbayani in Vallejo and told him about the connection between Maryanne Bernal and the Georges Valley AVA board. Dixon, being lead investigator, made the executive decision to add him to the task force. It was something she should have done upon the discovery that Bernal was one of the Crush Killer's victims. Vail certainly hadn't suggested it, nor had Brix, but Vail wondered if Dixon's relationship with Agbayani gave her pause. Still, the short delay in adding him had not had any ill effects on the investigation, and, their prior relationship notwithstanding, Agbayani appreciated the appointment.

"Are you okay with seeing Eddie regularly at the task force?"

"Hopefully, for our sake, this task force won't be around much longer. But as to Eddie, I imagine we'll have our awkward moments. The thing is, he's a really good guy. I miss him. I miss the intimacy, sharing things with a life partner I can trust. No games."

Vail chuckled, with a tinge of sarcasm. "I had a life partner once. Turns out I couldn't trust him and he had a whole arsenal of games up his sleeve."

"This is your ex?"

"Was my ex. Yeah."

"But now you've got Robby."

Vail smiled. "Yeah. I do. I lucked out." A long, hard yawn stretched her jaw wide. She shook her head. "Sorry. I need something to wake me up, I feel like my blood's gone stagnant." She turned to look out the window. "Is there a Starbucks around?"

"You won't find any chains around here." Dixon turned the ignition key and the engine turned over. "We've got some good cafés, but enough abusing your body." She twisted her wrist and grabbed a look at her watch. "I've got something better. We're entitled to a little downtime. Instead of breakfast, let's take an hour now."

———

THEY ARRIVED AT DIXON'S GYM, a Fit1! chain that featured a vast array of free weights, ellipticals and treadmills, and Ivanko machines. No saunas or juice bars. Plenty of sweat and body odor to go around, however.

While Vail bought an inexpensive pair of shorts and a T-shirt from the front desk, Dixon signed in, paid a one-day guest fee for Vail, then handed her a towel and locker key. "We'll do some weights, then shower. I promise, you'll feel a whole lot better."

Vail chuckled. "I'll feel better just from putting on the new clothes Robby bought." She slung the towel over her shoulder. "I was beginning to ease back into my regular workout routine after my surgery. You really think we can get in and out in an hour?"

"We'll do what we can do. My regular routine is about two hours a day. I usually come after work. No way would I get in a full workout before a long day at work."

Thirty cardio minutes later, sporting a reddened face and a half-drained water bottle, Vail joined Dixon in the free weights area, where Dixon was hoisting a curl bar loaded with iron discs.

"How goes it?"

Dixon puffed. "Good. Feels. Good."

"I'm gonna run to the restroom, then do a few machines."

"I'll. Be. Here," Dixon said as she strained the last rep.

Vail walked away and Dixon set down the barbell, then walked over to the shoulder press. She stacked the bar with weight on both sides, then sat on the bench. But she needed a partner to spot her. Given her irregular hours, she often did not cross paths with the same people when she was able to make it to the gym. Nevertheless, she usually found someone willing to help—and she never hesitated to return the favor.

Behind her, a lean, well-built man in a ripped tank top stood at the weight rack, large hands wrapped around thick dumbbells. He lifted them off the metal framework with a clean jerk, then proceeded to start curling.

He must have seen Dixon looking at him in the mirror, because he smiled.

Dixon grinned. A bit too much—it was her flirt smile. She stepped forward and said, "Sorry to interrupt."

The man set the weights down on the ground with a thud. His eyes flicked behind her to the bench, then back to her. "Need help with that? A spot?"

She smiled again. She rotated her body toward the bench, then back to her new acquaintance. "Would you mind?"

He waved a hand in front of him. "Not at all."

As he approached, her eyes widened. She liked what she saw. Raw attraction—she didn't even know the guy.

"You a regular here?" she asked.

"Every day for the past five years. You?"

"I try to get in at night after work, but I don't always make it." She extended her hand. "Roxxann Dixon."

"George." He removed his glove and took her hand in his. "George Panda."

*Soft hands, firm handshake.* "Thanks for doing this."

"Maybe I can get you to return the favor when you're done."

"I'm not sure I'd be much help spotting you." That was an understatement. Then again, he was probably flirting with her just like she was with him. "But sure, it's a deal."

Dixon slipped on her gloves, settled herself onto the bench, and placed her hands beneath the bar. She got a good grip, took a deep breath, and then realized she was wearing her lower cut fitness top, which, when she lifted the weight, might show significant cleavage. But as the song in *The Producers* says, "When you've got it, flaunt it."

Dixon hoisted the bar and huffed and puffed as it rose and fell. Panda kept his hands at the ready, but they weren't needed until Dixon strained for the twelfth rep, which went up slowly and with considerable groaning. She locked her elbows.

Before she could speak, Panda said, "Go one more. I'll help."

She lowered it slowly, then strained to raise it again. A yell escaped her throat and she arched her back. "Ahh!"

"C'mon, Roxxann," Panda said, "you can do it. Just a little higher." He had his hands under the bar, poised to take over if she got into danger.

She brought it up fully, her arms quivering involuntarily, and that was his cue. She gasped, "Take it!"

Panda did exactly that and settled the heavy bar into the weight cradles. She let her arms fall to her sides and stuck out her tongue for effect.

"Great job."

She shook her arms, then swung her legs around and sat up, facing him. "Thanks."

"My pleasure." He looked around, then clapped his hands together. "Tell you what—instead of spotting me, how about you let me take you to dinner?"

Dixon felt her eyebrows lift in surprise. "Wow. Uh, I'd love to," she said before she realized she was the one speaking.

"How about Saturday?"

"Saturday? I—well, maybe I could take a raincheck on that? Things are really busy at work, and I just don't know what my schedule's going to be."

"Hey, Bear, what's up?"

Approaching from the right was a large man, pushing six-four, a smidgen leaner than Panda, with a buzz cut and a military gait. He carried a near-empty Platypus two-liter water bottle.

Dixon turned back to her new workout partner. "Bear?"

"Roxxann, this is a buddy of mine. James Cannon. Bear's my nickname."

Dixon squinted. Then she tilted her chin back. "Ah. Panda. Bear."

Cannon gave Panda a shove. "George here didn't like it when I'd yell out, 'Hey, Panda,' in the gym. Some of the bodybuilders gave him a hard time. They thought it was a pet name or something."

"And let me guess," Dixon said. "Your nickname is Cannon."

"Actually, I go by 'Bob.'" He laughed. "Just messing with you. Name's Jimmy."

"I thought you were working out."

Dixon turned; Vail was coming up behind her, eyes bouncing from Panda to Cannon.

"We were. I mean, I was. Karen, this is George, and Jimmy."

Panda extended a hand. This time he didn't bother to remove his glove. "George Panda." Cannon shifted the water bottle to his other hand and took Vail's palm firmly.

"Karen Vail. Good to meet both of you. But," she said, nudging Dixon in the side, "we're running out of time. We should shower, get back to work."

"You two work together?" Panda asked.

Dixon swiped at her forehead with a towel. "I'm an investigator with the district attorney's office."

"I knew someone who worked for the DA." Panda shook his head. "That was a long time ago."

Cannon leaned back and appraised Vail. "Let me guess. You must be one of the attorneys."

Vail smirked. "God, no. I'm with the FBI. Out of Virginia."

"FBI," Cannon said. "Very cool."

"Visiting the wine country?" Panda asked.

"That was the plan," Vail said. "Work kind of got in the way."

Panda's gaze flicked from Vail to Dixon. "Uh-oh. Trouble in paradise?"

"Nothing we can talk about," Vail said. "And believe me, it's nothing you'd want to hear about anyway."

Cannon bent his head to the side and asked Vail, "I feel like we've met before."

Vail shook her head. "I've only been in town a few days."

"And what do you two do?" Dixon asked.

George tightened the Velcro strap on his glove. "I'm a consultant."

"Are you with a company, or out on your own?"

"Totally solo." He moved to the other glove, adjusted the strap. "I worked for a corporation years ago and swore that was the last time I was ever going to answer to anybody."

Cannon moaned. "Oh, not the big, bad corporation story again."

"I'm not gonna tell them the story, Jimmy, don't worry." Panda turned to Dixon and Vail and held out an open hand in explanation. "It's just that people think they know better than you, but they're either wrong or just plain clueless. I got tired of it, is all."

"And you?" Vail asked Cannon. "What do you do?"

He set the water bottle down at his feet. "I'm a winemaker. Herndon Vineyards."

Vail's eyes traversed his body. "You don't look like any winemaker I've ever met."

Cannon pursed his lips. "I'll take that as a compliment."

Dixon wrapped her towel around her neck. "Never heard of Hern—Hernd—"

"Herndon. Herndon Vineyards. You *will* hear of us, guaranteed. We're a closely held, private startup. We've got some of the best soil outside of Rutherford, with well-bedded sandstone and high gravel and volcanic content, and excellent runoff. Warm days, cool nights. We're planning to debut our first release in two years. It'll be the best Cabernet you've ever tasted. Believe me—couple years, everyone'll know who we are."

Panda shook his head. "You gave me a hard time about telling my corporation story and you bore these nice ladies with your company's sales pitch?"

Cannon gave Panda another playful shove. "My sales pitch beats your 'woe-is-me evil corporation story' any day. Beats your consulting stories, too."

"Speaking of which," Dixon said, "what kind of consulting do you do? What industry?"

Panda placed a hand on the upright of the shoulder press machine. "Despite what Jimmy says, I think consulting's a pretty good gig." He fiddled with the iron plate. "I do critical thinking, strategic solutions. Pay's damn good, so no complaints."

"I'm into critical thinking, too," Vail said. She pointed to her wrist, where there was no watch. "And we'd better get back to doing that. I'll meet you in the locker room." She extended a hand to Panda. "Good meeting you, George. Jimmy."

"Same here," Panda said.

Cannon quickly glanced from Dixon to Vail. "You, uh, you two doing anything for dinner?" He indicated Panda. "Maybe the four of us could—"

"Thanks," Vail said. "I'm busy. But thanks for asking." She made eye contact with Dixon and waved a thumb over her shoulder. "Meet you inside."

Cannon tucked his chin back and watched Vail walk off. "I think I just got rejected."

"New experience for you?" Dixon said with a laugh. "Don't take it personally. She's seeing someone."

Cannon turned to Dixon. His face seemed to harden. "Yeah." He bent down to pick up his water bottle. "Catch you later, Bear. I'm gonna hit the showers." He tossed a tight nod at Panda, did not acknowledge Dixon, then left.

Dixon swung her gaze toward Panda. "I didn't—I didn't mean anything by that. You think I hurt his feelings?"

Panda waved at the air. "Bruised ego is all. He'll be fine. He doesn't take rejection well."

"Who does?"

Panda grinned. "This is true."

Dixon blotted her face with the towel. "You done with your workout?"

Panda glanced around at all the equipment. "No, I've still got another hour or so on the weights, then I'm gonna do some cardio."

"Why don't I call you when I have a better handle on what my work schedule looks like?"

Panda nodded. "Sounds good." He gave Dixon his number.

She committed it to memory and told him she'd call him. "You want, you can always reach me through the DA's office. We're listed." Dixon gave him a broad smile. "Or maybe we'll meet up again here."

"I'd like that," Panda said.

Dixon winked. "Thanks again for your help. *Bear.*"

———

JOHN WAYNE MAYFIELD sat in his truck, slumped down in the seat, watching the exit to the Fit1! gym. Waiting around was not something he enjoyed, but it was often necessary in his line of work. So he continued to sit and surveil the entrance as the minutes ticked by.

Several men had left the gym, as well as a couple of women, but not the ones he was waiting on. He had followed Dixon and Vail to the gym, so he knew what car they had arrived in and where they parked. He had positioned his pickup so that he had a view of both the entrance and their vehicle. If they left through another exit, he'd still see them when they arrived at their car.

Mayfield checked his watch. *How long can they possibly be in there? Don't they have policework that needs attention? Haven't I given them enough to do?* As he sat there drumming his fingers on the dashboard, the front door swung open and out walked Dixon and Vail.

*About fucking time.* Dixon had a tote slung across her shoulder and a bounce in her step. He watched as the two of them walked to their car. Dixon shoved her key into the lock and lifted the trunk lid, then tossed her sport bag into the back and closed it.

*Your time will come, Roxxann Dixon. Very soon.* This afternoon? Perhaps. Perhaps not. He had much to consider—least of which was what approach would provide him with maximum impact.

He would use the time while tailing them to mull his options. Maybe something would come to him, a plan of action.

Mayfield turned the key and started the engine. He'd continue following them for now to see where they were headed with their investigation. That might help him formulate a cogent approach, ultimately making his job easier.

He pulled out of the parking lot and maintained a discreet distance. A mile or so down 29, an idea began to form. *Take the local first. Dixon. It'll throw everyone into a state of panic. I won't leave them a choice—they'll have to talk to the press. Because I'll leave the body in a very public place, posed, in front of City Hall, right on the stairs. Late at night, so when the bureaucrats arrive in the morning, it'll be like a blow to the throat. The press will swarm. Then I'll do Vail, an FBI profiler, and leave her body somewhere else, somewhere public. A double header. State and Federal. They'll fucking freak. The entire country will be tuned in.*

He rolled down his window. The blast of cold air snaked around his neck and made him shiver—exactly what he needed. He had to cool down before he did something he was not yet prepared for, something he would later regret.

*Enjoy your final hours, Roxxann Dixon. You may soon suffer a crushing blow to your life's ambitions.*

# THIRTY-FIVE

Vail walked out of Fit1! feeling refreshed, clean, and, at least for now, invigorated. The exercise had sharpened her mind and given her a renewed sense of focus. They each downed nutrition bars Dixon had in her gym bag and were now headed to meet with the AVA board president.

Once she had turned onto Highway 29, Dixon said, "I thought George was kind of cute."

"Really?" Vail faced the side window and watched the wineries pass to her right. "He didn't do anything for me."

Dixon laughed. "Well I can tell you that Jimmy wanted to do something for *you*."

Vail chuckled. "Yeah he did. Did I blow him off properly?"

"That watch thing was a bit obvious."

Vail feigned innocence. "Was I wrong? We're on a schedule." She smiled. "But seriously. Are you really ready to give up on Eddie? Is that over? For good? I thought you said you missed him, that you were just going to take some time off."

Dixon sighed. "I don't know. Sometimes I think it's over, then sometimes I think it's not. We love each other. That's not the problem. We just, I'm just not sure we're compatible."

"Was he good to you, did he treat you well?"

"Yeah, that was never an issue."

"So you two have some issues. All couples do. But you love each other, isn't that worth something?"

"If it wasn't, we wouldn't still be discussing this."

"So this guy in the gym—George. Is he better than Eddie?"

"Better? I just met him. How the hell do I know?"

Vail turned her body to face Dixon. "You're attracted to him."

"And that's a bad thing?"

"Of course not," Vail said. "My take? He'd be a good workout partner. But he didn't seem to have much depth to him."

A moment passed. "That's a pretty huge leap based on one short conversation."

"I make my living reading people," Vail said.

"And your read of Jimmy?"

"Please." She scrunched her nose. "He may be a winemaker, but . . . I wouldn't even want to work out with the guy."

Dixon drove another minute before speaking. "Why'd you bring it up?"

Vail rubbed her eyes. "Because I had a shitty marriage. It didn't start out that way, but it sure ended that way. So I'm pretty careful. No, I'm extra cautious. I wouldn't even think of getting involved with someone unless I knew certain things about the guy, about his heart. And his soul."

"And you know all this about Robby?"

Vail sucked on her bottom lip and thought a moment. "It's funny. I haven't known him that long, but we've been through a hell of a lot together. I trust him. Implicitly."

Before Dixon could respond, her phone rang. She pressed the hands-free device on her visor and answered the call.

"Roxx, it's Brix. I got an ID on the male. Where are you two?"

Dixon peered out her window. "Coming up on Opus One. We're headed to a meeting with someone from the AVA board."

"Fine. Pull into the Opus One lot. I'll be there in five. I won't keep you long. But you need to hear this."

———

BRIX WAS A LITTLE LONGER than five minutes out, but Vail didn't mind. When they arrived at Opus One, Dixon had phoned the board president and told her they would be delayed. During the call, she led Vail up to Opus One's terrace roof, which afforded a 360 degree panoramic view of the immediate valley. Parceled vineyards stretched in all directions, with the peaks of Mt. Veeder in the near distance.

The terrace was an arbor-covered walkway and patio bordered by rough-hewn limestone walls and planters lining the path. Ahead of them, over the edge, was a lush lawn that sloped gently downward, from the lip of the roof all the way to the parking lot.

"It'd be fun to roll down that," Vail said.

Dixon's phone rang. Glancing at the caller ID, she brought it to her ear. "We're upstairs on the roof." She listened, then said, "Yeah, meet us up here."

Thirty seconds later, Brix ascended the staircase and met them at the stone table. Off at the opposite end of the terrace, in a matching area containing tables, a couple stood beside one another at the wall, nursing a glass of wine and taking in the mountain view before them.

They took seats and Brix pulled out his notepad. "I've got a couple IDs for us. With all that's been going on, this kind of got lost in the shuffle. The male victim was Isaac Jenkins. Private equity fund manager who lives in Sonoma."

"And how did we keep *that* murder under wraps?" Dixon asked.

"Wife told his company, family, and friends that Isaac had a heart attack. Given what his business is like, and this market, there's enough stress for ten heart attacks."

Vail nodded. "Is he on the Georges Valley AVA board?"

"That'd be a 'no.' I had Ray check it out. He's got no connection to the board that we could turn up. Ray also followed up on the question of how the UNSUB got your cell number. He said there was no breach of the department's data backup, as far as the IT guys can tell. And all support personnel have been questioned. No one gave out our phone numbers, or any other information, to anyone."

"Then how did he get my number?"

Brix put his forearms on the round cement table. "I love this view. You can see for miles. And it's all gorgeous. This is a plot of land I wish we had for Silver Ridge."

"Redd," Dixon said. "The phone number."

He shook his head and refocused his gaze on Dixon. "Yeah. So Ray and I were thinking where else he could've gotten it. How about the Bureau?"

Vail leaned back in surprise. "Whoa, I didn't think of that. All he has to do is dial up the FBI Academy and ask for my cell phone number and they hand it right over."

"That's cute. But what I meant was, do you list it on your Academy emails?"

"Yeah, it's part of my signature, at the bottom of all my messages."

Brix raised his hands, palm up. "Then who the hell knows how he got it. Sending email is like putting an open envelope in the mail."

Vail nodded. She couldn't argue that.

Brix yawned, threw up a hand to cup his mouth. "I also have an ID on the female we found this morning. Or was that yesterday? I'm so fucking tired I can't remember anymore." He forced his eyes open wider, then said, "Name's Dawn Zackery. Thirty-two, single. And before you ask, no connection to the Georges Valley board."

Dixon looked at Vail. "I'm beginning to think that board is a dead end."

Vail stared out at the countryside. "Maybe, maybe not. If we haven't got anything else to pursue, then we'll turn over some rocks, see what we can find."

Brix began bouncing his knee. "I was thinking there was an angle we should look into first, something we kind of overlooked."

Dixon cocked her head. "And that is . . ."

"There's a guy," Brix said. "Someone we questioned early on. Scott actually wanted to bring him back in and talk to him. I resisted."

Vail brushed a lock of red hair behind her ear. "Why?"

"Well. . . ." He hesitated, then said, "Because he's an employee of Silver Ridge." He held up a hand. "I know what you're gonna say, and before you say it, you're right. I've got a conflict, and I think it colored my judgment on this. I'm sorry."

Vail waved it off. It wasn't something to be glossed over, but Brix came clean and there was nothing to be gained making him feel guilty about his error. "So this employee. Who is he?"

"The guy who found the body. Miguel Ortiz."

Vail leaned back. "I remember him. He gave me his flashlight. He seemed genuinely freaked by what he found. Then again, I didn't exactly have my guard up. I was on vacation. Could've just been an act, to deflect attention off himself."

Brix held out a hand. "There you go. Does he fit the profile?"

Vail bobbed her head about. "He's about the right age. Although the vast majority of serial killers are Caucasian, there have been a fair number of Hispanics. I can think of five just off the top of my head. That said, Ortiz is a low-level employee without the kind of access to information and people that our UNSUB's exhibited. From what I've seen, our offender is a much more complex killer."

"You thought of him, why?" Dixon asked.

Brix's eyes narrowed. "Not sure. Just a feeling. When I questioned him at the scene, he wouldn't look at me. He seemed very nervous."

"Maybe he knew you were one of the owners," Dixon said, "and he felt intimidated."

Brix twisted his lips. "Maybe. But he was the one who found Victoria's body. And Scott did a little checking before he—well, he did a little checking and he found that Ortiz didn't have an alibi for the other murders up to that point. But Ray thought we were wasting our breath. He just didn't think this was our guy."

"Because?"

"He said if there was a murderous Mexican looney on the loose, he would've heard about it in his community. He seemed pretty adamant that going after Ortiz was a waste of time."

"Serial killers are not 'looney,'" Vail said. "They're not insane or 'off their rockers.' They know what they're doing. Their actions are very purposeful. And they know murder is against the law. They just don't care."

"I checked with the HR person at Silver Ridge. She sees him from time to time when he's in the cave, rinsing the floors and washing out pails. According to her, he's always on time, works very hard and sends money back home to his sick mother. And if he needs something, like medical care, he pays for it. He doesn't live off the state. For what it's worth, in her words, he's harmless. A man with a good heart."

Vail smirked. "No offense to your HR administrator, but let's leave the threat assessment to us."

Brix shifted his weight on the bench. "There's something else about Ortiz." He paused a moment. "About an hour ago, when Agbayani arrived, I handed him the Ortiz lead and asked him to look into it. As soon as he heard the name, he thought it sounded familiar. Turns out Ortiz was a suspect in the Vallejo murder, Maryanne Bernal."

Dixon leaned forward. "No shit?"

Brix held up a finger. "Hang on a second. Before you get all excited, it was just an eyewitness account of a big guy with a white pickup. They picked him up and questioned him. He's got ties to Vallejo, a brother who lives there."

"An offender may dump a body in an area he's familiar with," Vail said.

Brix waved a hand. "Doesn't matter. It went nowhere. They had nothing on him. And he had no record, not so much as a misdemeanor. And he was one of about forty-five guys they ended up questioning who matched the description."

"So what did Agbayani think about Ortiz popping up again in connection with a murder investigation?" Vail asked.

"It wouldn't have been that big a deal. Except that someone fitting Ortiz's description was seen in the area at the time Isaac Jenkins was killed."

Vail lifted a brow. "You knew this? Why didn't you move on him?"

Brix let his gaze linger on Vail's. "I found out right around the time Scott was killed. We've been a little busy."

Vail held his gaze and didn't blink.

"Still," Dixon said, breaking the silent confrontation, "like what happened in Vallejo, a lot of guys fit his general description, so one witness account doesn't necessarily mean anything. Unless she picks him out of a lineup."

"She didn't see his face, only his body."

"His body?" Dixon sighed. "Make that a *poor* witness account. Well, it can't hurt to chat him up. Ask him about the two murders since then."

Brix shrugged. "It's probably not worth pursuing."

Vail slid her legs from beneath the cement table. "You've got a feeling about this. And we've got questions. I think we should go check it out. I'll call the AVA board president and tell her we need some more time."

Dixon rose as well. "Is Ortiz at Silver Ridge?"

Brix pushed himself off the cement bench as if he was lifting a heavy weight. "He's not working today. But he rents a room from a family off West Spain in downtown Sonoma."

"The male vic, Jenkins, he was from Sonoma."

"I'm aware of that," Brix said.

"How can we be sure Ortiz is going to be there?"

"I called the homeowner and she said Ortiz is home. She thinks he's sleeping."

"Does he know we're coming?" Dixon asked.

Brix shook his head. "If he is our guy—and I'm not ready to say that—then telling him we're coming by to question him may set him off. No, we'll go in quietly."

Vail led the way to the staircase, then glanced up one more time to grab a view of the vineyards. It was so peaceful up here. She hadn't felt an inner sense of tranquility since the day she and Robby arrived here. Her first visit to the Napa Valley, and it was marred by the rampage of a serial killer. Could she ever visit this place again and not be poisoned by memories of this case? It was a rhetorical thought. She already knew the answer.

"How do you know his landlord didn't tip him off?" Dixon asked.

Dixon's voice, echoing in the stairwell, pulled Vail out of her reverie. She realized she had spaced out, staring at the vineyards and mountains, smelling the soil-wet air. As she started down the steps, she heard Brix's voice somewhere below.

"I explained that we didn't want to make any trouble for her. But short answer is, we don't."

Vail's "short answer"—to her own rhetorical question—was more visceral. The magical Napa Valley would never be the same for her. The Crush Killer had ruined it. *Another reason to catch this bastard.* As she thought of all that had gone wrong these past few days, of all the victims this killer had now amassed, Vail realized she didn't need another reason to want to ratchet down a set of cuffs on his wrists.

━━━

THEY TOOK BRIX'S CAR and arrived in Sonoma thirty minutes later. The drive was as picturesque as any of the views they had seen along

Highway 29. Vineyards, rolling hills, mountains. And today, the hint of sun burning through the cloud cover.

"Welcome to Sonoma," Dixon said.

Vail craned her neck around, taking in the small and medium-sized residential homes. "Are there wineries in Sonoma, too?"

Despite the seriousness of their task ahead, Brix and Dixon, sitting beside one another in the front seat, looked at each other and laughed.

"I take it that was a stupid question," Vail said.

"That'd be a 'yes' twice over," Brix said. "First, it was a stupid question. This entire valley is wine country. Second, Sonoma is considered the birthplace of the California wine industry."

Vail turned away and looked out at the Readers Bookstore they were passing on the right. "Oh."

"Up ahead is the downtown plaza," Dixon said, as Brix turned right onto First Street East. "Besides historic wineries, Sonoma also has some interesting shops and galleries. And lots of good restaurants."

Vail pointed at a ground-hugging white adobe building with a large cross protruding from its roof. "What did that sign say? Mission San Francisco?"

"Mission San Francisco Solano," Brix said. "An old church."

Dixon threw Brix a look. "Give me a break. Calling that a church would be like calling Silver Ridge winery a 'grape juice manufacturing plant.'" She flicked the side of his head with a finger.

"Hey," Brix said.

Dixon turned to Vail. "California History 101. There are twenty-one missions. That one's the last one built—and the first one built under Mexico's rule, in the 1820s. It's also where the very first vineyards in the valley were planted. By monks who lived in the mission."

"Not to interrupt the history lesson," Brix said, "but we've got a *mission* of our own." He nodded ahead. "We're coming up on Ortiz's house." He slowed the car.

"Which one?" Dixon asked.

"Wait," Brix said, braking to a crawl. He leaned forward, peering in the right side view mirror. "He's right there. Behind us, I passed him."

Miguel Ortiz was walking the sidewalk, about thirty feet away. Brix pulled over to the curb.

Dixon popped her door. "You sure that's him?"

Brix shoved the shift into park and got out. He turned toward Ortiz, then caught Dixon's gaze. "Definitely."

Ortiz must have recognized Brix's voice, because he spun around. His eyes found the car . . . the look on Brix's face, the look on Dixon's.

And then he ran.

"Shit," Brix said. "Where the fuck does he think he's gonna go?" Brix jumped back into the Ford, jammed the gearshift into drive, and accelerated. He swung the car around. Dixon pursued on foot. And Vail unstrapped her seatbelt.

Ortiz crossed the street into the park that sat in the center of the square.

As Brix approached, Vail opened her door. "Let me off!"

Brix swung the car toward the curb and screeched to a stop. "Go."

Vail spilled out and fell into stride behind Dixon, who was about twenty-five feet off the pace. Ortiz was pretty quick for his size and was headed down the cement tile walk that cut diagonally through the park.

Off to their right lay a playground filled with young children climbing on the structures, mothers out for an early afternoon with their kids. If there was one thing the parents were not counting on when they arrived at the park with their children, it was finding themselves in the middle of a police pursuit.

"Miguel," Dixon yelled. "Wait up."

Vail quickly surveyed the kids. She yanked her badge from her belt and held it up, hoping the mothers would see and understand what was going down. Clearly, it had an effect, as a couple of them scooped up their children and swung them away from the approaching—and fleeing—suspect.

Vail to Ortiz: "We just want to talk!"

But he didn't stop.

A child ran out in front of him. Ortiz skirted the boy, who covered his face and ran back toward his mother, but Dixon was not so lucky—she shifted right, into the child's path—and went tumbling. She landed on her side amidst scattered sand and hard-packed dirt—narrowly avoiding a collision with a brick water fountain.

"Got him," Vail shouted, as she passed Dixon.

Dixon got back on her feet and slanted across the grass, taking an angle on Ortiz as he cut right onto the asphalt road that encircled the historic, stone-walled City Hall building. He ran past the structure into the front parking lot, then angled left, back into the park and across the grass.

*He's not going anywhere,* Vail realized. *He's just trying to get away. He's either our UNSUB . . . or he's done something wrong and does not want to face charges.*

Ortiz crossed East Napa Street—eliciting a blown car horn as he skirted by an Infiniti FX's hood—and ran straight into a narrow alley. No, not an alley—a covered sidewalk. A covered sidewalk that fed storefront shops.

*Great. Stores—and who knew what else. Is he cutting through here en route to a hiding place—or does he have a friend in a storefront who'll take him in and run interference?*

"Miguel," Vail yelled, "we just have some questions! You're not in any trouble—"

Ortiz ran underneath the ivy-covered archways. Vail followed—but there were no longer footsteps behind her. *Where's Roxxann?*

Vail passed beneath a sign that read, 42 Unique Shops & Services, slipped on the slick terracotta tile, then scampered past Chico's, an assortment of other stores, spas, and boutiques—thinking, *That blouse in the window would look good on me. I should come back here someday and browse, get a massage . . .*

Actually, Vail was thinking about her knee, which was beginning to balk. She heard her surgeon reminding her she wasn't supposed to be behaving like Lara Croft for at least another few weeks.

She passed a bubbling fountain, which tinkled splattered water on the slick tile, and she had to catch herself to keep from falling. *I'm sure the architect thought that was a nice touch, but he clearly didn't consider the danger it presented to a cop chasing a suspect on wet tile through an alley—*

The walkway dead-ended at a ramp, a salmon-and-pistachio tinted two-story stucco building directly ahead—and an oblong court that spread into a maze of more shops and buildings.

And more fountains. *Jeez, this architect is into water. What does that say about his childhood?*

Ortiz cut right, around a myriad of square columns that supported the various storefront overhangs, then ran into the two-story building's stairwell.

*Stairs, just what I need. Before I just wanted to question Ortiz. Now I'm not so sure. And where the hell is Roxxann?*

Vail followed him up and reached the second floor as her knee began throbbing. The staircase spilled out onto a covered outdoor veranda with doors that led to other shops and offices. *He could've cut left or right, but he chose to go upstairs. He must know something—or someone.* Her footsteps on the hollow flooring reverberated. If she had any thoughts of a stealth approach, it clearly wouldn't fly up here.

As she turned right, Vail saw Ortiz up ahead, grabbing a doorknob and pulling on it, then slapping the door. "Enrique, abre la puerta!" *Open the door!*

*This is where it stops getting interesting.* She pulled her Glock—she had no idea who Enrique was or what he had behind that door. Ortiz glanced back at her and his eyes found her pistol. If he wasn't scared before, his blood pressure must've just climbed a few dozen points . . . which was fine, because hers had now risen well above normal, as well.

But Ortiz abandoned his efforts to enter the store and continued on. Vail passed Enrique's door—marked Private—and watched as Ortiz turned right again and headed down the stairwell. Vail gave pursuit—and then heard shouting.

"Get down. Down on the ground!"

Dixon's voice. And she wasn't very happy.

Vail made it down the two dozen steps and there, spread eagle, face down on the ground, was Miguel Ortiz. Dixon, her SIG drawn and steadied out in front of her, stood fifteen feet away. Behind her, Brix pulled up along the side street and swung into the postage stamp parking lot. Jumped out, drew his weapon.

As Vail took a position to Dixon's left, Brix came up behind them. "Jesus Christ, Miguel. We just had some questions. What were you thinking?"

"I don't want to go back. Don't send me back!"

Vail and Brix shared a look. Brix closed his eyes, then holstered his weapon. "You ran because you're illegal?" He motioned to Dixon. "Let him up."

"But—"

"Miguel, get to your feet."

He stood up, keeping his hands above his head. "I thought you think I had something to do with that woman. In the cave. After we talk the other day, I was worried. I no want to go back home."

"If you had something to do with that woman in the cave," Vail said, "we'd arrest your ass. And believe me, you wouldn't ever see home again."

Brix stepped closer and banded his arms across his chest. "Miguel, we need you to tell us the truth. Will you do that?"

"Sí, sí."

Brix nodded at Dixon, who holstered her weapon and did a thorough pat down of their suspect.

She stepped back. "He's clean."

"You can put your hands down." Brix shook his head. "When you run from the police, we think you're guilty of something."

"No, no guilty."

"Okay, then. You haven't told anyone what you saw in that cave, have you?"

"No, you tell me not to. It was important, no?"

"Yes, that's exactly right. It's important. It's still important."

"I won't tell." He shifted his feet nervously. "Can I go now?"

"In a minute. First, tell us about Isaac Jenkins."

Miguel's eyes flittered between Brix, Dixon, and Vail. "Who?"

"What about Dawn Zackery?"

Miguel shook his head. "I do not know these people."

"Where were you yesterday?"

"In the vineyard, tending to the vines."

"Where?"

Ortiz pointed at Brix. "In yours. Silver Ridge, the Bella Broxton Cabernet vineyard."

"Who were you with?" Brix asked.

"Mr. Styles. We were putting sulfur on the vines and working the soil. For the cover."

Brix turned to Vail. "We sometimes use a cover crop between the rows as an early warning system. If there's something affecting the vines, the cover will show it first." To Ortiz: "When were you with Mr. Styles?"

"All day. From six in the morning to sundown."

"I'm going to ask Mr. Styles, Miguel. Will he tell me you were with him the whole time? Did you ever leave him?"

"We were in different rows of the vineyard. But we were talking the whole time. Yes, he will tell you that."

"And what about after you left Mr. Styles? Where were you and who were you with?"

Ortiz squinted, looked off at the parking lot behind them. "I went home, had dinner with Enrique. My friend."

"Anyone else see you?"

"The people in the restaurant. El Brinquito."

Brix nodded. "I know the place. I'm going to check that out, too. And what time did you leave?"

Ortiz looked down and rubbed at his forehead. "I think it was around eight. I went home. Miss Wright can tell you. And I stay there all night and then went to bed."

Brix pulled out his phone, flipped it open, and aimed it at Ortiz. The electronic click of a simulated camera shutter sounded. "You can go, Miguel. But next time when you see the police, don't run. Especially if it's me."

Ortiz nodded with an embarrassing shift of his eyes. He walked off, his head down. When he was far enough away, Vail said, "He's illegal. You knew that?"

Brix pocketed his phone, then lifted a shoulder. "If we got rid of all the illegals in California, it'd bring our economy to a screeching halt."

Vail watched Ortiz in the distance as he crossed East Napa Street. "If Ortiz were a serial killer, he'd fit more in line with a disorganized killer. Not very sociable, lower education, average intelligence at best, manual labor type job. But like I said before, our offender is more complex. He's predominantly organized. He brings the weapon with him. He's purposeful, he plans his kills. He's intelligent, sharp, and re-sourceful. Bottom line, Ortiz doesn't look like our UNSUB."

"I didn't think so," Brix said. "Still, I'll check out his story, just to be sure."

"And that means we're still nowhere," Dixon said.

Vail turned and headed into the parking lot, toward Brix's car. "Not nowhere, Roxx. Just not where we want to be."

# THIRTY-SIX

As they settled into Brix's Crown Victoria, Ray Lugo phoned to tell Brix he was on his way to Sonoma to hand deliver new information. His ETA was ten minutes.

While waiting, Brix emailed Vail his camera photo of Ortiz, and then she and Dixon walked over to the visitor's bureau, which backed up to City Hall in the square's parklike center. The interior office space was pleasant, filled with maps, signage for events and area promotions, and brochure racks.

Vail and Dixon showed the staff Ortiz's picture and asked if they knew him. Both women said they had seen him around, but had never observed any unusual or unruly behavior.

As they left, Vail said, "I didn't think that'd get us anywhere."

"You never know when you're going to run across a victim who escaped alive, someone who's too scared to go to the cops. Or one guy who heard another guy bragging about his kill."

By the time they returned to the car, Lugo was pulling alongside Brix, who was leaning against the front quarter panel of his Ford.

Lugo got out, holding a manila folder above his head. "Kevin called me. He was going through Victoria's things and found her file of board notes." He handed them to Dixon. "I started to go through them but then remembered you were meeting with the board president today."

"We were supposed to have already met but we pushed it back to chat with Miguel Ortiz."

Lugo shook his head. "Let me guess. Waste of time."

"It was worth a shot," Brix said with a shrug. "I've got some things to follow up on, but yeah. Looks that way."

Lugo nodded at the folder in Dixon's hand. "Hopefully that'll help you out when you meet with that board president."

Vail consulted her watch. "Speaking of which, let's get going."

Vail and Dixon took Lugo's car, leaving Brix to partner with Lugo, and headed to Wedded Bliss Estate Wines, where the Georges Valley AVA board president served as chief executive. While en route, Vail reviewed the file Lugo had brought them.

After several minutes of struggling to make out the handwriting and abbreviations, Vail stretched her neck and rolled her shoulders.

Dixon tapped the papers. "Anything in there?"

"Some of it's tough to read. Lots of shorthand and scribbles in the margins." Vail turned a couple of pages. "One thing stands out. Something about SMB. It says 'SMB better deal. No: VC, TN, IW. Won't carry.'"

"'Won't carry.' Sounds like a motion."

Vail traced backwards through the notes with an index finger. "Yes. Motion by PO. Second DY." She turned another page, then went back. "Doesn't say what the motion was."

"Is there a date?"

Vail flipped back to the prior page. "January fifteenth."

Dixon nodded. "Okay, we'll start with that. Keep looking."

A few moments later, Vail said, "There are notes talking about 'natural vs. fake. Big difference.'" She looked over at Dixon. "What do you think, are they talking about breasts?"

Dixon smiled. "There's definitely a big difference, but something tells me that's not what the board was deliberating."

"Probably not. But it looks like it was another point of contention according to the margin notes."

"Good," Dixon said. "We've got some things to discuss with our board president. Let's see what she has to say."

———

FIFTEEN MINUTES LATER, they arrived at Wedded Bliss Estates Winery. The driveway was long and narrow, and bordered on both sides by a continuous row of wine bottles, mounted single file and upside down, in the top of the wall.

"Neat idea," Dixon said. "That's pretty cool."

As they continued on down the road, Vail realized they hadn't yet seen the best Wedded Bliss had to offer. She pointed ahead. "Now *that's* pretty cool."

The building was carved into the side of a mountain—but that wasn't its most unusual feature. Where the mountainside once was, a fifty-foot glass enclosure now stood, forming the entire front of the winery.

"Looks like the mountain has a giant window built into it," Vail said.

They found a parking spot and headed down the crushed bottle-and-grout walkway that led to the entrance.

"I've gotta take Robby here before we head out of town."

"You're gonna bring your boyfriend to 'Wedded Bliss'? He may get the wrong idea."

Vail chuckled. "You ever been here?"

"I've seen pictures and read about it, but this is outside my jurisdiction and tucked away from the main drag. All I know is the building's won all sorts of architectural awards and the wine consistently scores over ninety points from *Wine Spectator* and a number of known wine critics."

They walked through the double wide three-quarter-inch glass doors, which slid apart as they approached. After moving inside, they both stopped—the view was breathtaking. The entire interior was made of glass—or its polymer equivalent. The staircase that spiraled up to each of the four stories, the elevator, the tasting stations . . . all pristine and clear.

"Must be a bitch to clean," Dixon said.

"Gives new meaning to the saying, 'I don't do windows.'"

Dixon pointed at the wall nearest them. "You can see the mountainside, through the glass walls. Like one of those cutaways, a slice right through the side of the mountain."

Indeed, the mountain was hollowed out to accommodate the large building, and the inner heart of the granite and dirt was visible. This place truly was an architectural marvel.

Vail pointed at something above their heads. "Look at those tree roots."

"Welcome to Wedded Bliss. May I help you?"

They turned to find a man dressed in a black suit, silver tie, and white shirt.

"Yes," Vail said. She splayed open her credentials case. "We have an appointment with Crystal Dahlia." Having said it aloud for the first time, Vail now wondered if that was the woman's real name. Given the appearance of the winery, she was beginning to doubt it.

They were led up the staircase to the second level, then down a hallway. The floor was made of sand-blasted glass blocks, preserving the building's look but retaining function. Walking on regular glass would be dangerously slick and the traffic of hard leather and dirt would eventually scratch the surface to hell.

The suited gentleman led them to a room and told them to wait inside, that Ms. Dahlia was finishing up a phone call. He stepped up to a wet bar, removed two glasses, and poured them wine.

"Oh," Dixon said. "I don't think we should. We're on duty—"

"Nonsense," Vail said. "I came to Napa to go wine tasting. We've had a few interruptions . . ." . . . *a few murders* . . . "but I think we've earned this." She reached forward and took the glass.

Dixon waved him off.

Before Dixon could object further, Vail put the glass to her lips and swallowed a mouthful.

"Haven't I taught you anything? At least do it right."

"Oh, yeah. Nose. Smell." She lifted the glass to her face and sniffed. "Hmm." Sniffed some more. "Raspberries. Berries. I'm getting berries. That's it." She took another drink.

"Small sips," Dixon said with the tone of a scolding teacher. "Let it float over your tongue. Taste it, swish it a bit."

"No matter how I do it, this is good." She took another drink, smaller this time, and let it float, then swallowed. "Yeah, that was a little better. But I'm still only getting berries."

"Actually, berries is correct. Fruit forward."

The voice came from behind them. They turned to see an attractive, slender woman in a white dress, a couple of years on the right side of forty.

"A hint of cinnamon," the woman said. "And a little cherry."

Vail rose and turned. A little too quickly, as the wine was already giving her a slight buzz.

"You must be Crystal," Vail said, struggling to keep a straight face.

"Are you Karen or Roxxann?"

"I'm Agent Vail. This is Investigator Dixon."

Crystal pursed her lips. "I see." She took their hands with a firm shake, then motioned them to follow her. They walked down the hall to a glass-enclosed suite. The doors slid open and revealed an office with photos of vines and grapes and wineglasses, in clear frames mounted on the wall with suction cups. At the end of the room was a desk. A . . . glass desk.

Crystal held out an open hand, indicating the two rubber-footed chairs at the foot of her desk.

"I'm curious," Vail said as she took her seat. "About the name."

"Oh," Crystal said with a wave and a bright smile. "Everyone asks. Yes, it's my real name. My parents thought it was cute. Me, I've grown to like it. And working here," she said with a sweep of her hand, "it kind of fits, now, doesn't it?"

Vail smiled. "Yes, it does. I hadn't thought of that." She looked at Dixon, who was squinting at her. "But," she said, turning back to Crystal, "I was referring to the name of the winery. Wedded Bliss. How does it fit with all the glass?"

Crystal waved a hand again. Grinned broadly. "Very simple, really. You want the winery tour version or the 'we're the police and we don't have time for that crap version'?"

Vail shrugged. "We don't have time for that crap, and, well, since we are the police . . ."

Crystal looked long at Vail, then nodded. Her smiled faded, but quickly returned. "Yes, of course. Short answer is that all our wines are blends, and we only use the finest grapes from Georges Valley. So it's a marriage of pure bliss."

*Who thinks up this shit?* Vail nodded. "Makes perfect sense. Surprised I didn't see that coming. One question, though. What's a blended wine?"

Crystal looked at Dixon.

Dixon scratched her temple. "She's new to the wine country. That was a serious question."

Crystal smiled again, wide and bright. "Well. A blend is a mix of two or more types of grapes to produce something of greater value than the parts would individually exhibit. We have an award-winning winemaker who created all our proprietary blends."

"Is he happily married?"

The smile faded from Crystal's face. "Is who happily married?"

Vail held out her hands, palm up, as if it were obvious. "The winemaker. Wedded Bliss. Surely he must—"

"We actually have some *important* questions for you," Dixon said. She looked at Vail and shook her head.

*Is she scolding me? Hey, I haven't had a whole lot of sleep. I'm punchy.* She realized Crystal was giving her a sympathetic look. *Did I say that out loud? Shit, Dixon was right. I shouldn't have had that wine. But it was so good. And I did deserve it.*

"Agent Vail?"

"Hmm?" Vail focused on Crystal, but her gaze was a bit unsteady. "What do you put in your wine? It's strong."

"The alcohol content hovers around 14 percent. It's not significantly different from any other fine wine. When did you last eat?"

"Eat?"

Crystal reached over, lifted her phone from its cradle, and asked the person at the other end to bring up some soda crackers to her office.

"Good idea," Dixon said. She looked disapprovingly at Vail, then turned her attention back to Crystal. "Nice to hear about Wedded Bliss, but we really need info on your board. Georges Valley AVA."

"Sure. But my term as president is due to expire next month. I'm not sure you want to be talking with me, or with the incoming president."

The doors behind them slid apart and the black suited gentleman who greeted them earlier entered carrying a silver tray. At Crystal's direction, he set it down on the desk in front of Vail and then left. Vail leaned forward and examined the spread. Soda crackers, as ordered. Sliced fruit, breadsticks, and cubed cheese.

"Please," Crystal said.

"Don't mind if I do. Very kind of you." *Jeez, I need to keep my mouth shut till I get some food in my stomach.* She took a napkin from the side of the tray, selected a toothpick and loaded up on cheese and crackers. Within seconds, she was munching away.

"Actually," Dixon said, "you're the person we want to talk with." She reached over and removed the manila folder from Vail's lap, then opened it. "Victoria Cameron was due to take over as president, right?"

Crystal's cheerful face hardened. Her eyes misted. "Terrible tragedy, Victoria. I—you just never know, do you? I mean, a stroke at thirty-seven? That's . . . it's just shocking."

"Yes, just shocking," Vail repeated as she reached for a breadstick and more cheese. *Got news for you, Crystal. If you find that shocking, I wonder what you'll think when you find out what really happened to her.*

Dixon sighed. "It was tragic. But with Victoria . . . deceased . . . who's taking her place as incoming president?"

"Well, it's all spelled out in our bylaws. Victoria was our VP of Administration—she handled administrative matters the board had to deal with, took minutes, distributed proxies, liaised with the VP of Budget and Finance to ensure we had our statements each meeting, that sort of thing. The Admin VP was next in line for president on a three-year rotation. If the Admin VP isn't able to carry out those duties, it falls to the Marketing VP. And that's Alec Crawford."

"Can we get a copy of your bylaws?"

"I'll have them emailed over to you, if you'd like."

"That'd be fine." Dixon dug out a business card and handed it across the desk to Crystal. "And a list of all the names of the board members, too, with phone numbers and addresses."

"We've got a phone tree I can send you."

"And a copy of your board's minutes for the past twelve months."

Crystal tilted her head. "Now that might be a problem. Our minutes are not public record. There are proprietary secrets discussed at these meetings. And I'm not at liberty to release that information."

"Well I'm at liberty to get it," Dixon said. "I'll have a subpoena issued if you think it's necessary."

Crystal leaned back in her chair. "I'm afraid it will be necessary."

Vail had polished off half the tray. Only the fruit was left—and she was already feeling more lucid. "We're not trying to be difficult. It's just information we think may be useful."

"Useful in what?" Crystal asked. "Is this about Victoria?"

"We're not at liberty to say." Vail winced. "Sorry, I'm not trying to be a wiseass." *At least, not right now.* "But this is a sensitive investigation and we can't say what it is that we're investigating." *Sure sounds like bullshit doubletalk to me, but what the hell, sometimes witnesses buy it.*

"Do I need my attorney? Or the board's attorney?" Crystal asked.

Dixon crossed one leg over the other. "Not unless you or your board has done something wrong. And we have no indication of that, if that makes you feel more comfortable."

"We're having some difficulties with our investigation," Vail added. "It's got nothing to do with Wedded Bliss or the Georges Valley AVA— but we're doing our due diligence in trying to cover all the bases."

"You're fishing," Crystal said.

Dixon shrugged. "Kind of."

"I'll see what I can do about releasing the minutes to you. I have to contact the executive committee."

"We appreciate it." Dixon looked down at the file. "Meanwhile, can you tell us what the abbreviation 'SMB' might stand for?"

Crystal held out her hands. "In what context? Sounds like someone's initials."

Vail didn't want to disclose they had Victoria's notes, and she hoped Dixon was on the same page. "Let's just say we came across it in our investigation. Something from January."

Crystal nodded animatedly. "Ah, then that would be Superior Mobile Bottling."

"Do you or any of the other bottlers who are members of your board use Superior?" Vail asked.

Crystal smiled. "Well, the way our AVA works is a little unusual. Our members pool their purchasing power. Wine making is a business like any other. Our goal is to make money while turning out a quality product. All businesses do well to carefully monitor their expenses. The more they pay out—"

"Thanks for the business lesson," Dixon said. "But the point is—"

"The point is that the more we order of something, the better our prices. We use the AVA as a means of keeping our bottling expenses low. So we contract with Superior to do the bottling for all our member wineries. And as a result, we get rock bottom pricing."

"You all use the same bottler?"

Crystal bobbed her head. "For the most part. There are a few who've had bottling facilities for years, so they don't participate, unless they have some specialty wines they need bottled a certain way."

Vail shook her head. "Let's back up a second. Bottling includes what, exactly?"

"Gas sparging the bottles, filling them with juice, corking them, applying the labels and capsules, and then boxing them into cases."

"And this is done at the winery, right?" Vail asked.

"That's what I was saying. Some larger wineries have the capacity to do this. Many don't. And many don't want to do it because it means committing a large amount of space to something that only gets used two weeks out of a year. And they have to maintain and upgrade the equipment every so often to increase capacity, or to accommodate new technology to increase efficiency. It's a lot of headache and expense. Easier, and usually more cost efficient, to let someone else worry about it."

Dixon nodded. "So the 'mobile' in Superior Mobile Bottling means they come to you."

"Exactly," Crystal said. "They have semi trucks that are outfitted with all the equipment. They come to your winery, hook up to your electrical grid, and eight hours later, you've got finished cases of wine. A state-of-the-art truck, like the kind Superior has, can do a hundred bottles per minute, about 2,500 to 3,000 cases a day."

Vail picked up a strawberry from the platter. "Sounds like a no-brainer."

"One would think."

"But there are some who don't get it."

Crystal slid her chair closer to the desk and leaned her forearms on the glass surface. "Our pricing power is contingent on us hitting certain volume goals. So if you have some who don't want to get on-board, it can cause some . . . *discontent* within the ranks."

Dixon pursed her lips and nodded. "Of course. So who in the AVA didn't want to get onboard?"

"A very small minority didn't want to renew the contract we have with Superior. They thought we should invest in building a few custom trailers of our own, that would then move from each of our wineries and do our bottling. But that didn't make a whole lot of sense. There's the initial build-out cost—five hundred grand to a million dollars apiece—and you'd still have to park them somewhere in the off-season. Not easy to find parking spots for sixty-five-foot trucks."

"And it puts you back in the business of maintaining and owning bottling facilities."

"Sort of. You don't have permit issues, which is a big deal nowa-days. Trying to get permission to build out new space to expand your bottling line is tough, if not impossible. So if we built trailers, we'd get around those issues. Still, there are other things that wouldn't make sense if we were to own our own trailers. Like some of our members have restrictions on the roads that lead to their wineries, so they'd need to have smaller trucks, which, obviously, have less bottling capacity. Su-perior takes care of all that for us. They have trailers that can accom-modate all our members' needs."

Vail swallowed the strawberry she'd been chewing and dabbed her mouth with a napkin. "What about the issue of natural versus fake?" She was trying to be nonchalant with the question, hoping to place less emphasis on it. Because she didn't really know what she was asking, should it involve something significant, she didn't want Crystal to feel the weight of the question and attempt to snowball them.

Crystal leaned back. "Well, that was another thing that led to in-tense debate. I'm not sure that got resolved. I guess we'll find out where we are at our next meeting."

"Why such disagreement?"

"What do you know about corks?"

Vail and Dixon shared a glance. Vail's look said, This is about corks?

"I don't know a whole lot," Vail said. "Wineries stick them in wine bottles to seal them. But my guess is there's a lot more to it than that, isn't there?"

Crystal smiled again—but this was not her promotional smile. It was a one-sided smirk that conveyed depth and irony. "Your guess is correct. It's sparked quite the debate in the wine community, and our board is no exception. There are those who are fervent supporters of natural cork, to the point of being fanatics. They claim that not using cork is breaking with centuries of wine-making tradition."

"What alternatives are there?" Vail asked.

"Synthetic corks or screw tops."

"Screw tops—like a twist-off on a bottle of soda or tea?"

"Yes. We don't like that model, for that reason. Screw tops solve a lot of the problems that come from natural or synthetic corks, but they're cheap looking. They fit more with a cut-rate label than the quality of a Georges Valley wine. There's something about a twist-off top that just doesn't fit with a fine bottle of Cabernet Sauvignon, Pinot Noir, or a highly regarded blend such as ours."

Dixon nodded. "Same could be said about those synthetic corks, right?"

Crystal's face firmed. "No. Not right. Not in my opinion. You still have the feel of opening the bottle with a corkscrew. The only difference is that the good ones are made of thermoplastic elastomer." She waved a hand. "That's not entirely true. There are other differences. Cork comes from tree bark, a very specific oak tree grown in the Mediterranean and Portugal—and the trees can't have their bark stripped until they're twenty-five years old. After that, they can only be harvested once every ten years or so. But there are nearly twenty billion bottles of wine produced each year. There just isn't enough natural cork to go around."

"So it's a supply and demand issue."

"On the surface, yes. But there's much more to it."

Dixon leaned back and placed a hand on her chin. "Doesn't cork allow some air to get into the bottle, which promotes natural aging of the wine?"

"It also allows TCA into the bottle, which causes what's called *cork taint*. It ruins the wine, gives it a moldy smell that tastes like wet cardboard."

"TCA?" Vail asked.

"Trichloro-something. It's a fungus that grows because of naturally occurring chemicals found in cork. Depending on who you believe, between 3 and 20 percent of bottles are 'corked.' Basically, those bottles are ruined by TCA contamination. The winery can avoid that by using the thermoplastic elastomer, or synthetic, corks that I mentioned. Some synthetics aren't as good, and they actually let more air into the bottle than natural cork. But the ones Superior uses are, well, superior. They don't have that problem.

"Then there's also the issue of cost. With our volume pricing, we can get these synthetics at about four cents apiece, compared to fifteen to seventy-five cents for natural cork. Add it up over the millions of bottles our members produce, year after year, and you're talking real money."

Vail hiked her brow. "So it seems like the synthetic would be the way to go."

Crystal grinned—that same deeper-meaning half-smile. "One would think. But there was considerable debate over whether to renew that three-year contract with Superior."

Dixon shook her head. "What does Superior have to do with the cork issue?"

"They only have one trailer that's still equipped to handle natural cork. They've refitted the rest of their trucks to synthetic-only because they've developed custom machinery that allows them to bottle faster with the synthetic."

"So," Vail said, "there are a couple people on the board who didn't want to renew the Superior contract. Did Superior know this?"

"Absolutely not. The business of the board and its member wineries is confidential and we don't discuss it outside the boardroom. We each sign confidentiality statements preventing us from discussing board business with anyone who's not a board member."

Vail wondered if Crystal had herself signed one of these statements—here she was telling them all about the board's deliberations. But she wasn't complaining. Still, it made her wonder who might also have thought it was okay to tip off someone at Superior that their contract renewal was in jeopardy.

"Who usually deals with Superior?"

"Our Contracts VP. Ian Wirth."

"And who's the board's contact person at Superior?"

Crystal hesitated. Her eyes moved between Vail and Dixon. "Why?"

"Same reason it was five minutes ago," Vail said. "We're investigating something and this information may or may not be germane to the issue we're looking into."

"I'm not sure—"

"This isn't confidential board business," Dixon said. "It's just someone's name at a company. We can call Superior and ask them the same question, but you can save us some time and effort. And we'd appreciate that."

Crystal reached to the right corner of her desk and removed a file folder from a standing portfolio. She opened it and traced a finger across a page. "César Guevara. He's their CFO."

Dixon pulled a spiral notepad from her inside jacket pocket and made a note of the man's name.

Vail sensed they were reaching the end of the interview. But there was one more piece of information they needed. "Who on your board," she said, "has the initials TN?"

"Todd Nicholson. Why? What—"

"Active investigation," Dixon said. "Can't say."

Crystal looked to be getting increasingly frustrated by their refusal to answer her questions. Vail didn't care—truth is, that's the way it was with the police. They asked the questions, the interviewees answered them and didn't get the opportunity to ask their own. Crystal clearly didn't understand the relationship. But she was getting the idea.

"And who on the board has a last name that begins with W?" Dixon asked. "Would that be Mr. Wirth?"

Crystal pursed her lips, clearly debating whether to keep answering these questions—then obviously deciding one more won't hurt. "Yes," she said.

"How is Mr. Nicholson?" Vail asked. What she wanted to ask was, Is Mr. Nicholson still alive?

"I spoke to him this morning."

"Nice guy?"

"Spineless, if you ask me."

"I just did." Vail forced a smile. "But if he's spineless, why did he defy the board and vote against the Superior contract?"

Crystal's jaw dropped. Before she could ask, Vail said, "You're not the first person we've spoken to about this." She shrugged. "But you can understand that, from our point of view, that doesn't fit. A spineless guy doesn't oppose the others. He goes along. He doesn't want confrontation."

"Yes. Well, I suggest you ask him about it."

"Last thing," Dixon said. "What's the status of the Superior contract? If there were only a few who opposed it, did they win the renewal?"

"Actually, no," Crystal said. "First, that was a preliminary vote. I wanted to see where we were. Second, because it affects everyone's business, it's one of the only things where we require a unanimous vote. As I said, this AVA board is very unusual in how it works. I don't know of any other AVA that works the way we do." She tried to smile—but it was only a half-hearted effort. "But it's worked for us."

Vail was the first to stand. She placed her used napkin on the food tray. "Thanks so much for your hospitality—and for the food."

Crystal rose from her chair. Dixon motioned her down. "No need to show us out."

"Yeah," Vail said. "The way out is pretty obvious. One might say it's crystal clear."

# THIRTY-SEVEN

As Vail and Dixon walked down the glass stairs, Dixon said, "'One might say it's crystal clear'? Were you trying to be funny?"

"I was trying."

Dixon shook her head. "Try harder."

They cleared the sliding front doors and headed toward the parking lot and Lugo's car.

"Three people opposed the vote on Superior's new contract," Dixon said. "If César Guevara found out about this, that's something to kill over. They'd lose millions in business. He does it himself or he hires someone to take out Victoria."

Vail stopped at the edge of the crushed glass path. "See, this is where this case doesn't make sense. Serial killers don't kill for money—I mean, there were a couple of exceptions, and they were women—but we're talking about a psychopath who's living out his psychosexual fantasies, which are rooted in a dysfunctional childhood. And what about this Todd Nicholson? He's still alive and kicking."

"Maybe he's the next victim." Dixon's phone buzzed. She flipped it open. "Text from Brix. They checked Ortiz's story. El Brinquito, the restaurant, confirms his alibi. Wants to know if we're still here. He and Lugo want to meet us here in five." She tapped out a message to him. Sent it. "What do you say we talk with Todd Nicholson, as well as one of the other board members who was in favor of the Superior contract? See what their take was."

"Board confidentiality might get in the way."

"Maybe, maybe not. Sometimes a couple of badges opens their mouths."

They stood there for a bit, alone with their thoughts, before Vail said, "Look. There are five vics attributed to the Crush Killer. There are few commonalities among them. We've got Victoria Cameron and Maryanne Bernal, whose wineries were members of the Georges Valley AVA. Victoria was an active board member. Maryanne was a former member. We need to find out more about Isaac Jenkins and Dawn Zackery. Ray was looking into Ursula Robbins, whose winery was in Georges Valley AVA."

"Do you see the common thread? Georges Valley."

"We'll see when we find out more about the other two vics. In one way, it makes sense because of the male vic—Jenkins. This type of killer wouldn't go after men. But looking at it from a for-profit motive, it doesn't make sense. That's just not what drives these psychopaths. I mean, severing sexual organs—like what this UNSUB's done with the breasts—that could point to an offender with mental health issues. But the rest of his behaviors are very well explained by his psychopathy." She leaned back against a pillar that separated the small entry plaza from the parking lot, staring out at the glass building, then shook her head. "This case . . . I can't get a handle on it. Things just aren't adding up the way they should be. Something's not right."

Dixon looked at her phone and pressed a button. "Email from Crystal." She scrolled and pressed the trackball. "Board roster."

"So let's pick someone who wasn't opposed to the Superior contract and start there. See if he or she talks to us."

"They're here," Dixon said with a nod to the lot's entrance.

They met Brix and Lugo halfway to their car and watched their reactions as they tilted their heads, taking in the winery. "I've read about this place," Brix said. "Never been here. Pretty impressive."

Lugo nodded appreciatively. "The photos I've seen don't do it justice."

Vail's phone rang: Art Rooney's number. "I've gotta take this."

"No problem. I'll brief them on what Crystal told us."

Vail stepped away and answered. "Art, what a pleasant surprise."

"Wait till you hear what I have to say. You might not think it's so pleasant."

"Go on."

"I was looking through the file we have here, and dipshit Del Monaco did his usual thorough job."

"What did he miss?"

"He ran the VICAP search too narrow. So I expanded it and added some stuff, and bingo. I got you another vic to run down. From '98."

"Where?"

"Frisco."

"Yeah, Art . . . I should've told you before. They don't like that abbreviation."

"Offer my sincere apologies. Meantime, I've spoken with an Inspector Robert Friedberg with the *San Francisco* PD. He's waiting to hear from you. I just emailed you his direct line."

"Thanks, Art. This case is really bugging me. Maybe this'll help."

"Anything you wanna run by me?"

"If we were in the same room, yeah. I'd sit down with you for a couple of hours and go through everything. Bottom line is nothing's adding up. Based on what we know, which is incomplete, this UNSUB might have a profit motive. But—"

"But that doesn't make sense. Not for a male SK."

"Exactly."

"Keep looking, Karen. You'll find something."

"Yeah, well, I don't have much longer. Gifford wants me home tomorrow night."

"I'm sure you'll find a way."

Vail turned back to Dixon and Brix. "I wish I was as confident about that as you are."

"Look on the bright side. If you head back tomorrow night, we can sit down in the same room for a few hours and hash this thing out."

"Thanks, Art. Talk to you soon." She hung up, scrolled to Rooney's email, and dialed through to Inspector Friedberg. She mentioned Art Rooney and Friedberg agreed to meet her in the Marin Headlands, just north of San Francisco.

Vail hung up and rejoined Dixon, Brix, and Lugo. "Did you tell them about Superior Mobile Bottling?" she asked Dixon.

Before Dixon could answer, Brix said, "I'm vaguely familiar with

Superior. Privately held, family-owned business. Like half of all the other businesses in the valley."

"Privately held," Vail said. "Meaning we don't know much about their operations. Their financing, investors, the people with skin in the game."

Brix nodded. "That's pretty much true. But they've been around a long time, as long as we've been contracting out bottling for Silver Ridge. Like most mobile bottlers, they own a fleet of semis outfitted to do bottling, corking, and labeling on-site at the wineries that contract with them. It's pretty lucrative, because they can turn out a lot of finished product pretty efficiently, and very reasonably. They make their money on volume. Kind of like the Costco model. Small margins, high volumes. And the wineries don't have to invest in the equipment themselves, so everyone's happy."

Dixon rubbed her eyes. "Any reason to look into them further?"

"Waste of time," Lugo said.

Brix raised an eyebrow. "Never heard of any complaints. You want more, we can have Agbayani do some checks."

Lugo shook his head. "I'm telling you. Waste of time. Just like Ortiz."

Dixon twisted her lips in thought, then said, "Give Eddie a ring, have him do some digging. Meantime, let's focus our energies on what's most likely to net us something useful."

"And on that front," Vail said, "we might have something. A VICAP hit in San Francisco. I've got us an appointment with the detective who's got a cold case from '98. Rooney already spoke with him. We're meeting him in an hour and a half."

"Then we better get our asses in gear," Dixon said. "Catch up with you later?"

Brix nodded. "Keep me posted."

# THIRTY-EIGHT

While en route to their meet with Friedberg, Vail looked over the roster of Georges Valley AVA board members. She called three and explained she wanted to drop by to talk with them. All three declined. But the fourth agreed to sit down with her: Ian Wirth, whose home was located near downtown Napa. Vail set a tentative time for their meeting, and told him she would call him when they were thirty minutes away so he had time to leave his winery and get home in time for their arrival.

Dixon, right hand resting atop the steering wheel, pointed out the windshield with her index finger. "Meeting place is just up ahead. We'll be there in a couple minutes."

Vail turned another page in the file Kevin Cameron had given them. "Can't say any of this is helpful, other than the Superior issue we covered with Crystal—which I'm not even sure was helpful at all. Problem is, a lot of this is in shorthand or some kind of abbreviation-speak Victoria devised for herself."

"We're not out of ammo yet," Dixon said. "And we may get lucky. That sit-down with the other board member might lead somewhere. And maybe this detective will have something that'll put it all into focus." As the freeway curved, she nudged Vail on the forearm. "Look up. You're gonna miss the view."

"Whoa," Vail said, leaning forward in the seat. The Golden Gate Bridge swung into sight behind, and between, the mountains that sat on both sides of the 101 freeway. "I've never seen it in person."

"Just wait," Dixon said. "Better views around the bend."

They drove up the two-lane mountain road and saw a knot of tourists walking along a dirt and gravel path. Dixon hung a left into the turnout parking area and slid her vehicle into the remaining slot.

Inspector Friedberg was standing beside his unmarked car in a black overcoat, a cigarette in his hand, and a chocolate brown woolly pulled down over his head. "Robert Friedberg," he said, shifting the cigarette to his left hand and offering his right.

"This is Roxxann Dixon and I'm Karen Vail."

Friedberg returned the cigarette to his smoking hand. "Agent Rooney said you've never been here before."

"Not really," Vail said. "Not any kind of trip that counts. This was supposed to be it—a vacation."

"Welcome to the Golden Gate. Come on, we can walk and talk, I can show you one of my favorite views in the state." He led them down a dirt path that curved and elevated, climbing toward a soil and cement plateau that opened up to a view of the Pacific.

Vail stopped and took in the 180 degree panorama, from the brightly glinting white and gray skyscrapers of San Francisco off to the left, to the scores of small white sailboats listing in the bay, heading back after a day on the ocean. Oh—and there was a huge orange-red bridge splayed out before her. Larger than life, it seemingly grew out of an out-cropping of mountain beneath her feet and spanned the bay to her right, landing somewhere on the San Francisco shore at two o'clock. A large cargo ship was passing beneath at midspan, moving slowly but steadily, leaving two parallel, relatively small wakes behind it.

From their perch, they were standing midway up the North Art Deco tower, looking down onto the roadway and the dozens of cars below.

She looked over at Friedberg, who was sucking on his cigarette. A stiff wind blew against her face. "Amazing view. I've never stood above a bridge and looked down on it from so high up. That color is so . . . dominating and unusual. Not quite golden, though."

Friedberg took another long drag, then blew it out the side of his mouth. The smoke caught the wind and rode around his neck. "Golden Gate refers to the strait below us, the entrance to the bay from the Pacific. The color's called International Orange, whatever that means. They've only repainted it once, since 1937. Know how long it took?" He turned to Dixon, who was standing slightly behind Vail. "You're from around here."

Dixon shrugged. "Haven't the slightest."

"Twenty-seven years."

Vail nodded. "Job security. And a great view."

"Now they've got an army of thirty-eight painters. Their whole job is touching up the bridge. It's the salt air. Very corrosive."

"You know a lot about the bridge," Vail said.

"A buddy of mine is one of those thirty-eight painters." He shook his head and laughed. "Marty says the damn thing can sway twenty-seven feet to either side on a windy day. And the roadway can drop about ten feet when fully loaded—"

"Inspector," Vail said. "I love the view. It's—" she turned and looked back at the expanse before them—"among the more beautiful I've ever seen. But the flip side to all this beauty is the killer Investigator Dixon and I are trying to find. While I'd love to sightsee and get the VIP tour, I just don't have the time. No offense."

Friedberg sucked hard on his cigarette. His eyes were riveted to Vail's. He blew away the smoke, then nodded. "Fair enough. Totally understand. So let me get right to it." He turned to face the bridge and stood there a long moment without speaking. Finally, he threw down his cigarette and ground the butt into the dirt. "Follow me."

Friedberg picked up the squished cigarette, then trudged off, away from the bridge, up the inclined frontage to a sunken, below-ground-level concrete complex. A low-slung steel pipe fence surrounded the area, most likely to prevent a kid or careless adult from falling over the edge and landing below on the cement ground.

Friedberg tossed the spent butt into a garbage pail, then led the way down a set of stairs. Directly in front of them was a twenty-foot raised circle of concrete, with an inner ring of thick, rusted bolts protruding from the surface. Off to the right, one level lower, was a central roadway that split barracks-style quarters on both sides. But the inspector headed left instead.

Vail took a step forward to get a better view of the ugly, flat-topped one-story buildings—oddly out of place against the green undulating hills of the mountain peaks behind them. "What is this place?"

"Battery Spencer," Friedberg said. "A gun battery that was used from the 1840s till World War Two. The military considered San Francisco Bay to be the most important harbor on the west coast. So they stationed three huge rifle guns here to protect the city and the bridge from attack. Right here," he said, motioning to the large circular platform in front of them, "was the emplacement for Gun 2." He stepped onto the gun mount and walked ahead. "But that's not what I wanted to show you. Over here."

Friedberg stopped in front of a slight overhang, at a cement outcropping that contained a rectangular horizontal iron door hinged at the top.

"A fireplace?" Dixon asked.

"Actually," Friedberg said, "I'm not sure what it was. It was a military installation, who knows what they did here. February 16, 1998, Marin County sheriff's office got a call a little after midnight. A terrible smell at Battery Spencer. A deputy sheriff was nearby, so he took the call, even though it was outside his jurisdiction. He followed his nose, which led him here." Friedberg grabbed the irregular bottom of the iron door with both hands and lifted it. The metal hinge squealed.

"Body dump," Vail said.

"Body dump. Take a look."

Dixon and Vail stepped forward and peered in. "Goes down quite a bit."

"Wasn't any fun getting the body out, I can tell you that much."

"How'd you catch the case?" Dixon asked. "This isn't SFPD jurisdiction."

Friedberg chuckled. "Jurisdiction around here is a freaking nightmare. Need a scorecard and map to keep it straight. A hundred feet in any direction, jurisdiction could change. Basically, it goes by who owned the land before it became a national park. So where we're standing is U.S. Park Police. They assigned a Criminal Investigative Branch detective, who ran the investigation and coordinated with the Marin

County sheriff's office. That's where I came in. This was a couple years before I hooked up with SFPD." He shook his head. "Let's just say I regretted working the case from day one. But I kept a copy of the file. I always hoped one day I'd solve it."

Vail stepped back and Friedberg lowered the cover. "ID on the vic?"

"Betsy Ivers. Bank teller, thirty-three, single."

"Any connection to the wine country?" Dixon asked.

"None I remember. But it's been a while since I reviewed the file."

"Did Agent Rooney go over the unusual things our killer does to the body?"

Friedberg clapped his hands to shake off the dirt. "I went to that FBI Profiling seminar in '06 that your colleague did, Agent Safarik. I know what to look for. He was really good. Great freaking class. How is he?"

"Doing well," Vail said. "He retired, but he's got his own company, still doing profiling, expert testimony, the whole shebang."

"Well, that's how I knew to fill out the VICAP form. Every cop in the country should take that course."

Friedberg led the way back toward the bridge, up the stairs and down the incline to the wood post and cable fence that prevented one from taking a header down the cliff, into the Pacific. The sun was setting and the temperature had dropped another few degrees. Headlighted cars streamed from the city across the bridge into Marin.

Vail took a deep breath. Cold, damp, sea breeze. Smell of salt riding on the air. "Any suspects?"

"Couple people we were looking at. One was a guy who was working for a local pest control company. I liked him, but he blew out of town after we questioned him. Turns out he used a fake ID, name, address. His whole employment app was bullshit. Couldn't find him—he vanished like water droplets in the freaking San Francisco fog. But just when we were about to start a goddamn manhunt, this other guy came on our radar. Billy Todd Lundy. Some psycho who'd been in and out of mental health institutions as a kid, went off his meds, and had all sorts of run-ins with SFPD."

Friedberg had Vail's attention. *Mental health issues. That could fit with the severed breasts.* "And what happened with Billy Todd Lundy?"

"We questioned him, there were holes in his story. He was seen around Battery Spencer a couple days before the murder, which fit with the estimated TOD. And he also lived down the block from Ivers's apartment."

"Violent tendencies?"

"When he was off his meds, yeah." Friedberg pulled a pack of Marlboros from his pocket and tapped it. Removed one, lit it. "But that's where things got screwed up. We didn't have enough to hold him, so we kicked him loose." He leaned on the fence's wood post. Took a long drag of his smoke. Nodded at the Golden Gate. "Did I tell you before about the bridge?"

Vail and Dixon shared a look. "Yeah, we went through all that. Your buddy the painter."

"No, no," Friedberg said, shaking his head urgently. "Its less glamorous side."

Dixon faced him. "I don't follow you."

"It's the most prevalent place in the country to commit suicide. Over *twelve hundred* a year. And those are just the ones we know about. Because of the dense fog we get here, and, well, times when no one'd see a jumper, like at night, some cops think the number's much higher." He pointed at the bridge. "Someone supposedly hooked up motion-detecting cameras that recorded the jumpers. Confirmed the theory that the rate was worse than we thought. Kind of morbid, don't you think?"

"Inspector," Dixon said. "The point?"

"Two days after we kicked Lundy, he jumped. Right there, by the north tower."

"Any chance he survived?" Vail asked.

"Who knows? I think a couple people have lived to talk about it over the years. But let's say the odds are against it. It's a two hundred-fifty-foot drop. He'd be going eighty-five miles an hour when he hit the water." Friedberg took another long puff, then held up his cigarette and examined it. "At least this kills me slowly."

Vail thought about that a moment, then said, "Yeah, I guess that's something."

# THIRTY-NINE

*J*ohn Wayne Mayfield finished "work" early—when Dixon and Vail headed out of town, he felt the risk of following them was too high. If one of them had taken note of his vehicle behind theirs in Napa, and the same vehicle happened to still be following theirs on the highway, thirty or more miles later, the chances of them dismissing it as a coincidence plummeted to unreasonable levels.

So when Dixon and Vail headed out of Napa, entered Vallejo and then Highway 37, Mayfield turned around and headed home. Now, as he settled down in front of his computer, a glass of fine '02 Cakebread Cellars Cabernet by his side, he had thinking to do—and tasks to complete before he planned his most high profile murders. There was considerable risk involved and there would be no turning back. He could still stop right here and come away clean. With what?

No, as he thought about it, there really was no turning back . . . even if he never killed again—which was just not going to happen.

He sat in front of the keyboard, staring at the screen. Took a sip of wine and let it linger on his tongue, savoring the complex Cabernet borne from Rutherford's exceptional soil and climate. He swallowed, then woke from his reverie. His task called to him, and though fraught with risk, it required his attention.

Everything had been leading up to this. He had no choice. He had to do it. He *wanted* to do it.

But wait.

As he sat there, an idea began to form. Perhaps there was another way. He'd give it one more shot, put forth one last effort, before he chose what he considered the "nuclear option." He thought it through, examining it from all angles, role-playing how it would go down once he contacted the cops.

This might just work—at considerably less risk. He'd take precautions, give them what they wanted . . . so long as he got what he wanted. It was a trade. Equitable. Fair. Just a reasonable business offer.

If he was going to do this, he had to do it right. He made a phone call to gather the particulars, then checked the wall clock. He had barely an hour before this copy was due. Not much time. And he didn't want to screw up, not this late in the game. Even if this was the path of lesser risk, if he wasn't careful it could end in disaster. He took a deep breath to calm his thoughts.

Then he opened a new document and started typing.

# FORTY

*D*ixon and Vail had left Robert Friedberg with a copy of his file in hand. They were headed back to Napa and their appointment with Ian Wirth. At the time prompt from Dixon, Vail had called and given the man the promised thirty-minutes' notice.

As they pulled into the circular drive of Wirth's three-story brown brick and stone-faced home, Vail tucked Victoria Cameron's file beneath the seat and pulled down the sun visor mirror to straighten her hair. The wind at Battery Spencer had done a job on it.

"Why didn't you tell me my hair looked like I just came out of a wind tunnel?"

Dixon shoved the car into park and turned to Vail. "I was driving. It's dark. I didn't notice." She pulled down her own visor and combed her hair into place. "How come you didn't tell me *mine* was a mess?"

Vail looked at her. "Guess we're even."

They popped open their doors and strode up the walk. "I'm starving," Vail said. She pulled her BlackBerry and texted Robby about meeting for a late—very late—dinner.

Dixon rang the bell. Within seconds, the large walnut door swung open.

"Good timing. Just got in a couple minutes ago." He extended a hand. "Ian Wirth. Come on in."

Wirth was a shade over six feet with small clear-rimmed glasses and a full head of close-cropped light brown hair. He turned and led the way along the dark wood floor into a paneled library. There was an ornate mahogany desk at the far end of the rectangular room and a smaller matching meeting table nearest the door. He motioned them to pristine glove leather seats. A pitcher of water and a pot of hot coffee sat in the middle of the counter behind them.

"Java?" Wirth asked.

"Sure," Dixon said. She eyed the freshly brewed coffee and said, "I thought you just got home."

"I called my housekeeper and had her take care of it before she left."

While Wirth poured the cups, Vail noticed a large, framed sepia photo hanging behind the desk. "Grandfather?" Vail asked.

Wirth swung his head around, then turned back, a smile broadening his face. "Great grandfather. Józef Wirth. That photo was taken in Bialystok, Poland, sometime around 1725. My grandmother told me that the genealogist who worked on our family history discovered that there were seven families that migrated in a group from Poland in the 1800s. There were others who decided to stay, and they were eventually swept up in the Nazi roundup in 1938. I've got a whole book if you want—"

Vail held up a hand. "Not that I don't find it interesting, Mr. Wirth, but—"

"Please, call me Ian."

"Ian," Vail said. "We've had a long day"—*make that a long week*—"and we just have a few questions to ask you. If you don't mind."

Wirth dipped his chin. "Of course." He removed a creamer from the counter and placed it on the table. "You said you had questions about the Georges Valley board."

Dixon dumped some milk into her mug and stirred it. "We spoke earlier with Crystal and she told us about Superior Mobile Bottling. The vote that turned a little contentious."

Wirth bobbed his head. "That's one way of putting it."

"How would you put it?" Vail asked.

Wirth lifted his coffee, warmed his hands on its sides. "We've had some issues lately on the board. I'm really not supposed to talk about this—"

"The confidentiality agreement," Vail said. "Crystal told us about it. It's okay. We're not taking notes. We're not going to share any trade secrets. We just want some background for our investigation."

"And what investigation is that?"

Dixon blew on her coffee. "Can't say. But it's got nothing to do with wrongdoing on the part of the board or its members. In fact, I doubt it has anything to do with the AVA at all. But we need some background. As Crystal put it, we're fishing."

"Just curious," Wirth said. "What'd you think of her?"

Vail hiked her brows. "Crystal? Nice lady. Very interesting." *Great body. She should be shot.*

"She's my ex-wife. Did she tell you that?"

Vail didn't know what to say.

"No," Dixon said, "she didn't mention it."

Wirth sat there a moment, lost in thought. Then he shook his head. "Sorry." Smiled, then nodded at the seat Dixon was occupying. "That was her favorite chair."

"Right," Dixon said.

"Don't worry, it won't color my answers. What do you need to know?"

"The acrimony on the board."

"Ah, yes. Well, Crystal probably told you all about the controversy Victoria was stirring."

"Controversy?" Vail asked. She felt a buzz on her belt. She stole a look at the display. Robby had texted her back:

call me when ur done. i'll pick a place and text u the address.

"Victoria was the most vocal opponent of using Superior. She was also an aggressive power broker. She was due to take over the presidency, as part of our board's three-year rotation. She was leading a group of three board members who wanted concessions from the other members of the AVA and they were using this Superior contract as leverage."

Dixon took a sip of her coffee. "Leverage for what?"

"She and her cohorts would agree to renew Superior's contract—if the board supported their efforts to convince the government to modify the proposed AVA law that sets forth the minimum grape requirement for our AVA standard."

Vail held up a hand. "Kevin Cameron told us something about this. The minimum requirement refers to that 85 percent rule?"

"Yes. The Alcohol and Tobacco Tax and Trade Bureau requires that a minimum of 85 percent of the grapes used in wines that are listed as coming from our AVA have to be from the Georges Valley district."

"Your minimum is 85 percent," Vail said, "but Napa's is 75 percent?"

"Correct."

"And the purpose is to protect consumers?"

"Well, yes—but it also supposedly protects the Georges Valley brand, because people who buy a Georges Valley wine expect a certain quality that comes from the area's soil, microclimate, and weather patterns.

"But," Wirth continued, "there are three higher volume vintners in our group—including me and Victoria Cameron—who want to be excluded from that minimum requirement because our brands existed well before the law was passed. But if they enforce the minimum, our brand, Georges Valley Estate Wines, Victoria's brand, F&M Georges Valley Family Winery, and one other, Georges Valley Reserve Select, would disappear overnight. Our business models are based on importing quality, but less expensive, grapes from the central valley."

"But there are no Georges Valley grapes in your wine," Vail said.

"That's correct. We couldn't charge what we charge for our wine and use predominantly Georges Valley grapes."

Vail set down her mug. "Isn't that misleading?"

"That's their argument. Our position is that our brands have been around for twenty years, well before this minimum grape law was proposed. It's unfair to penalize us—put us out of business by losing our brands—because of an administrative issue that some people have pushed through politically."

Dixon blew on her coffee. "Why would the government allow that kind of exclusion?"

Wirth shook his head, then held up a hand. "Exclusion isn't exactly the right term. We want our brands *grandfathered* in. But if our association doesn't endorse their application, the government probably wouldn't want to get involved in our own internal dispute."

"So," Vail said, "Victoria was trying to broker a deal in which she and her allies would ratify the Superior Bottling contract, and in turn, the AVA board would endorse the grandfather clause. And what's in it for the other members who don't have a stake in this grandfather clause?"

Wirth spread his hands. "They want Superior to get the contract. We've been using them for almost three years and they've done a good job. They turn out a quality product, they've got the best pricing on the market, and they're a one-stop shop."

As Vail reached for her coffee, her stomach rumbled. "Sorry." She threw a hand against her belly. "We haven't eaten."

"And we've taken enough of your time," Dixon said. She pulled a card from her pocket and placed it on the table. "If you think of anything else about what we discussed, give me a call."

Wirth took the card and looked at it. Vail sensed there was more he wanted to say. "Is there something else, Ian?"

"You can't tell me what the investigation is about, but you're asking a lot of questions. Questions that, when I put them together with the fact that Victoria is dead, lead me to think that you believe she was murdered."

"She had a stroke," Dixon said.

Wirth pursed his lips and nodded. Kept his gaze on the card. "My father was a cop, did you know that?"

Dixon and Vail shared a look. Vail had a feeling she knew where this was going. *We may have to come clean with this guy. He sees through this. And if we can convince him it's in everyone's best interest to keep it quiet, it might be better than if he were to talk to others about his assumptions . . . or worse yet, start investigating her death himself.*

"If the cause of death was not a stroke," Vail said carefully, "would that change what you've told us?"

"No," Wirth said. "See, I grew up with a father who was a cop, then a detective. In Sacramento. I spent a lot of time with him, I learned how he thought, how he saw people. How he saw the world." He looked at Vail. "I know to be straight with cops when they come asking questions."

"Good," Dixon said. "That's always best." She tapped her card with a finger. "Call me if you think of anything else that may be related to Victoria's stroke."

They stood from their chairs. "But if you have a theory on Victoria's death," Vail said, "I think it'd be best for all concerned if you kept it to yourself." She looked hard into his eyes.

"You were never here," Wirth said.

Vail nodded, shook his hand, and left with Dixon.

# FORTY-ONE

"**W**as that smart?" Dixon asked as she pulled out of his driveway.

"A guy like that, if we confide in him, he may confide in us. He understands what we're trying to accomplish. He may not be a LEO, but he grew up with one. I think he's an ally. We may now have a set of eyes in the enemy camp."

As Dixon headed down 29, Vail coordinated dinner plans with Robby. Dixon dropped her at Bistro Jeanty, advertised as "serving classic French haute cuisine" in Yountville, a pleasant town just off the main drag. With art galleries, gift shops, specialty restaurants, bed-and-breakfasts and modest homes, the area was its own little haven sporting an eclectic mix of young newlyweds and middle-aged empty nesters on a weekend getaway.

Vail settled down at a table with her back against the wall, facing the entrance of the restaurant. The place was still busy, despite the late hour. A few moments later, Robby appeared in the front door. His eyes scanned the tables, found Vail, and his face broadened into a wide smile.

He swung his hips through the narrow spaces between tables. He was wearing a long leather jacket, which, once he reached Vail, was slipped off his shoulders by a hostess who offered to hang it for him nearby.

Vail and Robby embraced and he gave her a kiss. His lips were warm.

"When did you get that jacket?"

"When I got us a new wardrobe, at the outlets. I saw it and said, what the hell, I'm on vacation." He settled into the chair and spread the white napkin across his lap. "This place okay?"

"Looks great."

They gave the waitress their dinner choices, then ordered wine—Whitehall Lane Cabernet for Vail and Rombauer Fiddletown Zinfandel for Robby.

After the woman collected the menus, Vail reached across the table and took Robby's hand. "So what'd you do today?"

"What I've been doing every day. Visit a winery, taste, have lunch, drive down the road and taste some more. Today I went into Healdsburg. Beautiful drive." He stopped and looked into her eyes. "Wish I was doing all this with you. I feel bad you're stuck working."

"Don't worry about me. I'm just doing my thing, trying to find another killer." She looked down at the table. "Except . . . I'm not—this one is different. I just can't get a handle on him. This offender is . . ." She shook her head. "I don't know. It just doesn't seem right. It's beginning to really bother me."

She recapped what they knew, and what they had learned about the potential monetary motives. As she finished, the wine glasses were set down in front of them. Robby took a drink from his Rombauer Zin, then nodded his approval. "This is really, really good. Try it."

Vail took the glass from him, swirled it, then sniffed. "Pleasing nose. Berry jam, I think." She tasted it, letting it drift over her tongue. Her eyes widened. "Yes, very good." She thought a moment, then said, "I'd describe it as fruit forward with sweet blackberries. And currants, too." She handed the glass back to him. "That's fabulous."

Robby eyed her. "For someone who's missed out on a vacation of wine tasting, you seem to have the lingo down."

"I squeezed in some tasting here and there with Roxxann. While we were out investigating, of course."

Robby grinned. "Of course."

Their server, accompanied by an assistant, slid their dinner plates in front of them. "Is there anything else we can get for you?"

"We're fine," Robby said. "Thanks." After the servers turned and left, Robby cut into his *côte de porc*—pork chop with caramelized onion sauce. "So, this case. Seems to me you're still missing some information. Maybe you need to dig a little more. Maybe one of the victims that doesn't seem to be connected to the AVA board is, in fact, connected somehow. A silent partner, someone pulling the strings behind the scenes." He dabbed at his mouth with the napkin. "Bottom line is, don't press. You may not be as far from the answers as you think. When you find the missing information, things will quickly fall into place."

Vail looked down at her wild mushroom pasta. "That's always the case, though, isn't it?" She shook her head. "This just feels different. I can't put a finger on it." Vail stuck her fork into the pasta and twirled it. "I'd better figure it out soon. Gifford's sending me home tomorrow night."

Robby sat back in mid-chew. "When were you going to tell me?"

"I—I guess I forgot. I've been kind of busy."

"What are you going to do?"

Vail shrugged. "Haven't thought that far. But just because he says I have to leave doesn't mean I have to. We still have some vacation left."

"Karen, be honest with yourself. If you're still here, do you really think you can divorce yourself from this investigation and go driving around wine tasting and sightseeing with me?"

Vail chewed her food and swallowed before answering. In a low voice, she said, "No."

Robby winked at her, then cut another slice of meat.

——

THE WAITRESS BROUGHT dessert menus and set them on the table. Robby caught her before she left. "I think we're going to get something to go."

"We are?" Vail said.

Robby nodded. "Yes, we are." To the waitress, he said, "We'll have the Montbriac. And the check."

Vail looked at the menu for an explanation: *Creamy bleu cheese from the Auvergne region, served with a sundried fruit compote.*

Robby handed the waitress his credit card. "Okay?" he asked Vail as the waitress collected the menus.

"Yeah, sure."

Robby leaned forward and took her hand. "Do you trust me?"

Vail's body tingled at the warmth of his touch. "Always."

# FORTY-TWO

obby stopped at the door to their room. Key in hand, he turned and said, "Wait here."

"Wait? For what?"

"You said you trusted me."

"I do."

Robby tilted his head. "Then wait here." He slid the key into the lock, slipped into the room, and shut the door.

Vail stood there, hands on hips. *What the hell is he up to?* She grabbed the knob, then withdrew her hand. In the next instant, the door pulled open. A dozen candles flickered around the room's periphery. They shimmered at the swoosh of air as Robby swung the door closed.

"What's this?" Vail asked.

"I think it's our room. Or did I take the wrong key?"

She gave him a mock punch in the shoulder. "I mean—"

"I know what you mean." He opened the bag containing the dessert and set it out on the table. "You've been working hard and haven't really had any time to just relax, clear your mind."

"The massage and mud bath—"

"Shhh," he said, then placed his fingers over her mouth. He removed her jacket and tossed it on the floor. Then he removed her blouse and carried her over to the bed.

The low-level, flickering yellow light from the candles provided barely enough illumination for her to see. He joined her on the bed, took the plastic spoon, and dipped it into the creamy cheese. Slathered it on her stomach . . . followed by the fruit compote, which he drizzled on top.

She giggled.

"You don't mind if I eat first, do you?"

She closed her eyes and relaxed . . . for the first time in days. "No, I don't mind. I don't mind at all."

# FORTY-THREE

The morning came and Robby was lying on top of her—or, just about. They had fallen asleep, the candles had burnt out hours ago, and they hadn't moved all night. The room's clock radio was on—probably set by the prior guest—and it was a good thing. She had not been in the state of mind to fiddle with it when she got into bed last night.

Vail gently rolled Robby over, slid off the bed, and shut the alarm. She would let him sleep in. She showered and dressed, gave Robby a kiss, and he stirred.

"I've gotta go. Roxxann is picking me up."

"See you tonight."

She winked. "Yes, you will."

———

VAIL CLIMBED INTO DIXON'S CAR. Dixon shoved her key into the ignition and turned over the engine. "You know," Dixon said, "it's been kind of fun working with you on this case. That sounds bizarrely morose, but when this case is over, I'm going to miss partnering with you."

"I feel the same way. But there's something I forgot to tell you. My boss, he wanted me to come home tonight."

Dixon, who had started backing out of her garage, stepped on the brake. "You—"

"Doesn't matter. I'm not going. I've got the time. I'm still on vacation. I just won't officially work the case. If push comes to shove, I'll just be an observer following you around. Okay?"

"Works for me." Dixon continued backing out, then headed toward 29. "So your boss. You gonna catch heat for this?"

"No doubt about it," Vail said. "But I've had hotter."

"You've . . . what? That doesn't make sense."

A few seconds passed. Vail giggled.

Dixon looked over at her. "You okay?"

"I've had hotter," she repeated. "Last night, with Robby. Oh, my god. You wouldn't believe—"

"You trying to make me jealous?"

"Sorry." Vail tried to wipe the grin from her face—but Dixon started to laugh, and then they both lost it. Five days of pent-up stress tumbled out in a tsunami of laughter.

Vail rested her forehead on the dashboard as her body convulsed—and then she began coughing. As she fought for breath, Dixon's phone began ringing.

Dixon cleared her throat to steady her voice, motioned to Vail to be quiet, then pressed the Bluetooth speaker to answer the call. "Dixon."

"Investigator Dixon, this is Ian Wirth. You told me to call if I thought of something else."

Vail and Dixon glanced at one another. Vail had to look away to avoid another laughing—and coughing—spasm.

"Absolutely."

"Can I meet you somewhere? I'd rather talk in person."

"How about at the sheriff's department? Do you know where that is?"

"I do. I can be there in fifteen."

―――

VAIL AND DIXON ARRIVED a few minutes after Wirth, who was already inside, at the second floor rotunda, in front of the glass reception counter.

"Follow us," Dixon said. She swiped her prox card, then pulled open the thick wood door. Dixon led the way to the break room, where Agbayani and Lugo were seated at a round table sipping cups of coffee.

Dixon nodded at them, then made introductions. "These detectives are on the task force, Ian. They can hear anything you have to say."

He scanned their faces. "Are you sure?"

Dixon placed a hand on Wirth's shoulder. "You're comfortable with law enforcement. I trust these guys with my life."

Wirth thought a moment, then took a seat. Dixon and Vail followed, filling out all the chairs at the table.

"Thanks for coming down, for calling us," Vail said.

Wirth glanced again at Lugo and Agbayani, then said, in a low voice, "Isaac Jenkins was talking with an attorney. I don't know if that's relevant or not, but I just thought you should know."

Vail and Dixon both leaned forward. "Isaac Jenkins?" Vail asked.

"Isaac Jenkins," Lugo said. "He was the male vic—" He stopped himself and looked at Dixon.

"*Was?*" Wirth looked from Lugo to Dixon to Vail. "Is he dead? Another *stroke?*"

Vail ignored the question. "How do you know Isaac?"

"Isaac's with Todd Nicholson. His partner."

"His partner. In business?"

"Isaac and Todd are a . . . couple. But yes, they're partners in business, too."

Vail felt perspiration sprout across her forehead. They were onto something. *Just like Robby said last night . . . a connection we weren't aware of.*

"What business?" Dixon asked.

"Isaac's the main investor in Georges Valley Reserve Select Wines. Todd's very . . . agreeable. Isaac's really the driving force behind Todd."

Vail rubbed her forehead. "Okay, I'm not clear on a few things. Todd was against Superior getting the contract, right?"

"It was more that Isaac was against it. Todd voted the way Isaac wanted."

"Why—wasn't it Todd's winery, too?"

"Todd loves the process, the challenge of growing quality grapes and turning them into reasonably priced, well-respected wine. That's why he's such a good winemaker. But he doesn't know anything about running a business. Isaac didn't really care about wine. I mean, he likes it, but he'd just as soon buy it than grow it. But it was Todd's dream, so Isaac, who's independently wealthy, bankrolled it. And he couldn't let Todd run the business, he'd drive it into the ground. So that was their arrangement. Todd knew how to make great wine. Isaac knew how to run a great business."

"Would you excuse us for a minute?" Dixon asked Wirth.

He nodded and Agbayani, Lugo, Vail, and Dixon walked into the hallway.

"This info's a game changer," Agbayani said. "We now have three people on this winery board who were against Superior getting this contract renewal. Two of the three end up dead. Although it doesn't explain the fact that our male vic, Isaac Jenkins, wasn't on the board."

Dixon shook her head. "Even though Todd Nicholson was the board member, it might as well have been Isaac Jenkins, because the person who was really calling the shots was Jenkins. So the killer knew this somehow and got rid of Jenkins to clear the way for Superior to get the contract."

"Whoa," Vail said, holding up a hand. "You're jumping to conclusions. We don't know that."

"It does look kind of obvious," Dixon said.

Vail rubbed a hand across her mouth. "No. I mean, yes, it looks obvious. But something's not right. Something isn't adding up."

"What's the huddle about?"

It was Brix, walking down the hall.

Dixon angled away from the doorway. In a low voice, she said, "We're discussing some new info we got from a witness." She canted her head, indicating Wirth sitting in the break room.

Brix's eyes flicked past her to their witness. "Well, let's do it in the conference room. I've got a techie waiting for us who's gonna go over texting stuff. I've been trying to get her in to talk to us, and she's billing the department a hundred fifty an hour. So if you're done with this guy, kick him loose and meet me in there."

Dixon and Vail rejoined Wirth in the break room.

"Ian," Dixon said, "we have a meeting we've got to get to. But you started to say something about Isaac hiring an attorney."

"Yeah. I don't know if it means anything, but he was looking at suing to get Crystal removed from the board."

"Remove Crystal—why?"

"You'd have to ask him. But I got the sense Victoria was involved with the attorney, too."

"The attorney's name?"

Wirth pulled his Windows Mobile Phone from its holster and poked at the screen. He scrolled, poked again, and said, "Marc Benezra. Downtown Napa."

Dixon wrote down the name. "Okay. Now listen to me, Ian." She shoved the pad back into her jacket pocket, then looked up at Wirth. "We're not sure what's going on here, with your board, and the players involved in its business dealings. But something's amiss. I can't say any more. But you seem like a good guy. Keep a low profile for now. Don't tell anyone you met with us. Don't say anything to anyone. Okay?"

Wirth looked at Dixon out of the corner of his eye. "Should I be . . . concerned?"

"A little bit," Vail said. "No one's said anything to anyone about you specifically. But just . . . be careful." She glanced at Dixon, then turned back to Wirth. "Ian, if we tell you something, do we have your word you won't tell anyone? And I mean, anyone. No one."

Wirth studied her face. His cheeks sprouted sweat. "I'm not sure I like the sound of this."

"I can understand that," Vail said. "I need you to summon those cop instincts you developed being around your father."

He bit his bottom lip and spoke with it sandwiched between his teeth. "Okay."

Vail leaned forward and held his gaze. "Remember we talked about Victoria's stroke? Well, Isaac also had a stroke."

Wirth's mouth fell open. "Are you saying—"

"I'm saying he had a stroke," Vail said. "Now, given that information, I want to reiterate that we have no direct information indicating you're in danger . . . of also having one. Having said that, of the three people who opposed Superior's contract renewal, two are now dead.

Be aware of your surroundings. Be careful. If something doesn't seem right, you call us. Okay?"

Wirth nodded without saying a word.

"Can we get him a uni to keep an eye on him?" Vail asked.

"I'll have to ask. I don't know if the sheriff will go for that."

"I have private security," Wirth said. "For the winery. Retired Secret Service. I'll take care of it."

Dixon called over to a deputy who was standing across the room at the coffee maker. "Greg, can you escort Mr. Wirth out?"

"Hang on to my number," Dixon said. "Remember, call if you need anything. Anything."

Wirth nodded uncertainly, then walked out with Greg.

"You're worried about the guy," Dixon said.

"His colleagues have been brutally murdered. And no one knows. The rest of them don't even know to be careful, that someone might be targeting them. I think we may need to get them all together and level with them."

"If we do, it'll be all over the news. If we're going to do that, let me find a way of using it to our advantage . . . as a way to catch this jerkoff."

Vail watched as Wirth disappeared into the stairwell. "You'd better think of something fast."

# FORTY-FOUR

Before joining the others, Dixon got Marc Benezra's phone number and explained to his assistant that they needed to meet with him today. The woman fit them into the attorney's schedule for ten o'clock, one hour from now.

"We're all set," Dixon said.

Vail, a dozen feet down the hall, was tapping out a note to Jonathan. "Excellent. Can you tell Brix I'll be right in? I've just gotta finish this email."

"Roxxi, you got a minute?" It was Eddie Agbayani, coming down the hall.

Dixon turned. "What's up?"

Agbayani stopped in front of her and shoved his hands in his rear pockets. He looked down at his feet.

Vail sensed the awkward tension and glanced up from her email.

"When this is over," Agbayani said, "when we catch this guy, maybe we could have dinner. Talk. Just the two of us."

Roxxann rubbed at her brow. "I don't know, Eddie. Yes. Maybe . . ." She shook her head. "Let me think about it, okay?"

"Is that where we're at? You have to think about whether we can sit down and talk?"

"Eddie, I can't do this. Not now. Let me—yes. I'm sorry. You're right, we should talk. As soon as we get some time, let's have dinner."

Vail shoved her BlackBerry in its holster, then pushed through the conference room door. The rest of the task force was there—Mann, Gordon, Lugo, and Brix. And a woman they hadn't yet met; presumably, she was the person they were there to see.

A moment later, Dixon and Agbayani entered and took their seats.

Brix stood at the front of the room by the whiteboard. Their assignments were still laid out in colors. A few had lines through them, while others were encircled because they were still pending resolution. Unfortunately, there were more circles than lines.

In the fluorescent lighting, Brix's sun-weathered, deeply lined face looked ashen. He resembled a man who was carrying the weight of several deaths on his shoulders—the unsolved murder of his boss's son and the pressure of going public with the Crush Killer versus the impact of keeping it under wraps. And time was running out before the decision might be made for him. Once that happened, his stress would increase several fold as the media descended on him.

Vail felt the same pressure. Billed as the expert in solving this case—the serial killer tracker, the famed profiler who has helped break the most heinous of crimes—she was impotent to provide useful, hard information that would lead to the apprehension of this offender. Making matters worse, she could not get a handle on what she was missing. And she was undoubtedly missing something.

Brix cleared his throat. "I've asked Austin Mann and Burt Gordon to stay on with us a bit longer, even though their work on the arson is largely done. We can use the manpower, and I'd rather not bring in fresh bodies that have to get up to speed. Hopefully we're closer to catching this UNSUB than we think." He extended his right arm and indicated the visitor. She rose from her chair and walked to Brix's side.

"This is Amanda Sinclair from AirCom Consulting. Amanda's here to explain text messaging, and give us a handle on how we can track, and hopefully apprehend, the UNSUB next time he contacts Karen." He moved toward his seat. "Amanda."

The woman, early thirties with frosted brown hair, took the center stage. "I know you've all used text messaging, or what we in the industry call SMS, or Short Messaging System. We don't think much about those little notes we send each other. But they can be useful in law enforcement if we know how to use them. And if the criminal doesn't. I think it's important for you to know what we can't do, as well as what we can do.

"So here's the crash course. And I'm leaving a lot out, so if you've got a question, don't be afraid to ask." She opened a file and set out some papers. "The texts that go through a wireless provider's system are not viewed by the carrier. They don't read them—they simply store the technical transmission information for varying periods of time. Very few carriers actually store the 'text' of text messages. The storage space required, multiplied by the billions of texts exchanged between users, is staggering."

"How long do they keep this transmission information?" Lugo asked.

"Good question. The answer depends on the carrier. Basically, there are several different systems for storing message information. The two most common are CDR and SMS Center. In CDR, or Call Delivery Records, the information is stored for seven days. These CDRs list information such as the time stamp—year, month, day, hour, minute, second, character length—and a variety of other technical info. The International Mobile Subscriber Identity, or IMSI, is also stored; it's like a thumbprint for the SIM card that houses all the phone's user specific information. You all know what a SIM card is, right? It's a little flash memory chip that fits into certain phones. You pull the card out of your old phone, slip it into a new one, and you're ready to go, without having to reenter all your contacts and such. With me so far?"

"Go on," Brix said.

"We also store the IMEI, or International Mobile Equipment Identity, a unique thumbprint for the exact phone equipment that's used. But it's got no permanent relationship to the individual subscriber. It's mainly used to identify valid users of the network, so if the phone is stolen, the carrier can shut off that IMEI and the phone will be a useless hunk of metal and plastic.

"The other commonly used system is the SMS Center, which is the E.164 address that lets everyone know which carrier the SMS is originating from or terminating to, the phone number the message is being sent to, how the digits were dialed, and so on. Here's an example." She moved to the overhead projector, set one of her pages on top, and turned it on. A document that resembled an Excel spreadsheet was displayed. A bar at the top read, SMS Center Log Window.

Everyone studied the screen. Vail and Lugo were taking notes as Amanda oriented the task force members as to what they were seeing.

"Any questions?" she asked.

"You said there are other ways of storing messages," Lugo said.

"Yes. Another common method is called SMSC, or Short Message Service Center. It shows where the messages originate and terminate from a carrier's system. This info is kept for a period of time based on message capacity. Sometimes, if there's a lot of messages, they'll only have the data for a week. Other times they may be able to go back a month."

Amanda slipped a different page onto the projector, showing a gray table with eleven columns aligned horizontally across the document. "The SMSC printout shows the millisecond messages are submitted from the handset and delivered out of the SMSC to the other carrier. It also shows the destination phone number. Now, it gets more complicated, because some carriers have third party vendors that send their intercarrier traffic for them."

Agbayani pointed at the screen. "Can we use this to determine the location of a perp who's transmitting a text message in real time?"

"Yes. If the carrier uses GSM technology, you can triangulate within a seven-to twenty-mile radius."

"Miles?" Lugo tossed down his pen. "You've gotta be kidding."

"Point is," Brix said, "we can determine the type of phone used and where he may've bought it."

"That *might* give us an idea as to where he lives or works," Lugo said. "But what do we do, watch weeks of surveillance tapes—if the store even has security cameras? We don't even know who we're looking for." He looked around at everyone in the room. "This ain't gonna help."

Gordon rocked forward in his seat. "I think we should plot the messages the asshole's already sent to Vail and set it up so we're monitoring her cell in real time. If and when this scumbag texts her again, we can at least triangulate on him." He spread his thick hands. "Better than nothing."

Amanda said, "Not to make things more difficult for you, but one thing you should be aware of is that the texts sent to Agent Vail's phone were from different disposable, pre-paid phones."

Mann slowly shook his head. "I think Ray's right. Waste of time."

Brix sighed. "Look, we do what we've gotta do. We use the tools available to us. Anyone got a better idea, now's the time."

Everyone looked at one another.

Dixon thanked Amanda for her assistance and dismissed her. She then recapped the information she and Vail had learned from Crystal Dahlia, Ian Wirth, and Robert Friedberg. "Karen's still got a problem with the motive because it just doesn't fit with how serial killers operate, their whole psychological makeup, and why they do what they do. But I think we should follow the course, see what we turn up."

"We're always learning and seeing new things," Vail said. "So this offender could be a new breed, or just something we haven't seen before. Right now, I wouldn't discount anything. I wish I could offer more, but I've had a hard time putting it all together."

"Let's have you guys stay on it, dig deeper into the AVA board and its players," Dixon said. "Karen and I have a follow-on appointment in half an hour with the attorney. We'll keep you posted."

Brix opened his notepad and flipped pages. "Last order of business. I've got something from the Special Investigations Bureau on the prosthesis request Karen had." He shot a glance at Mann, then Vail, and continued: "This is preliminary stuff, but there were a total of a hundred-fifty-seven males with upper limb prosthetics. Only eleven in the age range Karen specified. Two were alibied, three were out of town and unreachable and the other six are being interviewed, or are scheduled to be interviewed. Just going by their sheets and backgrounds, it doesn't look promising. But I told NSIB to ride it out. Questions?"

No one spoke.

"Okay, then. Keep at it. You find anything, let us all know."

# FORTY-FIVE

As Vail and Dixon descended the stairs of the sheriff's department, Marc Benezra's secretary phoned Dixon and moved their meeting to the nearby Artesa Winery, ten minutes down the road off Highway 12.

"You're in for a real treat," Dixon said. "Artesa has one of the more picturesque views of the valley. And judging by the weather and rainfall we had last month, you're going to get an eyeful."

Dixon took Highway 121, then turned left onto 12.

"Isn't this the same way we went to Sonoma?"

"It is. But not nearly as far. We're gonna turn off 12 in a few minutes, into the Carneros Region. Carneros is known for its Pinot Noir and Chardonnay. But Artesa is one of my favorite places to take guests when they come to visit. It's like an art museum rolled into a winery."

Dixon drove up the curving driveway and parked in the visitor's lot. "We're early. Let me take you the long way around, show you the view."

As they walked along the path from the car, they came to a large circular pond with a fountain shaped like a short martini glass. Water cascaded over the edges and landed in the surrounding pool. Large, glistening, silver railroad-spike-shaped sculptures stood erect along its periphery.

"What are those things sticking up?" Vail asked.

"Hell if I know. They're cool looking, that's for sure."

Beyond, the vineyard-blanketed rolling hills stretched for miles in all directions.

"Carneros," Dixon said, holding a hand against her forehead to shield the sun. "And the Napa Valley. Off in the distance is San Francisco."

Vail followed suit and brought up a hand as if ready to salute. "Stunning."

Dixon tapped her on the shoulder. "The view gets better as we go up." She led Vail up the four flights of cement stairs, which featured a trickling waterfall along its centermost rim. At the crest of the top step was a short landing and another flight of stairs. But just ahead was a cement bridge that featured an expansive pool on both sides, with water jets that shot bursts of narrow water streams at a 45 degree angle.

"Impressive," Vail said, slowing to watch the water arc through the air.

In front of them was the winery—and their appointment with Marc Benezra. The building was completely enveloped by clumps of wild grasses, save for the glass-walled entrance and a large V-shaped windowed bay jutting out by the left side of the mound.

They walked through the doors and found a richly appointed wood entry with freestanding metal and blown-glass artwork. They moved past the gift shop into the tasting room, an irregularly shaped area sporting smooth columns and floor-to-ceiling windows. Seated at one of the small tables on the far side of the room was a dark-suited man. He rose and buttoned his coat.

They approached and introduced themselves. Benezra was a shade over six two, with horn-rimmed glasses and a sharp-featured face that was all business. "Thanks for switching our meeting place," he said. "One of the employees here is a client I'm meeting at ten thirty, so this gave us more time to chat."

Vail took a seat in one of the ultramodern wood and metal chairs. "No big deal. This is my first time here, and if we hadn't met here, I probably wouldn't have gotten the chance to see it."

Benezra took his seat. "Quite the treat, isn't it?"

Vail looked behind Benezra at the wall of glass and the view beyond.

"We've got some questions," Dixon said. "About Isaac Jenkins and the lawsuit he and Victoria Cameron were discussing with you."

Benezra's face widened into a smile. "You must know I can't talk about that without my client present."

Dixon nodded, as if she agreed. But then she said, "Sorry to be the one to tell you this, but your clients are dead."

Benezra's mouth dropped open ever so slightly. "When? How?"

"Very recently. As to how . . . we can't say just yet. But their deaths are being kept quiet. For now. I'm going to have to ask you to respect that."

Benezra's eyes narrowed. "Why? What's—" He stopped, revelation relaxing his facial muscles.

Vail nodded slowly. He had just put it together. Cops coming around to ask about two clients who are suddenly dead. She figured he had realized there were suspicious circumstances surrounding their deaths. *And he'd be right.*

"So," Vail said, "I'd strongly suggest you help us. That's all I can say."

Benezra still looked stunned by the news. "I still can't discuss anything to do with Isaac's business. Does Todd know?" He reached into his inside jacket pocket and removed his phone.

Dixon placed a hand on Benezra's. "You can't discuss this with Mr. Nicholson."

"Excuse me, Ms. Dixon. Remove your hand."

Dixon kept it there. "This is a very serious matter, Mr. Benezra. Lives are at stake. This is much larger than your deceased clients."

Benezra sucked on the inside of his cheek, then nodded and dropped the phone back in his pocket. "I'm listening."

"Actually," Vail said, "we need to listen and you need to talk—"

"Agent Vail, I told you. I can't—"

"Let's do it another way. We're going to tell you some things and you're going to nod or shake your head. Don't say a word."

Benezra looked away. "This just isn't right."

"If I told you your life was in danger, would that change your attitude?"

The attorney's head whipped back to Vail. They locked eyes. "Are you saying—"

"We need to be asking the questions. First one. You were discussing a lawsuit to remove Crystal Dahlia from the Georges Valley board."

Benezra sat there a long moment, then nodded.

Vail continued. "You'd also been working with Victoria Cameron on the same issue."

Benezra's eyes wandered the room.

Vail rephrased: "You had some discussions with Victoria about this."

Nod.

"Okay," she said. "Did Victoria or Isaac say anything that might've led you to think they feared for their lives?"

Benezra shook his head.

"Were there any concerns about Superior Mobile Bottling, that maybe they were doing something illegal?"

Another shake.

Vail sighed and looked at Dixon. "Anything you want to ask?"

Benezra leaned forward. "Agent Vail, you're in the wrong forest. You understand what I'm saying?"

"I do. But I really need you to talk. We need to know what you know. I respect your legal responsibilities. But we're up against the wall here. We're trying to save lives. I promise you we won't disclose where we got this info. We're not interested in building a case against a suspect. We're just trying to catch a—a very dangerous person. Before someone else gets hurt. But we just need some answers. Tell us what you know."

Benezra sat back, then rubbed his face with both hands. A moment later, he said, "Let's go outside, take a little walk."

They rose from their chairs and pushed through the nearby glass door, which spilled out onto a long patio with multiple round aluminum tables and matching seats. The vista was clear and the hills rolled on for miles into the distance. A small, blue body of water was visible less than a mile way.

Benezra walked a dozen feet, then stopped and leaned his forearms atop the metal railing. Dixon and Vail did likewise. "I'm not telling you this. Right?"

"Right," Dixon said.

Benezra nodded slowly, then said, "Isaac and Victoria were very upset because of the AVA issue. You know about it?"

"The 85 percent minimum?" Vail asked.

"Apparently, someone from Congressman Church's office was involved. He was speaking in favor of the other members of the AVA board, trying to influence the Alcohol and Tobacco Tax Trade Bureau. The TTB. Familiar with it?"

"Yeah, it's come up before."

"Well, it was improper, to say the least, for the congressman's office to take sides. It had nothing to do, really, with his district. No reason for him to come down on either side of the issue unless he was politically motivated to do so."

Vail felt a pang of disappointment. While there could be the seeds of something underhanded—or merely politics as usual—it wasn't the smoking gun for which they were hoping.

"Interesting," Dixon said.

But Vail sensed the same emotion in Dixon's voice that she was feeling herself. *Interesting, but not relevant.*

"No," Benezra said. "What's interesting is what my PI found out. I hired an investigator to look into it. It just smelled foul. I mean, yeah, could've just been political horse-trading, but Victoria and Isaac were convinced something wasn't right. And what my guy discovered was worse than what they'd envisioned." He stopped, ran a hand across his forehead. "If I tell you what we found, everyone will know it came from me. I really can't—I need to talk with Todd."

Dixon pushed away from the railing. "Call him. Keep it short. Just tell him I'm investigating something regarding one of the congressman's advisors and I'm offering to exchange some information that you think'll be beneficial to your efforts. That's all true."

Benezra dug out his phone. He dialed, spoke with Nicholson, and did as Dixon instructed. He slid the phone back in his jacket. "He trusts me to do the right thing. Am I doing the right thing, Ms. Dixon?"

Dixon locked eyes with Benezra. "If you only knew."

Benezra sighed deeply. "My PI found payoffs to Timothy Nance, Church's District Director, in a private account. Two payments of twenty-five grand apiece. We think they came from Crystal Dahlia, which would make sense, but we're not sure. And it seems the fifty grand was shipped out of the account a couple days later."

"To where?"

"Don't know. My PI hasn't finished digging. It's . . . sensitive work. We have to be very careful. But it looks like Nance was taking a bribe to influence government legislation regarding the minimum grape requirement for the AVA."

Vail held up a hand. "Hang on a second. I'm not sure we can reach that conclusion. Those are pretty serious charges. Taking bribes, influence peddling. Corruption, graft."

Benezra looked away. "Congressman Church is close friends with the director of the Regulations and Ruling Division of the TTB. And they administer AVA designations. Does that change your opinion?"

Vail raised her brow. *Yeah, that'd change mine.*

"Kind of strange for a man who's thinking of running for governor to do something like this," Dixon said.

"Governor?" Benezra asked. "That's news to me."

"How deeply involved is Church in all this?" Vail asked.

Benezra shrugged. "I couldn't say Church is involved in *any* of this. Nance may've simply taken the money with the intent of convincing the congressman to talk with his buddy at the TTB. I wouldn't be surprised if Church has no idea what Nance is doing." He turned to face Dixon. "Can I trust you, Ms. Dixon?"

Dixon shoved her hands into her pockets. "I think you already have."

Benezra nodded. "Fair enough." He studied Dixon's face, then said, "One of your law enforcement colleagues also appears to be involved."

"Who?"

"Scott Fuller."

"Involved, as in the AVA issue, the bribery?"

"His name came up, more than once. But I'll leave it to you to look into it further. Fuller wasn't the big fish, so I told my PI to first concentrate on Nance and Church." Benezra tipped his chin back. "Now . . . the info you had to exchange?"

"Off the record," Dixon said. "And not for publication. Fuller, along with a guy named Walton Silva and Nance, were involved in an arson plot. Fuller's dead. Silva's in custody. Nance is implicated, but free. I'm not sure that helps you much."

Benezra considered that a moment. "I think it tells me this might be larger than we'd thought. We need to seriously consider turning this over to the Feds to investigate. Let them sort it out." Benezra looked down at his watch. "I have to go, my ten thirty."

Dixon extended a hand. "Thank you. This won't go beyond us. From our end, anyway, we'll keep you out of it. If you share this stuff with the Feds—and I do recommend you do that—they'll obviously want to see everything you've got."

Benezra nodded, bid them good luck, then walked back through the glass door.

---

VAIL AND DIXON headed to the sheriff's department in silence, both working through the information Marc Benezra had given them.

"I kind of liked the guy," Vail finally said. "He didn't have to tell us shit."

"Yeah, and what he did tell us . . . it kind of puts things in a different light. I'm now wondering about that arson. Silva and Nance lied to us."

"If you were taking bribes, would you tell the police? Either that or Silva was kept in the dark and Nance and Fuller kept the money for themselves, figuring the promise about getting a post in a governor's administration was enough for Silva."

Dixon cocked her head. "Yeah, but that's playing with fire. If Silva finds out they were taking money and not sharing it, he could get pissed and start talking."

"Playing with fire?"

Dixon winced. "No pun intended."

Vail shook her head. "I don't think he'd start talking—not only would he blow his chance at a major career boost, anything he'd say would implicate himself. And for what? It wasn't that much money, especially split three ways."

Dixon tapped her fingers on the dash beyond the steering wheel. "People have killed for a lot less."

"The jewel in this ring was the position they'd get in the governor's administration."

Dixon nodded. "Okay."

"So," Vail said, "let's back up. Nance and Fuller are concerned with my determination to go public with a serial killer on the loose in Napa. It brings in the media. More Feds. More scrutiny. And that's clearly something they wouldn't want because it'd jeopardize their future careers. Not to mention the nice payoffs on the side."

Dixon slid the car into a spot outside the sheriff's department. "There might've been more money on its way. Could it be the stakes were even higher than we know? Maybe Benezra's PI only uncovered one root of the tree. This may go deeper and farther."

"Sometimes a hammer is just a hammer, Roxxann."

"Either way, it still doesn't get us closer to the Crush Killer. Unless that tree is freaking huge, and we're missing more than we realize."

Vail got that stab in the gut again. "I think that's what's been bothering me."

# FORTY-SIX

*T*he rest of the task force was still in the conference room, making phone calls and tossing around theories. Coffee cups and crumpled lumps of paper littered the table. When Vail and Dixon relayed what they had just learned, they all leaned back in their chairs to digest it.

"Just when I think we're on the right track," Brix said, "something gets tossed into the mix that makes us rethink everything."

"You guys come up with anything on Superior Bottling?" Dixon asked.

"Record's clean," Lugo said. "None of their employees have ever had any brushes with the law. No complaints with the Better Business Bureau." He looked down at the pad in front of him. "Chamber of Commerce thinks they're model corporate citizens. I checked with a bunch of my winery contacts—from growers to vintners—at Oakville Winegrowers Association, Rutherford Dust Society, Stag's Leap Winegrower's Association, Oak Knoll Winegrowers . . . bottom line is, no one had anything bad to say about them."

"What you're saying is you didn't pick up any dirt on the grapevine," Vail said.

Dixon smirked. "That was bad."

"And," Mann said, ignoring Vail's pun, "I checked with my TTB office. No federal violations on record."

"Fine," Dixon said. "Then let's focus on what's most likely to give us something."

"I think we should at least go there, talk with them," Vail said. "Shake the tree."

"I agree," Brix said. He walked to the front of the room and dug through some papers. Pulled out a page and handed it to Dixon. "Here's some background on César Guevara. But there's something you gotta know. Silver Ridge uses them. So if you want me to hang back—"

"Why would you hang back?" Mann asked.

Brix put his hands on his hips. "All right, listen up. For those of you who don't know, I'm a silent partner in Silver Ridge. My brother handles all of its business operations. I have no say in any of it—nor do I want to. For this very reason. Keeps things clean and simple. This hasn't substantively affected Victoria Cameron's investigation. Has it, Roxx?"

"No."

"Anyone got any questions or concerns? Now's the time."

No one responded.

"Do you know anyone there?" Dixon asked.

"No, I don't know anyone there, and no one there knows me. But they'd recognize my last name."

Vail shook her head. "I think you should stay out of it."

Dixon bent forward, resting both hands on the table. "But your knowledge could be useful."

"Look," Brix said. "I've got a lot going on here. Ray's been as entrenched in the region as I've been. He practically grew up on a vineyard and is well versed in all aspects of wine production. Take Ray and you get the benefit of having an insider without the baggage I bring to the table."

Dixon turned to Lugo. "How about it, Ray?"

Lugo appeared to be shrinking into his seat. "I've got a lot to do here, Roxx. I really should stay behind—"

"We won't be long," Dixon said. "It's only a few minutes from here. C'mon."

Dixon pulled on the door and held it open. Vail walked through and looked back to see Lugo reluctantly pulling himself from his chair.

---

SUPERIOR MOBILE BOTTLING operated out of a large warehouse in an industrial area of American Canyon, a few miles south of the sheriff's department. Vail and Dixon left Lugo in the car and walked up to the concrete tilt-up building that featured an oversize gold crest above its entrance, emblazoned with a large seriffed S in the middle, sandwiched between a smaller M and B.

Dixon had decided on a straightforward, direct approach. If Guevara ducked them, they would leave and Lugo would then come in under the guise of a vintner inquiring about their bottling services and fee structure.

Dixon pulled open the glass door and stepped into a small, well-appointed reception room. Tastefully decorated with high-resolution photos of grapes on the vine, it also included industry-specific pictures of buffed stainless steel machinery involved in the various production steps of mobile bottling.

A woman with platinum hair and a face that had seen its share of facelifts walked in through a side door. "I'm Sandra. How can I help you?"

"Roxxann Dixon, Napa County District Attorney's office. This is my associate, Karen Vail. Is César Guevara available for a brief chat?"

"Do you have an appointment?"

"We were in the neighborhood and were hoping he could help us with a case we're working on."

"I'll go see if Mr. Guevara can meet with you. He was out back doing some maintenance on one of the trailers—"

"Perfect," Dixon said. "We'll just go on back ourselves. If he's in the middle of something mechanical, I'd rather not drag him away from his work. We just have a couple background questions. Around the side of the building?"

Sandra seemed a bit flustered. "I—yes, but I really should—"

"Thanks," Dixon said.

Vail was already through the door and signaling Lugo with a tilt of her head. Lugo slowly climbed out of the car and joined them as they walked down the asphalt roadway that abutted the long building.

Lugo slowed his pace. "Why don't I wait out here, have a look around the periphery?"

"We can look around after if we want," Dixon said, motioning him along. "I think you'd be more valuable with us."

"Or, I could talk with the front office personnel while you're in with Guevara. Sometimes they'll give you more than the main guy."

"We met her," Vail said. "I didn't get the sense she knew anything important." She gave Lugo a playful shove with her forearm. "You okay?"

Lugo swiveled to look over his shoulder. "Fine."

"They probably park the rigs indoors," Dixon said. "With the cost of that equipment, I'd imagine they don't take any chances with someone hauling off their trailers."

They walked briskly. Vail was sure Sandra had, by now, notified Guevara of their presence. Whether that mattered or not, she wasn't sure. It depended on whether Superior had done anything wrong. And all indications were they had not—other than being at the center of a contentious political squabble among business partners.

Dixon, a stride ahead, turned back to Vail and Lugo. "Security cameras." She indicated small surveillance devices mounted atop steel poles at various points in the lot. They were all aimed at the building.

A few feet ahead was a gray rollup garage door. It was in the up position, revealing three highly polished full-size semis parked alongside one another.

They walked in. A radio was playing music with a Latin beat. Vail knelt down and looked beneath the rigs. She saw two sets of feet a dozen yards away, one male and the other female.

Vail motioned to the others that Guevara was ahead, between the farthest two trailers. They turned left down the aisle between the trucks and saw a man of medium build, strong jaw and prominent forehead. He had a red flannel shirt on with the sleeves rolled up.

He turned to face them as they approached. Vail led the way, followed single file by Dixon and Lugo.

"Mr. Guevara?"

"Who wants to know?"

"I'm Karen Vail." She held up her credentials. Dixon moved alongside Vail and displayed her badge, then thumbed the area behind her. "And this is Sergeant Ray Lugo, St. Helena PD."

Guevara had a blue rag in his hands. His eyes narrowed as he moved his head to the side to see Lugo. "Is there a problem?" Guevara asked.

"We just have some questions," Vail said. "We're hoping you can shed some light on a few things for us."

Guevara spread his hands. "Ask away." His eye caught Lugo, and his gaze lingered there.

Vail turned to face Lugo, then swiveled back to Guevara. *Something's going on. Do they recognize each other from somewhere?*

"Why don't you tell us about your company."

Guevara stole a look at his watch. "Superior is the leading mobile bottling company in California. We bottle mostly in the Napa Valley, Sonoma, Healdsburg, and Mendocino, but if the price is right, we'll also do Contra Costa and El Dorado Counties. We've got eight rigs, all state of the art. Nobody comes close to the services we offer, the quality of work we do. And no one can match our prices. Simply put, we're the best."

Vail added it up. *There's a lot of money tied up in those trailers.*

"Now, what did you really come here to ask?"

Dixon lifted her chin. "We've been talking with the board of directors for the Georges Valley AVA. We know about the disagreement over renewing your contract. How has your relationship been with the board?"

Guevara's eyes flicked over to an area behind them. To Lugo. His gaze returned to Dixon and he shrugged. "No problems. We show up, we bottle, box, and offload. Bottle, box, offload. Same every year. They have lots of wineries. We work good with all of 'em."

"Any problems with any of the board members?"

"What do you mean?"

"I'm thinking, like, Victoria Cameron?"

Guevara rubbed his hands on the rag. "No. No problems."

"She was pretty much against you getting your contract renewed," Vail said. "You've got a lot of money invested in your equipment. Be a tough loss, a financial hardship, if she got her way. Any idea why she was so determined not to renew the contract?"

"I don't get involved in that stuff. That's their business. My business is bottling."

*This guy is sharp—but guarded. Why? What's he hiding? Is it related to the looks he keeps giving Ray?*

"Where were you last Friday, around six?" Vail asked.

"Here, cleaning the corking machine."

"How late did you stay?"

Guevara looked ceilingward. "About eight, I think."

"Anyone else here with you?" Vail asked.

"Sandra left at five. I don't know if anyone else was around. I'll have to check."

*Not the kind of answer we like to hear.* "Was there anyone here that you saw? Anyone who was scheduled to work?"

Guevara locked eyes with Vail. His jaw muscles tightened. "I'd have to check."

"You have to check if you saw anyone? Either you did or you didn't."

"I don't remember."

*This guy is beginning to piss me off.* "Who sets the schedule for your employees?"

Guevara folded his arms across his chest. "Why is that important?"

"It's important because I asked the question."

Another firm stare from Guevara.

"Ray," Dixon said. "How about you go have a chat with Sandra up front and see what she knows?"

"Do you have a warrant?" Guevara asked.

"For what?" Dixon said. "To ask questions?"

Guevara tossed the rag on the floor. "I don't know. It sounds like you think we've done something wrong."

Dixon shrugged. "We're conducting an investigation, Mr. Guevara. Right now we don't have reason to think anyone at Superior has done anything wrong. But you're being evasive in your answers, and that does make us suspicious. Like you're trying to hide something."

Guevara spread his arms. "I got nothing to hide. I don't remember seeing anyone here with me. But it's a short list of people who might've been here. I promise you I'll look into what you asked and call you back with the answers. Good?"

*Not really. But it's apparently the best we can get right now.*

"What about Monday? Where were you from noon till four o'clock?"

"I'll check that, too."

"And Wednesday, around six?"

"I'll have to get back to you."

"When was the last time you were in Vallejo?" Vail asked.

Guevara shrugged. "I drive through there once a week."

"Know anyone there, any family?"

"There's a supplier we use there. Other than that and the freeway, I've got no reason to go there."

Vail took a flier, played a hunch. "Mr. Guevara, is your mother still alive?"

Guevara's eyes narrowed. "What do you want with my mother?"

Vail shoved her hands in her back pockets. "Just a question."

"I can't see how she's got anything to do with this conversation."

"That'd be kind of hard for you to judge, though, since you don't know why I'm asking. Wouldn't you think?"

"My mother has nothing to do with me, my business, or my family. Next question."

*Interesting.*

Dixon dug into her pocket. "I'd appreciate if you get that other information for us later today or tomorrow."

"I'll let you know as soon as I have something to tell you."

Dixon handed over her card. Vail watched Guevara take it, then took special notice as his eyes flicked back over to Lugo. The look said he wasn't happy. Whatever was going on with Lugo, they would soon find out.

---

UPON LEAVING, Vail suggested they grab lunch while they could, since once they returned to the sheriff's department, they would likely get sidetracked with work. Dixon recommended Azzurro Pizzeria on Main Street in downtown Napa, a fifteen-minute drive from Superior Mobile Bottling.

"Best pizza I've had in a long time," Dixon said. "The flavors burst all over your tongue."

Vail laughed. "Burst all over your tongue?"

Dixon unfolded the menu. "You'll see. My fave's the Verde.

Spinach, garlic, chilies, and ricotta. If you like mushrooms, the Funghi is absolutely *killer*." She looked up at Vail. "Sorry. You've got me doing it now."

Lugo was quiet while they consulted the menu and then ordered. The waitress brought their iced teas and then moved off. Vail and Dixon made idle chitchat about the area, including their favorite pizza restaurants they'd eaten in across the country.

Finally, with Vail itching to address what was on her mind—it was bothering her like a piece of food stuck between her teeth—she turned to Lugo. "Ray," Vail said nonchalantly, "do you have a history with César Guevara?"

Lugo looked up, as if suddenly realizing others were at the table with him. "A history?"

"Do you know him?"

"Why are you asking?" Dixon asked.

Vail had to tread carefully. She had a knack for alienating people, and Lugo was a good guy and well liked. She didn't want to start something that would undoubtedly leave a bad taste with everyone on the task force. Clearly, Dixon had not picked up on the silent interplay between the two men. *Did I imagine it?* She tore open a packet of Splenda and dumped it in her glass. "I just thought I noticed Guevara giving him some strange looks."

Lugo took a drink from his iced tea. "Really?"

*He's not making this easy. Careful* . . . "So you didn't notice him giving you looks, like he was pissed at you or something?"

Lugo pursed his lips and shook his head. "No."

"So you don't know him then."

Lugo bobbed his head. "Sort of yes, sort of no. We worked the vineyards as migrant workers back when we were teenagers. But we weren't friends or anything."

"Have you seen him lately? Run into him somewhere, grab a beer?"

"I haven't talked to him in twenty years."

*Nowhere to go with that answer. He's either telling the truth or he's a good liar.* Regardless, without causing hard feelings, Vail had to drop it here. But the more she thought about it, the stronger her sense that there was something going on between the two men. If Superior

Mobile Bottling and/or César Guevara continued to remain under suspicion, she would have to convince Dixon to take the next step: check out their colleague's story. Get his phone LUDs and see if any of Guevara's contact numbers showed up.

Their pizzas came and Vail acknowledged the "bursting flavors." If there was one thing about this trip she found enjoyable—other than her limited time with Robby—it was the food. She even had to admit to Dixon that the Funghi pizza was "killer."

Now if she could just find the real killer—the Crush Killer—she'd be happy.

# FORTY-SEVEN

**W**hen Vail, Dixon, and Lugo returned to the conference room, all of the task force members were present except for Burt Gordon, who had left to follow up a lead. Brix finished a phone call, then riffled through a short stack of papers, removed a document, and brought it over to Dixon.

"The board list you got from Crystal Dahlia. We should divide up the names, start running backgrounders on them."

Vail rubbed at a kink in her neck. "Actually, if now's a good time, we've got some stuff to go over with the group."

Brix glanced around. No one was on a call, so he stood and said, "I need everyone's attention." He nodded to Vail.

"We just paid a visit to César Guevara, the principal at Superior Mobile Bottling. We didn't come away with anything concrete other than some strange vibes."

"How so?" Agbayani asked.

Dixon leaned back in her seat. "Evasive answers, nervous and defiant body language."

"Is he alibied for any of the murders?"

"That's where the evasive answers started. Whatever alibi he comes up with we're going to have to hit pretty hard."

"I got the sense there was something else going on," Vail said. She could not bring up the interplay with Lugo, but figured she would put it out there and see what came of it. "I think we need to look hard at Guevara, and separately at Superior Mobile Bottling."

Lugo spread his hands. "We already looked at Superior."

"Look harder."

"Before we get all hung up on hunches," Austin Mann said, "what do you think about this guy from a behavioral analysis perspective?"

Vail curled some hair behind her right ear. "César Guevara is in the right age range. He runs a successful company, and he was guarded in his answers. This tells me he's a smart guy—higher IQ—which fits with our offender. We need to run him through DMV, see what kind of car he drives. I'm betting it's something expensive and flashy."

Brix nodded at Lugo, who swiveled his chair over to the laptop on the conference table.

"He might have unresolved issues with his mother, which is common with narcissists. He's defiant, even when challenged by law enforcement. He's got a very healthy ego. If we can find out the history behind his company, we may know more. Did he start it or buy it? Does he have a partner or partners? We have to keep sight of the fact it's called 'Superior Mobile Bottling.' That'd be a name a narcissist might choose for his company."

"It could also be a name a normal businessperson might choose," Agbayani said. "All this stuff could be explained differently. He might just be a confident and cocky asshole. It doesn't mean he's a serial killer."

"He drives a Beemer," Lugo said, staring at the onscreen data. "A five series."

"Pricey," Dixon said. She leaned over and made a note on her pad.

"But," Vail said, "as Eddie pointed out, in and of itself, it doesn't mean anything. Successful guy, making good money, buys a nice toy. Status symbol. Fun to drive."

Dixon put down her pen. "Let's get some background on him. Married, kids, siblings, place of birth, known acquaintances. Ray, shoot us over a copy of his CDL photo."

Lugo went back to working the keyboard. "Emailing it to everyone."

Vail leaned over to Dixon. "There's something we're missing. I've had this feeling all along. I don't know what it is, but it's eating away at me."

"Any idea what it is?"

Vail thought a moment, then shook her head. "It's like something on the tip of your tongue. Your brain reaches out but it just can't grab the thought." Vail's BlackBerry vibrated. She checked the display: Gifford. *Shit. I know what this is about.* "I gotta take this," she said, then rose and left the room. Outside, she answered the call. "Hey, boss."

"Lenka's booked you on Virgin, the nine thirty-five red-eye out of SFO to Dulles."

Vail had to chuckle at the irony. That was the flight the Crush Killer supposedly took to Virginia. "I'm unfortunately familiar with that flight. But that's not why you're calling."

"Actually," Gifford said, "that is why I'm calling. Because I know that if I had Lenka call you, you'd blow her off or not answer it. Either way, it'd end up back on my desk and I'd be calling you anyway. So before you argue with me, here's the confirmation number—"

"Sir, we're closing in on the scumbag. We've got a suspect."

"Fan-fucking-tastic. Then the good men and women of the Napa Major Crimes Task Force can take it from here. I want you on that flight."

Vail did not reply.

"Karen, I know you heard me. Now, I want to hear you. Tell me you're going to be on that flight."

*So . . . do I tell him I'll be on it, when I'm not sure I will be? Or do I level with him? He's not interested in discussing it. I'd just be wasting my time.* "I still have vacation time left. I'm going to spend it with Robby. I deserve it."

Gifford laughed, a bellicose outburst. "Do you really think you're gonna be able to shut it out of your mind and relax while your former task force colleagues pursue these leads? I mean, are you thinking you can snow me, or are you deluding yourself?"

*Why does everyone think they know me so well?* "I think I can shut it down." *Okay, that's total bullshit. But did I at least sound convincing?*

A rustle of papers. "I can't order you home because you do, in fact, have vacation days left. And you are there on vacation. Or were." He sighed, audibly. "Karen, you've given me an ulcer, you know that?"

"I think you've already told me, sir. Again, sorry to hear that."

"Now *that* I know is a lie."

"Actually, in spite of everything, I like you, sir. You're a good man. And given everything that's happened recently, you've come through for me."

"I'm glad you realize that. But I wanna be perfectly clear with you so there'll be no misunderstandings later. You're there on vacation. This isn't some wink across the phone line for you to continue working this case. You're off the task force effective immediately. And I'm going to call Lieutenant Brix and let him know."

"At least give me until the evening, like our original agreement."

"I didn't realize we had an agreement—on anything."

"Sir, please. Let me see this one lead through."

There was a moment of silence while Gifford considered. "You have until 7 p.m. Then you're done."

Vail bit her lip. "I understand your position." And she did, though she didn't agree with it.

"Enjoy the rest of your vacation. Tell Hernandez I wish him luck, 'cause you're going to be a bear to live with the next few days."

Vail hung up, then texted Robby and told him the "good" news: that they were going to be able to spend some together on this trip, after all. She would touch base with him later about dinner because she was apparently going to be done by six. She sent the message, then pushed through the wood conference room door. She caught Brix's attention and motioned him over to the far corner.

"Everything okay?"

"Not really." Vail scratched at her head. "I've been ordered off the task force. Effective 7 p.m. My ASAC is going to call you."

"What? We're looking at Guevara, but we've still got nothing. He can't just pull you off. We need you."

Vail looked down at the carpet. "I tried, Brix. You know I tried." She turned toward the windows to her left. "I'll still be in town because I have vacation days left. But he specifically prohibited me from working with you guys."

Brix's phone buzzed. He locked eyes with Vail, then she walked away.

"Karen," Dixon said. "We got another fax from Crystal Dahlia. Board bylaws." She flipped the sheet and held up another page. "And here's the info Kevin Cameron had promised."

"Bad news, Roxx. Just spoke with my ASAC. It's official. I'm off at 7 p.m."

"Total bullshit," Dixon said.

Vail rubbed her eyes. "Maybe it's for the best. I'm really tired."

"You don't believe that."

Vail yawned. "I *am* very tired." She wore a weary smile. "But no, I don't believe that."

"Karen," Brix called out. He held up his phone. "That wasn't who we thought it was. Everyone, listen up." He waited for Agbayani, Mann, and Lugo to make eye contact. "Just got off the phone with my wife. I'd told her we were working with a profiler, she loves that show *Criminal Minds*—anyway, our UNSUB took out an advertisement in today's *Press*." He looked down at his pad. "It says, 'Karen Vail Photography. Get your profile taken, 50 percent off sale. Act now. Limited time offer.'"

"This may be our last chance," Vail said. "Can we get hold of a copy of the ad?"

"She's faxing it over right now."

"We need to call the *Press*," Lugo said, "see if the guy paid for it with a credit card."

"Do it," Dixon said.

"Was there a phone number or contact info?" Vail asked.

"Email address."

Vail pulled her BlackBerry and started to compose a message.

"What are you doing?" Dixon asked.

"Sending him a message. I think it's time to cut a deal." She looked up at the others. "Anyone have a problem with going public?" Vail knew it was a sore point: Fuller had forcibly objected—as did Nance—and both had since been discredited.

Brix shook his head. "If Guevara is our guy, we don't need to do that anymore."

"And if he's not," Vail said, "we blow this chance to make contact. I can at least promise it to him. Whether we follow through with it is something we can hash out later."

"Can we get a subpoena for Guevara's computer and Smartphone," Mann asked, "and any other email-enabled devices he may have?"

Agbayani said, "We should at least get someone on him, keep an eye on him."

Dixon pulled her cell and dialed. "I don't think we have enough for a subpoena, but I'll see what I can do."

Brix flipped open his phone and pressed a couple of numbers. "I'll call Gordon. He's only about ten minutes away from Superior. I'll have him keep an eye on the place, give him Guevara's Beemer plate in case he's our guy and he goes to a cybercafé to use an anonymous PC." He gave Gordon instructions, then closed his phone. Almost immediately, Brix's phone rang. "Caller ID says 703 area code."

Vail frowned. "My ASAC."

Brix silenced the ringer, then winked. "I'll have to call him back."

Vail smiled warmly. It really wouldn't buy her any time with her boss, but it made her feel good. When this case started, Brix wouldn't give her the time of day. Now, he was doing what he could to keep her on the team.

The fax machine in the corner of the room rang. As Brix retrieved the document, Vail pushed thoughts of Gifford's directive from her mind and concentrated on the wording of the message she would send. She closed her eyes and considered what she would say. *Keep it short. Unemotional. Build him up without being obvious.* She typed:

Got your message. Love the ad. Very clever. I want to take advantage of your offer. Let's make a deal. If you provide us with a list of all your victims—all of them—going back to the very first one, I'll have the Napa Valley Press here at our offices within an hour of receipt of the list, and you'll have a front page story in tomorrow's paper. Let me know if those terms are acceptable.

She read it back to the task force members, who had completed their respective phone calls. They asked a few questions, but the message was largely left intact.

"Any way we can track the email?" Agbayani asked.

Lugo nodded. "If we send it from Outlook through the county's mail server, yes."

"But he'll know it's not coming from me," Vail said. "That might spook him."

"I can set up a mail account for you here. I can spoof it so it'll look like your BlackBerry mail. But if he knows more than the average Joe about email, he may be able to tell."

Dixon rose from her chair and stretched. "If he's reading his mail in a cybercafé, I don't think he's going to take the time to dig into it." She stood behind her chair and leaned on the seatback. "I think we'll be okay."

Vail pointed at the laptop. "Do it."

"I'll need some help from IT," Lugo said. He lifted the corded room phone and dialed an extension. He pinned the handset against his shoulder with his head and configured the mail account per the tech's instructions. He hung up and said, "I'm ready. I've got tracking enabled. He won't know. We'll see when it's delivered to his mail server."

Lugo sent the message, then leaned back in his chair. "Now we wait."

The mail delivery receipt came back almost immediately; the UNSUB's response within thirty minutes. The familiar Outlook "mail received" chime sounded. Lugo slid his chair squarely in front of the laptop and yelled, "Got something." He opened the message and read: "I want TV news there, too. I will send you the document soon. You'll then have sixty minutes to get a TV reporter there. I'll know. I'll be watching."

"Call the news desk at KNTV," Dixon said to Agbayani. "Tell them we need a reporter and cameraman, in a marked van. Explain to them we have an exclusive breaking story that's fluid. But," she said, raising a finger, "do not mention the words serial killer."

Agbayani nodded, then pulled his phone.

"Ray," Brix said, "anything on the tracking?"

"Delivered to the mail server. I'll ask the IT guys to do a more thorough analysis of its path. But I would guess it'll end up at some generic wireless connection and he'll be long gone."

"We don't know if we don't try. Have them look into it."

———

FORTY MINUTES PASSED. The task force members performed follow-up on their various outstanding tasks, compared notes, and discussed the information they had amassed that had not yet been shared with the group. It didn't necessarily get them closer to identifying the Crush Killer, but it helped pass the time while they waited for some indication that the UNSUB was going to fulfill his end of the agreement.

A reporter and photographer from the *Napa Valley Press* arrived and were ushered to the morgue conference room on the first floor. They were told they would likely have a major story to write about, but the investigation was in a sensitive phase. Against the promise of an important scoop, they took seats and waited.

Vail stood to stretch when her BlackBerry buzzed. She nonchalantly read the display. *That's it.* "Text message. From the offender—"

package taped to silver ridge sign for you. cute trick with the email agent vail. don't deceive me again.

Vail read it to the group.

"Let's get a fix on him," Dixon said. "Triangulate that text."

Lugo grabbed the phone and started dialing.

"What's the point?" Vail said. "If he left something for us at Silver Ridge, we know where he was—or is. Why don't we check in with Gordon, see if Guevara has moved?"

"On it," Brix said.

Dixon said, "Ray, cancel the triangulation and get the closest LEO over to Silver Ridge ASAP. Call CHP, see if an officer's near. Or contact NSIB. Just get someone there fast."

A moment later, Brix ended his call. "Gordon went in and eyeballed Guevara after I sent him over there. No one's been in or out of Superior since. While we were on the phone, he checked in on him again. Still there."

"CHP was nearby," Lugo said, hanging up his phone. "They're about to pick up the package at Silver Ridge. I told him to take photos before he picks it up. But you think—should we call in EOD, at least alert the HDTs we may have a job for them?"

"HDTs?" Vail asked.

"Hazardous Device Technicians," Dixon said. "They handle all suspicious packages for the Explosives Ordnance Division."

Although this offender had not yet shown any proclivity toward bombs, it was always an option for your friendly neighborhood narcissist looking to grab attention. Vail was about to weigh in when Dixon spoke up.

"Let's first see what the package looks like before we call out the troops."

A moment later, they had their answer: A photo came to the sheriff's department in an email from the officer on-scene. The phone rang and Lugo picked it up. "Yeah, patch her through." He covered the receiver and said, "The officer's on the line. Putting it on speaker."

"Hello? This is Davina Erickson with CHP. I just sent you a photo—"

"This is Roxxann Dixon, Major Crimes Task Force. We've got the photo." She bent over the laptop and scrutinized the image. "Looks like a USB flash drive. Is that what it is?"

"Yes, ma'am. Secured with masking tape to the Silver Ridge landmark sign."

"Okay," Dixon said. "Carefully remove the tape and preserve any fingerprints that might be on it. Secure the area as a crime scene. I'll send a CSI to document it. But get that flash drive over to us as fast as you can."

"Lights and siren, got it," Erickson said. "Do you want me to leave before the scene is secured?"

Brix snapped his handset shut, then turned toward the speaker phone. "This is Lieutenant Redmond Brix. St. Helena PD just dispatched an officer to secure it. Soon as he arrives, get that flash over here."

"Ten-four."

Lugo disconnected the call.

Vail rose from her seat and paced. In a matter of minutes, they would have some answers. And hopefully some way of tracking the offender. But no matter what information they obtained from that flash drive, it would be more than they had now.

She glanced at the clock: 4:05. Less than three hours before she was supposed to walk out the door, officially on vacation. *How the hell am I going to do that? Can't deal with that now.* She turned away. "Anyone know how USB drives work?"

Agbayani looked up from his pages of notes. "Beyond the obvious, you mean."

"Yeah," Vail said. "Like what can we tell from the device?"

Lugo lifted the receiver. "I'll call down, see what the geeks can do for us."

As Lugo made the call, Agbayani held up his notepad. "Did anyone happen to notice when Maryanne Bernal was murdered?"

Dixon held up a hand in a gesture that said, *of course.* "About three years ago."

"And . . ." Agbayani said, as if they should all suddenly "get it." When no one replied, he said, "That was around the time the Georges Valley AVA board was discussing Superior Bottling's first contract. Right? It's now up for renewal. The initial term was three years. Maybe Maryanne was against it back when she was on the board."

"And she was killed because of her opposition to the contract?" Vail asked.

Agbayani nodded.

"I've got a problem with that. It just doesn't fit. Roxxann and I have been through this. Serial killers don't kill for money, they kill because it fulfills a psychosexual need that's rooted in their past." *Actually,* male *serial killers don't kill for profit.* For now, she was comfortable rejecting the possibility the killer was a woman. But if the offender was a man, it could mean they were seeing something different here. She had to be more flexible in her thinking.

"Still," Agbayani said, "I think we should look into it."

Dixon pulled her phone. "I'll call Ian Wirth, ask him about Maryanne and see if that was the case."

"I've got an answer for us on the USB device." Lugo leaned back in his chair and swiveled to face everyone. "We can track the device to a particular PC, maybe get a set of prints off the keyboard and desk if they haven't been used. But it doesn't give us a location, so unless we know where that PC is located, it won't tell us where to find it."

"So in a legal sense, if we know what PC he used, we can prove it in court by tracing the USB to a specific PC."

"Yes. According to Matt Aaron, when a flash drive is inserted into a PC, Windows logs it and writes a little bit of code to the drive to make a record of the device. This ensures the operating system doesn't get confused when you insert or remove it. It also records successful file transfers and even the file transferred and when. He also said the drives have serial numbers embedded in them as well as the manufacturer, model, and device characteristics. So once we get the UNSUB's file off it, maybe we can trace it, see where he bought the flash." He tossed his pen on the table. "As if that's gonna do us a whole lot of good. Other than wasting more time."

The conference room phone rang. Lugo looked at it, then sighed and leaned forward to pick it up. He listened a moment, then said, "Erickson just delivered the flash drive. Aaron's got it."

Vail leaned both elbows on the desk and ran fingers through her hair. *This has to be it. For me, at least, time is running out. Just like it could be running out on the next victim.*

---

MINUTES PASSED. The room phone rang. Lugo answered it, listened, then told the caller to hold.

"KNTV's downstairs. They're ready to go. But they want to know what the story's about so they can set up the shot."

Brix and Dixon shared a look. Vail knew what they were thinking. All the pieces were in place and things were coming to a head.

"Have them set up in the second floor lobby," Dixon said. "Tell them there might be a wait because we're engaged in sensitive negotiations. But we think it'll be worth their while."

After Lugo relayed the message and hung up, the tone from Outlook indicated a new email had arrived. He slid his chair forward and checked out the message. "Aaron sent us the document. It's a Power-Point file."

"Can you put it up on the screen?" Vail asked.

"Yeah," Lugo said. He thumbed the white remote control to his left and the screen unfurled from the ceiling. He pressed a couple of buttons on the laptop, the projector flickered to life, and the Windows desktop appeared on-screen. Lugo double-clicked the PowerPoint attachment and it opened.

"Napa Crush Killer" appeared in bold letters on the first slide.

"May I?" Vail asked.

Lugo handed over the remote and Vail advanced to the next slide: a list of nine names.

Vail felt a pounding in her head. "Holy shit. If this is real, he held up his end of the bargain. Which means we need to, also."

Dixon pointed at the screen. "Ray, print this page."

Lugo was staring at the screen, but didn't move.

Dixon looked over at Lugo. "Ray. Print the list."

"Yeah, yeah. Okay." His mouse movements appeared on-screen as he sent the page to the printer.

Vail scanned the list: there were names missing. It was incomplete— but she would worry about that in a minute. Next slide. A video file was embedded. "Double-click that," she told Lugo.

Lugo's mouse pointer skidded across the screen and found the image. The video jumped to life. Onscreen: a shaky, dark, grainy, moving image of a lifeless woman.

"Oh, shit," Agbayani said. "Don't tell me this is what I think it is."

Vail rubbed her forehead. It was exactly what Agbayani thought it was. She wanted to divert her eyes, but she couldn't. This was her job, what she signed up for. And unfortunately, watching videos of an offender's handiwork was becoming a more frequent occurrence.

"Audio," she said, her voice coarse, strained. "Is there audio?"

Lugo pulled his eyes from the screen and pressed a button.

Sound filled the room's speakers. But the offender wasn't speaking. His breathing could be heard, rapid. *The bastard's excited. He's loving this.* "Son of a bitch." Vail realized she was balling her right fist so hard her knuckles hurt.

The camera panned down and showed what looked like a hand— no, a wrist. Blood oozing. It ran a few more seconds, then ended.

Without a word, Vail pushed the remote to the next slide. Still photos of other victims she did not recognize. She paged through them, stopping long enough at each photo for everyone to get a look at the victim's face. "We've got a problem."

"Not all the vics are accounted for," Dixon said. "But there are plenty we didn't know about."

"No names on the pictures," Brix said. "There's no way for us to match up those photos with missing persons, unsolved cases. Shit, we don't even know if these vics are from California."

"I only recognize Dawn Zackery and Betsy Ivers," Vail said. She was reluctant to broach the subject, but sooner or later, someone would. "No photo of Fuller."

No one commented.

Finally, Vail said, "Okay, so we've got some questions that need answers. Let's keep the line of communication open with him. We should send him an email so he knows we're going to keep up our part of the deal and ask him who the hell these other vics are." She looked at Dixon for approval.

Dixon appeared distracted, staring at the screen and not responding. Finally, she said, "Do we want to do that? I mean, he didn't keep up his part of the bargain. We said *all* vics. We wanted a list of all his vics. He didn't give us that."

"You want to argue with him?" Vail asked. "At this point, I think that's the wrong move."

Dixon sat back hard. "Yeah, okay. Fine."

Vail looked around at everyone's body language. They were slumped in their seats. All were looking off, lost in thought. "Hey," Vail said. "This is good. We've got a lot more than we had an hour ago."

Failing to get a response, she pulled her BlackBerry and began composing a reply:

Thanks for cooperating. We need time to go through this. As promised, reporters from the press and kntv are here. We're calling the mayor and will keep up our end of the deal. There'll be something on the 11 o'clock news and a front page article in tomorrow's paper. We need your help with something. We're confused because there are victims we don't know about and we can't match their names to their photos. And I'm sure you can enlighten us as to why victoria cameron, ursula robbins, isaac jenkins, maryanne bernal, and scott fuller aren't on your list. Please reply to this email or leave us another flash drive. Thanks again for your cooperation.

Vail read the proposed message to the task force members. "Comments?"

Lugo turned to her, slowly. His face was hard, his jaw set. "I hate this fucker. Why are we sucking up to him? That email sucks. We should tell him to go fuck himself."

"Ray," Vail said calmly, "this offender is a narcissist. We'll get more by being subservient to him, by showing him respect and deference. Our goal, our only goal, is to catch the bastard. If we piss him off and he cuts off communication with us, we may not have another opportunity to achieve our one and only objective."

"Send it," Dixon said. She looked over at Brix, who nodded agreement.

Vail said, "I'm emailing this to you, Ray. Send it through Outlook, like you did before."

"But he didn't like that—"

"I want his response coming to you guys. In a little while . . ." She couldn't bring herself to say it. "I just want the communication to go to the sheriff's department mail server, not my BlackBerry."

Brix sighed deeply, then pushed himself from his chair. "I'll call the Mayor. And Congressman Church. And Stan Owens. We'll all need to huddle on this media story. I'll tell the reporters we'll have something for them around nine. Roxx, as lead, I think you should be the face of the investigation. Agreed?"

Dixon nodded slowly. "Yeah."

Brix pulled his phone to make the calls. Vail looked at the screen, where the image of an unnamed woman lay. The mask of death draped across her face.

# FORTY-EIGHT

**B**urt Gordon walked into the room and nodded at the people who looked up. "I handed off the Guevara surveillance to a couple guys from NSIB. But I have doubts about him being our UNSUB." He glanced at the screen, then froze.

"Hate to say it," Dixon said, "but it's beginning to look that way."

Vail felt like saying, "I've always had doubts about him. It just doesn't fit." But she didn't. She'd already voiced her opinion. And she hadn't had anything better to offer.

A call came through on the room phone. Lugo picked it up, then pressed a button. "It's Aaron."

Matthew Aaron's voice filtered through the speaker. "Redd, you there?"

Brix, leaning against the wall, said, "We're here, Matt. Got anything for us?"

"You're not going to like it. We've traced the flash drive to a PC right here at the SD."

Brix pushed away from the wall and walked closer to the phone's speaker. "What?"

"I watched the cybergeeks do their thing, and they're sure about it. I've had them lock down the room. I'm gonna go over there in a minute and start dusting."

Brix shook his head. "How can that be? It's a secure facility. You need a prox card—"

"Yeah, that's the thing. Turns out there was a prox card lost about three weeks ago. Shil-ray Simmons. I just talked with her, took her to task, questioned her pretty hard. She said she thought she just misplaced it and was afraid to report it lost. Nothing was missing, nothing was reported stolen in the building, so she figured it'd turn up, that it was just misplaced in a drawer somewhere."

Brix's face shaded red. "What the hell was she thinking? Evidence could've been tampered with, cases could've been compromised." He leaned a hand on the wall. "And what were you thinking, questioning her? You're a CSI, Matt."

"I was just trying to help. I uncovered the missing card, didn't I?"

Brix swiped a hand down his face. "We'll discuss this later. Have they deactivated the stolen card?"

"Already done."

"Fine. There are database records entries for every swipe each card makes. Get a printout of that log. Which doors, which times, which days." He motioned to Lugo, who clicked off the call.

"So our UNSUB's got someone on the inside," Vail said. "Or he *is* someone on the inside and he used Simmons's card to cover his tracks. He had to know sooner or later the card would be reported missing."

Brix nodded. "Ray, have Lily in HR print us out a list of all county employees. I want to know everyone who's had access to the sheriff's department facility. Include contract workers. Everyone."

Lugo made a note on his pad. "And you want this tomorrow, I take it."

"No," Brix said with a tight mouth. "I want it today."

"And have them pull the surveillance video for the past week before it gets overwritten," Dixon said. "We're gonna have to go through it all, correlate it with the doors that card opened, see if we can ID the fucker who stole it."

"They already pulled the video when Karen got that letter," Lugo said.

"That may be all we need," Agbayani said. "Have Aaron look at the date the PowerPoint document was created and last modified. That'll tell us when the UNSUB was in the building."

"Yes, yes," Brix said. "Perfect. Then match it up with the swipes of that prox card. And find out what's taking them so goddamn long with that video. Did they find anything or not? Got all that, Ray?"

Lugo tossed down his pen. "Yeah. Got it." He swung his chair around, rose, and walked out of the room.

Dixon watched him leave, then said, "Is it me, or has he been on edge lately?"

Brix walked to the whiteboard. "We've all been on edge. With everything that's gone on this past week, I think we're holding up pretty goddamn good." He waved a hand. "Ray'll be fine. Besides, we've got other things to worry about. We don't know for sure this card was used by our UNSUB. But it's highly probable. Now I'm assuming no one on the task force is our guy. But that still leaves a lot of county employees, a lot of 'em in this building, who could've palmed that card. So from this point forward, no one's to share any information with anyone. Have it go through me. I'll control all info in and out. So don't leave any important papers lying around."

Vail snapped her fingers. "That's how the offender got my phone number, how he started texting me. Those sheets you printed up and gave out with everyone's cell numbers. He was here, in this room."

"Shit." Dixon looked around, acutely conscious of her surroundings. "What else could he have taken or seen? The whiteboard—"

The door swung open. Lugo stood there, his face crumpled in thought.

"Forget something?" Brix asked.

Lugo stepped in and let the door close behind him. "Your PC has all sorts of personally identifiable information buried in it. Like what Eddie was saying, about the date the document was created. But there's a lot more info on there. Every single document you create embeds info that it takes from your computer."

"I know a guy at Microsoft who's helped me out before," Agbayani said. He checked the room clock. "It's late, but maybe I can catch him."

"Do it," Dixon said. "Burt, can you run down and take care of that other stuff Ray was doing? The video, county list—"

"Got it," Gordon said, then left the room.

Agbayani settled himself in front of the conference room laptop and logged in to Windows Live Messenger. "Cool, he's online. We're in business." He clicked, Start a live video call. It rang through the speakers, then the ringing abruptly stopped and a face and torso filled the screen.

"Tomás, how goes it?"

"Eddie, my man. Still catching bad guys?"

"That's what I'm calling about. I've got a thing here and I need to pick your geek brain."

"I'm out the door for a meeting in the EBC—I mean, the Executive Briefing Center. A delegation of security people from China are here to discuss a new relational database. My boss will have my head if I try to cut out early. Can it wait?"

Agbayani looked off to Brix, then back to the screen. "The sooner the better. We're really under the gun on this one. It's bad."

"What's the deal?"

"We got an Office document written by a serial killer," Agbayani said as he opened Outlook and started a new email. "PowerPoint. We need you to crack it. The embedded info."

Tomás tapped his #2 Black Warrior pencil on the desk. "Okay, send it over. I'll get started on it as soon as I'm done with the meeting. How about I get back to you in two hours or so?"

Agbayani hit Send and the Crush Killer's files were on their way. "That'd be great, Tomás. Looks like we've got RoundTable in the sheriff's department here, so we can video conference with the task force. And—same as before—this is confidential shit, don't be circulating it around the campus. And for your sake, don't view its contents. It'll chill your flabby geek ass."

"That's a geek ass of steel, bro." The Outlook chime sounded and Tomás's eyes canted down, away from the camera. "Got the email. Be good. Catch you later."

The Live Messenger webcam screen went blank.

"Great work, Eddie," Brix said. "Ray, email a copy of that PowerPoint file to the video guys and have them analyze the clips. Maybe something in the background'll tip off the UNSUB's location—a site-specific sound, a landmark sign, whatever. Eddie, you, me, and Burt, when he gets back, will work on the vics in the file. Austin, Roxxi, Karen, why don't you three take a break, grab some dinner, meet back here in a couple hours. I think we're gonna be here all night. We'll work in shifts."

Vail caught his gaze and silently reminded him she would need to leave them at seven. Brix nodded, the twist of his lips indicating disappointment.

She thought of sticking around to help out. But there was nothing more for her to do at the moment. They now had a dialogue going with the offender, and the key would be in his reply to their email. Her advice at that point would be critical, but until then, her expertise was not needed. And she would be back before her deadline to lend whatever final thoughts she had to offer.

Brix turned toward the whiteboard to make some notes. "Oh, Roxx—bring back a few of those pizzas."

"From Azzurro?" Dixon asked.

"Best in town."

Dixon glanced at Vail. "We just had that for lunch."

"Hey, life's tough all over. See you in a couple. Maybe by then we'll have something back from Microsoft."

# FORTY-NINE

A ustin Mann had an errand to tend to, while Vail and Dixon ran over to Fit1! for a quick workout. They put their clothing in lockers, then headed out onto the gym floor. Because it was dinner time, only a few dedicated gym rats were still there, pressing weights and cycling.

Vail migrated to the Life Fitness elliptical to get in some needed work on her knee, while Dixon headed to the Ivanko barbells and Hammer Strength machines.

Vail punched the program buttons, then began pumping her legs and moving her arms. Five minutes in, her mind cleared and her thoughts turned to James Cannon, the guy she met here yesterday. Something about him. What is it? That whole exchange bothered her. What was it? *Think . . . He'd said, "FBI, very cool . . . I feel like we've met before." Did he say that because he'd sent me letters and text messages and emails? Is that what he was implying? Or was he just hitting on me?*

Vail stopped moving and stood there on the machine, sorting it through. She climbed down off the elliptical and went back to her locker, pulled her BlackBerry, and dialed Lugo.

"Ray, it's Karen. Listen, can you check something for me? You've got your ear to the ground in the wine country, right?"

"Yeah, pretty much."

"Ever hear of Herndon Vineyards?"

"Doesn't ring a bell. Where's it located? The Valley? Sonoma, Healdsburg—"

"Don't know. All I can tell you is they have great soil for growing Cabernet. Not sure that helps much."

"Actually, it might."

"Winemaker's name is James Cannon."

"Two *n*'s or one?"

"Your choice. No clue."

"Anything in particular you're interested in?"

Vail narrowed her eyes as she thought. "Nothing I can put my finger on. Just some vibes. Probably nothing. This guy, James Cannon. Roxxann and I met him yesterday. Said he was a winemaker for an upstart winery named Herndon Vineyards. They're due to put out their first bottles of wine in a couple years."

"Okay."

Vail flashed on the letter the UNSUB had sent them. "He knew about the historic wine cave where we found Ursula Robbins."

"Who, James Cannon knew?"

"No, no. Our UNSUB. I'm thinking out loud. The letter the UNSUB sent to me a couple of days ago. He knew about that vintage wine in the cave that had collapsed a hundred years ago. And he talked about 'the crush of grapes.' He might be someone who'd know his way around a wine cave like the one at Silver Ridge." She stopped a moment. "I—I didn't think of this before, but he's dumped his bodies in vineyards and wine caves. Maybe there's some significance to that. A guy who's spent years plying his trade in vineyards and wine caves is comfortable there. I kept thinking it had to do with access, but . . ." She thought a second. "I don't know. Maybe this is bullshit."

"I'm looking up Herndon now. I don't see anything. No press releases, nothing online in public sources. That's not unusual, though I'd think they would've issued a press release either announcing the winery, or the purchase of land and their business plans. I'll have to do some more digging in the law enforcement databases." Vail could hear the clicking of keys. "Zippo on a James Cannon. I'll run him, too. I should have something in an hour or two, definitely by the time you get back here."

"Thanks, Ray."

Vail put her phone back in the locker and took a deep breath. It was probably nothing. But they were desperate, grasping at things they may not normally give any serious attention. Working out often helped clear her mind, got her thinking in ways she couldn't do in the stress of the moment. She grabbed her towel and headed back out to the elliptical.

DIXON, AT THE FAR END of the gym, worked her lower body with the assistance of her new workout partner, George Panda.

Vail approached, dabbing a towel at the perspiration rolling off her reddened face. "Hey, George. Didn't realize you were here."

"Roxxann texted me, told me she was here. I'd been chained to my desk all day and hadn't gotten in my workout, so she did me a huge favor. My office is only a few minutes down the road."

Vail tilted her head back and appraised Dixon. "Now I know why you wanted to 'squeeze in' a workout today."

Dixon blushed. "Karen—"

"Just giving you shit," Vail said. She stole a look around. "Jimmy with you?"

Panda glanced at the wall clock. "Should be here in a little bit."

"I'm gonna go shower and dress. I'll call in the pizzas so we can grab and run. Meet you out front."

"I'll catch up with you," Dixon said as she bent over to wipe the bench with her towel. "I'm just gonna snag five minutes in the steam room."

As Vail headed toward the lockers, Panda said, "You doing upper body tomorrow?"

"Who knows." Dixon tossed the towel across her shoulder. "Work has a way of interfering. But if not tomorrow, maybe the day after."

Panda pulled a plate off his bar and set it down. "Last minute works, too."

Dixon's conversation with Agbayani flashed through her thoughts. She pushed it aside. She needed to find out if there was anything in George Panda worth pursuing. "You know," she said as she tossed her towel into the hamper, "we should schedule a time to go to dinner. I may not be able to commit to a full evening until this case breaks, but I'm sure I can get away for an hour or two."

Panda grinned. "I'd like that."

AS EVENING FELL ON NAPA, it was a common time for people to get in their exercise after leaving work. But John Wayne Mayfield was heading *to* work, in a sense—a swing shift of sorts.

He stood outside the women's locker room, his pulse pounding. Killing someone in a public place, where anyone could walk in on you, at any time, was the ultimate challenge. The ultimate *thrill.*

But he would have to be careful—being discovered in the ladies' shower and dressing area, if there were women in there, was risky at best—and irreparable at worst. If caught, he would do his best to feign surprise at his bone-headed mistake of walking into the wrong locker room. Hopefully he could sell the "stupid me" act well enough to get him out of there without a call to the authorities.

Mayfield had already scoped out the women's lockers during a slow time when almost no one was in the gym. He was thus familiar with the layout, and, as it was, he would enter and hang an immediate left, which would take him to the steam room. Veering right would instead take him to the locker area.

He wished he'd had time to watch the door, so he could know how many women were in there. But because of the room's layout, he'd be able to enter and turn toward the stream room without being seen by others in the vicinity. That's where he would go first.

Seconds ticking. Pulse pounding.

Mayfield pushed through the locker room door slowly, his head down. He moved in, turned left, all the while listening. The echoing sizzle of a shower in the distance. Eyes scanning the floor around him, looking for feet—for trouble.

He strode purposely down the narrow corridor, his shoes squeaking against the wet cement floor. There it was—on his left—the glass door to the steam room. It was opaque, the view impeded by thick vapor. He pushed in. The loud hissing of the jets and dense steam deadened all noise.

The odor of eucalyptus oil stung his nose. He hated that smell. It made his throat close down.

He stood there a second, his eyes darting around, looking for a body. There—sitting on the top step—was Roxxann Dixon. He moved forward, the swirl of steam moving aside as he approached, fearful of his presence. Like *she* should be—would be—in a matter of seconds.

# FIFTY

**B**rix was looking at a database onscreen with Agbayani when an instant message came through:

I told my boss what you needed and he let me leave early. still in the executive briefing center. you ready to login with roundtable?

Agbayani typed back:

you bet. give me a sec.

"Hey," Brix said. "We've got Microsoft online. Have a seat and Eddie will link us all in."

Mann, Gordon, Brix, and Lugo took their chairs while Agbayani opened Office Live Meeting and got RoundTable online.

All of the task force members appeared on the large, wall-mounted flat screen. The 360-degree panoramic camera and associated software knitted them together into a virtually seamless image.

"Cool stuff," Lugo said.

"We're on," Agbayani said. "Everyone, meet Tomás Palmer, Senior Security Program Manager at Microsoft." Agbayani made introductions of the task force members. "The way RoundTable works is that you're all on camera in the video panorama at the bottom of the screen. Whoever is speaking loudest will appear in a close-up at the top left." He turned back to Microsoft's RoundTable device, a small circular unit about the size of a dollar bill, with a central telescoping extension that contained the camera. "Tomás, it's all yours."

"I've got some pretty cool technology here, so I may as well use it to show you what I've got so far on your document."

"Sounds to me like an excuse to play with the new toys," Agbayani said.

Tomás smiled. "You know it." He sat at the far end of a long, empty conference table. Behind him was a flat panel that nearly filled the wall. "I've got a monitor in front of me. I'm seeing what you're seeing on the large screen behind me." Images popped up; Tomás flicked them aside with his fingers.

"Whoa," Brix said, staring at the screen. "What is that?"

"Surface technology. C'mon, Eddie, you haven't told them about Surface?"

"Another time. The documents—"

"It's okay, bro. I can multitask. Surface is a PC that's embedded in a tabletop with Microsoft's touch interface. There's no keyboard or mouse. You move things across the screen with your hands and fingers. Like the technology Hollywood envisioned in the movie, *Minority Report*." He swiped his hand across the monitor. Icons whisked by and spun across the screen. He spread his fingers apart and the image in front of him instantly enlarged. "Okay, here's the document you sent me."

"This is the PowerPoint file, right?"

"Yeah, and now I know why you told me not to look. Bad shit there, bro. Be really cool if I could help you catch this psycho sicko."

"It'd be more than cool. You have any luck?"

"First thing I did was to take the jpegs that are embedded in the file and applied some new technology out of Carnegie Mellon. This stuff is gonna blow your mind. The computer analyzes the image and determines where in the world it was taken."

"There are a few photos we really need to place," Brix said. "If you could help with that, you'll be my new best friend."

Tomás's eyes swung left, then right. "Right. Well, in spite of that, I do have some answers."

"What does it do?" Lugo asked. "Look for similar shapes and landmarks?"

"No, not landmarks. That'd be too limiting. It records the distribution of textures, colors, lines, vegetation and topography in the photo and then compares it to the database they've created using GPS-tagged images in Flickr."

"The online photo album site?"

"Yup. So here's what I've got. The first three photos appear to be from Albuquerque, New Mexico, the next two from Southern California and the last two from Northern California."

"Ray," Brix said, "when the dust settles, contact Albuquerque PD and tell them we have the killer of three of their unsolveds. Pull the jpeg images from the PowerPoint and email them the photos. Do the same for SoCal."

Mann pointed at his pad. "Other than his trip up north in '98, looks like he came from Albuquerque, shot west along I-40 to L.A., then worked his way up the state." He touched the pen to the paper with each location, as if it were a map. To Tomás, he said, "Can this image analysis technology also date the photo?"

"No," Tomás said. "But it's funny you should ask. I started thinking, if your bad guy took any of these photos with a GPS-enabled phone, the time, date, and place of the picture would be embedded in the photo. When I looked at the individual image files, some were taken with a regular digital camera, and they're time-and date-stamped. I've got the camera model and exposure for each photo, but that's not going to help you.

"I can't be sure the dates and times are accurate because it depends on whether the owner input the correct data when he set up the camera. But as it turns out, the later pictures were shot with a GPS-enabled camera phone, and one was taken near downtown Los Angeles. We've also got a scanned photo, and when you scan film prints, the scanner leaves behind embedded data in the digital file that's created. This picture was scanned March 9, 1998."

Brix shot a glance around the room. "That would fit with the Marin County vic found near the Golden Gate."

"What can you tell us about the document itself?" Agbayani asked.

"Lots of good stuff," Tomás said. "First, let me ask you something. What do you think this killer's deal is? You think he wants publicity?"

Lugo looked up from his notes. "Yeah, that's exactly what we think. Why?"

"Well, I assume if he wants publicity, you want to minimize that, to reduce panic."

"That's one theory," Brix said. "Why do you ask?"

Tomás shrugged. "This killer could post the PowerPoint document on some websites with unique tags and let search engines 'find' it, then use a kiddy script virus kit to create a virus that would then spread. It'd be disseminated from thousands of computers."

Brix sighed deeply. "Well, that's fucking great." He rubbed his eyes and said, "Let's hope our UNSUB is not that tech savvy. Can you tell anything from the document that would indicate his level of sophistication?"

Tomás bobbed his head. "I'd say he's more knowledgeable than the average computer user, but he's not a hacker or anything like that. So if his intent is to try to wreak the most havoc possible, and he knows something like that virus kit exists, he'd still have to research it. But you can find out how to build a bomb on the Internet from household items, so yeah, it's possible he could create this virus even if he's not an expert."

"What about the document itself?" Mann asked.

"Okay. Here's the deal. Office documents contain more information than what you see when you open the file. There's a good deal of PII—Personally Identifiable Information—that's kept in the document to help the user. It's called metadata, like that embedded time and date info in the digital photos. Metadata's stuff like word count, number of lines and characters, and so on. It'll also tell you how many times the document was revised, how long the author spent editing it, who saved it, when it was printed, and what printer printed it.

"You can cleanse the document, but you have to know this metadata exists in the first place, and then you have to know what to do to get rid of it. Your killer used Office 2007, which has a built-in feature called Document Inspector that scrubs away just about all PII. But it's something you have to actively apply, and lucky for us, your guy didn't use it. That's why I think his level of sophistication is good, but not high. Anyway, I used some custom cracking tools—including my favorite, the

Palmer Plunger—and a couple other security tools from our Honey Monkey project." He looked at the camera and winked. "Silly sounding stuff, I know. But if it works, the embedded PII becomes the bread-crumb trail your killer left behind for us."

He flicked a document aside and spread his fingers to enlarge a printout that looked like rudimentary computer text.

"So here's the info we've got." He moved his finger toward the top of the screen and the long document scrolled top to bottom. "You want the name of the guy who created this document?"

Brix sat forward in his chair. "You got the killer's name?"

Tomás moved the page a bit and zoomed in on lines of text. "I've got the name of the computer user who registered the software on this particular PC. If it's a real name or an alias, I have no way of knowing."

"And?" Brix asked. "What's the name?"

Tomás looked away from the camera, said something to someone off screen, then turned back to Lugo. "I've got it right here." Tomás zoomed again and a name filled the screen. "John Mayfield."

Brix's eyes widened. "Holy shit. We've really got a name?" He reached for the phone.

"Hold it," Tomás said. "Before you make any calls. There's another name embedded, so I asked the licensing team to check the database used for binding the registered user to the software. Just to try to ver-ify if that name is real or not."

"And?" Agbayani asked.

"And the software *was* registered to a John Mayfield. So Mayfield appears to check out. But I don't know what to make of this other name. The document's author. Both names could be real, or they could be fake, I've no way of telling."

"What's the other name?" Brix yelled.

"Right here." Tomás flicked the screen and it scrolled down. Tapped it again and it stopped. Zoomed. "There. The document's author."

# FIFTY-ONE

*T*here she was. Naked. Hair clipped back. Dixon looked up—surprise—

"George—what the hell are you doing in here?"

Panda smiled disarmingly and stepped forward, then grabbed Dixon beneath her armpits and threw her across the room, into the opposing wall. A flat tile wall, perfect for his needs.

Dixon slipped on the wet tile and went down hard. Panda turned and grabbed her. She shook her head, fighting through the momentary daze. He lifted her off the ground and pounded her against the wall. Clamped his left hand across her mouth. Grabbed her left bicep and squeezed. "Very good, Roxxann. Very nice."

Dixon yelled and kicked, her right foot slipping on the moist floor—and landed a knee to his groin. But it didn't matter because he was wearing a cup. It landed impotently against the hard plastic.

That didn't stop her. She kicked again, in the thigh, and then again. The last one knocked him back a bit—she had powerful legs. He'd have bruises for sure, but again, it was nothing he couldn't handle.

He brought his right forearm out in front of him and grinned, then bent his elbow and slammed his arm into her throat. Her body rebounded against the tile, but his forearm bounced back. Her neck muscles had prevented the crushing blow.

Panda leaned back and thrust forward again, and this time he had greater impact, because her eyes bulged and she coughed. Hard.

But a crashing blow to his right cheek knocked him back and temporarily blinded him. *What the fuck was that?*

She yelled—hoarse, loud—

But it disappeared into the deadening fog.

And then she landed another blow, from the left, across his jaw—blinding pain—and he staggered back. He saw her darting around his side. *No—can't let her get away—*

He reached out and grabbed her arm—slipped off the wet skin—but he'd gotten just enough because she went sprawling forward. He swung hard, connected with something, and he felt her body jolt. He wasn't sure what he hit, but all that mattered was that it was her. And he wanted to do it again.

Panda reached back and swung again, and hit hard flesh again. He thought he heard a cry, but in the jet-noise and dense fog, it was swallowed whole, absorbed into nothingness.

He leaned over for a better look—he'd finish her on the ground if need be—and saw a blur of skin in front of him—reached out and grabbed—felt a breast and pulled her body against his. She was facing away, which would not do. He needed to watch her face. As he squeezed the life out of her.

# FIFTY-TWO

*T*he air in the locker room was damp, with a musty, stale smell. Vail sat on the brown resin bench to tie her shoes, the repetitive beat of some inane pop song droning through the speakers. The workout refreshed her, gave her a jolt of needed energy and a renewed outlook that they were going to catch the Crush Killer . . . sooner rather than later. Hopefully Agbayani's Microsoft contact would be able to extract hidden information from the document. But even if he couldn't, she still had the sense they were getting close.

Vail was reaching back into the locker for her phone when the BlackBerry buzzed. "Vail."

"Karen, it's Brix. I tried Roxxann, but she didn't answer. Where the hell is she?"

"We're at the gym, working out. Why?"

"We got an ID on the killer—the document he sent, that Microsoft guy said that unless he's using an alias or someone else's PC, the name we've got is John Mayfield. My sense is that's his real name. But there's another name embedded. George Panda. We're putting out an APB for both—"

"Wait—George Panda, are you sure?"

"Yeah, he's—"

"He's here, Brix—at Fit1."

"Fucking A. Keep an eye on him. We're on our way. Do not engage until you've got backup. You hear me, Karen? Do not—"

# FIFTY-THREE

*J*ohn Wayne Mayfield—a.k.a. George Panda— struggled to turn Dixon around while maintaining a tight hold on her body, determined not to let her land anymore punches. They did an awkward dance as he drove her forward, smashing against the tile seat. She swung her elbow back, landing a soft blow against his left bicep. He continued to wrestle with her—until he finally gained leverage and spun her fully onto her back.

He was now over her.

And there was little she could do to hurt him. He clapped his hand over her mouth, but she knocked it away, then clawed at his face, scratching his cheek. It reminded him of a rough sexual encounter he had as a child. *Sexual encounter my ass—the bitch raped me.*

He growled—fuming at the memory. Yet relieved he finally had Roxxann Dixon where he wanted her. "Say good-bye, Roxxann," he said close to her face, then slammed his hand over her mouth again. He would squeeze her carotids, cut her blood supply, then have his way with her body. It wouldn't be what he wanted, but at this point, he had to think about survival: If he got caught, it'd all be over. And as good as he was, the longer he remained in this steam room, the higher the risk he'd get caught. Better to get rid of her, then live to kill another day.

He clamped his large right hand across her neck and squeezed. She should feel the pressure building in her head. In five seconds, her brain would be hungry for oxygen. But there won't be any. And then, sleep. Unconscious.

But Dixon swung her arms upward, slamming against his forearm and knocking his hand off her neck. Fuck—he withdrew the hand from her mouth to catch himself from falling over—just as she swung her head forward and slammed it into his nose. He heard a crunch—his vision blurred—his hearing blunted—and he staggered back and off her, twisting around, where—

—he could see, at the door, a dark, amorphous silhouette.

The steam room jets stopped. Numbing quiet.

But then, somewhere in the distance, Dixon was yelling and kicking, trying to get his weight completely off her legs.

He felt a blow to the back of his neck—not enough to make him go down, but the door, now a foot from his face—was swinging open. He powered forward and lunged, slamming his weight against it. The glass shattered into hundreds of pieces and the wood frame flew open, into the person who was behind it.

He stumbled out, down the corridor, toward the exit. Right now, it was about survival.

*Another victim*
*Another day*
*Survival—*

# FIFTY-FOUR

*V*ail picked herself up off the damp floor—her pants were now wet—and watched as the man—*Panda?*—ran down the hall.

"Hey, stop!"

"Karen—"

Vail turned, her shoes crunching and slipping in the glass fragments. Standing naked in the steam room, steadying herself against the doorway, was Dixon.

"Roxx—you okay?"

"Get him—Panda—he's the killer—"

*Yeah, I got that. A little late, but I got it.* Vail took off.

"Meet me out front at the car—" Vail yelled back at Dixon, then burst through the locker room entrance, nearly running over another woman heading toward her. Vail pushed her aside and saw Panda running out Fit1!'s front door. Vail ran across the padded rubber workout flooring and hit the door before it closed. In the glow of the parking lot's lights, she saw Panda in the street, running along Highway 29. He veered too far right into the roadway. Headlights. Blaring horn. And the oncoming car swerved around him.

Vail looked back, hoping to see Dixon emerging—with the keys to the car—but she wasn't there and Vail couldn't risk losing him. Bad knee or not, she took off after him. Pulled her BlackBerry. The glow of the screen reflected off her face and fried her night vision.

She pulled up the call history, felt for the trackball, then accidentally hit the Call button—*crap, who'd I just dial? Probably someone on the task force.* But it wasn't. It was Robby's cell. Right to voicemail. "It's me. Need your help. In pursuit of Crush Killer. John Mayfield, a.k.a

George Panda . . . foot pursuit along 29—" She glanced over her right shoulder, then coughed. "Leaving Fit1, somewhere near Peju, that place we went a few days ago with the yodeling wine guy—hurry!"

Mayfield was still visible, but he was a stride faster than she and the gap was widening. She struggled with her phone, pressed the Call button again and found what she thought was Brix's number, coughed hard again, then dialed Brix.

"Ray Lugo."

*Lugo. That works.* "Ray—Roxxann and I are in pursuit of John Mayfield. Need backup." She gave him the location, told him to call Brix and the rest of the task force. He was thirty minutes out. The others were already en route, he said, but not a whole lot closer.

She pressed End with her thumb and shoved the phone into its holster. *This fucker is not getting away. Even if I have to shoot him in the back, I'll answer for it later. But he's not going to crush anymore throats. I'll take whatever heat they give me—*

Except that she was getting winded—not surprising given the smoke she'd recently inhaled—and she was falling further behind. She thought about yelling for him to freeze, but who was she kidding? Would he stop? That didn't even require an answer.

Over her left shoulder, she heard the clanging rumble of a large moving object approaching. She turned and saw the lone headlight of The Napa Valley Wine Train blazing its trail along the tracks. And in that instant, she realized what was going to happen. Mayfield was going to hop the train.

Vail angled left, toward the tracks, running through scrub, on uneven terrain, gravel and angled dirt—something she was specifically advised against doing for awhile, until the knee was completely healed. In a perfect world, she would do exactly as told. But with men like John Mayfield on the loose, this world was anything but perfect.

She angled closer to the train—and for the first time realized how massive it was. Traveling in a car, at a distance, as she had been with Dixon when she had first seen it, the restored railcars didn't look so imposing.

But running alongside it, feeling the shudder of its tonnage as it passed over the iron tracks, was intimidating. In some ways more so than staring down a serial killer in lockup. Because there the offender was in shackles. But here, with the unbridled power of the locomotive bearing down on her, knowing she was going to have to jump onto this moving monster, she started to have doubts she would be able to carry through on her plans. And that didn't happen often to Karen Vail.

The train rumbled by her, first the locomotive and then the dining cars. She fought the urge to shut her eyes, to tell her there wasn't a train barreling down the track to her left. Step the wrong way and she'd be crushed. Or worse.

And up ahead, just as she had suspected, John Mayfield moving closer to the train. The bastard wasn't going to make this easy. As she started to feel the burn of the cold night air in her lungs, Vail realized she had no choice. It was either that or shoot him. And while that was an option, it was not a good one. She had a chance to catch him— ethically. When she reached the point that plan was no longer viable, she would raise her Glock and fire. But not yet.

As she mused on that thought, John Mayfield reached out and grabbed the iron railing on the third car, jumped, and pulled himself aboard.

# FIFTY-FIVE

There were some things about being a profiler Karen Vail did not enjoy. She had made a list once, then folded it and shredded it. She didn't need to be reminded she was dealing with the extremes of human depravity.

But one thing that was not on the list was jumping onto a moving train.

The wine train did not travel at the same speeds as a traditional train—because, after all, its purpose was to leisurely troll the five cities it passed through en route to its turnaround point, to allow its passengers ample time to enjoy the lush countryside, mountains, and vineyards, while savoring a wine-paired, freshly prepared meal at the hands of a renowned, onboard chef.

That's what she kept telling herself as she pumped her arms harder, catching up a bit to the last car, reaching up for the railing—lifting herself up—and getting thrown back against the train's siding. She held on, whipped around and stretched her right arm onto the opposing handle while feeling for the wide metal steps she knew lay somewhere near her feet.

She lunged forward—and slammed her shin into the hard edge of the step above. But at least she was aboard. She had a feeling that would not be the hardest part of catching John Mayfield.

A sudden, spasmodic coughing fit wracked her body. She bent forward while straining to hold on, hacking away until her throat felt raw. A moment later, she was able to stand erect, the spasm passing. She risked taking a deep breath, squared her shoulders, then wiped her mouth on her sleeve.

*Inward and onward. Mayfield's inside.*

Vail pushed through the door, then reached for her handgun—but it wasn't there. Neither was her backup weapon, which had been burned in the fire. Her Glock was locked in Dixon's vehicle, where she had left it when they went to work out. There were no fixed Bureau rules on where to leave your sidearm when you were not able to carry it with you—so long as it was secure. Leaving it in a gym locker did not qualify as "secure"—so she'd left it in the car.

*Fuck.* Given Mayfield's size—and what he does to his victims—she would have to be extremely careful, unarmed and in the close quarters of a train. Not much room to maneuver, to duck and roll—or run. Not that she shied from a conflict—this was Karen Vail—but cooler heads had to prevail, and if the circumstances were not to your advantage, you changed those circumstances so they would help you achieve your goal.

Vail apparently did not have that luxury.

She looked around, then stepped into the rail car and pulled her credentials case. Held it up to soothe the minds of the passengers and to identify herself should a fight with Mayfield break out. At least they'd know who to root for.

As she moved forward, the creds raised to eye level, the passengers waved and gave her a thumbs up. Actually, they did neither. Most sat there, some squinting confusion. The presence of an FBI agent who no doubt wore a very serious expression did not spell good news for the rest of their expensive wine train journey.

None of them presented a threat, so Vail moved on. She walked through the car, headed toward the end of the train, searching the seats—below and behind—for the big man who, until recently, went by the moniker of "UNSUB."

But Mayfield was no longer an "unknown subject." They knew who he was. And, at the moment, they knew where he was.

Except that Mayfield was not in this car. Vail turned around and walked toward the front of the train, the slight side-to-side sway of the car throwing off her balance as she stepped toward the doorway. Into the next car, also one with large, plush, fixed rotating seats that faced the windowed sides. And above, a glass ceiling.

But this was not time to dream about the vacation that could have been, the one that John Mayfield had stolen from her and Robby. Now was the time to catch the bastard, make him pay for the people he had murdered.

So she moved forward, suddenly realizing that while she was making her way through the train, there'd be no way to know if Mayfield had jumped off the train. *Fuck. I hadn't thought of that. I hate it when I blow something. And I blew this. But what was I to do? No backup. It was just me and my two eyes.*

Vail pulled her phone and moved to the nearest window. Normally, the patrons in the gold velour seats would've moved aside at the sight of her big, black handgun. People tended to do that, FBI badge or not. But those who were unaware of who she was merely threw dirty looks at this pushy woman who was bullying her way past them to grab a window view. *C'mon, people, it's dark out now. Not a whole lot to see out there.*

While standing there, nose against the glass, hoping to see a large man dressed in gym clothing bathed in a car's headlights, she phoned Dixon. Dixon answered quickly, as if she was expecting the call.

"Yeah—"

"I'm on the train. You see Mayfield?"

"Who the hell's Mayfield?"

"Panda," Vail said. "Panda's other name—his real name, I think—is John Mayfield. He was onboard, but I lost sight of him and have no way of telling if he's jumped off."

"Haven't seen him. I'm in the car, coming up alongside the train now."

"Good. Keep pace with it. I'll let you know if I find him."

*If I go flying through the glass, that would likely serve as your first clue.*

Vail signed off, shoved her BlackBerry into its holster, then crossed into the next car. No windowed skylight in this one. But a well-restored and meticulously maintained interior nonetheless. Carpeted interior, paisley fabric seats . . . and curtains on the windows. *I could enjoy this,* she thought, if Robby were here and she wasn't chasing a serial killer through the Napa countryside.

*Focus, Karen. Catch the fucker.*

She moved between cars, hearing the rhythmic clanking as the wheels struck the rail joints, thump-thumping as the train barreled down the track. Vail scanned the car she was in. People seemed to lean away when they caught a glimpse of her—she was no doubt looking pretty ragged . . . hungry, tired, stressed, and, oh, yeah, there was that gold badge she was holding out in front of her. She hoped people still respected authority.

Vail forged forward into the next car, where patrons were sitting at tables, gold velour curtains blanketing the mirrorlike windows, beyond which lay the Napa countryside—actually, probably now Rutherford, on its way toward St. Helena, if she remembered her map correctly. There was a hint of light out the left windows, to the west . . . a silhouetted vineyard flicking by.

Gone, blurring past her, signaling the metaphoric passage of time.

Then she had a feeling. John Mayfield was still on the train. Somehow, she just knew.

So she moved forward. Stopped to ask a man in his forties if he had seen a large man dressed in gym attire moving through the cars. Yes, he said, and he pointed "thataway." Vail couldn't help thinking she was in some inane children's cartoon, asking "Which way did he go?"

But she continued on nonetheless. Because this wasn't an ink and celluloid drama. It was an honest to goodness race to find a man who murders people. Innocent people.

She moved into the next car and saw the door ahead close suddenly. Was it possibly her offender? Impossible to say. She pulled her phone and called Dixon. "Anything?"

"If he came off the west side of the train, no. If he came off the east, I have no fucking clue."

"I think I just saw him. Who's en route?"

"Task force is lights and siren, but probably at least fifteen out. I just called St. Helena and Calistoga PDs."

"Ten-four. Wish me luck."

Vail signed off and hung up. For now, it was her ballgame. Hopefully she could stay in the game until the others arrived. And being on a train filled with people—who paid handsomely to be here—didn't make her job any easier. If Mayfield wanted to make this a hostage situation, there'd be little she could do to stop, or defuse, it. So she kept moving forward.

As she climbed through the doors of the next car, she grabbed the waitress and asked a question she should've thought to ask earlier. "Just how many goddamn cars are on this train?"

The answer told her she was in the last one before the locomotive. Mayfield was either here—which he was not—or he was in the locomotive. Or he had bailed out. Vail looked west first and did not see anyone—but in the near darkness, there was no way she could be sure of what she was seeing. To her right, the east was totally black.

Yet she sensed Mayfield was still aboard the train.

Vail pushed forward into the connecting area between the car and the locomotive—and saw, to her right and now behind her as the train continued on, John Mayfield, standing in the middle of the road, carjacking a vehicle.

*So much for intuition—*

She pulled her BlackBerry, but Dixon was already calling through.

"Got him—" Dixon said. "Two cars ahead. Silver SUV—"

"I see it."

Dixon pulled right, around the car in front of her, along the shoulder of the winding road.

"I'm getting off," Vail said. "Pick me up."

She yanked open the side door, looked at the descending metal stairs, and stepped down. *Damn. It's not enough I had to jump onto the train, now I have to jump off it.* If she didn't hate Mayfield before, she sure hated him now.

Glanced right. Saw what looked like Dixon's car.

*Why haven't I heard back from Robby? Where the hell is he?*

Vail stepped down to the lowest rung, then sprung off the train and into the brush, rolling onto her shoulder as she landed. Cushioning scrub or not, the impact still stung.

She pushed herself up, saw Dixon's head poking through the window, yelling at her.

"Hurry the hell up!"

Blaring horns. Vail ran onto the roadway and got into Dixon's car.

Dixon floored it as soon as the door closed, throwing the seatbeltless Vail backwards and sideways. She grabbed for the door handle and righted herself. Pain shot through her left shoulder.

Dixon's engine was revving, groaning as she kept the pedal against the floor.

"Don't lose him," Vail shouted. As if she had to tell Dixon to step on it. Dixon was driving along the rough hard-pack shoulder, which made for a less than comfortable ride. But neither of them cared, not with their quarry in the SUV ahead of them, speeding along this twisty-turny stretch of Highway 29 that was now out in the suburbs, vineyards on both sides illuminated by Dixon's headlights.

Suddenly, a buzz on Dixon's phone.

"Get it," she yelled.

Vail reached over, grabbed Dixon's cell, and flipped it open. "This is Vail."

"It's Brix. I'm en route, passing Pratt Avenue."

*Now there's a street that rings a bell.* "He's at Pratt," Vail said to Dixon. To Brix: "I don't know where we are—"

"Sounds like he's a couple miles back," Dixon said. "Tell him we're passing Ehlers."

"We're—"

"I heard," Brix said. "I'll be there soon."

Vail ended the call, shoved the phone back into Dixon's pocket—and that's when she realized her partner was wearing the bare minimum: gym shorts and shirt, no bra, and tennis shoes without socks. But she had her sidearm strapped to her shoulder and her phone holder clipped to the shorts' waistband. It looked bizarre—and downright geeky—but who the hell cared?

Vail caught a sign on the left—Bale Grist Mill State Park—and realized the area was becoming more rural as they drove down 29.

Dixon tightened her grip on the wheel. "He's speeding up, I think he realizes we're behind him."

"Where's your cube?"

"In here," she said, banging her right elbow on the large armrest.

Dixon lifted her arm and Vail reached into the deep receptacle. She pulled out the device, flipped the switch, and the blinding light filled the interior and reflected off the windshield. It made them both recoil.

"Jesus—"

"Shit, sorry about that." Vail rolled down the window and set the magnetic base on the roof.

"Two-way's in the glove box. Tell dispatch we've got a code 33. Give our twenty."

Vail located the radio, then saw something that brought a smile to her face: her Glock. *Missed you, big fella.*

She keyed the two-way and followed Dixon's instructions. " . . . Code 33, stolen silver Nissan SUV headed—"

"North."

"North on Highway 29." She lowered the radio. "Get us closer, let me grab the tag."

Dixon pressed the accelerator, the engine roared louder and the vehicle closed on Mayfield's SUV.

"Roger," the dispatcher responded. "Code 33 on primary. All non-emergency traffic go to red channel."

Vail leaned forward and squinted. "I see a five. X-ray, Tom, Robert—" Vail moved the radio back to her lips. "License on the stolen Nissan. California plate. Five X-ray Tom Robert."

Mayfield swerved left to avoid a motorcyclist, who leaned right, onto the shoulder.

Dixon gave the man extra room and cut back into the lane. "I hate high-speed chases. Too fucking dangerous."

The headlights caught a large sign up ahead and off to the right. Vail pointed. "What do you say we forget the chase and go see Old Faithful spew her wrath?"

Dixon veered right around a stray cat. Vail grabbed the dashboard with her left hand, then set the radio between her thighs when Dixon slammed on the brakes and yelled out—

"What the fuck!"

A cruiser, light bar flashing, was approaching from the opposite direction. Dixon's car dovetailed, her rear end flying right while she coaxed the front end left, back into pursuit of Mayfield.

"Mayfield saw the cruiser, turned left," Dixon said. "Right into the Castillo del Deseo."

"The what?"

"Castle of Desire," Dixon said. "A dozen years to build. Looks and feels like a real Spanish castle." She accelerated up the inclined cement drive, the taillights of Mayfield's SUV still barely visible around the bend. She sped past the seedling evergreens, then crested the hill. Ahead, in the darkness, was a large, dramatically lit brick structure.

Vail craned her neck to take in the enormity of the approaching complex. "Robby said he went to a castle a few days ago. Wish I could've seen it with him. Just a guess . . . but this won't be nearly as fun."

Dixon swung the vehicle in behind Mayfield's parked Nissan. "Let's go."

"Where?"

Dixon nodded ahead, toward the castle. "You're gonna get your wish."

# FIFTY-SIX

**W**eapons drawn, Vail and Dixon rushed out of their car and approached the Nissan from behind, beneath window level. The headlights from Dixon's car lit them up like precious jewels against black velvet. They moved up alongside the SUV and pulled open the doors. The dome light was disabled, but there was enough brightness from Dixon's headlights to check the interior.

"Clear," Vail said.

"Clear," Dixon repeated.

They looked out into the darkness.

Vail spotted him first. "There!" She threw out a hand to the left of the castle, at what appeared to be a grassy knoll with thick elder trees peppering the hillside. A large man was running alongside the massive building.

They took off in that direction, trying to keep an eye on Mayfield while watching for hidden ruts, low barriers or other structures that would lay them out face down on the ground.

Dixon pointed. "Over there, by the opening in the wall—"

They ran forward, across the grass and through the stand of thick-trunked trees. In the shadows of the dim lighting hanging from various points of the castle wall, the trees looked eerie, like witches ready to pull their roots from beneath the grass and start walking.

They pulled up against the high, rough hewn brick wall. Vail peered around the edge. "Clear."

They fell in, through the opening, which was a back lot of the castle, with machinery and stainless steel white wine casks arranged against the far wall of the large square. To their left was another building constructed of the same materials and architecture. By the looks of it, it was a miniature castle all its own, perhaps a private residence for the winery's owner.

Vail and Dixon moved into the square and squatted to get a better view of the area. There were only a few places where someone could be hiding. Mayfield didn't have enough of a lead on them to sprint across the lot to the stainless steel casks. And he couldn't have made it to the residence. But to their right, twenty feet away, was a service entrance into the castle.

Two heavy, ornate wood doors were swung fully open, inviting them in. As they approached cautiously, Dixon's phone rang. Dixon mouthed "Brix" to Vail, who pressed forward.

Dixon remained where she was and answered the call. "We're at the castle, around back," Vail heard as she moved into the room. More stainless containers stood on thick metal stands, hoses coiled on the cement ground beneath them. Metal steps led up to a catwalk, where workers could presumably monitor the huge vats of Chardonnay and Sauvignon Blanc.

Vail knelt down and swept the area, then proceeded forward up a couple of steps . . . into the castle. Immediately to her left was an ornate plaza, with dim lanterns providing enough light to be romantic— and authentic—but far from useful when conducting a foot pursuit of a serial killer.

Clearly, that was not in the original designers' plan when they sketched out the lighting requirements for the facility. Shame on them.

Vail heard a noise behind her—swung around hard—and saw Dixon.

She leaned in close toward Vail's ear. "Brix and Agbayani are here. They're coming in through the front. Cruisers are in the lot, making sure he doesn't leave with his car."

"I wish that was comforting, but there's a lot of rural real estate out here. I'm not sure we caught a break when that cruiser forced him off the road."

Dixon's head was turned, taking in the area in front of them. "There's an iron fence that surrounds the property, so if we don't get him in the castle, it's not likely he'll be able to get away without going past one of our people."

"Even armed, I'm not sure a one-on-one confrontation will be to our advantage." Vail pointed with her Glock. "You go left. Into the plaza. I'll go right."

Dixon nodded and Vail headed down a stairwell that sported slightly improved lighting—but opened into what appeared to be a gift shop. A large armored knight exoskeleton stood guard to her right, against the wall. To her left was a series of catacombs, all illuminated with mood lighting. Filling the main space and directly ahead was a well-camouflaged sales counter and tasting area. Two women stood there, one pouring wine for a husband and wife and the other exchanging a charge slip with a customer.

Vail stepped forward, her pistol by her right thigh and her badge now clipped to her belt. She unfolded her credentials, held them up and played show-and-tell. "FBI. Have any of you seen a bodybuilder come through here dressed in gym clothes?"

The two women and the couple shook their heads. "Okay, leave what you're doing and get out of here. Move to the parking lot and wait there. Don't scream. Go quickly, but don't panic. You hear me?"

Their eyes, wide with fear, registered their understanding and they moved off.

Vail continued on, through the gift shop, into tasting stations that were tucked into small rooms off the main hallway. She felt her anxiety bubbling up, the pressure in her chest, the sense that she had to get the hell out of here.

*Claustrophobia sucks. And it's goddamn inconvenient.*

*I don't have time for this shit.* She pressed on, following the tasting room into what was apparently a wine cave. The hallways were narrow, the ceiling was low, and the lighting was dim.

Hundreds of wine bottles were stacked horizontally against the wall, twelve rows high and several dozen wide. Up ahead, oak barrels rested on their sides along the walls, making the rooms seem even narrower. She turned down another bend and entered a similarly slender hallway. With only one bulb now every twenty or so feet, it was getting darker. And she was finding it more difficult to breathe.

*This is ridiculous. Mayfield could be anywhere. He must've known this place. Maybe the cruiser didn't force him down this road. Maybe he knew how many caves and corridors and hidden rooms there were down here.*

*How are we going to find him?*

Vail kept wandering through the maze of passageways, the anxiety and dread now consuming her thoughts. *No. Focus on Mayfield. On Mayfield. He could be anywhere. Stay focused—*

Up ahead—a larger room. Time to breathe, regroup. Think things through.

She stepped into a vast brick-encased vault—filled with oak barrels. It was brighter in here, and the ceiling was higher. She continued in, eyes scanning every corner and the subrooms created by the stacks of barrels. It was not unlike the thousand square foot barrel room she had been in at Silver Ridge.

When they found Victoria Cameron. When this whole mess started. In a sense, she had come full circle.

She walked down the wide, main aisle, her head swinging from side to side, trying to ensure John Mayfield didn't ambush or blindside her. A few feet more and then she stopped. Turned 360 degrees, then backed against the nearest wall. Crouched down and pulled her Black-Berry. She had minimal service—one bar—but hopefully it was enough.

She looked for messages. Nothing. Robby had still not replied. What was up with that? That was a pretty frantic message she left. He wouldn't ignore it. He'd never ignored any message she left him. Ever.

With her Glock in her left hand, she thumb-typed Robby a quick text:

where r u. need help

Then she texted Dixon and Brix, Lugo and Agbayani:

in large room filled with oak barrels. past gift shop. somewhere in tunnels. no sign of mayfld. ur 20?

As she reholstered her BlackBerry, she heard the tone of a cell phone. It was more than nearby—it was damn near next to her. She rose from her crouch and started searching. Whose phone had rung? It wasn't a prolonged ring, as if someone had called. It was more like a quick, repeated beep. Then nothing.

A text.

She had just sent a text. *Shit, this is not good.*

Vail tightened her grip on the Glock, then moved slowly forward. Looked left, into a smaller room—also lined with oak barrels—and saw a body. Lying supine. With a shiny, thick liquid beneath it.

Vail rotated her head, checking as best she could around the barrels. Finding nothing, she inched closer to the body, still keeping an eye on her immediate vicinity. She moved to the far wall and cleared that completely, then kept her back to it. Directly in front of her was the victim. Male, well-dressed.

She advanced, in a crouch, her eyes still scanning below the barrels for feet—or movement of any kind.

Looked back to the body. And then she saw the face. It was Eddie Agbayani. In this light, it was impossible to determine much about cause of death. She lay her index and middle finger across his neck to check for a pulse. Nothing. But she felt something that confirmed her suspicions.

Vail pulled her BlackBerry. Using the light given off by the LCD screen, she scanned Agbayani's throat area. Palpated the cartilage. And concluded—to be confirmed later under more optimal conditions—that the detective was the latest victim of John Mayfield, of the Crush Killer.

His left wrist had been sliced, the blood moist around the wound. He was killed moments ago—which meant Mayfield was likely still nearby.

Agbayani's boots were on his feet—but at this point, it didn't matter. Mayfield didn't need to leave his calling card. They would know who was responsible.

As she glanced back up—she'd taken her eyes off the room too long—a text came through. Brix:

covered east upper level and turrets. zip.

Then Dixon:

courtyard and surrounding rooms, banquet room clear. on second floor. no way of knowing if he's still here

Vail replied to all:

still here big room. found a db. still warm.

She sent it without saying it was Agbayani—the revelation would no doubt upset Dixon—but then realized she had no choice. They needed to know one of their boots on the ground was now, literally, on the ground.

She took a deep breath, looked over at Agbayani, and typed a new message:

sorry, rox. vic is eddie

Tears filled her eyes. She knew Dixon would take it hard. And though she didn't know him well, he seemed to be a good guy.

If Vail were to follow standard crime scene procedure, as was her duty, she needed to secure the area and remain with the body. But that was a low priority. Her greater duty was to find the killer. Besides, they knew who did the murder. And Agbayani was dead. No sense in remaining. No one was going to walk up to a dead body.

Vail rose and moved back into the larger room. That's where she stood while she figured out what to do, where to go.

That's where she stood when the lights went out.

# FIFTY-SEVEN

*D*ixon was on the second level, her neck aching and swollen from Mayfield's attack in the steam room. The adrenaline had masked the pain, but now, as time passed and the inflammation increased, she could no longer shrug it off. Her throat was narrowed and she was having difficulty swallowing and breathing.

And her neck's range of motion was diminished. She had to twist her torso—which was also sore—because the cervical muscles were bruised and in spasm.

Dixon left the room she had just cleared and moved back into the corridor when her phone vibrated. She pulled it from her belt. A text from Vail:

> in some kind of large room filled with oak barrels. past gift shop. somewhere in tunnels. no sign of mayfld. ur 20?

Dixon shifted her weapon to her left hand and texted back.

> courtyard and surrounding rooms, banquet room clear. on second floor. no way of knowing if he's still here

Flipped the phone closed, proceeded carefully. One run-in with John Mayfield was enough. She felt fortunate to have escaped; trying to pull off a second miracle in the same night might be asking too much of her Creator. Another buzz. Pulled her cell, flipped it open. Text from Vail:

still here big room. found a db. still warm.

*Goddamn it.* She took a deep breath. They had to find this monster. *Fast.* Phone in hand, Dixon steadied her weapon with both hands and moved forward a few feet, toward a doorway that led to a balcony overlooking the square below. Black iron lights hung at various intervals from the brick walls, under alcoves and from rusted brackets, throwing romantic—but minimal—light on the courtyard.

Her phone buzzed again. She twisted her right wrist and read the display.

sorry, rox. vic is eddie

Dixon stood there staring at the message. *What? How can that be?* Read it again: vic is Eddie. *Eddie?*

She started walking, unsure where she was headed, moving toward a staircase that would take her down. Dixon wasn't paying attention to where she was going or what was in front of her. She kept moving, through corridors, across the square, down a staircase. Someone bumped her. Brix. She looked at him.

"Roxxi, I'm so sorry—"

She blinked away tears. Looked off ahead of her. "Where. Where is he?"

Brix took her by the arm and led her around the gift shop, through tunnels and small rooms lined with barrels and wine bottles. He pulled his Maglite and turned it on, twisted the beam to a wide spread.

*Eddie. Dead?*

*I'll kill that bastard. I'll break every bone in his body—*

"Roxxi, calm down," Brix said in a low voice. "Relax."

*He must've felt me tensing.* "I'm gonna kill him, Redd—"

"Shh," he said, placing a hand over her mouth. "Hold that thought," he whispered. "Let's catch him first."

They were moving down a long, narrow corridor when suddenly the lights went out. They both stopped. Brought their handguns up, adrenaline flooding their system.

Ready for a fight.

# FIFTY-EIGHT

*V*ail backed up against the nearest wall and crouched down low, into as small a target as possible. Unless Mayfield had night vision goggles, she would be nearly impossible for him to find. But she could not rule out him having NVGs—because, thus far, he seemed to be prepared. And because his ending up at the castle might've been by design.

But it couldn't be. He did not have NVGs. He was as much in the dark as she was.

Then why would he cut the lights?

*Unless he knew where I was when he took them out. Move—I have to move.* Vail clambered to her left, attempting to be quiet, but the scrape of her shoes against the cement flooring, the fine gravel and detritus from the people who'd walked through here today made stealth difficult. But that worked both ways.

She continued left, bumped into a wall—brought up her right hand and felt around—barrels. Took a step forward to move around them—and stopped. Someone was coming. Noise in the distance.

Vail rose, backed up behind the barrels and brought her Glock in close to her body, holding it low, so it couldn't be easily knocked from her hands.

Waited. Footsteps.

━━━

BRIX HELD HIS SIG-SAUER out in front of him, the Maglite alongside the barrel, illuminating the area in front of him. In such narrow quarters, Dixon had to follow single file behind him. She was a good five feet back, giving adequate spacing.

Up ahead, she saw the mouth to another, larger room. Brix stopped. Dixon stopped.

---

Vail listened. Moved forward slightly, peeked around the edge of the barrel. Saw the flicker of a light. Then it went out.

Her heartbeat accelerated. She felt it pounding, an aching in her head, a pulsing in her ears. She backed up a step away from the edge and listened.

---

"What?" Dixon whispered.

Brix shut his light. "A room up ahead."

"Could be the one Karen's in."

"If so, Mayfield could be in there, too."

"Split up?"

Brix nodded, leaned in close to her ear. "I'll take the light. If he goes after someone, it'll be me because he'll know where I am."

Dixon gave a thumbs up. Brix lit up his Maglite and pressed forward. The room ahead appeared to be large, with curvilinear brick ceilings, like multiple gazebos launching from thick square columns.

As Brix disappeared into the room, Dixon started ahead herself, wanting to shout into the dark, "Karen, you in here?" But she knew that was the absolute wrong thing to do. She didn't even dare open her phone in the darkness, as that would surely give away her position.

But just as she'd gone about fifteen paces into the large room, she saw Brix's flashlight go flying from his hand. He let out a sickening thump and, in the twirling and carnival-like swirl of his light as it spun on the ground, he appeared to drop to the floor with an even louder thud.

Dixon started to rush forward, then stopped. Mayfield was here. She had to get to him before he killed Brix—if he hadn't already. She had to risk it. "Karen!"

---

VAIL SAW THE LIGHT advancing into the room, footsteps approaching. She backed up further, Glock out in front of her, taking an angle on the imminent arrival of her guest. The light was moving, bouncing the way it would with someone's gait. Or if it were held out in front of you against your gun.

But she didn't dare call out.

A noise—skin on bone—and the light went flying to the ground. A bump. Something hit the cement. A body?

"Karen!"

Vail looked out into the near darkness. *Dixon.* "Over here!"

And then she saw something dark spring toward her, a mass like a football player plowing into her, a crushing blow that knocked her back into a wall of barrels. Her air left her lungs.

And the Glock flew from her hands.

# FIFTY-NINE

In the distant light that was off somewhere in the background, Vail saw John Mayfield in silhouette, his massive hand over her mouth. He had her shoved against the barrels. And she knew what was coming.

*Vail swung, struck his meaty shoulder, then*
*kicked him in his groin—hit something hard,*
*kneed him again, and*
*again,*
*writhing her head from side to side, trying to open her mouth to bite—*
*reached up and grabbed for his face, got hold of his nose but*
*he yanked his head back and*
*she threw her left hand up in time to block a massive thrust into her neck.*

*It struck her hand and forced it against her throat and she coughed. Spasmodic. Coughing—*
*And then she heard a nauseatingly sick bone-breaking crunch.*

---

"OVER HERE!"

Dixon tried to locate Vail's voice—but in the chamber, with its uneven and gazebo-rounded ceilings, she couldn't triangulate on her position. She moved quickly into the large room, using whatever light was being given off by the fallen Maglite, hoping she wouldn't run into Mayfield. Because right now, she was sure he was here. That's what had taken down Brix.

She saw barrels to her left and moved toward them, her right hand aiming her SIG and her left feeling the metal rims surrounding the flat oak faces, forward, forward, a few feet at a time.

And then scuffling, struggling, muted yells—off to her right. *Karen!*

Dixon ran in the direction of the noise. Around the bend, she saw, in the relative darkness, John Mayfield, legs spread, straddling something. She couldn't see Vail, but Mayfield was easily twice her width.

Given Mayfield's well-documented MO—which she'd experienced firsthand—she didn't have to see Vail to know where she was, or what Mayfield was doing to her.

There wasn't a good angle to take him out with a clean shot—especially in the poor lighting, she couldn't be sure what she would hit. And a man like this wouldn't respond to her plea for him to put his hands above his head. Based on what Vail had told her about narcissists, "surrender" is not in their ego-driven vocabulary.

So with Agbayani's demise in the forefront of her thoughts, Dixon went for the more personal approach. She came up beside him, lifted her right leg, and brought her foot down, with all the force she could muster, against the side of Mayfield's locked left knee, driving it to the right.

He recoiled in pain, the bone-crushing blow tearing ligament, cartilage—and probably fracturing his tibia and fibula.

As Mayfield's knee buckled, he yelled out in pain, crumpled backwards. Dixon grabbed his thick wrist and brought her right forearm across her body and forward, through Mayfield's elbow joint. It hyperextended and snapped. She yanked down on his fractured arm, then backhanded him across the face with her SIG-fisted hand.

Mayfield, dazed by the blow, stumbled awkwardly on his broken leg, then collapsed and hit the ground hard.

Dixon stepped forward and brought her leg back like a place kicker and planted it in his jaw. It was a cheap shot, she knew, because the man was already unconscious.

Then she brought up her SIG and aimed.

# SIXTY

fter hearing the first crunch, Vail felt Mayfield release his grip on her mouth. She saw and heard movement—and Mayfield was suddenly yanked to the side, followed by another bone-snapping sound. A blow to the face. And then he was stumbling backward.

Standing there was Dixon. She stepped forward and kicked him. Just to make sure the Crush Killer would not be doing any more damage.

Vail rushed over to the fallen flashlight and picked it up. And that's when she saw Dixon aiming her pistol at Mayfield's head.

"Roxxann!"

Dixon, her blonde hair matted and mussed and half-covering her face, brushed it aside. Her chest was heaving, her left hand still balled into a fist.

Vail stepped forward. "It's okay, Roxx. It's okay." She brought Dixon against her body, gave her a hug and a reassuring squeeze, and felt her tense body relax.

But Dixon suddenly pushed back. "Brix—" She scrambled to her left. "Light!"

Vail swung the Maglite around and, twenty-five feet away, found Brix on the floor, facedown and alongside a stack of barrels. Vail knelt down and pressed her fingers against his neck. "Strong pulse. Call it in."

As Dixon opened her phone, Vail reached for her handcuffs. But they weren't there. Of all the things she'd replaced, she had forgotten to get a new set. She went back to Brix, felt around his belt and found his cuffs, then brought them over to the unconscious Mayfield and clamped them down, extra tight. When he awoke, there was no way he was getting out of those. Especially with a fractured arm.

Vail pulled her BlackBerry and checked for messages from Robby. Nothing. "Call Ray and the others," she said to Dixon. "Let 'em know we have the suspect in custody and he needs transport to county." She looked over at Mayfield, who was stirring, regaining consciousness. "He'll need medical attention on arrival."

———

As Dixon pocketed her cell, Brix slowly sat up. Dixon extended her arm, locked hands with Brix, and pulled him up. He swayed a bit, then steadied himself against the barrels and looked over at Mayfield. "Bastard clocked me from behind."

"You okay?" Dixon asked.

He stretched his neck and rolled his shoulders back. "I'm fine."

"You missed all the fun," Vail said. She brought a hand to her throat and rubbed it.

"Where's Eddie?" Dixon asked.

Vail locked eyes with Brix. He frowned, then said, "Take her. I'll stay and keep watch over the douche bag."

Vail led Dixon to the next room, created by walls of barrels, and stood there while Dixon approached the body. She knelt down, her back to Vail, started to place a hand on his chest—and stopped. No doubt, her "cop instincts" trumped her emotions and she knew not to contaminate the crime scene. But did it really matter?

"It's okay, Roxx," Vail said. "You can touch him. Pay your respects."

She reached out again, placed the back of her hand against his cheek, then his forehead. Gently closed his eyes. Said something to him, and her back heaved in sorrow.

Vail remained where she was, giving her friend some space.

A moment later, Dixon stood up and, wiping away tears, squared her shoulders, brought up a hand and moved her hair off her face.

"Let's go," she said, walking past Vail.

## SIXTY-ONE

**B**rix called one of the officers who was watching the castle's periphery and had him secure Eddie Agbayani's crime scene. The paramedics, clad in light gray tops, darker pants and ball caps, transported Mayfield, under heavy guard, to the Napa Valley Medical Center ER, not far from the Napa Police Department. Brix refused treatment, saying he was "Just fine now, thank you very much."

Vail chucked it off to male ego, embarrassment to having been taken out, but then she realized she'd probably behave the same way. She chided herself for looking for male-female gender issues in every situation. It was something she would have to work on, because she knew, invariably, it would sneak into her thoughts, despite her best efforts to keep those attitudes in check.

On the way to the hospital, Dixon and Vail stopped at the Heartland bed-and-breakfast in Yountville. Robby was not there. Nor was his car. In fact, he had not been there the entire day—other than the maid service straightening the bed and cleaning the bathroom, the room was as she had left it when she locked up this morning.

"I take it it's not like Robby to ignore your calls," Dixon said.

Vail stood at the foot of the bed, hands on her hips. "No, it's not." She turned and faced the new suitcases Robby had purchased at the outlets a couple of days ago. Flipped his open, moved aside his dirty underwear and socks. Hit something hard and flat. Dug it out and held it up.

Dixon joined Vail at her side. "His cell phone?"

Vail did not reply. She flicked it open. It was powered off. She turned it on, waiting for it to boot and then find service. When it had finished, she scrolled to the incoming log. All the messages she had left him stared back at her.

She turned to Dixon. "The only messages in his log are from me. No one else called him?"

"Did he get other calls while you were with him—at any time during your trip?"

Vail thought. "No." She thumbed the mouse button. "But at some point he would've received a call, and there's nothing. Nothing here before today."

"Maybe he deletes his logs regularly. I have a friend who does that. What about outgoing calls?"

Vail played her thumb across the buttons again. "Nothing there either. That's not right." She held up the phone. "There's *nothing*."

"Either he regularly deletes his logs, or—"

"Or someone deleted them for him." Vail stood there staring at the phone, as if doing so would magically restore the log entries. "I can send the phone to the Bureau lab, see if they can grab data off the chip. There's gotta be a computer chip inside, right?"

Dixon shrugged. "I would think so. But would the Bureau lab do that? It's not a federal case. I mean, it's not a case at all, not yet."

"His friend," Vail said. "Robby's friend. Maybe he knows where he is." Vail scrolled to the phone book. "What the hell was the guy's name?" She watched the list roll by. "Sebastian, I think."

"Is he there?"

"No." Without another word, Vail carefully closed the phone and slipped it into her pocket.

"We can't explain the log," Dixon said. "So let's approach this another way. If Robby left the phone here, he wasn't planning on being gone long. Does he run?"

"Yeah." She looked around, found a pair of new dress shoes. No sneakers. "Okay, maybe he drove somewhere and went for a run and left his cell. Or he just forgot it."

"Sure. He's on vacation, you're swamped with a case. He's on his own. Makes sense."

"So why didn't he come back?"

Dixon surveyed the room. "Too bad the maid cleaned the room."

Vail nodded. She knew what Dixon was getting at: If there had been a struggle, a cop would immediately recognize the telltale signs, but to a cleaner it might look like a messy room . . . or the aftermath of a rough morning of sex. Regardless, what it looked like then—along with whatever clues there might have been—was now lost as far as the information it might have yielded.

"I'll try to locate the owners, see if we can question the maid. For what it's worth. Who knows, if it was obvious, things knocked over, she may remember."

"Fine, do it." Vail got down on all fours and examined the carpet, looking for trace blood. After making a circuit of the room and finding nothing suspicious, she moved into the bathroom to examine the sink and shower drains.

Dixon hung up and joined Vail in the bathroom. "She's going to have the maid call me." She crouched beside Vail. "I'm gonna call Matt Aaron, get a CSI in here to find what he can. If there's latent blood or prints, he'll find it. Other than maybe vacuuming, making the bed and running a sponge over the countertops, I don't think the cleaners do a whole lot till you check out." She tapped Vail on her knee. "C'mon. Let's get out of here before we contaminate the scene more than we already have."

Vail followed Dixon out of the room—took one last look back—then pulled the door closed.

# SIXTY-TWO

O utside, Dixon called Brix and asked him to have someone at the Sheriff's Department issue a BOLO for Robby's car. They weren't sure of the license plate, so Vail gave him the name of the rental company and their arrival date. A deputy would chase down the registration. Brix, being briefed on what was going down, also issued a countywide alert to law enforcement officers, across all local jurisdictions, that Detective Robby Hernandez was to be considered missing. It was far short of the time frame whereby they would normally issue such an order, but Brix said he had no problem bending the rules for another cop, especially one he'd come to like.

Before leaving the bed-and-breakfast, Vail and Dixon knocked on the doors of the other rooms, mindful that some of the guests might still be out on the town, at a late supper. Napa largely shut down in the evening, apart from the restaurant scene, and people often ate leisurely dinners that lasted longer than usual.

Vail and Dixon spoke with couples in four of the eight other rooms. No one was around during the time frame Vail estimated Robby might have left the room. No one saw or heard anything unusual. In short, no one had anything of value to offer.

They left Dixon's card stuck in the doors of the rooms that did not answer their knock, with a note to call as soon as they returned. With that, they got back in the car and headed for the emergency room.

———

THEY ARRIVED at the Napa Valley Medical Center and entered the emergency room through the ambulance bay. As they passed the

367

nurses' station, where a woman was talking quickly into a corded red phone, Vail heard the beeps of heart monitors, medical orders and countertalk between doctors and nurses, and the firing of a portable x-ray unit. The composite sounds reminded her of Jonathan's recent stay at Fairfax Hospital. They weren't fond memories.

A gurney wheeled by in front of them, causing them to pull up and wait while the staff descended on the patient.

It didn't take long to find the area where John Mayfield was being treated. Gray and blue curtains were drawn, but three Napa County deputy sheriffs, dressed in black jackets and pants, stood a few feet back from the foot of the gurney. Vail and Dixon badged the three men, then stepped around the curtain. Another two deputies were inside, beside the doctor and nurse, who were dressed in powder blue scrubs. A portable x-ray tube stood off to the side. A stocky physician, presumably the radiologist, was holding up an x-ray to the fluorescent lighting.

"I'll give this a better read on the lightbox, but it's pretty clear." He pointed with an index finger; his colleague, a slender physician, looked on. "See? Here, and here."

"Set it and release," the thin doctor said.

The radiologist lowered the film. "That'll do it." He looked down at his patient. "Someone did a number on your elbow and knee, Mr. Mayfield."

"That someone is me," Dixon said. She stood there, thumbs hooked through her belt loops. Daring anyone to comment.

Everyone in the room turned to face her. No one spoke.

The doctor turned back to his patient. "We'll get you stabilized, but you're going to need an orthopedic consult. My best guess is surgery will be required to reduce that tib-fib fracture and repair the torn ligaments, but that'll have to wait till the swelling's down. It's possible, even with surgery, that you'll have some reduced mobility."

"Get the violins," Vail said.

All heads once again turned in their direction.

"I gotta listen to this bullshit?" Mayfield asked.

"Excuse me," the radiologist said. "You mind waiting out—"

"No," Vail said, "excuse us. Your patient is a serial killer who's brutally murdered several innocent people. Still concerned about the *reduced mobility* of his left arm?"

The doctor pulled his eyes from Vail, took a noticeable step back from Mayfield, and glanced at his colleague. "Well, as I said, I'm going to give these a closer look on the . . . on the lightbox." He turned and pushed past the nurse and deputies and left the curtained room.

"Shall I call Dr. Feliciano?" the nurse asked.

The remaining physician took a step back himself. His eyes found the handcuffs that were fastened to the gurney. "Yes . . . Dr. Feliciano. Let's get Mr. Mayfield casted and on his feet. So to speak."

———

TWO HOURS LATER, Dr. Feliciano had finished casting both limbs—without incident, and, at his patient's insistence, without pain killers. Shortly thereafter, Mayfield received an expedited release and was cleared for transport to the Napa jail.

Earlier, while Mayfield was being attended to by Dr. Feliciano, Dixon fielded calls from the maid for the Heartland bed-and-breakfast. She did not recall anything unusually out of place in Vail's room, but she couldn't be sure because she cleans four different B&Bs per day, and they all tended to run together. There was one that was in significant disarray, but she thought it was down the road from Heartland. Dixon tried to get her to commit, but the woman could not swear the tossed room was Vail's.

Dixon also took three calls from other guests at the bed-and-breakfast. No one recalled anything out of the ordinary.

Vail checked with the hospital nurses to make sure a man matching Robby's description hadn't been brought in for emergency treatment. He had not been. They called over to Queen of the Valley Medical Center and Santa Rosa Memorial Hospital, Level II trauma centers, which is where Robby would've been airlifted had there been a major accident. They, too, had not treated or admitted anyone resembling Robby. The nighttime administrator made a call, herself, to other area hospitals that might have received him. But she came up empty.

As Vail and Dixon drove to the Napa County Department of Corrections, Vail was quiet, replaying in her mind the last conversations she'd had with Robby. Nothing stood out. She'd been preoccupied with the Crush Killer case. He had been entertaining himself, going here and there . . . and she'd been too busy to really listen to what he was saying in terms of what he'd seen and where he had been. Other than visiting the castle, she couldn't even remember if he'd told her anything about specific places he had visited.

Dixon must have sensed her mental somersaulting, because she reached over and nudged Vail in the shoulder.

"Hey."

Vail pulled her numbed gaze from the window and turned to face Dixon.

"I'm sure he's fine. Maybe he just had something to deal with. You said he knew some people out here, right? Maybe he went over there to help them."

Vail pulled her BlackBerry and called Bledsoe.

"Karen," Bledsoe said with a hoarse grogginess. "If you're gonna be in California much longer, you've really gotta get the hang of that three-hour time difference. It's almost . . . 2 a.m."

"Sorry."

"What's wrong?" His voice was suddenly strong, his mind wide awake. He knew her pretty well.

"I . . ." She sighed deeply, trying to find the energy to form the words. "I can't find Robby."

"What do you mean, you can't find him?"

"He's disappeared. Gone."

"Hernandez is a big boy, Karen. I'm sure he's somewhere."

"No. I've been trying to reach him all day. I found his phone in our room, turned off. The logs were wiped clean. No apparent sign of a struggle, but we're not sure. His car's gone. I take it you haven't heard from him."

"Not since the thing with Jonathan. How's it going with that killer?"

"We got him. Tonight."

"Congrats, Karen. Give yourself a pat on the ass."

"I'll let Robby do that. As soon as I find him."

"You check air, car rentals—"

"Air. No, I totally spaced—"

"Look, I'll take care of it. Flights, car rentals, I'll check it all. I've got all his info in the file, down at the office, from Dead Eyes. I'll go down there right now. I'll call you if I find something."

She wished Bledsoe was there, by her side. Right now, she needed something close to home. For some reason, talking to him felt better. "Call me even if you don't find anything."

She hung up, let her head rest back on the seat. They had arrived at the Department of Corrections' Hall of Justice complex on Third Street.

"You wanna come in, or wait here?"

Vail sat up and rubbed her face. "I should be nearby when Mayfield's questioned." Her voice was tired. Truth was, she was exhausted, mentally and physically. And whatever remaining energy she did have was focused on Robby, not on John Mayfield. "I should probably be the one in the room with him. Narcissists need to be handled differently than most suspects."

"Assuming Owens goes for it." Dixon was staring at her. "Are you in any condition to go face-to-face with Mayfield?"

Vail popped open her door and got out. That was her answer.

They stowed their guns in the lockers, then met Brix, Lugo, Gordon, and Mann at the long, window-enclosed booking office. Timothy Nance was there as well. He did not look pleased. Vail had the fleeting thought of wondering why he was still around, but decided her waning energies were better spent on more important matters than scum like Nance.

Lugo looked particularly worn. His face was taut and his gaze was focused on the ground.

Normally, the arresting officers discharged their duties and returned to patrol once their prisoner was brought into the jail and turned over to prison personnel for processing. But in this case, the task force members were not about to let anyone handle John Mayfield. He was their collar, and they intended to see this through to the end.

Austin Mann stepped over to Dixon and Vail, then nodded at Mayfield, who stood off to the side in prison blues, getting his fingerprints digitally scanned. "Property and medical intake's been done. And the nurse already came down to clear him."

Vail folded her arms across her chest. "He just came from the hospital. The docs released him. What'd they need the nurse for?"

"Liability," Brix said, joining the huddle. "CYA, that's all. But because of his injuries, they're gonna house him separately, outside the general pop. In case someone were to attack him, he couldn't defend himself."

"That'd be a damn shame," Vail said.

"Wouldn't it," Mann said with a chuckle. He glanced over at Mayfield, who obviously heard his comment, then turned his body slightly, away from the arrestee. In a lower voice, Mann said, "Watch Commander's cleared us to interview him in the Blue Room."

"Yeah," Brix said. "About that." He touched Vail on the elbow. "Can I have a word with you?"

As he moved her aside, out of earshot of the others, Mayfield was escorted down the hall and through Door 154, which separated the booking area from the prison.

"When I saw him, I felt like I'd seen the guy before, but I couldn't place where. Then it all made sense. Asshole is a pest control and mosquito abatement technician. He used to spray around the department when we'd get ants in the winter, after the rains. I think I even spoke to him once or twice."

"Here's one better. Yesterday, Roxxann and I worked out with the guy." Vail didn't say anything about Dixon's considering a date with the man. "I saw the guy, Brix. I looked the monster in his eyes and I didn't know. I'm supposed to be able to recognize evil. If I'd only—"

He held up a hand. "Don't. We're not perfect, Karen. We're just cops. We do the best we can with what we've got. Yeah?"

She sighed deeply. "Yeah."

Brix leaned in close. "Listen . . . the sheriff wants you to take the lead on Mayfield's interview."

"The sheriff?" After what had happened with Fuller, Vail figured she'd be the last one on his list to reward with the prized interview. The detective who nailed the killer was the one who usually did the interview. In this case, Vail figured that'd be Dixon.

"The sheriff. He says you're the best man for the job. No offense."

Vail tried to smile. "No offense taken."

"Last thing. Are you okay with being alone in the room with him?"

Vail sucked on her bottom lip, glanced over at her fellow task force members. They were all looking at her, including Dixon. "No big deal. Let's do it."

# SIXTY-THREE

The task force members settled into the video monitoring room down the hall from the Blue Room. It contained a faux wood media cabinet outfitted with a Sony television, videotape recording facilities, and several chairs.

"You'll need this," Brix said, handing her a file. "Oh—the prick insists his real name's John Wayne Mayfield. We did a quick records search. Looks like he added the middle name himself."

Vail snorted. "Yeah, that definitely fits."

"Karen," Brix said. "Good luck."

The rest of the task force members nodded their agreement. Dixon dipped her chin.

Vail closed the door and walked across the hall into the Blue Room, where John Mayfield sat behind a round table. She carried the manila folder against her chest; she entered and set the file down on the table and looked at the arrestee.

Mayfield's left arm was casted from the thumb to a point above the elbow. An equally large plaster cocoon immobilized his left leg. As a result, only his right arm was handcuffed to the belly chain that was wrapped around his waist. The other cuff, which normally would've been on his left wrist, was instead secured to the metal armrest of his chair. His left arm and both legs were free.

Knowing firsthand what this man was capable of, Vail couldn't help but wonder: *Is he effectively restrained?*

But she couldn't worry about it. She had a job to do and she sure as hell wasn't going to back down now, in front of the men on the task force. Besides, in the mood she was in, she thought she could kill him if he got loose and came at her.

She flipped open the file. "Says here you claim your name is John Wayne Mayfield. That a joke?"

Mayfield squinted. "The only joke in this room is you."

Vail pouted her lips and nodded slowly. "Okay, John, I hear you." She made an exaggerated motion with her neck of examining the room. It was immediately clear why this was called the Blue Room. The cement walls and floor were covered with a tight, thin blue carpet, which had a peculiar sound absorbing effect.

Vail sat in the brown chair to the left of the table. Mayfield was across from her. Behind and above Vail's head was a small camera lens, embedded in a wall-mounted, cream-colored apparatus that resembled a smoke alarm. It was beaming real-time video to the task force members in the video monitoring room.

"I hope you like your new home. I guess if you've gotta do time, might as well be in Napa. Then again, who knows where you'll end up after you're convicted. Probably someplace nowhere near as nice."

"What I've done is take advantage of an opportunity. And I'm just getting even for what was done to me, sweetie. I'm balancing the scales of justice, is all."

"Is that right? So in killing these people, you've done a good thing."

Mayfield shifted in his seat, threw out his chest. "Damn straight."

"How did killing make you feel?" Vail didn't really need an admission—the charges against him, assault of a federal agent, attempted murder, let alone the murder of a law enforcement officer—Eddie Agbayani—would put Mayfield away for a long, long time. But any opportunity to get inside the mind of a killer was too important to ignore.

"How'd it make me feel?" Mayfield glanced around the walls, then shrugged. "Depends on who it was."

"Victoria Cameron."

Mayfield pursed his lips, thinking. "I didn't feel a whole lot with that one."

*That one.* The objectification, the treating of people as objects, was classic among narcissists. It wasn't much different from the attitude of powerful leaders—political, corporate, military, it didn't matter— though most of them weren't killers.

"What about Ursula Robbins, Isaac Jenkins, Mary—"

"Special cases. And special cases deserve special attention because of who they are. Or were."

"I'm not following you."

Mayfield's mouth rose into a grin. "Of course you aren't."

"Was Scott Fuller a 'special case,' too?"

"You know, you people should be thanking me. I *helped* these people." He tugged on his chain. "And this is the thanks I get?"

Vail knew that narcissists felt they helped their victims by improving them, removing imperfections, and cleansing them of the evil they committed during their lives. Truth was, they were really cleansing their own souls.

"You'll forgive me if we're not more demonstrative in our gratitude." Before Mayfield could respond, Vail forged ahead. "I don't think you killed to help them, John. I think you killed for a different reason. I think you have some issues with women in your life. You're angry at them. More than anger. Rage. And killing them allows you to exert control over something in your life you didn't have control over. You gain control by dominating them, then degrading them by cutting off their breasts."

Mayfield smiled and looked at her a long minute before answering. "You think you've got it all figured out, don't you, Special Agent Vail? Well, I checked you out, too. And I know all about your son, whose name is very similar to mine. Isn't that something? Maybe your son and me, we're more alike than you know. We both had mothers who weren't around. Because I'm sure you're busy with your career, and looky here. You're on the other side of the fucking country, trying to catch people like me when you should be at home taking care of your boy."

Vail clenched her jaw. She couldn't let Mayfield see what she was feeling. Truth was, she wanted to jump out of her chair and put her hands around *his* neck. She forced a smile instead.

"I had you there for a while, Vail, I know I did. You thought I was in Virginia, at Jonathan's middle school. Bet you called your buddies, had them go apeshit protecting your precious little son. Looking for a phantom killer who wasn't even there."

Vail nodded. "That's right, that's exactly what I did. Because I'm not like *your* mother, John." She noted his facial twitch. She leaned back and opened the file. "So you're a mosquito abatement technician for the county of Napa. Pretty clever. You had access to all sorts of places without suspicion."

He placed his left arm on the table. Vail watched but fought the urge to flinch. He smiled back at her. "I've been killing more than just mosquitoes."

Vail nodded thoughtfully. "Indeed, you have. How many people have you killed?"

"Look it up. I sent you that list."

"Yes, you did. Thanks for that. It was more important than you'll ever know. But I know there are other names that aren't on the list. Because narcissists like yourself lie. They lie all the time."

"Oh, poor Agent Vail," Mayfield sang. The smile evaporated from his face. He leaned forward, a sneer crumpling his mouth. "You think you got it all figured out. Well, fuck you. You ain't got shit. There's more to this than you know."

Vail was usually able to let the slime of a serial killer slide off her as if she were made of Teflon. But John Wayne Mayfield, or George Panda, or whatever he wanted to be called, sent the creeps crawling up her spine. She couldn't let him know, or even sense it.

She countered her repulsion by leaning forward, closer to him than was advisable. He could easily head butt her into oblivion. And given her fatigue, she wouldn't be able to react fast enough to lessen its impact. A guy like Mayfield had nothing to lose. Doing more damage, adding another count of assault on a federal officer, was meaningless.

Mayfield shook his head, a *tsk-tsk-tsk,* shame-on-you movement. "You've missed the point, *Karen.* But you'll probably get it eventually. And when you do, I think it's probably safe to say this will have been unlike anything you or your profiler friends have ever seen before."

Vail checked that off to a narcissist's need to show he was better than everyone else. Superior. Special. *Fine, I'll give that to you if it makes you answer me.* "Obviously," Vail said, "you're a superior killer to any we've dealt with in the past. So why don't you tell me what I'm missing?" She shrugged. "I'm just a fuckup. Humor me. What don't I know?"

Mayfield leaned back—the restraints offered no resistance. "Ask nicely. I want to hear you beg."

"I'm sure you do." She looked at him, trying to read his expression. But the image of his large face, leaning into hers in the cave as he attempted to squeeze the life from her, kept invading her thoughts. She was speaking before she knew what she was saying. "But that just ain't gonna happen. I'm not going to beg. Because I think you're bullshitting me."

Mayfield shrugged. "Maybe I am. And maybe I'm not." He leaned forward again. "But aren't you curious? It's going to eat away at you, every night when you get into bed and turn off the lights. You'll think of me, of this conversation. You'll think about the lost opportunity to get to the bottom of this. And it'll eat you up inside."

Vail couldn't argue with that. *That's exactly what's going to happen. Goddamn it. This scumbag seems to have some kind of periscope into my thoughts.*

Vail had to change the rules. She realized now she had approached this interview incorrectly. She was too close, had too much invested—*the fucker tried to kill me*—to be objective. She should have tried to strike a chord within him, talk to him and touch him like he'd never been touched before. *I need to get him to connect to me in a way John Mayfield has never connected with anyone before. Is that possible, given our history?*

She closed the file folder and pushed it aside, but kept her left hand on the table. "You know what? I want to back up for a minute. I've been rude to you, and that was wrong." She placed her hand on the exposed, noncasted area of Mayfield's, careful to avoid quick or awkward movements. She was trying to establish a connection with him and didn't want anything disrupting it. "Can we start over?"

Mayfield looked down at their hands. He looked up at her, a distant look in his eyes. Confusion.

Vail pressed on. "Tell me something." Her voice was soft, nonthreatening. "Tell me about your mother, John." His eyes narrowed. He was listening. Like taming a lion, his tremendous power was suddenly neutralized. "Your mother is sitting right there," Vail said, nodding toward a seat to her right, in the corner of the room. "It's empty, but she's sitting there. Say something to her."

Mayfield turned his head slowly, his eyes remaining on Vail. For the first time, he looked unsure of himself.

"Go on, look at her. I'm not going to judge or hurt you. No one else is here. Just you, me, and your mother."

Mayfield's eyes remained on Vail a long moment, then they swung to his left, toward the empty chair. He quickly looked away, then back at Vail. "I can't."

"You can," she said soothingly. "Tell her what you feel, what's on your mind. Tell her what you've always wanted to tell her."

Mayfield turned his entire head this time. Facing the empty chair, staring at it, his eyes moistened. A minute passed. Then two. Finally, he said, in a low voice, "You let it happen. Why did you let him do that to me, Ma? Why?"

Vail leaned in, ever so slightly. "John, what was it that she let happen to you?"

"My father. It was my father." He licked his lips. Hesitated, sat there quietly another moment before continuing. "I was thirteen. He wasn't happy with me. I was a scrawny kid, unsure of myself. I walked slumped over. I disappointed him. He wanted me to play varsity football but I was too small. Guys in the neighborhood would spit on me, they beat me up, stole things from me. Made fun of me." He stopped. The tears flowed down his cheek. "He called me a little runt."

"It's okay," Vail said, barely above a whisper.

Mayfield sniffled. Still looking at the empty seat. "My father wanted to make me a man. So he hired a hooker, a whore. I ran out, but he caught me in the kitchen and dragged me back into the bedroom. Tied me down."

Vail knew where this was going before Mayfield said it. "She raped you?"

"He said I needed to be a man. He stood outside the door and listened. I saw his feet underneath the door. Standing there." He dragged his nose across his shoulder. Face down now, he talked to his lap. "But I was a man now. I'd had sex with a woman, with a *whore*. And my mother let it happen."

"Was she there, too?" Vail asked softly.

"There?" Mayfield shook his head. "She was always working. She was never there. My father couldn't keep a job, so he was always at home, getting drunk and smoking pot and playing cards. My mother was never around. But she knew what was happening, and she did nothing." He lifted his head and turned to the empty chair. Took a deep, uneven breath, slumped forward and put his right elbow on the table.

"I don't think your mother knew. I don't think she'd let that happen to you, John. Did you ever . . . tell her?"

Mayfield swung his face toward Vail's. "I couldn't."

Vail nodded slowly. "I understand." And, honestly, she did understand. What thirteen-year-old could face his mother and tell her he'd been raped by a prostitute? The details of how it happened were unimportant. It was too embarrassing for most thirteen-year-olds to admit. Telling your mother something that personal, face-to-face, was out of the question. The evolution of John Mayfield into serial killer was now clear. She lowered her eyes, saddened by the series of events that led to this man in front of her having taken the lives of so many innocent people. People who had nothing to do with John Mayfield's failed upbringing.

Piercing the quiet, the moment, was the grumbling vibration of Vail's BlackBerry. Both she and Mayfield reflexively jumped as she lifted her hand off his and fumbled to answer it. She cursed herself for forgetting to silence it.

The display said it was Bledsoe. *Goddamn it.* Take it or not? What if he had critical information on Robby? Mayfield had revealed to her some of the most crucial details: why he killed. But she hadn't yet gotten into the equally important questions of how and why he chose these particular victims.

*Why the male?*

And the document he'd sent that listed victims they didn't know about—who were they?

Then there were those affiliated with the AVA board—the *special cases.* What the hell did that mean?

Phone vibrating. *Answer Bledsoe's call or not?*

She may never have a chance to reestablish the connection she'd developed with Mayfield. But the decision was made for her. Mayfield yanked back, pulling his arm off the table.

His reaction took Vail by surprise. In that instant, she thought he was going to hit her, and she recoiled, nearly fell backwards in her chair. The phone stopped ringing. *Fuck. Lost the connection—to Mayfield and to Bledsoe.*

"I'm done talking," Mayfield said. "You're a whore just like my mother. Pretending to care, to be there for me. I should've killed you when I had the chance. Just like I killed the others. Guess I'm a fucking man now, huh!"

Vail shoved the BlackBerry into its holster and rose from her chair.

Mayfield tried to stand. But his leg cast—and the restraint cuffed to the armrest—forced him to fall back into his seat. "Remember, Vail. There's more to this than you know. And I'm beginning to doubt you're smart enough to ever figure it out."

The door to her right swung open and in stepped Ray Lugo. He lifted his right hand, revealing a black SIG-Sauer pistol.

And it was pointed at Mayfield.

"Ray!" Vail lunged for the gun—but Lugo fired. The blast in the small room was deafening.

Vail grabbed Lugo's pistol and wrapped her hands around it, trying to force it toward the ceiling. But Lugo was intent on keeping the SIG on target.

"Drop it. Ray. Drop. The. Fucking. Gun!"

Lugo twisted back, but Vail held on, ducking to keep her face from the barrel of the pistol. "Leave me the hell alone—" he yelled, then yanked down hard and drove his left shoulder into her chest.

Vail bounced into the wall

fell to the side

*Mayfield—blood—yelling—*and

Lugo fired again.

As Vail got to her feet, Lugo crumpled and fell backwards into the wall. He grabbed for his neck. Blood was spurting, soaking the carpet and Vail—Vail pulled off her blouse and pressed it against Lugo's neck.

Banging on the door. "Karen!"

*Brix.*

He was trying to get into the room, but Lugo's body was blocking the doorway.

"Ray's been shot," Vail yelled. "He's been shot!"

Holding her shirt tight against Lugo's neck, she dragged his body a few inches to the side . . . an opening just wide enough for Brix to squeeze through.

"What happened?"

"I don't know. A ricochet?" Vail grabbed Lugo's neck to apply firmer pressure. "We've gotta get him to the ER. Help me carry him—"

Brix lifted Lugo into his arms—not an easy task because the man was thick and it was a cramped space—but they managed to get him out of the room and down the hall. Vail tried her best to keep pressure on his neck wound.

"What the hell happened?" Dixon asked, following closely behind. "I was watching you on the monitor. I looked away and then there's a gunshot."

They stumbled through the metal door and hung a left into another corridor. "We need to get him to the hospital," Vail said. "He's been shot—"

"Get the van," Brix yelled. "Bring it around Main. By the Sally Port. He's fucking heavy. And call an ambulance for Mayfield!"

There were shouts in the hallway as deputies cleared the way and scattered.

"Bring the van around!"

"Hurry!"

"Call the Med Center," Brix yelled. "Tell 'em we're en route. LEO with a GSW to the neck . . ."

# SIXTY-FOUR

*T*hey loaded Ray Lugo into the back of a state Department of Corrections specially outfitted Ford E-350 Super Duty van. The passenger compartment was lined with a thick gray-metal cage, so there wasn't much room. Nevertheless, Dixon and Vail squeezed in, alongside Lugo. Vail's head pressed tight against the ceiling.

The claustrophobic crush of being in confined spaces began building in Vail's chest. *Shit. I can't deal with this now. Focus on Lugo, keep pressure on his neck.*

Brix hoisted himself in and pushed onto the bench seat beside Vail as the van screeched away from the building. Shoulder to shoulder, they swayed with the vehicle's jerky movements. Her head repeatedly struck the roof with each bump in the road.

Vail was covered in Lugo's blood, the slick liquid coating her arms and face, shoulder, bra—

*Concentrate. Keep pressure on his neck.*

"All right," Brix said. "What happened? Ray stowed his gun, I saw him do it."

Dixon patted down Lugo's jeans. "Me, too." Her hands stopped moving and she squeezed his left ankle. Drew back his pant leg, revealing a holster. "Backup piece."

"Fuck."

"But how did he get hit? If he was aiming for Mayfield—"

"He fired twice," Vail said. "Must've been hit by a ricochet."

Brix nodded. "The Blue Room walls are cement. Makes sense. But why—why Mayfield?" Brix leaned forward. "Why, Ray?"

Lugo's breathing was labored. His lids parted and his eyes rotated toward Brix. "Him. He . . . started it."

"Who started it? Mayfield?"

"May . . . field. Kidnapped."

"Kidnapped?" Vail asked. "Who? Mayfield kidnapped you?"

He fluttered his eyelids. "Wife. Son. He was . . . going to . . . kill them. Made deal. He lets 'em live."

"You made a deal with Mayfield?" Brix asked.

"Told me. Can't escape . . . him. Will find us." He licked his lips. "Scared . . ."

"He scared you," Dixon said, "so you cut a deal? With a goddamn killer, Ray? You're a cop, a sergeant, for chrissake."

"No . . . Tried finding . . . him. No leads. Couldn't . . ."

Dixon leaned in. "What kind of deal did you cut with him, Ray?"

"Looked. Couldn't find. He . . . found out. Warned me." He coughed.

Blood leaked. Vail pressed her shirt harder against the wound.

"What kind of deal," Dixon repeated, this time louder, firmer.

Lugo did not answer at first. Finally, he said, "Helped. Left wife . . . son . . . alone."

"That's why you shot him?" Brix asked. "Because you helped him? You thought he'd rat you out?"

"Helped him how?" Dixon asked.

"Had to."

"Had to, what? Had to shoot him, or you had to help him?"

"Ray," Vail said. "What did Mayfield mean when he said, 'There's more to this than you know'?"

His eyes swiveled to Vail, then toward Brix. "Look . . . after. Wife. Son." Lugo's voice was low. He was gurgling his words. "Or . . . he . . . wins."

"What?" Vail looked to Brix for confirmation of the meaning of the garbled words. Then she dropped her gaze to Lugo. "Ray! Mayfield wins? Why?"

Lugo closed his eyes. Vail grabbed his shoulder and shook. "Ray! Stay with us. Why is there more to this?"

Lugo opened his eyes. Brix leaned in close. "Was Mayfield the Crush Killer?"

"Yeah . . . but . . ." Lugo sucked in air. Blood bubbled on his lips. "Disc . . ." His body convulsed, then went limp.

*Oh, my god.* A horrifying thought suddenly formed in Vail's mind: Had Mayfield killed Robby? Did Lugo help him? *Is that what Ray was talking about? Is that what Mayfield meant?* 'There's more to this.' *Am I going to find Robby dead in some vineyard, missing the second toenail on his right foot?*

Dixon looked at Brix. "Did he say, 'disc'? What disc?"

Vail grabbed Lugo's wrist and felt for a pulse. She looked away. Brix did the same, but nothing needed to be said. Everyone in the van knew that Lugo was gone.

Brix's phone buzzed. He looked down, glanced at the display. "Ambulance is en route with Mayfield."

"Still alive?"

He reread the text message. "Barely. Probably not going to survive the ride."

Vail slumped back against the van wall, her head and shoulders bouncing with the bumps in the road. Brix had his bloody hands on his face, elbows on his knees. And Dixon just sat there, staring at Lugo, at the man she had known for so long. Yet hadn't known at all.

The van pulled into the ER parking lot and stopped with a lurch. They didn't move. The back doors swung open. Two hospital personnel in scrubs peered in and apparently read their body language. "Is he gone?" one of them asked.

"Gone," Brix said.

"You sure?"

"I fucking know when a cop's dead. Now close the goddamn door and leave us alone."

The van was dark again, save for the parking lot light filtering through the tinted rear windows.

They sat in silence until Vail's phone vibrated. And vibrated. She ignored it. Seconds later, it vibrated again.

It pulled her back to rational thought. With blood-smeared hands, she reached for the BlackBerry. Put it against her ear. "Yeah."

"Karen, it's Bledsoe. I checked everything. Airports, flights. Credit cards. Car rentals, hotels, area hospitals, morgues, police and sheriff departments in a hundred mile radius. I can't be totally sure because it's the middle of the night, but I came up empty. I got nothing. There's no sign of Robby."

Vail dropped the phone to her lap. Bledsoe was still talking, but it didn't matter. His words resonated and repeated in her head: *There's no sign of Robby.*

Exhausted, famished, emotionally drained, and covered in a dead man's blood, she closed her eyes.

And she cried.

# A NOTE FROM ALAN JACOBSON

I know, I know . . . I left a few loose threads hanging on this garment. Fear not, they will be tied together, neatly trimmed or tucked away in the next Karen Vail novel.

Go now (yes, now) to **www.crush.alanjacobson.com** for a short video featuring yours truly discussing the ending to *Crush*. But that's not all—you'll also find a few other surprises there. See you soon.

—ALAN

# ACKNOWLEDGMENTS

As always, I could not have written this novel with the accuracy and credibility I strive for without the assistance and cooperation of the following professionals:

**Senior FBI profiler Supervisory Special Agent Mark Safarik** (ret). Mark, now Executive Director of Forensic Behavioral Services International, started as a vital resource fifteen years ago and became a close friend. His knowledge and expertise in the field of criminal investigative analysis is tops among his peers. I value his friendship, his input, our discussions, and his detailed and critical review of the manuscript.

**Senior FBI profiler Supervisory Special Agent Mary Ellen O'Toole** (ret). Mary Ellen provided key information regarding her experiences dealing with narcissistic serial killers, including their offender character traits, crime scene behaviors, and the interview techniques she has used with them. Moreover, the stories Mary Ellen shared with me over the years relative to her long career in the profiling unit helped me understand Karen Vail's challenges and opportunities.

**Sergeant Matt Talbott**, St. Helena Police Department. Matt was my first law enforcement contact in the valley. He helped orient me as to the Napa County Major Crimes Task Force and its makeup, operations, procedures, and background, as well as the various policing and jurisdictional nuances of the Napa Valley.

**Captain Jean Donaldson**, Napa County Sheriff's Department. Jean not only gave me a comprehensive tour of the Sheriff's Department facility, including the morgue, task force conference room, and all points in between, but he graciously answered my unending follow-up questions about department procedures and operations.

**D. J. Johnson,** Assistant Director of the Napa County Department of Corrections. D. J. took me on a comprehensive, behind-the-scenes tour of the Napa County Hall of Justice, particularly the jail and courthouse, and provided detailed explanations of the Department of Corrections' operational procedures.

**David Pearson**, CEO of Opus One Winery. David assisted me with understanding appellations, AVA associations, their boards, and the politics that permeate the wine-growing regions. A longtime wine industry veteran, David took me on a fascinating personal tour of Opus One, and subsequently reviewed pertinent portions of the manuscript for accuracy.

**Tomás Palmer**, Senior Security Program Manager at Microsoft. Tomás provided detailed explanations regarding embedded data in Office documents—and kept it on a level a nonprogrammer could comprehend. During our ongoing exchanges of information and "what if" scenarios, I found Tomás to be a creative and outside-the-box thinker—an invaluable resource to a thriller novelist. He also reviewed relevant sections of the manuscript to make sure I didn't mangle what we'd discussed.

**James Patton**, Deputy Director of Global Trade Compliance at Microsoft. Jim ran point, putting me in touch with Tomás and arranging mind-blowing behind-the-scenes tours of the Microsoft campus facilities, which included a fascinating look at the company's cutting edge research. In addition, thanks to **Bryan Rutberg**, Director of the Redmond Executive Briefing Center and **Dominic Trimboli**, Group Manager Executive Briefings, for showing me around the Executive Briefing Center and teaching me how to use the Surface computer.

**Jonathan Hayes,** a senior forensic pathologist in the Office of the Chief Medical Examiner in New York City, and a clinical assistant professor at NYU School of Medicine. Jonathan, author of the thriller *A Hard Death,* provided information on body decomposition and advised me on the drug BetaSomnol. Before I start receiving emails due to concern over conveying actual dosages about real pharmaceuticals, it was best to invent a drug—no harm in a little creative license—and get on with the story. Both Jonathan and I will sleep easier.

**Amanda Montes**, Translations Switch Technician for CellularOne

Arizona. Amanda provided information regarding text messaging, storage, law enforcement standards, access, and terminology.

**Senior Special Agent Susan Morton**, of the Arizona HIDTA (High-Intensity Drug Trafficking Area), and **Law Enforcement Specialist Marybeth McFarland**, at the National Park Service's Golden Gate National Recreation Area, for background on the complex jurisdictional issues relative to the park. As the fictional SFPD inspector said, you really do need a map and scorecard to keep it straight!

**Jeffrey Jacobson**, Esq., former prosecutor, Assistant U.S. Attorney, current Associate General Counsel for the Federal Law Enforcement Officers Association . . . and my brother. Jeff answers my procedural questions when pesky legal issues interrupt the telling of my stories.

**Jeff Ayers**, author, librarian, media escort, friend. Jeff connected me with James Patton, and shuttled me around Seattle like a pro.

**Kevin Fagan**, *San Francisco Chronicle* staff writer, for timely assistance with the Zodiac case. **Greg Miller**, for a primer on appellations, AVAs, Napa politics, and police jurisdictions.

**Roger Cooper**, my publisher. I'm extremely fortunate to have the ongoing opportunity to work closely with Roger. His forty years in publishing are an invaluable resource; more than that, however, Roger is a visionary, a tireless worker, and someone who has earned my limitless respect. I am guided by his insight and knowledge.

**Georgina Levitt**, Vanguard Press associate publisher, and **Amanda Ferber**, publishing manager. Georgina and Amanda are my lifelines throughout the publishing process. It is truly a pleasure to work with two very professional, efficient, and special individuals.

**Peter Costanzo**, Vanguard's director of online marketing, for producing such a fine and functional web site; and the entire **Vanguard sales force and production staff**, who busted their tails behind the scenes to assemble a first-class product—and then get it sold into the stores.

**Kevin Smith**, my editor. Kevin and I are of like minds when it comes to suspense. He understands my characters and what I am trying to accomplish with each novel. For *Crush*, his vision and astute observations helped me find that razor's edge.

**Laura Stine**, my project editor. Laura is the embodiment of dotted i's and crossed t's. With so many moving parts at the production end of publishing a novel, it's essential to have a chief at the helm making sure the hard work gets packaged into a polished final product.

**Anais Scott**, my copy editor. There are an unfathomable number of details to keep straight across four hundred pages, and having someone trolling my sentences with Anais's extraordinary attention to detail is vital.

**Jen Ballot**, my publicist. Jen did an unbelievable job setting up a successful, aggressive, and full-scale book tour in the most challenging retail and promotional environment in decades.

**Joel Gotler** and **Frank Curtis**, my agents. As fortunate as I am to have Roger Cooper as my publisher, I'm equally as blessed to have two agents with the decades of experience Joel and Frank possess. They have freed me to think less about the business of rights, subrights, and contracts—and more about creating unique stories and characters.

**Gil Adler** and **Shane McCarthy**, the producers who bought the film rights to *The 7th Victim* and my (eventually) forthcoming novel, *Hard Target*. They have made my first Hollywood experiences special, memorable, and enjoyable. I couldn't have asked for better people to work with in this process.

**Jill**, my wife, best friend, and editor. I've joked that there's a lot of me in Karen Vail . . . but there's also a fair amount of Jill in Karen Vail. Jill's influence is felt throughout the manuscript, not just from our trips to (and experiences in) the wine country, but also behind the scenes, in her critical review of the story and characters. She has put up with me being sequestered in my office toiling away at these pages all day and night, and well into the morning hours. Thanks for being patient.

To **my readers** . . . Thanks for your support, for spreading the word about "Alan Jacobson" to friends, family members, neighbors, colleagues, book clubs, and bloggers. My promise to you is that I will always try my best to entertain you with unique characters and interesting stories. Come out and see me sometime at one of my signings. I'm here for you.

Thanks, as well, **to those who went above and beyond to help sell my books**: Nanci Gill, Carey Pena, Gretchen Pahia, Larry Comacho,

Dave Anderson, Helen Raptis, Leslie Martin, Kelly Jackson, Dan El-liott; Marianne McClary, Nick Toma, Mark S. Allen; Bill Thompson; Tom Hedtke, Beth O'Connor, Vicky Lorini; Colleen Holcombe; Jeff Broyles; Terry Abbott; Pam Chadwick, Doran Beckman; Mary Ann Diehl; Judy Wible, Jackie Kelly; Gunjan Koul; Douglas Thompson; Jean Coggan, Kristine Williams; Shana Pennington-Baird; Russ Ilg; John Hutchinson, Virginia Lenneville; Ruth and Jon Jordan; Alex Telander; Jared Martin; Debbie White, Alison Meltcher; Torey Harkins; Jeff Bobby; Joel Harris; J. B. Dickey, Maryelizabeth Hart, Terry Gilman, Patrick Heffernan; Joan Hansen; Bobby McCue, Linda Brown, Pam Woods, Kirk Pasich; April Lilley, Christine Hilferty; Lorri Amsden; Jeffrey Jacobson; Corey Jacobson; Russell and Marion Weis; Marci and Paul Ortega; Len Rudnick; Wayne and Julia Rudnick; Marc Hernandez, Ronny Peskin; Marc Benezra (fifty times over); Bill Kitzerow (you da man!); Mikel London, Tim Murphy, Dennis Hoover; John Hartman; Perry Ginsberg; Florence Jacobson; Pete Bluford; Andrew Gulli; Art O'Connor; Sarie Morrell; Anthony and Herta Peju, Peter Verdin, Katie Lewis, Stacee Cootes, Alan Arnopole, Robert Sherman, Helena Frazier; Micheal Weinhaus; C. J. Snow; Aaron Matzkin; Heather Williams; Mike and Betsy Schoenfeld; Josh and Debbie Sabah; Dena Benezra; Richard Grossman; Mimi Graham-Rose; Susanna Yao.

**Author's note**: For obvious reasons, some of the locations mentioned in the novel are fictitious; many, however, are real. For those of you visiting the region, stop by the real wineries and restaurants mentioned in *Crush* for some world-class Napa Valley wine (for a list of these wineries, wines, and restaurants, visit www.crush.alanjacobson.com).

I've attempted to ensure accuracy—but despite my best efforts, it's likely I've blown some fact somewhere among these four hundred pages. This is not a function of the aforementioned esteemed professionals I consulted, but rather my own error. If I unwittingly omitted anyone from the acknowledgments, please forgive me.

**ALAN JACOBSON** is the national bestselling author of the critically acclaimed thriller *The 7th Victim,* which was named to *Library Journal*'s "Best Books of the Year" list for 2008. Alan's years of research with law enforcement, particularly the FBI, influenced him both personally and professionally and have helped shape the stories he tells and the diverse characters that populate his novels.

Both *The 7th Victim* and one of Alan's forthcoming thrillers, *Hard Target,* are currently under development as major feature films with an A-list Hollywood producer.

Visit Alan at www.AlanJacobson.com.
For more information on Crush, visit www.CrushNovel.com.